BALLAD OF THE REVERIE ORGAN

Spectacle of the Extension
-a novel-

One night, a young artist's painting comes to life, its presence causing her to question the decisions she's made and her relationship with reality.

As the creature travels through the artist's world and she is drawn ever deeper into its own reality, they both unearth secrets about each other and the worlds around them.

Cover art by Julia Y (JuliaY.com)

Visions from the Dream Gyre
-short stories & poems-

Travel through dreams, through time, talking to crotchety old frogs and majestic trees. Discard worlds and personalities only to don the next in a series of tales each possessing its own flavor of dream logic.

Cover art by B.K. Jenkins

BALLAD OF THE REVERIE ORGAN

THE AGENTS OF ::VOLUME II::

Andy Reynolds

Published by Mosquito Publishing
ISBN-13: 978-0692044094
ISBN-10: 0692044094

Cover Art by Andy Reynolds

Author Photo by Mars

First Printing: 2021

Find Andy Reynolds:

AndyReynolds.net
Facebook.com/AndyWritings
Patreon.com/AndyReynolds
YouTube Channel: AndyWritings

This volume is dedicated to
friends who fall away.

May they thrive in their paths
& give something great
to this world.

File (-1) :: [Todo]

Smoke hung lazy and thick in the air, meandering about the large room and judging the current inhabitants—gamblers, murderers, con artists, thugs. No one was innocent in this place. Red velvet covered the walls, decorated with giant paintings of brothels and gambling halls, lit by gas lamps mounted between the paintings. An antique and immaculate *fleur-de-lis* patterned carpet covered the entire floor, holding up various pool tables, poker tables, blackjack tables, as well as a dozen other pieces of gambling paraphernalia. Against one wall was a long, wooden bar with giant mirrors stretching across the back of it. Faces carved into the wood above the mirrors looked down with the disdain of souls pulled from life too early. Next to a woman playing the grand piano in one corner was a large, wooden target at which a few unsavory individuals threw knives and small axes. The *thock, thock, thock* of steel sinking into wood was barely audible over the piano and the murmuring of four-dozen humans, creatures, entities, and ghosts conversing over the buzz of the crowded room.

This was not your average gambling hall—this was The Den, run by Nimble of the Two Sisters. Some nights the only thing keeping a person from being outright killed where they sat was Nimble's utter insistence that the floor be kept pristine by all who stepped inside. Several individuals who had spilled blood on the floor were never seen again. Even the toughest brutes in The Den were *extremely* careful with their cigars, cigarettes, and cocktails, making sure neither a stray ash nor a drop of their drink touched that antique *fleur-de-lis* pattern.

Todo sat at a poker table with four other gamblers and the dealer. He was not a pretty man, his face and arms scarred from various run-ins with good luck that ran out faster than he himself could run. Both his hands were missing two fingers, giving him a grand total of six digits.

Some would deem Todo a cheat. In fact, several people in that room would sooner stab him than gamble with him. But their minds were narrow. The very *rules* of games, gambling, and the world have *cheating* built into them. Cheating is nothing but the hidden ruleset of the game. Sure, cheating could get you beat up and left in an alley; it could get you killed or held down while someone cuts *another of your damned fingers off* while you scream awful things about the cutter's family (about which you know nothing). But those consequences were merely more hidden rules of the game, and Todo had gotten better at side-stepping said consequences, though it had taken him a couple of decades (and digits) to do so.

Even his name was sliced up. Years ago, when he lost the middle and ring fingers of his left hand, the denizens of the gambling halls dubbed him *Trois Doigts*, or "Three Fingers." Over the years, his nickname became slurred, shortened, and bastardized until it became what it was now—Todo.

Todo had learned to embrace his reputation. Often these days, he didn't actually cheat, but would lead others to believe that he *was* in order to throw off their game, getting them to overreact and make poor decisions.

He licked his lips and smiled, eyeing his cards and the other gamblers at the table. He only had a half-decent hand, but he was feeling lucky. And if he was wrong about that luck, there were a few cards hidden around his person which would definitely tip luck in his favor, as long as he could get to them without being noticed.

A silence fell over the far side of the room, near the doorways leading further into the establishment. Todo glanced up, expecting to see a fight break out, or perhaps Nimble making one of his "demonstrations". The other gamblers glanced over too, and Todo used the opportunity to swap a few cards from his hand with those hidden around his body. Seems he was right about his luck.

Then he heard the music. It sounded like the damned calliope that played from the steamboat docked on the Mississippi. Except the music he heard now was out of tune and creepy as hell, like someone had broken the calliope's back and was playing horror music with it. And hadn't he heard that the calliope had been destroyed or stolen in the last week? The music reached into his head, tickling something at the back of his skull.

The gamblers around him tensed up, and Todo glanced across the room, watching as people began collapsing off their chairs and bar stools, cocktail servers twisting and falling limply to the floor, glasses shattering.

Todo kicked into survival mode, instantly aware of everyone around him as he ripped open the two top buttons of his shirt, grabbing the necklace underneath. On the strip of leather hung two large alligator teeth with symbols carved into them—something he'd won in a bet with someone who didn't know what they had (not that Todo had known what the hell the necklace was, just that it was powerful. He'd experimented for months to figure out exactly how it worked). He squeezed the two teeth in his fist, grinding them together, and a thin layer of blue liquid spread quickly over his body. It felt gross, but he was growing used to it.

The gambler to his left jumped to his feet, backing away from Todo. "*What the hell?*" The calliope music got louder, and the man's head reeled back as he collapsed to the floor.

Todo slunk out of his chair, ducking behind the table as everyone else in the room fell to the ground. He grabbed a satchel belonging to one of the other gamblers, dumped it out, then reached onto the table and began shoving all the poker chips he could find into the bag. Everything he touched got smeared with blue liquid.

In his experiments with the necklace, he'd discovered that it kept him from being as physically harmed as he'd otherwise be. He would get a bruise instead of a cut, or a cut instead of a broken bone. This was the first time the necklace had the chance to protect him from whatever was happening to these other people. Hell, even the *entities* and *ghosts* were down.

Staying low, he rushed to the next table and began shoving more chips into the satchel.

Seeing movement across the room, he crouched lower behind a large gambler. Everyone on the floor seemed to be alive, staring at the ceiling like they were dreaming with their eyes open. And their faces… they were all either *smiling* or *in awe*. What the hell was going on?

Through a doorway across the room walked a figure donning a huge helmet and a long cape made of various animal hides. No, that wasn't a damned helmet, it was a massive *skull*. The skull had large tusks spreading out into the air, but Todo didn't think it was an elephant skull. He had no clue what it was. There were symbols carved up and down the entire skull, but he was too far away to make them out.

Something big was strapped to the figure's back, under the cape, with brass pipes coming up from their shoulders, and a keyboard hung from a strap across their chest. They played the keys, and the broken-sounding music emanated from the pipes sticking up through the animal hide cape.

From another doorway walked Nimble, and Todo ducked lower behind the gambler. The dark-skinned man wore a purple button-up shirt and a burgundy vest, his hair in tight rows across his scalp. Nimble gazed across the room of prone, open-eyed would-be gamblers. As per usual, an enormous smile stretched across his face.

Todo didn't *know* Nimble, but he'd watched him from a distance over the years. If he'd never seen Nimble before, he would believe that Nimble had *planned* whatever was happening—for what else could the smile on his face mean? The man looked *ecstatic* with the situation. But having witnessed Nimble's reactions a handful of times before, Todo would wager that Nimble was actually ecstatic over the chaos that someone had brought into his carefully tailored and guarded Den.

Nimble turned to the skull-masked figure, still a dozen yards from him, and held up a short sword in his hands, pulling it from its sheath. A blue light flared from the blade, and the skull-masked figure froze in place, their limbs shaking, their fingers vibrating against the keys of the keyboard.

Nimble spoke and walked towards the figure, stepping over bodies, but the twisted calliope music drowned his words before they reached Todo's ears.

The symbols on the giant skull pulsed bright gold, and appearing from nowhere throughout the room were four... *beasts*. They had the bodies of colossal bears and the heads of lions, with spiraling elephant trunks and long tusks curving into the air. Their hides were a patchwork of different animal furs, as well as scales and rough skin. Todo's heart raced. Just looking at the creatures made his stomach cringe.

Suddenly he realized that the skull the intruder wore was the *skull* of one of these creatures, and the cape was one of their *hides*.

Two of the beasts descended upon Nimble, snarling and swiping. Nimble used an elbow to knock one of their swinging paws away, but the other caught him in the chest, lifting him up and slamming him into a wall.

The blade fell to the ground, and the intruder broke free from the blade's effect. Their fingers left the keyboard as they backed away. The gambling hall was silent except for the growl of beasts and the murmurs of the half-conscious gamblers.

Nimble grabbed the blade from the ground and held it up. The two beasts closest to him froze. He laughed loudly, still bent over from being hit so hard in the chest. "*I'm telling you, we could work something out!*" he said to the skull-masked figure.

The symbols on the skull flared to life once more, and a fifth creature appeared behind Nimble, already leaping through the air. It's massive jaw latched onto the shoulder of Nimble's knife hand, wrenching its way down his arm as he twisted and hit the ground.

The skull-masked figure looked around, their body visibly heaving, and they screamed into the room: "*Eat! Eat all their dreams!*"

It was unmistakably a man's voice.

The creatures pounced on the unconscious bodies, ripping into them. But it wasn't flesh they were eating—it's like the beasts were eating the very *souls* of the gamblers. Even with the violence of the beasts' rending and swallowing, the bodies of the gamblers remained somehow unscathed, unlike the body of Nimble as he stood and began fighting two of the beasts at once. Blood seeped quickly across his vest and shirt from his wounded arm, which was shredded down to the bone.

Still, that smile never left his face.

Todo realized that he'd watched the endeavor for roughly twenty seconds too long. Grabbing the satchel, he quickly crawled towards the entryway and the red metal front door.

The three burly guards were on the ground. Todo began hastily unlocking the fifteen bolts and chains which secured the door. He heard the snarl and turned just in time to see the beast hurling itself through the air. It collided with him, as did his body with the door, the force so intense that the metal buckled, snapping the hinges as he and the door flew across the nighttime alley of Exchange Place, slamming into the wall of the next building. The satchel he'd been holding exploded against the wall, poker chips flying, bouncing, and rolling down the alley in all directions.

Todo rolled across the ground, coughing. "Am I still alive?" he muttered. But when he spit out a wad of blood, it was mixed with the blue liquid of the necklace, and he remembered exactly *why* he was still alive. He was pretty sure some of his limbs were broken.

Looking up, he saw the massive jaws of the beast above him as one of its paws firmly pinned his shoulder to the ground. Its trunk sniffed at his face, hot saliva trailing over Todo's nose and mouth. The beast bent down to dig its jaws into his torso, and Todo winced.

But nothing happened. It rose above him with a mouthful of blue liquid. It shook its head, trying to shake the blue liquid from its jaws, roaring so loud that Todo's ears began ringing.

The beast turned and ran off, back into The Den.

"This *was* a lucky night," Todo muttered, just before passing out.

File (0) :: [Edith Downs]

Edith opened the hand of the massive metal Extraction Glove to let go of the memory file, which melded back into the head of the wounded man along with hundreds of other glowing, square memory files. A light blinked on the side of the Extraction Glove, letting her know that the glove copied the memory. The man shuddered and looked up at her, half-conscious. "Are the beasts gone?"

She shook her head and stood up. "I don't know." She wore a gray tank top and dark cargo pants, the pockets filled with bits of useful equipment. A duffel bag was strapped to her back. Her black hair was in a ponytail, a lone streak of sepia-colored hair falling down the side of her face.

"Beasts?" asked Julius, the leader of The Agents Of. "What kind of beasts?"

"Nothing I've ever seen," said Edith. "They were horrifying, like six or seven different animals mashed up together." She motioned to the bent up red metal door lying on the ground amid hundreds of spilled poker chips. "One of them smashed through this using Todo here. He only survived because of that necklace."

Julius walked up to Todo and crouched. His mechanical leg was much quieter than it had been in previous weeks, being tinkered with by both Roman and Mars. The leader of The Agents Of wore a dark trench coat, torn up pants, and boots. His hair fell in braids nearly to his shoulders, giving him the look of the lion god which dwelled within him. The new mechanical arm strapped to the stump of his missing arm was *not* quiet, constantly hissing and clicking, and he often dropped things with its three-clawed hand.

He reached out with his real hand, grabbed the necklace, and pulled until the leather snapped. One alligator tooth was cracked and missing pieces, the other nearly pulverized to dust. "This has seen the last of its protecting days. Anyway, it belongs to the Riverwalkers. I'll see that they get it back." He pocketed the broken necklace and walked through the open doorway to The Den.

Edith followed Julius. It was her first time inside Nimble's Den. Dark red velvet covered the entryway walls, and small fountains adorned each corner of the room. Several people were on the ground, their eyes barely open like they were half-dreaming.

Julius pointed at one of them. She knew what the pointing meant—that this one didn't work for Nimble, so they were fair game. The pointing also meant that Julius knew a dark secret or two about the individual.

She squatted down next to the man.

"Who are you?" he muttered, half-awake.

Edith pushed strands of sepia-colored hair behind her ear with one hand while twisting her other hand inside the Extraction Glove, letting the glove hum to life around her arm. Liquids sloshed through hoses, and lights pulsed up and down the side of the glove. The man's memories lit up before her like cards in an over-sized Rolodex.

"I am Edith Downs, member of The Agents Of and Protector of the Memories of New Orleans."

The man looked up in horror as Julius approached. "What the fuck is going on?"

"Tommy Butera," said Julius.

"How... how do you know my name?"

"In two-thousand-four, you aided a woman named Blessed Bianca in a botched robbery scheme which nearly resulted in a tear in time so big it would have swallowed the Irish Channel, sending it to who-knows-when. Your actions put a significant portion of the city at tremendous risk. Under the terms of The Fair Memory Act, your memories are forfeit."

"My... my memories?"

"I'm just going to look at one memory," said Edith. "Your memory of tonight. Before you heard the calliope music. Bring that memory up, and I won't have to go through any others."

Julius spoke up once more: "I, Julius, am a licensed Louisiana notary. I agree to witness this extraction, viewing, and/or copying of memories."

"What the fuck..." muttered Tommy Butera.

"Think of the calliope music," said Edith. "This'll just take a second..."

BALLAD OF THE REVERIE ORGAN

The events of this book, the second Volume detailing the actions and accounts of The Agents Of, begin about seven weeks after the heroic events transcribed at the end of The Agents Of, Volume I: The Axeboy's Blues. All thoughts, emotions, and memories used in the making of this volume were given freely with the permissions of the owners or extracted in the presence of a licensed Louisiana notary under the terms of the Fair Memory Act.

File 1 :: [Mars]

Mars stepped carefully over the muttering bodies scattered about Nimble's Den, vaguely aware of Roman across the room doing the same. Roman had told her that they might only have seconds to be alone at the scene, so there wasn't time to gawk at the massive paintings of gambling halls and speakeasies adorning the walls, or all the corsets and suits that Mars would die to wear.

She wore a leather jacket over an Empire Strikes Back T-shirt, her red dreadlocks spilling over her shoulders. Gadgets hung from straps on her belt; a duffel bag full of more devices hanging from her back. She held up a Reader—a round device that looked uncannily like a makeup compact. When opened, several tiny colored lights flashed on the display, the color and number of flashes telling the user all manner of things about the immediate area.

Roman was also holding a Reader across the room from her. The pale half-human, half-Collector wore his long, dark coat, with his black hair pulled back into a tiny ponytail[1]. Unlike her, he was actually *using* the Reader he held in his long-fingered hand.

Mars was *pretending* to use the device while using her abilities. She tapped into her sight, into the way she could watch energy moving through living beings. She watched the lines of energy flow through the people on the floor, counting how many were human, how many were entities, and how many were other creatures—distinctions Roman had been teaching her to recognize[2]. Green energy pulsed and sparked inside their bodies.

[1]   Collector – Short, near-invisible creatures that run through the city collecting and eating the fruit called Wonder, which grows from the heads of people experiencing awe. Roman isn't short, but can be near-invisible when he's eaten a bit of Wonder.

[2]   Entity – Sometimes, the memories of a building or place gain a sense of self and take on a bodily form, occasionally interacting with the world with said body. For more information, please see The Agents Of, Volume I.

She watched that same green energy float through the air of The Den like cigar smoke.

Julius and Edith walked in from the entryway.

"Should I do one more?" Edith asked Julius, looking around.

People were waking up, confused. Some got to their feet; some merely kept lying on the ground, staring up at the ceiling. Some were crying, some muttering to themselves.

In all of their eyes, Mars could see a void—something was ripped out of them or crushed. Like part of their soul had been taken.

Mars realized that half-an-hour ago most of these people, entities, and creatures would have gladly killed her if they could have gotten away with it. Now, what were they? She only saw broken minds. Maybe the effect was temporary, but she had a feeling none of them would be the same after this point in time.

Goosebumps cascaded across Mars' skin as a man entered through a doorway across the room. One arm of his purple button-up shirt was bloody and ripped to shreds, the arm underneath riddled with deep gouges and gore. Across his face stretched a large smile, but his eyes were like two tiny holes into Hell, if Mars had believed in such a place. Thin lines of blood trailed down his hand, trickling from his fingertips to the beautiful carpet. This must be Nimble.

Upon seeing the Agents, his smile somehow became even wider. "Ah! *The Holy Knights of Bes*! I am so glad you stopped by. If only the NOPD were so quick."

"What happened here?" Julius asked.

"Oh, you know how games of shuffleboard can get wildly out of hand after a couple of whiskeys."

"I'm sure."

Looking at the energy coursing through his body, Mars realized she was looking at a creature she'd never seen before. No, more like a *mix* of different creatures fighting to claim dominance over what he was. He had the floating sparks of energy distinct to humans, which Mars was just beginning to learn to see. Yet he also had the lines of vertical energy which she'd only seen inside of entities. The green mist-like energy she'd seen inside the others was also inside of him, but he was *full* of it, and it was leaking up into the air from the wounds in his arm.

"What attacked you?" asked Julius.

"I haven't the faintest idea." Nimble turned to Edith as if he was going to speak, but he merely looked at her for a single, dreadful moment, never losing that smile. Edith grew pale, and Mars balled one hand into a fist. If this fucker felt like messing with Edith, Mars was going to punch him and deal with the consequences.

Then Nimble spoke, quiet and slow, his eyes never leaving Edith:

"Why don't you ask your *memory thief?* That is why you brought her, is it not? Perhaps she can enlighten us all about the debacle that has befallen my fine establishment."

Edith kept his gaze, though Mars could see the sweat creeping down her forehead.

Julius was about to speak, but Mars turned to Nimble and spoke up first: "*Gods!* Doesn't the whole *being-creepy-all-the-time* thing get boring? You ever think about just doing it around Halloween? Seems like keeping it seasonal would be way more effective."

Nimble turned his gaze to Mars. She smirked in an attempt to cover the tension in her body as his eyes dug into her. He was about to speak, but Mars cut him off:

"I know what you're going to ask. They brought me because I'm the muscle."

He nodded, laughing. "Oh yes? Wow, I like you."

She took a step forward, the hairs on her neck and arms sticking straight up. "*You won't,*" she said through clenched teeth, "*in the end.*"

Nimble's smile faded to only a half-smile, and it's like he was peeking out from behind that plastic persona of his. What Mars saw in his face was even more horrifying—not just intense violence, but violence mixed with utter *indifference.* If she didn't already know what a sociopath was, she'd have a pretty good idea by now. "Looks like this one's got me all figured out." And then his smile returned, stretching across his face. "Speaking of muscle..."

The roar of motorcycles was so sudden and loud that Mars swore they were going to drive through the entryway and into the gambling hall. One by one, the engines shut off, then a group of eight people entered The Den from the alley. Most wore leather jackets or long coats, with weapons, devices, and artifacts strapped to their bodies, several of them still wearing their black helmets.

At the head of the group was a beautiful Asian woman who Mars figured must be Nemu, the Sleeping Assassin, wearing black-padded clothing with nine blades strapped to her person, the largest being a full-on katana. Her eyes were closed as if she were in a deep, peaceful sleep.

Nemu ignored the Agents as she stepped up to Nimble's side.

Nimble turned to her. "We were attacked."

"By whom?" she asked, her serene voice somehow calming Mars despite the dangerous situation.

"Not a clue. We've got a mess to clean up. Block off the alley and set up a perimeter around the block."

She nodded and turned to the other seven. Nemu made a circle with one finger, and they turned, making their way back to the entrance.

Julius spoke to Nimble as the motorcycles outside revved back to life:

"Here's where you pretend you'll call us if you find anything out. Like who attacked you and your place, which, like you said, you don't know."

"But of course," said Nimble through his smile. "And Bes, I like the new arm. It suits you." He looked down at his own thrashed arm. "If this doesn't heal right, perhaps I'll just cut it off and have Roman whip me up one of those."

Julius motioned for the other three Agents to make their way towards the entryway, turning back to Nimble. "Sure thing. You investigate the mysterious, unknown person who attacked you, and we'll start fixing you up an arm."

"Sounds like a devil's plan," Nimble said from behind them.

Stepping out into the night air, Mars immediately felt her body relax. Three of Nemu's people were in the alley, one of them sitting on a Yamaha motorcycle where the alley opened up onto a busy Canal Street. The person wore their motorcycle helmet with the tinted visor down, but Mars could feel the person's eyes on her as they passed.

Once on Canal, they made their way towards the river. Every block they walked was another weight lifted off Mars' shoulders. So many emotions surged through her—wanting never to go back there, wanting to go back immediately and burn the place, wanting to take Nimble down along with everyone associated with him.

She wanted to punch something, and she wanted a shower. She felt gross. So many questions buzzed through her mind, but Julius had told them beforehand not to talk when leaving Nimble's place, in case they were followed.

Finally, they walked over the streetcar tracks and up the stairs to the dark and empty Spanish Plaza—the ferry terminal on one side, the Riverwalk Mall on the other, and the Mississippi River just ahead. The river was as still and dark as a secret, reflecting the building lights of Algiers Point across the way.

They walked past plants and trees, then down the stairs to the giant fountain, surrounded by cement bench-seats depicting dozens of Spanish coats of arms.

Roman pulled back his sleeve and plunged his arm down into the fountain's water, opening the submerged metal box and pulling a lever. A section of walkway around the fountain descended into the labyrinth of hallways underneath, and The Agents Of walked down into their headquarters.

As soon as her feet touched the stone floor and the gas lamps began flaring to life around her, Mars blurted out: "*What the fuck!? That was Nimble!!*"

"Who cares about Nimble!" said Edith. "What about those

monsters?!"

"Wait... what?" asked Mars.

Julius just pointed forward and kept walking. "The planning room."

File 2 :: [Julius Marcos]

The planning room was a place they'd barely used since Edith and Mars joined The Agents Of. At its center stood a circular, wooden table surrounded by a half-dozen wooden chairs. Covering one wall was a corkboard with notes tacked all over it about current problems and possible future incidents of the city. Another wall had a second cork board used for any big problem they had, which was empty. A third wall had a floor-to-ceiling map of the city, and a fourth had a large, empty blackboard.

Mars placed a six-pack of Charming Wit on the table, which she'd gotten out of the fridge in the break room[3]. She tossed a can to Edith, then offered one to the other two. Julius shook his head. She tossed one to Roman, then opened her own. All of them stayed standing, still wired from the immediate danger of Nimble's Den.

Julius leaned back against the empty cork board, folding his real arm and metal arm as best he could. "Well, you've met Nimble."

"Yeah, fuck that guy," said Mars, swigging her beer.

"Mars, you first. What did you see?"

She set her beer down. "The people in the Den were a mix between humans, entities, and ghosts, with a few other creatures I've never seen before. By squinting, I could see this greenish mist in the air—it was all over the place and inside the people on the floor. When I looked at Nimble, he looked like a mix between human and entity, and had the green stuff leaking out of him into the air."

Roman looked between Julius and Mars. "You sure it was leaking out of him?"

"Yeah, like he was bleeding it. I don't think all the stuff in the air was coming out of him though—it was textured different."

3   Charming Wit – A refreshing witbier, or white ale, brewed by Urban South Brewery in the Garden District of New Orleans, the neighborhood where Edith Downs resides.

Julius nodded to Roman. "What did you see with the Reader?"

"Large quantities of dream energy throughout the entire Den—that's the green energy Mars was perceiving. There were other energy types, but too many to count and in too small of quantities to deem relevant. Most likely traces from weapons, devices, and substances people had on them. Since I consumed Wonder beforehand, I too was able to see the dream energy in the air, though I did not perceive it emanating from Nimble."

Julius nodded. "Edith, what did you see?"

Edith took a deep breath, staring down at the table like she was prying open her own thoughts. "The two people whose memories I copied were both gamblers at The Den. Everyone was gambling, drinking, and talking. A song began to play, coming from deeper within the building. It sounded like the calliope, but broken... or out-of-tune. Hearing it made everyone fall to the floor, like we found them when we arrived. Todo, the guy outside in the alley, used a necklace to shield himself from the effects."

"A necklace?" said Roman.

Julius pulled the busted alligator tooth necklace from his pocket and tossed it to Roman. "Riverwalker design. You can give it to Elsh next time you see her. I know Donish doesn't like Riverwalker artifacts running loose[4]."

Roman studied the carved alligator teeth, and Julius motioned for Edith to continue.

Edith told them the rest of the story—the man wearing the giant skull and animal-hide cape, Nimble talking to him, the *monsters*. How the man yelled out, "*Eat! Eat all their dreams!*" How the monsters took bites out of people, but somehow did no physical harm.

"Holy shit!" said Mars.

"How did the music affect the gambler who wasn't protected?" asked Roman.

"Julius said to be quick," said Edith, "so I barely glanced at the memories as I copied them. From my glance, I'd say he fell asleep, but I'll have to take a closer look and see."

"Did the monsters bite him too?" asked Mars.

"I don't know."

"I need you to find out tonight," said Julius.

Edith nodded. "Easy enough."

Julius walked over to the chalkboard, grabbing a piece of chalk with his real hand. He wrote and underlined *Calliope* on the top left, *Skulled Man* on the top middle, and *Monsters* on the top right.

---

[4] Riverwalkers – Amphibious part-human creatures who live in the swamps, rivers, and lakes of Louisiana. The Riverwalker tribe residing in the Mississippi River is led by Donish. Another member of that tribe is Elsh, a longtime acquaintance of Roman's. For more information on the Riverwalkers, please see The Agents Of, Volume I.

Under *Calliope* he wrote:

> *Calliope*
> • *Stolen 1½ weeks ago by Banshee Dave*

Julius turned to them. "Alright, we already know the calliope atop the Steamboat Tchoupitoulas was disassembled, most of its pieces ransacked[5]. We know the culprit to be the ghost, Banshee Dave. We know where he'll be later this week. We were already going to pick him up and try to get the calliope back. Now we're going to pick him up and find out who he *gave* it to."

"Um, what if Banshee Dave still has it?" asked Mars. "What if he's the one wearing the giant skull. Ghosts could do that, right?"

Julius shook his head. "When you meet Banshee Dave, you'll understand. He's essentially a kleptomaniac and thrill-seeker and definitely not organized enough to take down Nimble's Den. I also highly doubt that he'd ever confront Nimble. If anything, he'd rob Nimble while across the city and then hide for six months in hopes Nimble forgets him."

"Got it," said Mars. "So someone was using Banshee Dave to get the calliope."

"That's the idea," said Julius. "Roman, enlighten us about your calliope modifications and how they could put dozens and dozens of people into some kind of unconscious state."

Roman took a long swig of beer, then set the can down. Julius could tell his old friend was using the beer to counteract the Wonder he'd eaten before Nimble's Den, pulling himself closer to his human side.

The half-human, half-Collector reached into his coat and pulled out a piece of the fruit called Wonder. The colors of orange and green pulsed around it, the orange traveling into his hand as he held it. Roman set the fruit on the table. "In nineteen-seventy-nine, a few years after the Steamboat Tchoupitoulas began traversing up and down the Mississippi, I modified the calliope atop one of the steamboat's upper decks. I altered it to amplify and pump out Wonder through the city, along with its music. I've also done this with the fountain of Spanish Plaza, so no one can perceive us going up and down the ramp of our headquarters. As you all know, I've modified over a dozen fountains and devices across the city, to make certain that locals and tourists keep experiencing awe and producing

---

5   Tchoupitoulas – pronounced *chop-ah-too-lahs*. It is an alternate spelling of Chapitoulas. The Chapitoulas were a Native American tribe who moved up and down the Mississippi River. The name is thought to come from the Choctaw language and to mean, "those who live by the river." Tchoupitoulas Street is one of the main streets running through New Orleans, and hearing tourists mispronounce the street's name is a favorite pastime of locals.

Wonder, to keep the city's Wonder levels at a high enough frequency.

"Using my modifications to the calliope, there are at least forty-three ways, off the top of my head, that those pieces could put a large room full of people into some kind of dream state. Somebody would just have to use the pieces to amplify an effect that already exists—an effect that would make one person slightly sleepy, for instance."

"So the calliope could be hooked up to a bottle of melatonin?" asked Mars.

Roman pondered a moment. "It would be more complicated than that, but essentially, yes."

"So there's no way to figure out what the skulled man is using?" asked Julius.

"I could come up with many theories, but it would be a waste of my time," said Roman. "It may take me days, and I'd merely have dozens of possible methods. We still wouldn't know which method was actually used until we found more information, which is how my time would be more aptly spent."

Julius nodded. As per usual, he didn't need more convincing from Roman. His friend was usually as good a judge as Julius was, if from a unique perspective.

He returned to the chalkboard. Under *Skulled Man* he wrote:

Skulled Man
- *Nimble and him know each other*
- *Uses skull to control monsters*
- *Plays Calliope*
- *Obtained Calliope from Banshee Dave*

Julius turned back to the table. "Edith, describe everything you can remember about the monsters."

Edith took a deep breath. "Well, they're obviously large enough that a man could wear one of their skulls as a helmet. They were kinda like really big bears with elephant heads. They had tusks and trunks, but their eyes were like lion or tiger eyes. Their bodies were covered in different patches of fur and scales and rough skin."

"What the hell..." muttered Mars.

"They sound like *chimera*," said Roman. "Chimera is a very broad term which applies to creatures that are a mix of two or more animals. Like a gryphon being made of lion and eagle."

"But that's Greek mythology," said Edith.

Roman looked at her like he expected her to keep talking. When she didn't, he continued. "The word comes from Greek mythology, but the definition is not limited to creatures from Greece." He looked to Julius.

"There are some books focused on different types of creatures down in the First Quarter laboratory. Also, I have a few books here that might be helpful."

"I'll look through them," said Mars.

Julius nodded. Turning back to the blackboard, under *Monsters* he wrote:

> *Monsters*
> - *Chimera – elephant, tiger/lion, bear, snake(?)*
> - *They eat dreams?*
> - *Controlled by skull of one of their own.*
> - *Can disappear and/or travel by non-physical means.*

"You forgot one," said Mars. *"They can hurt Nimble."*

Julius set the piece of chalk down. "That doesn't tell us what they are or how to find them; it only tells us about Nimble."

"Is Nimble made out of dreams?"

Julius twisted his mouth and glanced at Roman. "No. Between Roman and I, we've got several theories. Nimble's tied to dreams just as he's tied to many things. We'll go into our theories with the two of you soon, just not tonight. For now, we need to focus on what's on the board. Any other questions?"

Mars shook her head, and the other two were silent.

"Brew up some coffee; it's going to be a late night. Mars is on research. Edith, you're going to study those memories, see if you can find anything else we can use. Roman and I are going to scout and try to find more information on the streets. Maybe someone saw The Skulled Man or the monsters leaving the area."

File 3 :: [Edith Downs]

Piano notes slunk through the air, parting the opaque cigar smoke like curtains. Chatter swirled to either side of her as she tread across the antique *fleur-de-lis* carpet of The Den. Gamblers threw dice or tossed down cards while they sipped cocktails. Knives and hatchets launched through smoke towards a thick wooden target in the corner.

The broken and disjointed calliope music, at first faint and indecipherable, grew louder until people at one end of The Den began to collapse. Gamblers, cocktail servers, and game dealers fell to the floor, their eyes glazed and their mouths open or locked into smiles. Edith stood amidst them as they fell in a giant wave, moving past her. The broken calliope music made her twitch with its shrill notes and incongruous keys, but she didn't feel its effects.

The Skulled Man waltzed into the room only thirty feet away from her. She raised the humming, glowing Extraction Glove, and he *froze* along with everything else in The Den.

All was quiet now, people behind her suspended in the air mid-fall.

Edith tried to make out the symbols running up and down the monster skull worn by The Skulled Man. Though she was close, the symbols blurred as she squinted at them. She was inside the memory of Todo, a gambler somewhere behind her at the far edge of the room. Any details his eyes didn't pick up were lost to her.

She rotated her hand in the glove and let the memory move forward and pick up speed. Nimble came in through a door and began conversing with The Skulled Man, though Edith couldn't pick up anything new from the conversation. The parts that Todo couldn't hear, Edith couldn't hear.

The monsters appeared, fighting Nimble, and Edith froze time again. She took note of the monsters, what animals they seemed to be made up of. In some ways, they were each similar, but in others, they differed. Each one had the tusks and trunk of an elephant. They seemed to have some kind of wild cat head, whether lion, tiger, or jaguar. As for their coat, each one had a different layout of fur, scales, rough skin.

She turned her attention to the one they fought.

Even knowing this was a memory, it was difficult to make herself face the black holes of Nimble's eyes. She swore this memory-Nimble watched her in its frozen state, that any second it would jolt to life, slipping behind Edith and pressing a blade to her throat.

She shook away the thoughts, ignored the memory-Nimble as best she could, and kept looking around for anything she may have missed.

After searching for a while and finding nothing new, Edith raised the Extraction Glove and closed her hand into a fist. Light streaked towards her as the glove sucked the entire memory into itself, leaving her standing at one end of the laboratory in the headquarters of The Agents Of.

The long room was lit by gas lamps mounted to the stone walls. Cabinets and shelves lined the walls, each one full of books, jarred specimens, tools, and devices in various states of completion. The middle of the room was full of long lab tables and stools.

Mars sat at a lab table nearby, a stack of large, dusty books in front of her, pouring through one of them.

On the table behind her was the bulky pair of VR Goggles she'd been tweaking over the last several weeks[6]. Next to the goggles was a partially disassembled device she'd created herself, the *Dust-o-Bot 5000*[7]. So far, the Dust-o-Bot 5000 had cleaned the entire laboratory as well as a few smaller rooms, but Mars was constantly thinking of new ways to improve how efficient it was at cleaning, or how fast it moved.

Edith switched off the glove, suddenly aware of all the mems in objects around the lab, along with the memories in Mars' head[8]. She grabbed her coffee mug, walked over to the small coffee maker, and gave herself a warm up.

"How's it going?" asked Mars.

Edith rubbed her eyes. "It's going alright, I guess. No new revelations. I wish I could show you these memories, though; it's a trip walking through them when they're frozen or moving in slow motion. You'd get a kick out of this."

---

[6] Originally designed by Roman to hold several types of lenses, these were goggles available to each member of the Agents. Mars had tweaked her pair to an absurd degree, making the goggles big and bulky, with many movable lenses. Tiny levers stuck out of each side of the goggles. She named them Very Rad Goggles, or VR Goggles for short.

[7] A crab-like device designed to walk up walls as various cleaning apparatuses emerge from the device's belly to clean the layers of dust covering the entire headquarters.

[8] Mems – memories instilled into objects which manifest as tiny blue figures who have communicated with Edith since she was a little girl.

"One day," said Mars. "Roman or I will create a device to look at the memories you copy."

"Do you think that's possible?"

She shrugged. "Or we'll make a device that works with your ability, that alters it, letting you show us what you see. That's probably the way it would work, if it works at all."

Edith sat down on a stool, taking a long sip of coffee. "What about you? Find any monster candidates?"

Mars twisted her mouth. "Maybe. So I started with Ganesha, the Hindu Elephant-headed deity, because it was the only elephant-related deity or creature I could think of. Going through Indian and Hindu creatures didn't get me anywhere, but I found some interesting creatures from Thai mythology."

She held open one of the old books to an ornate depiction of what looked to be a lion with a long neck and an elephant head. "Two creatures that look like this. The... *Kochasri* and the... *Tukkar Tor*. So far, I can't find out any info on them, just the pictures and that there are many paintings and statues of these creatures."

Edith studied the picture. "Maybe the monsters are Thai. Doesn't quite look like what I've seen, but maybe these are loose interpretations."

"Maybe. Well, I've got a lot more books to look through."

"Yeah, I should get back to studying these memories."

"Good luck, space cadet."

Edith smirked. "You too."

She twisted her hand inside the Extraction Glove to power it on, feeling the fluids being pumped through the tubes inside and out. She looked at the storage cartridge latched into the side of the glove, two glowing dots alongside it, one dot for each memory stored. She pushed the dot of Tommy Butera's memory.

She opened the glove's palm, and the glowing, square memory file appeared, floating just above the metal fingertips. She'd already gone through the brief memory a few times, but one more time couldn't hurt.

With a twist of her gloved hand, the memory burst into shards of light and wrapped around her, replacing the entire lab with an illusion of Nimble's Den. Edith stood near Tommy Butera, a burly, dark-haired man. He'd just been let in by the men guarding the red metal door leading to the alley of Exchange Place. He was about to step foot into the main gambling hall when he stopped, knowing something wasn't right. At the far end of the room, people dropped in that strange wave which Edith had watched now so many times.

He took a step back, the calliope music tickling the back of his skull, stirring up his memories and wishes like a dark stew. The world of the gambling hall went dark, Tommy still standing in that darkness with Edith next to him.

She watched fear grip Tommy's blue eyes.

"Tommy?" It was a woman's voice. "Tommy, is that you?"

He spun around, looking through the darkness, completely ignoring Edith. Then the woman was there, curly brown hair spilling down the shoulders of a black evening dress.

"Angela..." he whispered.

"You've done it," she said. "You got it all back."

The lights turned up, and they were standing in the giant living room of a mansion. White leather couches and chairs, a large television, a wall of windows overlooking a yard with a pool on one side and a fountain on the other. Photos of Tommy, Angela, and a little girl were up on the walls.

"Daddy!"

Tommy turned as his little girl jumped into his arms. He lifted her up, tears streaming down his face.

"Are we together forever now?" she asked.

"Yeah," he said. "I think we are."

Edith slowed the memory to a crawl and began walking around. The room was very detailed for a dream. It was made up of his memories of the real place, which he'd lived in for years.

At the moment, Edith was keeping Tommy's emotions from affecting her, but she'd gone into his emotions earlier, experiencing the memory as he'd experienced it, with his thoughts and feelings. She knew this was the life he'd had years ago. When his business dealings went south, he turned to crime and gambling in a struggle to keep the life. But all that backfired, leaving Tommy jumping from one poor decision to the next, until debt collectors took his house and his wife took his daughter and moved away.

Tommy stayed in a rut for a long time. Just in the thoughts passing through Tommy's mind in this little slice of memory, Edith saw some truly horrific acts that he'd committed. But he was currently trying to crawl his way out. He was still gambling, but he was doing so with careful strategies that he'd developed over the last year. He was winning more than he was losing, and he was paying off his debts.

She looked at the pictures of the three of them, then turned and looked at Tommy holding his daughter. His wife moved in slow motion towards embracing him.

This wasn't just a dream; it was the attainment of the goal he craved the most. This was everything to him. He just wanted his old life back. He wanted his wife and his little girl.

Edith wiped a tear from her cheek.

She was torn. This guy had murdered. He'd hurt people. Part of her wished him luck with getting his family back, and part of her hoped his wife and child found a place to live their life free of the darkness that this man dragged around.

In the end, Edith had no say in it. For this, she was glad.

She twisted her glove slightly, letting time flow forward at half-speed. After the three of them embraced, the dream shifted to them eating a small feast in a large dining room, telling stories and laughing. Here she slowed the memory, stopping it right at the point where one wall of the room is ripped away. Long triangle pieces of white wall hung down like a ripped tapestry, beyond which was utter darkness, like the beginning of the dream. Edith walked into the hole in the wall, looking through it and into the dark beyond. Of course, there wouldn't be anything back there. Like any memory, she was bound by Tommy's perception of the event, and he was sitting at the table.

With nothing new to study, she let the memory play forward slowly. Tommy, his wife, and his daughter were screaming at the suddenly-missing wall. The next section of the room to be ripped away was the one farthest from Tommy. This included the end of the table where his wife was seated.

Edith studied the white triangles hanging from the ceiling where the room now stopped, as if the entire room consisted of nothing but cloth that could be so easily shredded and pulled apart.

Tommy jumped to his feet, his chair clattering to the ground behind him. He reached out and grabbed his scared daughter's arm, pulling her towards him.

Then she was pulled, ripped from his grasp. The food, the table, the dining room were all gone, replaced by a thick sort of darkness—the kind of darkness you don't find your way out of.

Tommy crumpled to his knees, shaking his head as tears bled from his eyes and mouth. He heaved and screamed out, his large, empty hands splayed out in front of him.

Edith looked away, into the darkness, wiping her own tears away. He'd been given everything, even if it was just a dream, then had it ripped away.

She thought of The Skulled Man's words: *Eat all their dreams.*

Was this what each person in The Den experienced? Did the broken calliope show them the attainment of their goals, attainment of their hopes beyond all other hopes? And did the monsters then eat and destroy everything they were dreaming?

How horrifying.

Edith shuddered and flicked her wrist. The darkness broke apart and was sucked back into the Extraction Glove.

File 4 :: [Edith Downs]

The sharp ring of the alarm clock plunged into Edith's mind and yanked her out of a deep sleep. This time she was engaged with dreams of her own, rather than those of a gambler-kinda-ex-criminal. Her eyes opened to morning sunlight splashed over her bedroom.

"Thanks! I'm awake!" she said. The two brass bells on top of the old-fashioned alarm clock stopped ringing.

She'd been using the same round, broken clock for over a month now. The mems inside kept it going and woke her up whenever she asked. Edith had initially bought a digital alarm clock but kept finding it unplugged after accidentally sleeping in. Figuring Maurice was playing with the cord at night, she duct taped the plug into the outlet. When she woke up to find her glass of water had traveled from one side of the bed to the other and poured itself all over the digital clock, destroying it, she realized the mems of the old alarm clock were feeling neglected.

Edith sat up and stretched her neck, then swung her legs off the bed.

Maurice barely stirred from where he slept at the foot of the bed, halfheartedly moaning in complaint of her waking up so early, clearly before his stomach had the appropriate time to wake up and contemplate its own cavernous and empty depths.

She got up and went into the kitchen, pouring water in the teakettle and setting it to boil. She poured food into Maurice's bowl as he sauntered in half-awake, complaining about how she was forcing him to eat so early. Yawning and walking into the bathroom, she brushed her teeth and washed her face, looking at herself in the mirror. No longer did she wonder if the streak of sepia in her eyebrow would go away, nor the discoloration of her eye. She also knew by now that the hair at the top corner of her forehead would continue to grow in sepia strands, probably for the rest of her life.

She'd stood still for most of her life, unknowingly, and now there was only forward momentum. Her life had no time for sitting still.

Smoothing her hair back, she took a hair band and tied it into a ponytail. She was still wearing the gray shirt from the night before (or morning before, rather). Grabbing a pair of blue running shorts from a metal rack above the toilet, she pulled them on, threw a small towel over her shoulder, and went into the kitchen.

Edith ground some coffee in an electric grinder, then poured it into a French press. Since she no longer went to the coffee shop every morning, she'd had to upgrade her coffee situation at home. When the water was ready, she poured it into the glass cylinder and put the lid on top. After a few minutes, she pushed the filter down through the cylinder, then poured the coffee into a big mug, along with cream and allspice.

Taking a long sip, she let the coffee and spices reach through her chest and down her ribs, bringing her bones to life like curling, stretching tree roots. Exhaustion from the late night of studying memories weighed heavily on her. Maybe she'd squeeze some extra sleep in later.

Grabbing a bottle of water, she took her coffee and walked to the front door, stopping at the coat rack to grab the grappling hook and coil of rope hanging from it. Hefting it over one shoulder, she walked out the door and down the stairs to the side yard of her building.

Edith walked across the yard, tossing the grappling hook and rope onto the bench underneath the large oak tree and wiggling her toes around in the wet grass. After going through the twenty minutes of stretches Adelaide had taught her, she stood sipping her coffee and staring at the bench.

A woman was sitting there, crying in the misty rain, wearing a bathrobe with her hair a mess, the distant notes of an accordion dancing on the wind.

Edith smiled, feeling the heat of the coffee mug in her cupped hands, wanting to hug the woman, but not wanting to take anything from her. The woman needed this experience.

And then the *cricking* sound came through the tree branches all around, and Edith's head jerked up, but the sound was only memory. It was too early for the cicadas in this area of the city to need winding up. Her eyes fell to the younger version of herself on the bench. It dispersed like smoke, the wind stealing it away. "It's going to get better," she told the old her, just in case her voice could crawl across time.

Edith set her coffee on the bench, picked up the coil of rope, and backed away from the tree, swinging the grappling hook through the air before launching it upwards. It wrapped around a branch about fifteen feet above the ground, one of the hooks catching onto the rope. She pulled it taught. It had only taken her one try the last few days. Walking up until she was under the branch, Edith leaped up and grabbed as high as she could, then wrapped the rope around her feet and climbed, using both her arms and her legs to propel herself. Moving slowly, she paid more attention to her form than speed.

Get your form down, and the speed will come on its own, the words of Adelaide whispered just over her shoulder.

Reaching the top, she grabbed onto the branch and moved her legs away from the trunk and the grappling hook, then proceeded to do chin-ups. She still couldn't do that many, but her body was feeling stronger all the time.

Then she turned, swinging her legs up to hook around the branch and letting go to hang upside-down. Grabbing the bottom of her shirt, she tied it into a knot over her ribs so she didn't flash anyone who might walk into the side yard. Curling her upper body up towards the branch, she began a series of hanging crunches.

When she finished, she reached over, grabbed the rope and, careful not to scratch her bare legs too much on the bark, unhooked them and swung towards the trunk, pushing against it with her feet as she climbed down using only her hands. She was still clumsy, but she was glad at how fast she was progressing at Adelaide's routines.

"Hello, Edith."

Her heart jumped up in her chest. She looked up to see Wole approaching in the treetops, his dark skin shimmering with golden dust[9]. As per usual, he wore a pair of faded trousers with an open black vest.

"I didn't mean to interrupt," he said. "I was heading up to Riverbend and thought I would see if I could catch you."

"You're not interrupting." Edith jumped up and grabbed the rope, climbing up as he walked closer, branch to branch. When he reached the branch her grappling hook latched onto, he crouched and swung down, holding onto the tree's limb with one hand so he was eye level with her, his other arm snaking around her waist and pulling her close. Their lips met, and she melted against him, feeling her weightlessness in his arms. Even if she let go, he would hold her against himself with no effort.

In his lips she tasted decades upon decades of history—cicadas in times of war and tranquility, trees growing beneath his feet as his boots withered under each step, the surrounding city blooming like a garden.

"I was wondering if we could have a night soon," he whispered.

"Of course."

He bowed his head into the crook of her neck, and she shivered from his warm breath on her skin. He kissed her neck, then her jaw. "Good."

They kissed again, and she looked into his dark eyes, biting her lip. "I'll leave you a note as soon as I can."

"Farewell then, Edith." He slowly let her go, making sure she had a

---

[9]   Pronounced "whoa-leh."

grip on the rope before he did so. He used his arms to walk himself backward toward the tree trunk, then climbed up onto the branch.

Climbing down and dropping to the wet grass, Edith backed away from the tree, still holding the rope, watching as Wole vanished into the distant treetops. Then she flicked the rope so it made a wave towards the branch. On the fourth try, it came free of the hook, and with another flick, she got the grappling hook to swing up over the branch without hurting the tree.

She sighed and licked her lips, still tasting Wole and his past. She could still smell his scent mixed into the sweat of her shirt. She shook her head, smiling, shaking memories of him into the background of her mind.

After stretching again, Edith dropped to the ground and began doing push-ups. When she finished, she took a long drink of water, then picked up the rope and spun the grappling hook, launching it up towards the branch so she could do another round.

*   *   *

Back in her apartment, Maurice lay sprawled out on his bed by the sofa, catching up on all the sleep he'd lost by being woken so early. Edith refilled her water bottle and took a long drink, then walked towards the bathroom but stopped, frozen.

Under her window, sitting on the floor next to her television, was a black antique telephone. It was tall and slender with a round base and a cradle for the earpiece to sit. She'd seen many phones like it in her black and white noir movies.

Her heart raced, and she became hyper-aware of the surrounding room. There was no way that all the mems in the apartment would let anyone sneak in. She thought of the Extraction Glove, which lay quietly in its bag on the loveseat.

She looked up at the shelves of antiques above the television. "How did this get here?"

Blue light shimmered around a couple of the objects, and a few mems emerged. One of the three-inch-tall blue figures stepped forward, sending her an image of a shield and of several blue stick figures.

"Yes, I know who I am," she said, trying to keep her voice calm. "How did this telephone get here?"

It sent her an image of a window.

"Who brought it? How long has it—"

The telephone flickered with dim blue light, and two mems walked out of it. They took a couple steps towards her, and then each dropped to one knee. They sent her a picture of a shield, then of blue stick figures, then a question mark.

"Yes, I am the Protector of Memories. Who brought you here?"

They sent her a picture of an "X".

"I don't understand. Who brought this telephone?"

The two mems looked at each other, then sent her a picture of two blue stick figures.

Edith moved closer and crouched down, getting onto her knees. "You... you two brought your own item here? To my house?"

One of them nodded.

Edith looked up at the shelves. Many other mems had emerged from all her antiques. Addressing the newcomers again, she spoke slowly: "You... *belong* to someone. I can't have other people's property in my apartment. You were in a house or an antique shop or... or maybe a storage unit, right? I need you to take your item and put it where it belongs."

One of her first mems, from the baby blue apron, walked up and conversed with one of the antique phone mems. They conversed, though Edith heard nothing. The apron mem turned to Edith, weaving more complicated pictures for her: A tall house with a yellow bulldozer moving towards it. There was a big arrow pointing at the roof. Then there was a picture that looked like an attic, with a drawing of the phone and an arrow pointing behind a beam. Then two blue stick figures carrying the phone away from the house as the bulldozer broke through the side of it, the house collapsing.

"Ah, I see. So no one owns you, is that correct?"

The new mems nodded.

"Then you are welcome here, of course."

They sent her a picture of a pink heart.

"Make yourselves at home. I've got to get ready for work."

Edith got up, walked into the bathroom, and started up the shower.

File 5 :: [Mars]

Mars sat on a folding chair on the raised flat section of roof just outside the door to her attic apartment, from which the thumping beats and gravelly voice of Tricky poured out to join the songs of the cicadas. The night air was warm and breezy, the kind of air you want to pull around your body and roll around in.

Mars intently studied her hand of cards. "Ha!" She slammed her cards down on the cardboard box she'd set up as a table. "Rummy, son!"

The Function sighed and leaned back on his plastic folding chair, tossing his cards down on the box. "You don't say 'rummy' when you win; it's when you're playing a card on something another player put down."

"Really? 'Cause I think I just rummied the fuck out of you."

"You should not have won that hand."

Scape, being a giant mosquito, stood on a plastic crate, wearing a purple velvet vest and looking over the cards held by his two front legs. He set his cards down on the box.

The Function pushed Scape's shoulder (or would have had Scape owned a shoulder). "That was nice of you to finally let her win a hand, but maybe you could let *me* win once too?"

Scape shrugged, his large feathery antennae waving about. He picked up his mason jar of vodka soda, unfurled his proboscis until it dipped into what was left, and slurped the rest down.

Mars reached over and took all three empty jars. "Time for another round."

The Function started speaking, but Mars was already walking over to the makeshift stairs of plastic crates leading down to the door of her attic apartment. "Don't worry about money; I know Serendipity doesn't hardly pay the two of you. I got this round. I know the bartender, she'll hook me up."

She fixed three more vodka sodas in her kitchen, squeezing lime into each one and using a chopstick from her dish rack to stir them, then headed back up.

"I was trying to say that Scape's gotta go soon," said The Function. "So he doesn't have time for another game."

"Oh, come on!" said Mars, setting the drinks down. "Scape, you know I was just getting warmed up. You don't have to be scared just 'cause you're gonna lose again."

The Function laughed. "No, really, he's got work to do tonight."

Scape nodded.

"Alright, alright," said Mars, sitting back down. "But you said soon, not now." Mars took a sip of her vodka soda, looking deep into Scape's many eyes. They blinked at her like two spherical fields of green-yellow diamonds. "I know you speak, Scape. I want you to say something to me."

The Function leaned over and put a hand on her shoulder. "Whoa! You don't know what you're asking, Mars. Scape doesn't just speak—he can't. He *alters* you."

She didn't take her eyes off Scape's. "He talks to *you*, F."

"Yeah, but I'm used to it. So is Roman. So is Julius."

Mars licked her lips. "And now it's my turn." Then, to Scape, she said: "Do you have something to tell me?"

Scape's eyes held hers as he nodded. He walked forward, off the crate and onto the cardboard box. His proboscis uncoiled and raised, brushing the side of Mars' cheek as he opened something akin to a mouth underneath—a deep, dark hole. When Mars gazed into that darkness, it was like a mirror, and she was gazing into herself. She saw the slats of a wooden fence, those slats being the thin layers of fake persona she displayed to most of the world, with gaps of realness shining through from between them. Somehow Scape conveyed to her that many people had no gaps between the slats, or that they had a full on brick wall between them and the world—they revealed nothing of what they actually were, and perhaps had forgotten themselves entirely. He let her know that what shined through was interpreted by others as Mars' beauty, but it was only a fraction of what she truly was.

Boom.

She was a child, and she crouched down next to the fence, grabbing the sides of her head, her breathing coming short and fast.

Boom.

The man on the other side of the fence slammed his entire body against the wooden wall, bits of the brown-painted wood splintering off and raining down around her, getting into her short brown hair, which stuck up all over.

Her hair had been long and glorious. She'd taken a serrated knife to it, and the man had gone insane.

Boom.

She closed her eyes, then her ears screamed with the howling of wind, the force of which picked her up and threw her against the wall of the house, pain ricocheting through her shoulder. She crumbled into the grass, tears streaming down her face, the wind and noise stopping. The silence was palpable, her ears ringing as she looked up with dread at the approaching man. But this man was unfamiliar, not the man behind the fence.

She flinched and pulled away as he crouched down next to her, his old gray coat wet with dark red spots, which grew like galaxies in the fabric. His blue eyes were far older than anyone she'd ever met. "You never have to be afraid again," he said. "No one is coming after you."

"Who are you?" she asked, tears streaming down her cheek and into the grass.

"I don't have a real name, but I'm called The Function."

Her mouth folded in an ugly way, and she shook her head. "That sounds like something a person with a stupid name would say."

He smiled and then laughed. "Yeah, I suppose it does."

*   *   *

Mars was curled sideways into her plastic folding chair, staring at the remnants of the last rummy game, the sputtering candles illuminating the scattered cards and mason jars of vodka and soda.

The Function sat across from her, the plastic milk crate next to him empty. "Scape had to go."

Mars wiped the tears from her cheeks. "S'alright. I could tell he was afraid of losing again."

He nodded. "You're probably right."

Mars took a deep breath and whispered: "Can you hug me?"

The Function put down his mason jar and walked around the makeshift table, knelt, and put his arms around her. She grabbed onto his arm and squeezed, pushing her face into his shoulder and silently weaving her tears into his shirt. He put a hand on the back of her head, his fingers pressing into her dreadlocks, and kissed her head. "You never know what'll happen when Scape speaks."

She rolled her face against The Function's shirt, drying her face a little, then pulled away. "I wish I could have thanked him."

"You'll have plenty of chances to do that."

Mars looked at his soaked shoulder streaked with red and black eyeliner. "Oh gods, I'm sorry."

The Function smiled. "Don't worry about it. I hardly take my coat off, anyway."

"I know, but you only have one shirt, and I've ruined it. You're going to have that ugly Mars stain on your shoulder until the end of time. It might be even harder for you to get laid."

He shook his head. "Well, you've ruined yet another moment."

She looked up at him and smiled. "I learned from the best."

"Yeah, I suppose that's true."

Letting go of his arm, Mars said: "Thank you. I'm good now."

The Function kissed the top of her head again. "Good, my knees are going numb."

"Old age just creeps up on you, huh?"

"Shut up." He got to his feet and went back to his folding chair, scooting it around the box so that his chair faced hers. After sitting down, he picked up his mason jar of vodka soda and raised it to her.

Mars uncurled from her fetal position, reached over, and grabbed her own jar, raising it. "To love, unending friendship, and sass that won't quit."

The Function smirked, and their glasses tapped together, then they both thunked their glasses on the cardboard box and took a drink. The vodka tingled as it crawled around her insides.

She stretched, giving the vodka more room to maneuver through her, then looked deep into The Function's eyes.

"Really?" he said. "I thought the heavy conversation was over."

Mars shook her head. "It doesn't have to be heavy. When did you meet Scape?"

He took another long drink, his eyes darting up to the swaying trees around them.

"F. You've already protected me—more times than anyone deserves to be."

Leaning back in his chair, he looked at her and shook his head. "I know you can take care of yourself, but I will never give up on protecting you."

Mars leaned forward and placed her hand on his knee. "I know, but keeping knowledge from me is no longer protecting me. In fact, ignorance of any kind is dangerous for me now."

He nodded and took another long drink, then set his jar on the box beside them. "Ask anything you want."

"When did you and Scape meet?"

The Function licked his lips. "Nineteen-twenty-three."

Mars took a deep breath. She knew The Function was old, aging slowly, but had never heard him admit it. Some small piece inside of her held onto a belief that there would be some rational explanation—some puzzle piece that would make all of her suspicions moot.

"Where did you two meet?"

"In the swamps far south of here. There was a cult, a cult of human monks. They worshiped Scape as some kind of prophet or force of enlightenment. Serendipity sent me to find him."

Mars nodded slowly. "How old was he at that point?"

The Function shook his head. "I don't know, I never asked. It's impolite to ask someone their age. Your generation seems to have forgotten that."

"Pshhh. You set yourself up for this one: How old are you?"

The Function smirked. "I don't know."

Mars raised an eyebrow. "You said I could ask anything."

"*Really*, I don't know." He shrugged. "Thirty-eight? Forty? Forty-five? Something like that..."

Mars sipped some of her drink. "How can you be that young? That doesn't make sense."

The Function took out his flask, unscrewing the cap and taking a swig, then handed the flask to Mars. She turned it around in her hands, running her fingertips over the endless dents and scratches.

"That keeps me going," said The Function.

"Chartreuse?"

"Serendipity fills it. I don't know if it's the same as the stuff you can buy at the store."

"Then you're older than forty-five."

He shook his head. "When you were twelve, I sent you to San Francisco."

"I'd have to get a lobotomy to forget."

"I said I'd check on you and never did."

"Yeah. You fucking left me out there. You forgot me."

"No, I died." He looked up at the sky and tongued the inside of his mouth. "Serendipity sent me to bargain with the Swampwalkers, and... well... it didn't end well. There were other factors at play that Serendipity didn't know about." He waved the air like he was waving away memories. "The story's longer than it is interesting. And then you moved back to New Orleans, but you didn't see me right away. Actually, you didn't see me for years."

Mars squeezed her temples. "You showed up about four years ago. Somehow found my apartment and knocked on the damned door."

He reached over and tapped the flask in her hands. "That's when Serendipity brought me back."

Mars brought the flask to her nose, but she only smelled the sweet spices of Chartreuse. "And then when you vanished again for nearly a year?"

"Oh, that was a street performer who came back from the dead, then beat the hell out of me, shattering most of my ribs. I was probably gonna die anyway, but he threw me into the river, and I drowned. For some reason, he had a dozen or so talking squirrels following him around, but I never figured that part out. They *did* speak only in rhyming poetry, so maybe that doesn't count as talking."

Mars looked down at the flask. "But she brought you back."

"Yeah. Eventually, she always does."

"You showed up a few months ago... she brought you back because of Rachel."

"The Agents of Fateful Encounters were wiped out. Serendipity brought me back to help fill the void in the city."

"Gods, how long have you been doing this?"

"A long time."

"And when you die, you don't age?"

"No one ages when they're dead."

She reached out and took his hand, holding it. "I'm so sorry. No one should have to go through that."

"Don't be sorry. If I hadn't gone through it, I never would have met you."

Mars smiled, a tear falling down her cheek. "But to die over and over again..."

"Oh, I've died so many times; it's really not so bad. I mean... no, that's a total fucking lie. Dying is *horrible*—I wouldn't recommend it. But I've kind of gotten used to it. It's coming back to life that's *truly* excruciating. Like being dragged across a street of broken glass."

"Yikes."

"So, in conclusion, don't die. But if you do, definitely don't come back." He grinned. "Unless it's 'cause you miss me. And you don't mind the whole broken glass thing."

She squeezed his hand in hers. "I'm sorry."

"It's not your fault."

"No, I've yelled at you, I've said terrible things. I couldn't understand how you could just vanish from my life. I'm sorry for the things I've said."

"I could have told you the truth."

Mars wiped tears from her cheek with her shoulder. "No, I don't think you could. That's not who you are."

The Function chuckled. "You are the only person who might know who I am."

"That knowledge is quite the burden, let me tell you."

"Oh, shut up."

Mars reached over and grabbed Scape's full mason jar of vodka soda and used it to top off their glasses. "Ok, one more question for tonight."

The Function sighed and took a long drink. "Alright, make it a good one."

"When were you born?"

The Function shook his head and looked at the scattered playing cards beside them. "I... I'm not sure."

"When's your birthday?"

The Function leaned forward, holding his mason jar in both hands, looking down at his boots. "There are certain things I just haven't thought about for a long time. And you have to understand; time moved slower back then. People didn't live as long. At thirteen, you were an adult. Things are a little hazy."

"Damn, how long ago are we talking about?"

His eyes met hers. "I can tell you when I met Serendipity—when I began working for her. That date is easy to remember."

"And you were an Agent back then?"

He shook his head. "I've held the title of Agent, sure, but I've always been Serendipity's wild card, her ace. Since early on, there was a fissure between Bes and her, a struggle for the direction of the Agents, until she split off entirely, taking me with her."

"So then tell me, when did you meet Serendipity?"

The Function took a long drink, then stared down at the jar in his hands. "January eighth, eighteen-fifteen. The Battle of New Orleans."

"Holy fuck."

"Yeah."

"Were you a soldier?"

He shook his head. "I'm not good at taking orders. Usually."

"How old were you when you met her?"

Turning the glass around in his hand, he thought a moment. "Sometimes, looking back, I think I was fifteen, sometimes twenty. But I could have been younger. Like I said, time moved slower."

Mars took a long drink, then studied the features of her best friend—how he held himself. "Besides the old coat, you don't look or sound like you're from back then."

"I'm good at adapting, always have been. Anyway, how many people do you know from 'back then'?"

"Point taken. But good at adapting? Seems like you've died a lot."

He shrugged. "I've died fewer times than Bes. You gonna tell Bes that I'm not good at adapting, but that he's even worse?"

Mars raised an eyebrow. "Did you just talk shit about a god?"

"Wouldn't be the first time."

Mars laughed, swaying in her seat and realizing how much vodka she'd had. Raising her jar, she said, "Cheers to that."

The Function tapped his jar to hers, then they both took a long swig.

File 6 :: [Roman Wing]

The streetcar squealed to a stop, the doors folding open onto the nighttime street. Roman made his way to the front of the empty streetcar. "Thank you, Henri," he said to the elderly black man in the driver's seat.

"Any time," said Henri, rubbing his gray beard. "You want me to wait?"

Roman shook his head. "I don't know how long we'll be."

"Alright, then you two be careful now."

Roman stepped out of Henri's streetcar and onto Frenchmen Street. Edith followed behind, already wearing the Extraction Glove. The afternoon sky was gray and cloudy.

Metal streetcar tracks rose up from the cracked street in front of the streetcar as it accelerated into the night. The tracks melded down into the street behind it, back into the past whence they came.

Usually, Frenchmen Street at night was rife with live music. Jazz, brass bands, and guitar would spill together in the street, coming from every club, street corner, and bar. Tonight it was hauntingly quiet. People in every direction were lying on the ground, gazing up at the club ceilings or the sky. Perhaps a thousand people.

"We don't have long," said Roman, pulling out his Reader and flipping it open. "Not between people waking up and law enforcement arriving."

Edith powered on her glove. "It's weird to be here again. Feels like wandering the rooftops with Adelaide happened years ago. It also feels like last night."

Roman smirked. He hadn't been eating as much Wonder since Nimble's Den and wholly related to Edith's sentiment. "It feels like last week when I too wandered the rooftops of the French Quarter with Adelaide."

"You mean like in the '30s?"

He nodded.

"I can't even fathom that."

"Stick around a while, and you will. In one way or another."

Edith walked up to a cluster of young musicians lying on the sidewalk, brass instruments cradled in their hands. They were in a state similar to those found in The Den, yet something was different. The looks on their faces radiated euphoria and happiness.

"What about the Fair Memory Act?" Edith asked Roman.

"I'm probably not going to know any of these people or their past deeds, so we have to get their permission."

Edith crouched down, figuring out who was closer to being conscious and asking if she could see their memories. One, though confused, said yes, and she began copying their memories of the past fifteen minutes.

Roman continued watching the Reader for any information it gave to him. He stayed highly aware of any movement going on along the street, keeping watch over Edith.

"How many should I get?" Edith asked him after she'd copied two.

"Seven would be ideal, from down the block. We don't know where The Skulled Man was. Maybe we could get someone who saw him."

She walked down the block with him, dipping into a club and talking to people who were waking from whatever dream state the Skulled Man had thrust them into. Edith found a woman her own age, a black apron tied around her waist, and spoke to her through the haze of the woman's dreamy state, getting permission to copy her memories.

File 7 :: [Delia Sadler]

Like any afternoon, the Frenchmen Street club was full of jazz music and chatting tourists, with the occasional local sprinkled in. Delia poured drinks behind the bar as the five-piece jazz band played on the little stage across the room. When there was a break in customers, she grabbed her cigarettes from underneath the bar.

"Hey Mark, I'm smokin'," she told her fellow bartender.

"Damn right you are," he said, then turned to an approaching customer. It was a joke they'd had going on for months now. Mark didn't even smoke, but he still said, "I'm smokin'" when going on break, and Delia would retort with, "Yeah, you right," or something in that vein.

She walked across the club, pulling out her lighter as she came up to the large windows and front door. Her stomach dropped as she saw people running in terror past the club and down the street, away from something. She stopped at the doors, ready to shut and lock them in case it was a shooting. She hadn't heard shots, though, had she?

More people were running past. She grabbed one door, swinging it shut and reaching up to shove the bolt into the doorjamb. Then she saw it —an animal like nothing she'd seen before—charging down the street, howling as it knocked a man to the ground with a swipe of a massive paw, his body hitting the ground with a loud *crack*. The animal was a mass of fur and scales and rage, with curving tusks, a coiling trunk, and a mouth full of teeth.

"*Jesus fuck!*" she yelled.

The jazz musicians behind her stopped playing as the screams from the street grew louder. Someone with a giant skull over their head walked up behind the animal, followed by another two of the beasts, each animal with a person limply dangling from their massive jaws.

The person wearing the skull was playing a keyboard, the dark and surreal music tickling the back of Delia's skull. She reached for the other door, her hand resting on the handle. Then her fear vanished like the flame of a snuffed-out candle.

The first beast she'd seen reached down with its jaws and picked up the man it had knocked down, then all three of the beasts vanished along with the people they carried. The man wearing the skull kept playing, and Delia realized that none of it mattered. The only thing that mattered were those dreams she'd somehow misplaced in the last thirty years. But there was nothing to worry about, was there? Because there they were, her dreams, buried just underneath the path she walked upon. She reached down, dug into the dirt at her feet, and picked one up. The dirt fell off the dream with the slightest shake—it shined even brighter than it had when she was a little girl.

It was the single most beautiful thing she'd ever seen, and she knew that everything was going to be alright.

File 8 :: [Roman Wing]

People were waking from whatever dreams The Skulled Man had brought them. Some looked skeptically at Edith and Roman, and the sound of sirens rose into the air. Edith was in a doorway hunched over a service worker, the woman dressed in black with an apron around her waist, a pack of cigarettes and a lighter lying next to her open hand.

"*Holy shit,*" whispered Edith.

Roman walked up and touched her shoulder. "Time to go."

The sound of revving motorcycles flooded the waking street. The dark riders came from both ends of the street, six in total, all of them on slick street bikes. Roman approached the one bike that rolled ahead of the others. The rider pulled off their helmet. If he didn't recognize her from all the blades strapped to her body, he would have recognized her by her closed eyes and long, black hair.

Nemu, the Sleeping Assassin.

Roman had always felt a kinship with Nemu, enjoying the immense calm that she emanated. The kinship didn't go deep, though—he never understood how someone so relaxed and orderly could work for Nimble. Roman was fairly certain that she made Nimble's operations stronger, bringing a layer of order to his chaos.

Nemu's entourage parked their bikes along the street. They scattered, pulling out devices and artifacts to investigate the area. Nemu herself dismounted her bike in the middle of the street as Roman approached, Edith at his side.

"You should let us know what you find about the culprit," said Nemu.

"And why is that?" asked Roman.

"When we find him, he'll disappear. He'll never again bother the citizens of New Orleans."

"So we're cooperating," said Roman. "Who is he? What's his name?"

Nemu merely stood there, her eyes closed, her face aimed at Roman.

"If he goes away, we both win."

"What about the creatures?" Roman asked. "What are they?"

Her face twitched, just the smallest wrinkle in her mask of serenity, gone in less than a second. "We'll take care of the creatures. You should tell us anything you know. We want this taken care of just as you do."

"I'm sure, only for different reasons. We got what we came for. If you feel like cooperating, you know how to contact us." Roman walked past Nemu, followed by Edith. He was acutely aware of Nemu's position and movements, in the off chance that she pulled a blade and attacked.

He scanned the others of her crew, one of them using a short spear artifact, possibly of Riverwalker design, which emitted a blue light onto everything they pointed it towards. Some kind of reading device, probably scanning for dream energy.

He led Edith towards the French Quarter, which was mere blocks away. Once they were far enough, Roman broke the silence. "Did you see her face?"

She answered in a whisper, as if Nemu could hear them. "Yeah, when you mentioned *creatures*."

"I haven't had many interactions with her, but I've never seen her display emotion before. She has a stake in this."

They crossed Esplanade Avenue and made their way alongside The Old U.S. Mint, which doubled as the Jazz Museum, where The Angel of Death had stolen Louis Armstrong's first cornet mere months before.

"It should be safe to talk now," said Roman.

"The beasts knocked people out and kidnapped them."

"Kidnapped?"

"Yeah. I barely glanced at memories as I copied them, for the sake of time, so all I saw at first were the charging beasts. Seems The Skulled Man showed up and let at least five beasts loose to charge into the crowds, knock people down, and pick them up. Then he began playing the calliope device, and everyone fell into their dreams or whatever."

"Did you see the beasts feed?"

"No, I don't think they had time to. The Skulled Man didn't stay long. Maybe the creatures were taking those people to feed on later."

"Perhaps he was afraid of the authorities arriving too quickly."

"Or us."

"Or Nemu, for that matter."

They turned towards the river and headed into Dutch Alley, which ran parallel to it, and walked up to a payphone. Roman grabbed the receiver, dropped a few coins in, and hit some numbers. It rang a few times.

"*Agents of Badass, how can we save the city today?*"

"Mars, tell Julius we're having a meeting," said Roman. "Edith and I are getting on the streetcar in a minute."

"*You got it.*"

He hung up the phone, and they headed towards the river where the streetcar tracks (the current ones, not the past ones) lay waiting.

"The phone thing still weirds me out," said Edith.

"You'll get used to it."

Edith shrugged. "If you say so."

Roman pulled out an ancient streetcar token and flipped it into the air, catching it as they walked up to the tracks. A moment later, Henri's streetcar squealed to a stop in front of them, the accordion doors sliding open. "That was fast after all," said Henri. "Where to?"

"Spanish Plaza."

File 9 :: [Julius Marcos]

Julius and Mars were only in the Planning Room for a few minutes when Edith walked in. She pulled off her Extraction Glove and set it on the table.

"On your three," said Mars, tossing a beer can spinning through the air. Edith caught it, opened it one handed, and took a long swig.

"Where's Roman?" asked Julius.

"He's headed to Nimble's Den. Said I could speak for him."

"Alright, what have you got for us?"

"The Skulled Man hit Frenchmen Street. I need to comb through the memories I copied, but it seems he appeared near Decatur and Frenchmen with at least five of the beasts, causing chaos as people ran in terror. The beasts ran through the crowd and took one person each, knocking them out and picking them up in their jaws. The beasts vanished and The Skulled Man played the calliope device, sending hundreds of people into good thoughts and dreams."

Julius flexed his mechanical arm, wanting to take it off. Most days he felt like all it did was *itch* and get in his way. "What did Roman say?"

"He read the same dream energy at Frenchmen as he did at The Den," said Edith. "He went to The Den in case The Skulled Man shows up there again tonight. Also to watch for Nemu. She showed up to Frenchmen Street with her thugs. Asked Roman to let her know what we knew. He asked her about The Skulled Man and the creatures, but she didn't answer. When he mentioned the creatures, though, her face twitched. She had an emotional reaction to that."

"Interesting. Did Roman say anything else?"

"He votes that we contact The Nor."

"Oh fuck," said Mars. "Those *kids* who run through fog with freaking swords, disappearing whenever they want?"

"There's no need to fear them," said Julius. The itching of his metal arm became too much. He pulled the leather straps loose, taking it off and dropping it on the table. "Sun's coming up soon, so it'll have to be tomorrow evening. The Nor are best contacted at night. You'll go to Jackson Square around midnight tomorrow. You'll ask for them."

"Jackson Square? And who exactly are we supposed to ask?" said Mars.

"The cats," said Julius.

"Oh," said Mars. "Yeah, that makes complete sense, just like everything else."

File 10 :: [Edith Downs]

Late the next night, Edith and Mars made their way down Decatur Street. Drunken laughter spilled from bars, thumping bass spilled from cars. As they passed the empty pedestrian walkway along one side of Jackson Square, Mars patted Edith on the shoulder to stop.

"Collectors," she whispered, looking down at her boots but nodding her head down the stone walkway. "Look out of the corner of your eye. There are a couple down by the bench doing something."

Edith looked down and saw out of her periphery the small, blurred figures in the light of the street lamps. There were at least three. She wanted to get used to seeing them, so she knew when they were around, but with all the other tasks constantly rumbling around in her mind, she hadn't quite gotten the hang of always paying attention to her periphery. She heard a splash and then a loud, hoarse laugh.

"Oh, hell no," whispered Mars, turning and running down the stone walkway. *"Hey! That's gross! We told you to stop doing that!"*

Edith turned to look but saw nothing except Mars running, so she looked away as she followed behind Mars, careful not to trip on the stones. The three blurry figures laughed and split up, one bolting towards Pirate's Alley, one hopping the fence into the park of Jackson Square, and the third scaling up the side of the Pontalba Apartments.

Catching up with Mars, Edith saw the pile of discarded plastic cups and colorful plastic containers known for containing sickeningly sweet boozy drinks from Bourbon Street.

"Jackasses," said Mars.

"They pour them under the stones, is that it?"

Mars nodded, pushing her boot down slowly on one of the stones, liquid splashing up from underneath. "Some stones are loose. The Collectors gather abandoned drinks from around the Quarter, bring them here, lift the loose stones, and pour the alcohol underneath. When someone steps on the stone, the liquid splashes up onto their foot."

"*Eck.* Gross is right."

"Roman says they've been doing this on and off for decades. I'm gonna freaking stop them, though."

"Good luck with that. They don't seem easily convinced."

The two Agents picked up the empty cups and containers, tossing them into a trash can. Then they walked up to the side gate of the park. Through the bars they could see the trees, benches, and pathways of the park, along with the statue of Andrew Jackson atop his rearing horse. To their left, the Saint Louis Cathedral rose into the night sky.

Mars motioned to the massive Extraction Glove covering Edith's arm to the elbow, with all of its vials and tubes. "I like that you wear that all the time."

"It helps me," said Edith. "The weight of it reminds me what I'm doing—why I'm an Agent."

"Well, it's your trademark now, so you're not allowed to get tired of wearing it."

"I don't think I *could.*"

"Good. With you wearing that, it's like I have to be more badass to compensate." Mars shrugged. "And I like being more badass, so it's a win-win, really."

"Glad to help."

Mars pulled out what she now called "the Skeleton Key"—the device she'd used to "borrow" the party buses they'd taken to the Tartarus Realm to stop The Axeboy. Roman had designed it to turn on most kinds of machines, but she'd modified it to also open simple locks. It was a six-inch metal rod with buttons along one side. The lock to the gate opened right up, and they were inside the park.

A half-dozen cats suddenly turned their way, their eyes gleaming from the Square's light posts. Some were peeking out from behind or inside bushes; others were merely lying sprawled out on the park's pathways. Edith took a deep breath and let her awareness reach out to the living memories in the park, feeling the firecracker-like memories of the stray cats, and she sensed that there were more than a dozen cats in total.

"Are we supposed to talk to a certain one?" she asked Mars, who shrugged and licked her lips before raising her voice to address them:

"Cats of Jackson Square! We apologize for stepping into your nightly domain. I am Mars, this is Edith, and we represent The Agents Of. We were wondering if you would be so kind as to deliver a message to The Nor. We seek an audience with them."

One cat, stretched out and moonbathing on the pathway near the statue of Andrew Jackson, rolled up onto its feet. It stretched and yawned and then bolted off in a lakeward direction.

Mars nodded to the remaining cats. "Our many thanks. Let us know if there is anything we can do to repay you."

The cats, each one a different color, size, and type, merely stared at them with mixed expressions of abject boredom.

"I can't tell if they're annoyed at us," whispered Mars.

Edith shook her head. "No, I think they're just cats."

"Ok."

Edith motioned to some metal benches. "Feel like sitting?"

"Sure."

As they made their way to the benches, Edith noticed a couple small piles of cat food hidden behind some bushes. "Who do you think feeds them?"

"Oh, that's Tomas," said Mars. "The entity who's the Caretaker of Jackson Square. You might have seen him before—bald guy, overalls, usually talking to the plants here. I don't think he's around at night very much."

"He's the one who gave you the flower?"

Mars pulled back the sleeve of her leather jacket and looked at the daisy with its stem coiled around her wrist. "Yeah, for protection. Gave it to me to thank me for helping him out."[10]

"Does it work?"

Mars shrugged. "I haven't broken any bones or died since I got it."

"It still looks really fresh."

"Yeah, the perfect gift for me, a plant that I never have to water and that won't die."

They sat down on a long, curved bench in the park's corner. They had a picturesque view of the statue, the cathedral, and all the gorgeous architecture around them, not to mention the giant old trees stretching their branches into the night sky.

Edith sat back with her arms on the back of the bench and her legs crossed. Mars leaned back, stretching her back and neck.

"Mars, how are you doing?" asked Edith.

Mars looked over at her, about to laugh, then her smile faded. "Oh, you're asking a real question. I was about to give one of my token answers, like 'Badass as usual,' or something like that." She looked out over the Square, then back at Edith. "I'm good. Really good. I love being an Agent, and I feel like Julius and Roman are the compasses I've been needing for a long time. They aren't perfect, but I'm learning so much from them. I like the direction of my life."

Edith smiled. "It makes me happy to hear that."

"What about you, girl?"

---

[10] See The Agents Of, Volume I.

Edith bit her lip, thinking. "I enjoy being an Agent, and learning more about my memory abilities. And I love the Extraction Glove...."

"But..."

"But I really want to help the memories of the city. I want to protect them, to keep them safe. And I've helped some of them. They're safer than they were months ago. I just can't help but wonder if my idea to protect them is too big. Maybe it's beyond me."

"Oh, hell no. You're the *Protector of the Memories of New Orleans.*"

Edith reached over and pushed Mars' shoulder. "Oh, shut up."

Mars shrugged. "You know what we need? When was the last time we hung out and got nice and plastered? Let's go dancing or something."

Edith sighed. "I'd love that."

"Oh, how's Wole?"

"He's freaking great."

Mars laughed. "Damned right he is."

Edith tapped Mars on the shoulder, pointing towards the dense fog rolling out of the alleys beside the cathedral and through the wrought-iron fence of the park.

"That was fast," whispered Mars.

More fog came from behind them, from the river. It covered Decatur Street and blanketed the whole Square, though it remained thickest on the far side of the park from Edith and Mars, leaving the Saint Louis Cathedral like a floating castle in a river of clouds. The two Agents got to their feet, watching small, shadowy figures running back and forth through the approaching mist.

Cartwheeling out of the mist came a small person with a bowler hat. The young person stopped their cartwheel in a handstand, looking across the pathway at the two Agents from an upside-down face covered in white mime makeup. The mime pushed off into the air with their arms, flipping to land in a crouch.

Edith realized it was a girl, a young black girl. White makeup covered her face, with black smeared around her eyes, and her lips painted dark blue. The white makeup was choppy at the edges, like she had smeared it on with fingers. The girl wore a white button-up shirt, a dark red vest, black slacks, and boots. She stood up and reached over her shoulder, pulling out the black walking cane which was shoved through the back of her vest, then twirled it in her fingers.

Two boys walked out of the fog behind her. They wore frayed shirts and shorts, along with boots. One had a civil war sword hanging from his belt, the other a machete. Edith guessed the age of the girl and one of the boys to be about eleven, with the other boy around nine. Though they looked like kids, she was well aware that The Nor were as ageless as they were dangerous. These three "kids" could easily be far older than Edith.

The mime stepped forward, her cane suddenly stopping in her fist, stretching horizontally in the air. The cane's handle was a crouching, silver frog. She bowed her head and reached her free arm towards Edith and Mars. Her bowler hat tipped off her head somehow, rolling down the length of her arm and into her hand. "You have called for an audience with The Nor." Her hair was sticking up in a multitude of two-inch black braids.

"*Damn*," Mars whispered to Edith. "We've gotta up our style game."

Edith followed Mars' lead as they walked closer to the three Nor, behind which several more shadows darted through the fog. As the two Agents got closer, Edith could see tattoos covering what little she could see of the girl's dark skin—up her neck and along her wrists.

Mars nodded. "I'm Mars, and this is Edith. We're The Agents Of. We were wondering if we could ask you a few questions."

The mime flicked her wrist and the bowler hat rolled back up her arm, where she bumped it with her shoulder, sending it flipping back to land on her head. She reached up and pressed it down over her braids. "My name's Keaton. Ask away."

"Damn you're cool," said Mars.

"Thanks," said Keaton. "But… I'm kinda busy."

"Of course," said Edith, elbowing Mars.

"Someone stole pieces off the calliope," said Mars. "They modified those pieces to enhance dreams and aspirations in some way. Then this person attacked Nimble's Den, using the device along with several beasts that may be able to feed on dreams."

"Heard about that. And that's a problem?" asked Keaton.

"Well, no," said Mars. "But then he hit Frenchmen last night. Innocent people were affected, and five were hurt and kidnapped."

"He's affecting dreams," said Edith. "We wanted to ask if you knew anything, if you'd noticed anything, since you deal with dreams."

Keaton looked back at the two boys, who each shook their heads. "No, I don't think we know anything about this. We'll look into it and let you know if we find anything."

"Thank you," said Mars.

Keaton motioned towards Edith's Extraction Glove. "You Agents always have the coolest shit. What does that do?"

Edith glanced at Mars, who shrugged, then turned back to Keaton. "It's an Extraction Glove. I use it to copy memories from peoples' heads."

Keaton whistled. "Dark and messed up. I like it."

"Well, I usually get the person's permission," said Edith.

"*Usually* is a fun word," Keaton said with a smirk.

One boy behind her held back a laugh, while the other failed to do so.

Keaton used her cane to point at the multicolored goggles strapped to

Mars' forehead. "Anyway, it looks like Roman's still quite the tinkerer."

"Roman made the base, but most of what you see are my modifications. Roman's a good teacher."

Keaton nodded. "Groovy. Well, tell Roman I say hello. And Serendipity. Though I don't know if she'd remember me, that was long ago."

Edith spoke up: "We don't work for Serendipity."

"The Agents used to," said Mars.

"Oh?" Keaton turned, tossed her cane to one of the boys, and walked up to the other, holding out her hand. He pulled the civil war sword from his belt and handed it to her, resting the blade over his palms. She took the sword by the handle and walked towards Edith and Mars.

Edith's heart quickened, but she held her ground, waiting to see if Mars was going to react.

Keaton flipped the sword so that the blade was downward, then thrust it into the dirt pathway. She took a step back and looked at Mars. "Indulge me. Pull it out of the ground."

Mars shook her head. "As Agents, we do not use or touch weapons."

Keaton looked to Edith, who also shook her head.

Keaton pulled the sword from the ground. "Not touching weapons is Serendipity's rule. You sure you don't work for her?"

"Yeah, pretty sure," said Mars.

She turned and tossed the sword to the other Nor, who caught it by the handle just as the third Nor threw her the cane. The two boys walked into the fog, joining the other shadows, and Keaton turned to Edith and Mars. "I'll let you know if we find your calliope thief."

"Thank you," said Edith.

"If you ever need anything," said Mars, "don't hesitate to call on us."

Keaton smiled, stepping back into the fog. "Oh, I don't know if the Agents can help with the things we deal with, just as The Nor can't do much to help you. But you ladies keep Roman and Julius out of trouble."

The fog swallowed her up until she was nothing but shadow. One by one, the shadows of The Nor disappeared until only the fog remained.

"And I say again," said Mars, "we've gotta up our style game."

Edith glanced up at the cathedral's clock. "Well, we're done before one in the morning. That's a win, at least."

"You got that right."

They turned and walked towards the opened gate of the park. Mars locked the gate back up, and then they strolled towards the river.

File 11 :: [Mars]

Mars walked into the break room, followed by Edith. She opened the fridge and threw Edith a beer, then raised her own.

Edith tapped her beer to Mars', then they knocked them on the table, and both drank. Roman walked in with his sleeves rolled up. His arms and the front of his shirt were splattered with a glittery green liquid. He'd obviously cleaned his hands, which were mostly devoid of the green and glitter. Traces of it were even smeared on his face.

"Lose a fight with some ectoplasm?" asked Mars.

Roman's face twisted up, then he smiled and laughed.

Mars froze, her beer can slipping from her fingers. It clinked on the ground and fell on its side, and she quickly crouched to pick it up. She looked over at Edith, who was also looking at Roman wide-eyed.

"Um, Roman, did you just laugh at a *Ghostbusters* joke?"

Roman's laugh shrunk into a smile. "Ghost-what?"

"I've never seen you laugh like that," said Edith. "I mean, I've seen you laugh a little, but not that much."

"Well, it was quite funny," said Roman.

"But you don't know the movie *Ghostbusters*?" asked Mars.

He shook his head, then looked at their beers. He opened the fridge and grabbed one for himself.

"But *ectoplasm* is funny?" asked Mars.

"Yes, of course, in the context," said Roman, taking a sip of beer. "Ectoplasm used to be a largely debated phenomenon in the early 1900s. It was really a catch-all word for many substances related to completely different phenomena, so most of its supposed properties were a kind of amalgamation of properties from those various substances. The Scientist, who is the Agent I've mentioned to you before, conducted many studies on the substances attributed to being ectoplasm. Of course, he wasn't publishing in scientific journals or anything, so most of his research is kept around our various headquarters, as well as his old lab down in the First Quarter."

"Huh," said Mars. "I'll have to work on more ectoplasm jokes. Noted."

"Is Julius here?" asked Edith.

"He's out questioning some of his contacts," said Roman. "Did you meet with The Nor?"

"Yeah, about that..."

"I hope they weren't too aggressive. Some have a tendency for shocking people rather than talking to them. A bit like the Collectors in that respect."

"The meeting went well," said Mars. "We spoke to Keaton, who says hi. She said they don't know anything, but she'll look into it."

"Keaton," said Roman, smiling. Mars knew he was already leaning towards his human side with how he'd laughed so hard, and she could tell that the beer was pulling him even further in that direction. "I'm so glad she's still around."

"Ok," said Mars, pointing at Roman with her beer. "I want to hear that story. But first, maybe you can tell us *exactly* what The Nor are."

Roman took a long swig of his beer. "Very well. The Nor are... guardians, in the same way that The Agents Of are guardians. The Nor guard *dreams* and *ideas*. They guard the potential of imagination within New Orleans. They are also very closely tied to Carnival and Mardi Gras. In fact, in the 1930s and '40s, they had their own parade, called The Mystic Krewe of N.O.R., which was the first parade that consisted of children. In the context of the parade, 'N.O.R.' stood for 'New Orleans Romance', the word 'romance' back then meaning *fantastical*, like the worlds of fairy tales."

"But they've been around longer than the '30s," said Edith.

"Quite right. They formed in the late eighteenth century, though you can't ask a Nor—dealing so much with dreams, they don't have a clear concept of time."

"And kids can just join them?" asked Mars.

"Kids who have lost a lot are sometimes found by The Nor and asked to join. A child who becomes Nor stops aging, and by most definitions, ceases being human. They *see* the real world of New Orleans, but they do not *inhabit* it. They inhabit the city's dreams more than anything else, which can be infinitely more beautiful, or infinitely more terrifying."

"Do they have a leader?" asked Mars.

"Their leader is chosen by some sort of challenge system and always takes on the name King Nor."

"Keaton's not their leader, is she?"

"If she were, I believe she would have introduced herself as King

Nor."

"How do you know Keaton?" asked Edith.

"After the last incarnation of Bes died, and before Julius turned fifteen and remembered who he was, I led the Agents. During this time, I had the task of finding a replacement for The Moon."

Mars coughed. "What?"

Edith walked over to the fridge. "I think this segue calls for a second beer."

"Speaking my language," said Mars as Edith threw her one.

Edith motioned to Roman, who downed the last of his beer and took one from her before continuing:

"You met The Angel of Death, of course. And Edith knows Wole. There are many jobs throughout the city which have to be passed down for one reason or another. The Agents are sometimes called on to help in that process. In the late 1970s, we were charged with facilitating the passing on of the job of The Moon. Two of The Nor, Keaton and her brother Quill, came to us and asked us to consider their mother."

"Keaton is the daughter of the freaking *Moon*?" asked Mars.

"Keaton and Quill were twins who both became Nor, but about ten years ago, Quill died. The Nor, like the Agents, live quite hazardous lives."

"Damn," said Mars.

"Were The Nor started by kids then?" asked Edith.

"No, they were started by a very old *entity* named Revel. The oldest entities of the city are not tied to buildings or places like The Wellington Bank or Jackson Square. These old entities are more like physical representations of *aspects* of the city, rather than of a place. I'm not certain whether they were ever tied to a place at all, except for New Orleans itself."

"Serendipity's one of those old entities, isn't she?" asked Mars.

Roman nodded, taking a sip of his beer.

"Serendipity started the Agents," said Edith, "and Revel started The Nor."

"Yes. Two great fires nearly destroyed the colony of New Orleans in the late eighteenth century. One fire in seventeen-eighty-eight and the other in seventeen-ninety-four. The colony, Spanish at the time, had only been founded seventy years earlier by the French, and consisted of the area which is now The French Quarter. The fires were not normal fires; they were forces that burned the very reality of the city, ripping apart the city's core. Serendipity and the Agents at the time did what they could, but the city was going to be lost for good. Revel, who had frequently worked with the Agents, came up with an idea. Since reality was breaking apart, she stepped *physically* into the dreams of the city. Mixing her own dreams with those of the dying city, she wove them together like rope, creating what are now called the *dream tethers*. She used these dream tethers to bind reality together, a kind of net keeping the reality of the city from falling apart.

"While her dreams and subconscious integrated with those of the city, she found she could connect with children, since they are much closer to their dreams. She found children who had no reason to care about the waking world—the abandoned and the neglected—and she enlisted their help to wrap reality in dream tethers. Those were the first of The Nor, the guardians of the dreams of New Orleans."

"Wow," said Mars. "Holy shit, that's epic."

"So that's why reality can be so dreamlike in this city..." said Edith.

"Yes, the waking world is thinner here than in any other city I know of." Roman took a swig of beer, looking over the two of them. "Do you have further questions?"

All were silent for a moment, Mars figuring Edith was still processing everything like she was.

"I think I'm answered out," said Edith.

"Wait," said Mars. "The First Quarter, where the Riverwalkers live at the bottom of the river—did Revel put that there?"

"I believe so. But it's best not to mention it to anyone. Whoever put it there had their reasons and has never come out to claim the deed. My theory is that The First Quarter was placed in the river to *hide* something, possibly evidence pertaining to the two great fires. Elsh is one of the few people who knows my theory. She and I have scoured much of The First Quarter, but we've never found evidence to support my theory. Of course, since I believe Revel put The First Quarter in the river, I'm not worried about whatever is down there with it—it's more of a curiosity. I trust Revel's judgment and whatever plan she may have."

Mars nodded. "Ok, I might be answered out now too. Speaking of dreams, mine are going to be freaking crazy tonight."

Edith yawned. "Mine too."

Roman stood up straight and stretched his shoulders back, which made him look a bit not-human with the way his muscles and bones moved. "Well, you know where I'll be if you have more questions."

File 12 :: [Roman Wing]

The next evening was both warm and cool, the dual currents swimming around one another to flirt and nuzzle each other like cats. The last bit of light in the sky was nearly extinguished, yet seemed to hold on indefinitely, like somebody blowing out a candle too slowly to put out the flame.

Julia Street was full of meandering locals, some dressed casually and some rather fancily as they mingled, drank wine, and poured into and out of the art galleries lining both sides of the street. The street was blocked off to traffic, creating a pedestrian mall for the night. Plastic tables selling drinks lined the middle of the street, as well as small stages hosting performance art and glowing sculptures of paper and light. Looming high above the galleries in every direction were tall warehouses, business buildings, and hotels.

Roman followed Elsh out of one gallery and over to an empty section of sidewalk. People chatted and strolled all around them. Elsh turned to him, smiling, her long black hair spilling over her shoulders in different-sized braids with vines and leaves woven into them. Her dark skin gleamed in the light of the paper sculptures, and the parts that were silvery and scaled reflected the light like pools of liquid metal.

Her long, flowing dress was pieced together from a sail she'd found on the bottom of the Mississippi along with rope netting, fashioned into a kind of gown that reminded Roman of movie starlets of the 1940s. There were slits cut into the sides to make way for the fins protruding from her shoulders and the sides of her torso. Also emerging from the slits were the plants which grew from within her, seaweed and flowering vines spiraling up and around her body. The plants were much less active outside of the water, only occasionally twitching or trying to eat an insect.

Elsh's green eyes were beaming. "So many emotions wrapped into this artwork, I'm not sure how much more I can take!"

Roman pointed down the street with his plastic cup of red wine. "We haven't even seen half of the galleries."

"And these galleries just sit here, full of art, all the time?"

Roman laughed. "That is why they're here." He felt the smile on his lips, and his breath caught.

"What's wrong, Roman?"

He reached up with his long, pale fingers and felt his own lips, acutely aware of the vivid elation churning up the center of his body. "Nothing." He looked back at her, at her smooth skin, at the gills along her neck and shoulders stretching in a way that emoted how happy she was in that moment.

Elsh reached out and touched the arm of his long, blue coat. "Are you getting overwhelmed? Do you need to eat some Wonder?"

He sighed, feeling how hard his heart was beating in his chest, his eyes having trouble pulling themselves away from her. "No, I don't want Wonder. Not tonight." His sudden desire for her was so strong, so blinding and intertwined with emotions that he never let come to the surface, that he wasn't even sure exactly what he wanted. His mind was like a small room with a dozen people all talking at once—he didn't know how to pry these desirous emotions apart, didn't know how to interpret them. Neither did he care.

He took a deep breath, attempting to calm the feelings inside.

Elsh turned to the wall of windows and peered into the gallery they'd just walked out of, her eyes falling on the piece in the center of the small room. It was a gown with a hoop skirt, reminding Roman of a painting he'd seen in a mansion many years ago. The gown was completely white, suspended by wire, with projections running all across it from the inside. The projections depicted blue water with an animated drawing of a little girl endlessly swimming across it, her legs kicking slowly, her face serene and calm.

A shiver ran up Roman's arm as Elsh's webbed fingers slid along the back of his hand. He closed his eyes for a moment and let his hand wrap around hers.

Opening his eyes, he suddenly noticed his and Elsh's reflection in the window—her dark and silvery skin dressed in white, next to his own pale countenance wearing a long, dark coat and trousers, the image of the little girl swimming endlessly between the two of them.

"I like this piece," she said softly. "It speaks to me."

Roman swallowed. "I can see if it's for sale."

In the reflection, she shook her head. "Seeing it right now, standing here with you, this is perfect."

He took a deep breath and gently squeezed her hand. "I'm not sure I know what 'perfect' is anymore. Or that I ever did."

They stood there in silence for a moment. Her green eyes could have been locked right on his, or she could have been watching the swimming girl—he couldn't tell with the quality of the reflection. She looked so together, so sure of herself, standing there holding his hand as if she were invulnerable. Usually, Roman felt confident, but standing there next to Elsh, looking at their reflection, he felt like a sack of broken pieces.

She turned to him, but he kept his eyes on her reflection. "Maybe that's not true," she said. Reaching over, she placed her other webbed hand against his chest, right over his heart[11]. "Maybe you know what perfect is, but it's not time yet. And that's completely alright."

Finally, Roman turned to her, reaching up and pressing her hand into his chest. He was suddenly very aware of the surrounding crowd, and beads of sweat began forming on his forehead. Closing his eyes, he took a deep breath and willed himself to stay calm, trying to imagine that they weren't on an extremely crowded street. "Would you want some fresh air?"

"Yes."

He opened his eyes and looked around, trying to peer through the thick crowd of chatting and drinking bodies for a way out, but Elsh pulled his hand and started leading them in the other direction, through the crowd.

She looked back at him. "Let me guide you for once. I saw a spot over here when we passed this way earlier."

Having her pull him through the crowd allowed his anxiety to relax a bit, and he focused his awareness inward instead of at the people all around. He also focused on her hand, on the difference between her skin and his, how they were each made of such different material. Her hand always felt slightly wet and slick, even though it was mostly skin.

Then they were veering off down Camp Street, past a few more galleries off the main strip and into a parking lot squeezed between buildings.

Normally Roman wouldn't like being surrounded by cars, but the parking lot was empty of people except for a wandering parking lot attendant, which was quite preferable to a crowd at the moment. He let go of Elsh's hand and stretched, taking a deep breath. "Thank you."

She looked up at the nearby buildings, several of which were only one-story tall[12]. "The air will be fresher up there."

Roman smiled. *"A woman after my own heart."*

Elsh laughed at his joking use of a very human saying and pushed his shoulder awkwardly, a human action that they both found strange and

---

[11] Elsh knew, through their endless conversations, that Roman's heart was slightly to the right of center and a little low—the middle point between where a Collector's heart and human's heart would be.

[12] Of course, having high ceilings, the buildings were closer to one-and-a-half stories tall.

humorous.

Roman laughed and gestured to the rooftops. "Lead the way." He followed her between two cars and up to the brick wall of a building with a nice, flat roof. "Do you want help up? I know you're not wearing the best climbing clothes."

She looked at him and raised an eyebrow. "Do *you* want help up? I know you're getting pretty old." Then she turned and leaped through the air, her sail-gown billowing about her as she reached down and touched the roof with her hand before landing in a crouch.

They had spent so little time above water together that Roman realized quite suddenly how little he knew about her capabilities while on land. She was not one of the warrior Riverwalkers, but she was still a Riverwalker.

He easily jumped up through the air and landed next to her. "Are you alright with heights? Because we could do this more often if you'd like."

Elsh stood and looked up at the higher buildings around them. "I'm not sure, but I suppose we'll find out."

"I suppose we will." Roman took in the open space around them, his lungs and skin breathing it all in. She was gazing at him, the lights from lampposts and buildings reflecting across her eyes and the silvery parts of her skin. His heart felt so large, so vast, yet like it was tearing in half. "I'm sorry. There's just so much in my head, so much that I can't—"

Her fingertips were on his mouth, silencing him. Her face was so calming; he wanted to let go and melt into her eyes. "Tonight's not about anything that happened before tonight."

Closing his eyes, Roman let her words dig into his muscles and relax him. He reached up and held her fingertips on his lips, inhaling the scent of plants and water on her skin. She stepped closer to him, his heart beating madly as he felt skin against his cheek, then her warm kiss slow against his jaw, his neck, then back up to his cheek. He let go of her hand and wrapped his arms around her, opening his eyes and seeing her braids with vines woven through them. It had been so long since he'd been close to someone in this way, and he'd never been this close to Elsh. She kissed his neck again, and he put his hand on the back of her head, feeling her braids, feeling the vines moving against his palm.

She pulled her head back, and Roman saw his pale reflection swimming in her green eyes. Their lips met, her eyes closing and her body easing into him. Her lips pressed into his, and he felt the poison they released spreading through his veins, relaxing him, unwinding his anxiety, and dispersing his thoughts.

Kissing her was like reaching through time. It was becoming a past version of himself and kissing someone he should have kissed years ago.

After a few moments, they pulled away from each other, and both smiled. He felt so *young*. Months of anxiety and worry and guilt had momentarily vanished.

She bit her lip. "I fucking needed that."

Roman laughed. "I did too. I think the poison in your lips is good for my emotional well being."

She shook her head, reaching up to push stray strands of hair away from his face and behind his ear. "I didn't use any poison."

His eyes widened, then he searched her eyes and felt around inside himself. He wondered how much her poison had ever affected him when she'd kiss his hand in the past.

Down in the parking lot a car alarm erupted, cutting through the quiet.

Roman held Elsh and looked up to the higher rooftops. "Do you want to get some even fresher air?"

She pressed her cheek to his. "You can take me anywhere."

"Anywhere?"

Elsh pulled away and followed his gaze to a thin tower the color of sand, piercing the sky only a few rooftops away. The tower was steeped with ledges and got thinner the higher it went, with narrow stained glass windows going up the center of each side. Crowning the tower was a small battlement, like the top of a European castle, with a waist-high wall which had gaps in it, or crenels, for archers to fire between. As far as Roman knew, archers had only used the tower four times, and only twice in his lifetime.

"What is that building?"

"Saint Patrick's Church. It's one of my favorite views of the city."

"Can we get up there?"

"How are you at climbing rope?"

"I imagine I'd be alright. You brought rope?"

Roman ran a finger over Elsh's hip, across some rope and netting which held the surrounding sail in the shape of a gown. "I always have rope. But you brought rope tonight as well."

She raised an eyebrow. "That line might have worked on girls in the 1920s, but you're gonna have to try a little harder to get me out of this."

He pulled her close and kissed her, feeling his body melt all over again.

She kissed his chin, then his neck. "Ok, maybe you won't have to try that much harder."

Roman felt his cheeks flush and pulled her towards Saint Patrick's Church. They made their way across a few flat rooftops and up onto a two-story building next to the main body of the church. The church's roof was steeped, but not sharply. They leaped onto it and walked towards the front of the church, where the tower rose high into the sky. Roman crouched down and unlaced his boots, pulling them off his pale feet. His toes were slightly longer than a human's, and he flexed them against the surface of the roof. "There's not much to grip onto, so I need more than just my hands."

He pulled his boot laces through a belt loop on his hip and tied them together, so his boots hung against his thigh.

Elsh looked up at the tower. "Um, it seems weird to say this to you, but be careful."

Roman smiled, still feeling like he was fifty years younger. He took her hand and kissed the back of it. "This is the safest thing I've done all week." He turned and walked up to where the tower met the roof. "When I throw the rope down, let me know if you want me to come down and help you."

Then he leaped high into the air, reaching out to grab the edge of a tall, thin stained glass window. His hands and feet easily latched onto the wall, even the near-flat parts. He jumped up from steeped ledge to stained glass window to steeped ledge, then pulled himself up over the short crenelated wall and into the parapet. He unlaced his boots and set them on the ground, then pulled off his long coat and laid it on top of them. Strapped to the inside of the coat were various pouches and small pieces of gear, and he unsnapped a coil of long, thin black rope. He tied the rope around one of the merlons (the higher sections of the wall) and then tossed it down to Elsh.

With the wind, it took her a few tries to grab onto it. She pulled on it, walking up to where the tower met the roof, then climbed several yards, her webbed feet on the stone wall. She shifted, adjusting her grip, getting used to the rope and her weight while on dry land. Then she ascended rather quickly. If she were human, Roman would think she wasn't climbing in the most logical manner, but he wasn't quite sure how a Riverwalker would best climb the side of a building with rope. If the height was bothering her, she gave no sign. She began jumping upward from each ledge, grabbing onto higher sections of rope each time and landing with the balls of her feet against the wall once more.

Then she was climbing over the wall and into the parapet with Roman, breathing heavily and stretching her arms and legs. "Wow, those are muscles I rarely use." She looked out at the view and gasped. Roman smiled as they looked out at the Central Business District and beyond. There were dozens of skyscrapers much higher than them, and through the gaps between those buildings, they could see most of the city. Elsh gasped again when she turned and saw the river, the closest parts barely visible at all from across the building tops. Their eyes followed it as it snaked up under the bridge of The Crescent City Connection, the bridge linking the East Bank of New Orleans to the West Bank. In the other direction, the river curved around Algiers Point to disappear behind the trees along

Algiers' levee.

"I..." Elsh shook her head, holding her hand to her chest. "I had no idea. I didn't know that it was also beautiful from far away."

"I'll show you the river from a dozen angles, each one beautiful in its own way."

Elsh turned to him, grabbed his face in her webbed hands and kissed him hard. Roman could do nothing but stand there a moment, kissing her back. Then his arms wrapped around her. He felt her back and shoulders through her gown, some of the skin smooth, some rough with scales. Then the plants which grew from her slowly uncoiled from her torso and began sliding up around him, around his back, one of the vines slipping between the buttons of his shirt and sliding over his ribs to hook around his hip, pulling him even tighter against her.

Each moment he kissed her some old cage unlocked within him, heavy chains falling to the ground, old parts of him waking up and squinting from the light. Energy and vitality surged through his body, desire beating in his veins like drums. He realized that the age he'd been feeling wasn't age at all, but merely the feeling of cutting himself off from pieces within, of holding onto things that didn't resonate with who he really was. No, Elsh's kiss hadn't been poisoning him—he was the one who'd been poisoning himself. Her kiss was reminding him of what it was like to be Roman.

They kissed, feeling each other, coiling themselves about one another upon that tower piercing the night sky, in the midst of the city, yet so far away from it.

They kissed like old lovers and like new lovers. They kissed like old friends. They kissed, they touched, their breathing becoming a song that surrounded them, and they both felt more alive than they had in a very, very long time.

File 13 :: [Elsh]

She lay curled up in Roman's arms, his long fingers slowly trailing up and down her forearm. The noises of the city seemed miles away. She drifted as close to dream as she was able while out of the water.

The traffic sounds mixed with the indecipherable voices of people, which mixed with the songs of cicadas, which mixed with the deep whistle of a steamboat along the river. Behind these sounds, the familiar melody of the calliope grew in the distance.

Roman's body tensed around her as her breath caught.

The calliope.

They both got to their feet and looked out from their perch.

"It's coming from Julia Street," said Roman, just as a wave of people along the street fell to the ground about three blocks from them. They could only see slices of Julia Street between the other buildings. "It's not close enough yet to affect us."

Elsh could feel a tickle at the back of her head. "I can feel it. If he moves this way, we might be out."

Roman pulled on his pants, his boots still tied to the waist. He grabbed his coat, unrolling it on the floor. Elsh was clothed in nothing but the plants that grew from within her, twisting around her body.

Roman unbuttoned pouches and slid pieces of devices out of the coat. "See if you can get an eye on him. He may be wearing a big animal skull like a helmet, he'll definitely be playing a keyboard hanging from his shoulder."

She grabbed her dress and slid it over her body, then looked out towards Julia Street. Being a Riverwalker, she could see a decent amount of detail at that distance. There were hundreds of people on the ground, their eyes open like they were locked in daydreams. She listened to the traveling sounds of the calliope on the wind.

"I can't see him," she said, "but I can tell where he is by the sound.

He's just on the other side of that building." Her eyes scanned all around. "Wait, there! I can see his reflection in one of the gallery windows."

"Any monsters?"

"Not that I can see. Just him."

Roman was beside her with a four-foot-long device that looked like a mix between a slingshot, a sniper rifle, and a crossbow. It had a tripod base, which he set atop the wall. A thick elastic band was pulled nearly three feet back, attached to a leather cup holding what looked like a golf-ball-sized wad of gray string.

"That whole thing was in your coat?"

"In pieces," he said. "I knew the calliope player would have to be taken down at a distance, so I've been carrying this around."

Roman knelt down and looked through the scope on top of the device, turning a few knobs on the side of the scope.

Elsh found her eyes wandering to the scars running along his sleek, pale torso. Her cheeks flushed, and she forced herself to turn towards Julia Street. "Do you see the reflection?"

"Yes," he said.

"He moved but stopped, still just out of sight. Maybe he'll move again. Or we could go down and get a line of sight..."

Roman raised a hand, like he was feeling energy laced into the air, his eye still against the scope. "Elsh, hold your breath."

She did so.

She watched as his body took a breath and held it. Then he swiveled the device slightly to one side, away from the building that blocked their view. He pulled the trigger, the ball of gray string hurling through the air so fast that she could barely follow it. It curved above the buildings, pushed by the wind, then soared around the building that hid their target from them. In the reflection, she saw the ball hit the ground right next to the skull-wearing man. The ball exploded in a ten-foot radius, covering everything around it in a thick mess of stringy gray goo. It covered the man's skull helmet, his arms, and his legs. He jerked and struggled as he fell to the ground, hitting the back of his skull helmet on the curb.

The calliope music stopped.

"You got him!" said Elsh. "He's down!"

Roman got up and threw on his coat, leaving his shirt, and tossed the rope back over the side of the tower. "You don't have to come."

"I'm going."

"Alright." He jumped over the edge and slid down the rope. Elsh wasn't so confident in her above-water rope skills just yet. She climbed over the edge and made her way down quickly. When she was halfway down the tower, she jumped onto the roof, landing in a crouch. She saw Roman leaping over rooftops a block away, nearly to Julia Street already.

She ran, her eyes scanning the rooftops as she figured out the best route. Leaping from rooftop to rooftop, then down into an alley, she jumped a fence and was standing in a street covered in a thousand prone people, still deep in whatever dreams they'd been thrown into.

Then she heard the roars. The calliope player was on the sidewalk wrapped in gray goo, completely still, and three of the creatures Roman had described to her appeared between the calliope player and Roman. They were horrifying—lion, elephant, bear, and a few other animals, their tusks and trunks curling into the air. One was chewing through the gray goo that trapped the calliope player, and the other two charged at Roman.

He leaped quickly against the wall of a gallery, jumping off it to elbow one creature in the neck, sending it crumbling to the ground. He faced off against the second as the wounded creature raised its trunk into the air and howled. Three more of the creatures appeared close by.

One lunged at Roman. He jumped straight up, well over the creature, tossing another ball of gray string between two of the creatures. It exploded and wrapped around both of them, sending them twisting and writhing to the ground. Three were down, counting the one that was prone and coughing from Roman striking its neck. The three others were very much active.

Elsh was overwhelmed. She'd only been in combat a handful of times, and it had always been underwater. Her fear for Roman being in danger was like a tightening fist embedded in her chest. But she knew all her emotion and doubts in herself would only hinder her, further endangering Roman and herself. She took a deep breath, feeling her body, her clenched fists, her pounding heart.

Two of the creatures turned on Roman, but the third one was struggling to rip the gray goo off the calliope player. If it freed him, this would all be for nothing.

She charged. It spun around towards her, its trunk flailing in the air as it roared. Elsh reached between its tusks and grabbed the end of its trunk in her fist, coiling it around her wrist. The creature reeled back from the pain, swiping with its claws and tusks, but Elsh leaped above its attempted blows and came down punching with the hand gripping its trunk, striking one of the creature's eyes and sending its head colliding into the ground.

The enormous glass window of the gallery next to her shattered as a beast head-butted Roman through it, the creature following through to land upon him. They were surrounded by statues, paintings, and people lying on the ground.

"Roman!" screamed Elsh. She moved to jump through the broken window but suddenly found herself on the ground, holding her jaw, seeing violet spots on the outskirts of her vision. Something had hit her hard. Then a creature was on her, pinning her shoulders down with massive paws, its claws sinking into her skin like long, rusty nails.

She heard Roman cry out, and she gritted her teeth. The creature above screamed into her face, giving her a full look at its sharp teeth, red tongue, and slick gums. Elsh gathered a large wad of poisonous phlegm from her throat and spat it into the creature's wide maw. The creature coughed and choked, and she knocked it off of her.

 Elsh sat up, looking through the broken window to see Roman facing off against the beast. He swung out and struck the creature in the head, but it bounced back and sunk its jaws deep into his chest. "No!" screamed Elsh. There was no blood, but she swore its teeth were *inside* of him. He stumbled back, knocking over two paintings as he tried to keep his footing.

She was on her feet and moving fast. Elsh flew through the window, grabbing the creature's curving tusks and using her momentum to spin its head down, its body twisting behind as she drove the beast's skull into the ground with a loud *crack*.

A ripping sound tore through the air, and she turned. One creature had ripped the unconscious body of the calliope player from the gray goo. The substance was still all over him, but he was no longer attached to the sidewalk and street. The creature held him in its mouth, its trunk coiled around his waist.

Another creature from the street howled into the air.

Elsh ran and leaped out the huge, broken window, but the creature vanished along with the calliope player. One beast entangled in the gray goo had freed itself and was ripping the other one free. They both vanished together. The choking one Roman had hit in the neck vanished. Elsh turned to the gallery and the one she poisoned, still coughing, grabbed the one she'd knocked unconscious. They were both gone, leaving her and Roman in a street filled with people waking from some kind of dream. Roman slid down the wall to sit on the floor.

She stumbled back into the gallery through the window, not caring if the glass on the ground cut her feet, and collapsed next to Roman. She touched his shoulder, looking at his unscathed torso. "Roman, are you alright!?" He kept blinking, taking short, deep breaths.

Next to her, someone on the ground was going through their cell phone, confused and trying to call someone. Elsh pulled it easily out of their hand, her fingers dialing a number she'd had memorized for decades. She pushed the call button and held it up to her ear.

"Yes?"

"Julius, it's Elsh." Her voice broke as her body shook.

"What's wrong?"

"Come to Julia Street. The calliope player. The beasts did something to Roman. There are a lot of people here, down but waking up."

"Stay safe, we're on our way."

File 14 :: [Julius Marcos]

Julia Street was relatively close to the Spanish Plaza headquarters. By the time Julius and Edith arrived, the art walk crowd was awake, yet dazed. Music spilled from some galleries, and everyone was comparing stories of what happened.

"Does this look like Frenchmen Street?" he asked Edith as they walked. "The look in their eyes?"

"Yes." She seemed in awe of the emotion surrounding them. "These people are full of hope, they're radiating it. They were given their own dreams, and those dreams were not ripped out of them or eaten."

They approached the shattered gallery window, the sidewalk in front of which was covered in the shiny gray goo of webs. Julius was pretty sure he knew where Roman had acquired those webs.

Elsh and Roman were out front of the gallery, Roman leaning back against the wall like he was drunk. Elsh wore a gown made of netting and thick cloth, her shoulders bleeding from what looked like claw marks. Roman was missing his shirt, only wearing his coat and pants, with his boots tied to his hip. His hair was messy, half out of its ponytail. Neither one of them seemed badly injured.

"Edith," said Julius. "Try to get consent to copy peoples' memories."

"Ok, I'll see what I can do."

He approached Elsh. "Are you alright?"

She nodded, barely taking her eyes off Roman. Julius could smell her worry.

He directed his words towards Roman. "You alright there, friend?"

Roman blinked rapidly, then stopped. "I am... fine, technically. My thoughts and emotions are severely altered in some areas of my psyche, while they are completely normal in others."

Julius watched his friend's jaw tense over and over. "The monsters got you?"

Roman nodded.

"We almost got the calliope player," said Elsh. "The beasts can vanish at will. Roman knocked the player out, but they took him."

Julius looked at the shattered window, the gallery inside a wreck. "I'll call Mars. She's down in the First Quarter looking through the books there, trying to figure out what the creatures may be. We'll have a meeting and update our plans."

"They're from Japan," said Roman. "Tell her that and she'll figure out what they are fairly easily. I used to know what they're called. They're the *dream eaters*, I think."

"They're Japanese?"

"When the chimera freed The Skulled Man, holding him in its mouth, some webbing had come off of him. The symbols going up and down the skull, they're Japanese Kanji and Hiragana. They're sentences, I think. As soon as I saw the Japanese, I remembered reading about the creatures many years ago."

Julius reached out and put his real hand on Roman's shoulder. Roman met his gaze. "What did the monsters take from you?"

Roman's eyes teared up. He blinked rapidly again. "I can't *believe*... I just... I can't believe."

"You can't believe what?" asked Elsh.

He turned to her, a tear sliding down his cheek. "In The Agents Of."

File 15 :: [Mars]

Less than an hour later, The Agents Of convened around the large wooden table in the Planning Room of their headquarters. Julius stood with his real and metal arms folded, leading the meeting.

Mars stood because of the adrenaline coursing through her and imagined that Edith was standing for the same reason.

Roman was sitting. Every so often, his eyes blinked quickly for about three seconds, freaking Mars out more than a little bit. He wore a button-up beige shirt with his boots still tied to the belt loop of his pants. Bruises welled up along one of his arms and on one of his cheeks.

Elsh had gone back to the First Quarter, Mars missing a chance to finally meet her. Though, given the circumstances, Mars was glad not to have to interact with a stranger right now.

Roman had just finished telling them his account of what happened—taking down The Skulled Man from up high, fighting the monsters, getting a chunk bitten out of his psyche, the monsters disappearing.

Julius turned to Edith. "Tell them what you told me about the memories you looked at."

Edith glanced down at The Extraction Glove sitting on the table in front of her. "I copied memories from five people. The earliest memory I saw is of The Skulled Man walking through the crowd of Julia Street, no monsters in sight. It seems people thought he was doing some kind of performance art. He started playing the calliope device, and people went into their own dreams and dropped. From a memory of someone several blocks away, The Skulled Man appears to have played the device for nearly a full minute before Roman took him down. Then the monsters showed up."

"So Roman's the only one who got their dreams fucked with," said Mars.

"I think so," said Edith.

"The Skulled Man might see the chaos he brought to Frenchmen Street as a mistake," said Julius. "So instead of siccing the monsters on people and then playing the device, he plays the device first, putting everyone to sleep, and *then* has the monsters eat."

"That seems logical," said Roman.

"Any word on the kidnapped people from Frenchmen?" asked Mars.

Julius shook his head. "No one's been reported missing yet who was around Frenchman Street or the Quarter that afternoon. It's only been two days, though."

"Do you think the monsters *only* eat ideas?" asked Edith.

"I don't know," said Julius.

"They seem pretty freaking physical," said Mars. "They might need to consume more than just aspirations to survive. Maybe that's why they vanished with those people." The thought of those people being taken somewhere to be gorged on by those creatures made Mars nauseous.

"All the more reason to hunt down The Skulled Man," said Julius. "And Mars, you've figured out what the monsters are?"

She picked a big, dusty book off the chair in front of her and set it on the table: *The Encyclopedia of Creatures Presumed Unreal*. Opening it to a bookmarked page, she pointed at a picture. "They're called *Baku*, or sometimes Dream Eaters." The three others leaned in to analyze the picture. The Baku depicted was like a bear with an elephant head and a mouth full of sharp teeth under the trunk. It circled a child sleeping on a mat on the floor of a room, looking like it had crawled in through the open window.

"That looks like them," said Edith. "Except the ones we're dealing with are much bigger."

"Does the book say why they're called Dream Eaters?" asked Julius.

Mars nodded. "Little children in Japan are sometimes taught that if they wake up from a nightmare, they can call a Baku to come and eat their bad dreams. But they've got to be careful—if the Baku is still hungry after eating their nightmares, it may turn on the child and eat *all* of their hopes and dreams as well."

Mars spun the book around to face her and turned the page. "Get this —it also says that supposedly you can take the pelt of a Baku and use it as a defense against other Baku. You can nail a Baku pelt above your bed and Baku can't come and eat your dreams."

"Explains The Skulled Man's pelt cape," said Julius. "So maybe he's not exactly friends with these *Baku* after all, if he uses the pelt as protection from them." He walked over to the chalkboard. Next to *Monsters*, he put a dash and the word *Baku*. Then, at the bottom of the list under *Skulled Man,* he added:

- *Uses Baku hide-cape to protect himself from the Baku.*

Julius turned back to them. "Unless anyone has more to add, I think we should call it a night and let Roman get some rest. You two should rest as well. Tomorrow night you'll be following up on the Banshee Dave lead. Hopefully, we can get some more answers."

"*What?*" said Mars. "I've been waiting this whole time to hear what happened to Roman. I can't sleep not knowing if Roman's alright."

"He'll be better after a night's sleep," said Julius.

Roman raised a hand to Julius. "It's alright. I have a better idea of what's happened to me. I can speak about it." He looked so weak and tired, somehow even paler than usual.

Mars heard Julius growl under his breath, but she didn't give a shit. "How are you?" she asked Roman.

"A bit mixed up," he said. "The Baku took a bite out of me, creating a sort of vacuum inside that sucks up any positive emotions or thoughts about certain subjects, most notably the subject of The Agents Of and its future."

"Your aspirations," whispered Edith. "Like Tommy Butera. But it only took a bite out of you, rather than gorging on you like the Baku did to the gamblers in Nimble's Den."

Roman nodded. "And my dreams were not magnified like the gamblers' were because I was not being affected by the calliope device. Perhaps if I had been affected, my dreams would have been closer to the surface and the Baku would have done more damage."

"What kind of damage are we talking about?" asked Mars.

Roman closed his eyes for a moment before continuing, like he was looking inside himself. "It ripped out a piece of my belief. As of now, I can no longer believe that any of this," he motioned around the table to the three of them, "is worth pursuing. With *logic* I can see that there is much value in this, that the city needs us. But as soon as I step into *emotion*… it's like the darker forces of the city have already won. It's like we're playing a fixed game. Like we're wasting our time."

Mars fought back against the tears wanting to well up in her eyes.

"It's funny," said Julius. "You got me out of a similar slump only weeks ago. I said the Agents were over, drowning my failure in alcohol."

"The irony has not escaped me."

Mars could see Roman pushing his mind into his hyper-logical side to keep clear of his emotions. As far as she knew, he hadn't been eating as much Wonder lately. She guessed that he was leaning into his logical side without much use of Wonder, instead relying on utter willpower.

She closed the book, not realizing she was slamming it until it was too late. "Alright, if we're done here, I need some sleep too."

"Mars," said Julius, "are *you* alright?"

"Peachy keen," she said, walking around the others and out the door, leaving *The Encyclopedia of Creatures Presumed Unreal* on the table. "See you tomorrow for the Banshee Dave Dance Party."

The gas lamps along the stone hallway lit up as she walked. She thought of going to the lab, but realized she needed to get away from things reminding her of Roman for a few minutes. Also, she needed some fresh air. She made her way to the exit and pulled the lever embedded into the wall. The ramp leading up to the fountain of Spanish Plaza descended. After making it halfway up the ramp, she heard footsteps and turned.

Edith stood there holding the Extraction Glove under one arm. "Hey Mars, I just wanted to see if you're ok. If you want to talk, or if you just want a ride home, I'm here. If not, I can leave you alone."

Mars nodded and approached her friend. Then she threw her arms around Edith and hugged her tight. Edith hugged her back with her free arm.

"I'll be alright," said Mars, pulling away. "Just a lot of thoughts and emotions right now." She took a deep breath, the night air so much nicer than the air inside the headquarters or down in the lab of the First Quarter. "Hey, I really need a drink. Or three. If you happen to be in that kind of mood, I wouldn't mind not drinking alone."

"Definitely, I could be down for a drink. *Maybe* three, but we'll see." She hefted the Extraction Glove under her arm and stepped back down the ramp. "I'm just gonna go grab my things."

Mars nodded, the chilly night air beginning to crawl along her arms. "And could you grab my jacket! I left it on the back of my chair, like an idiot..."

File 16 :: [Edith Downs]

Edith drove them through the French Quarter and into the Marigny, where Mars ran into her apartment to grab a small backpack, into which she shoved a bottle of freezer vodka, cans of soda water, limes, and two plastic Muses cups[13]. Then Edith drove them out of the Marigny and through the Bywater—a quirky neighborhood full of shotgun houses, small mansions, and dive bars—parking on Poland Street near the edge of the neighborhood.

They walked a few blocks further, past more shotgun houses and apartment complexes, and came up to some train tracks. Straight ahead was a giant, grassy hill rising up over a dozen feet, and to their right, walled off by a fence, was a large parking lot and an even larger building covered in graffiti. The building was maybe eight stories tall and as big as a downtown building.

"What's that?" asked Edith.

Mars laughed. "You don't know where we are?"

"Are we close to Elizabeth's Restaurant?"

"Yeah, that's maybe ten blocks from here. We're really close to Bacchanal, the wine place."

"I keep meaning to go there."

"We should remedy that. You get to drink wine in a beautiful courtyard listening to live music."

"Sounds like my kind of spot."

Mars pointed to the large abandoned building covered in graffiti.

---

[13] Krewe of Muses is an all-female Mardi Gras krewe created in 2001. Muses' parade is one of the most unique during Carnival season, their floats including a giant high heel shoe and a giant bathtub full of bubbles. The hand-decorated high heel shoes that the members throw from atop the floats are some of the most coveted parade throws of Carnival. They, like many krewes, throw krewe-specific plastic cups adorned with artwork that changes year to year. Many New Orleanians have at least one cupboard shelf dedicated solely to plastic cups from various Mardi Gras krewes.

"That's the old Naval Base. Giant navy ships still dock there, but the buildings are all abandoned. I guess they still own the docks. With the bend of the river, you can see the docked ships from the Quarter."

"Oh yeah, I've seen them docked there over the years."

Mars led them up to the top of the grassy hill. The hill then descended into a thin body of water. They were on a levee. Across the water was another levee, with trees and houses beyond. To their left was a large bridge traveling high above the water, cars going back and forth along it.

"*Oh*," said Edith. "This is the Industrial Canal.[14]"

"Yep."

"So that neighborhood is Holy Cross and the Lower Ninth?"

"Yep again."

Mars led them across the top of the levee, the canal down below them on one side and the abandoned military base on the other.

"I've only seen this area while driving over the bridge. I didn't realize you can go down here."

"Oh yeah, people come up here all the time. Walking their dogs or just wandering or hanging out."

They walked down to the end, and Edith's breath caught. The dark, shining Mississippi spread out in both directions under the night sky. Across the river was the neighborhood of Algiers, but she was seeing it from the side, rather than head-on from the French Quarter. From that distance, it looked like one of those perfect miniature towns built for model trains to pass by.

Ahead of them, the levee slanted down towards the water. To their left, the river curved further around towards neighboring cities and the swamps beyond. To their right were clusters of trees. The remnants of a small bonfire left a dark circle burned into the grass.

"This place is called the End of the World," said Mars.

"It's gorgeous out here."

"Yes, it is." Mars tapped Edith's arm and gestured for her to follow. They walked towards the cluster of trees. "Be careful," Mars said as she led them towards the trees, then down past some twisted driftwood until they reached a beach.

"What the hell? There's a *beach* here?"

"A tiny one, only when the tide's low."

Edith walked up to the edge of the river. She could see the bright French Quarter beaming in the distance on the river's curve, with the tall

---

[14] The Industrial Canal is a waterway that bisects a section of New Orleans, connecting Lake Pontchartrain to the Mississippi so that ships can travel between the two. The beasts which roam the Mississippi above the First Quarter originally only inhabited Lake Pontchartrain, but after the Industrial Canal was finished in 1923, dozens of younger beasts slipped through and took up residence in the curving river.

buildings of the CBD just beyond.

"*It's gorgeous*," whispered Edith.

Mars sat down on a washed up log, pulled out the contents of her backpack, and began making them some drinks. Edith sat down next to her and Mars handed her a cup of vodka, soda, and lime.

Mars raised her cup. "To outlaws and fame."

"Outlaws and fame," said Edith. They tapped their cups together, tapped them down on the log, then drank.

"I love you, girl," said Mars with a laugh. "Julius and Roman are great, like really great, but I don't know how I'd be an Agent without you here. We've only known each other a few months, but I can't imagine not having you as a friend. Or having you in my life."

Edith smiled, reaching an arm around Mars to hug her. "I love you, too. I can definitely imagine you being in a trio of Agents with Julius and Roman, but could you imagine *me* working alone with them? That would be nothing but awkward."

"Well, it definitely wouldn't be as *fun* without me, that's for sure."

"Cheers to that," said Edith, taking another sip. She slid apart from Mars. "So, how are you doing?"

Mars was silent for a moment. "I'm… um…" She took another sip of her drink. "Ok, story time. So last week I was playing cards with F and Scape. I was kinda buzzed, and I asked Scape to *talk* to me. F warned me against it, said talking with Scape changes a person, but I needed to know. And you know how I get when I want something…"

"All too well."

Mars burst out laughing. "Damn right you do. Alright, so Scape's mouth opened and… this might sound crazy, but I was a kid again, living this kind of dream-version of my past. And… and it really threw me."

"Was it a bad sort of past?"

Mars took a long drink. "Yeah. Yeah, it was. My mom passed when I was really little and my dad was a horrible, horrible person. I don't know if he was always that way, or if he snapped after my mom died."

Edith put a hand on Mars' knee. "I'm sorry."

Mars shook her head. "It's alright. By now I've gotten used to living with it. But Scape made it feel more alive, more present. Which is fine, because it's part of me, but now it's been combined with other things, and my mind is all jacked up on emotions and memories."

"Does this have to do with Roman?"

"Yeah." She took another long drink, then stared out at the small waves crashing on the shore. "My father got really bad. He drank a lot, hit me a lot. He always said I had my mom's beautiful hair, so one day I took a knife and cut it all off. And… he just lost it. I really think he was going to kill me."

She looked up at Edith with red, watery eyes, and Edith fucking lost it, crying while gritting her teeth. Edith wanted to console her friend and to murder this man, in just about equal measure. She stayed silent for the moment, open for her friend's memories and words. She put a hand on Mars' knee.

"F, The Function—he saved me. He showed up and stopped him. That's how we met."

"Holy shit," whispered Edith. "I had no idea."

"I think... I think he killed him." She reached down and held Edith's hand on her knee. "I've never had the courage to ask F. I'm not sure that I want to know, either way. I don't want to know that my friend murdered my father, or that my father is alive."

Edith took a deep breath. "Yeah, I'm not sure I'd want to know that either."

Mars downed the last of her drink. "You up for another round?"

Edith's drink was still half full. "Sure," she said, drinking half a cup in one go.

"Well, alright then." Mars fixed them up two more drinks. They cheersed, hit their cups on the log they sat on, then took a drink.

Edith was definitely feeling the alcohol now.

"F and I became good friends. I wanted, or *needed*, him to be part of my life. But he kept disappearing." Mars shook her head, smirking. "We ironed all that out, but it really fucked with me for a long time. Then, when I joined The Agents Of..."

"You found Roman and Julius."

Mars nodded.

"You found structure."

"I found structure. Structure in the form of role models I'd had since I was a kid, because of all the fantastical stories F would tell me about the Agents."

"So Roman losing faith..."

"I'm kinda fucked up by it. It shook me and I hate it. I see the apparent string going back to my father. Oh, boo-hoo, Mars just needs a fucking male figure to hang her damned securities onto. I know what it looks like, and I fucking hate that too. I *hate* it all." She took another long drink.

"I don't think it looks that bad," said Edith. "I think it just looks human."

"Sometimes I hate being human."

Edith raised her cup to Mars. "Don't we all." They cheersed again and drank.

Mars shuddered and leaned into Edith. Edith put her arm around Mars and held her.

"I'm sorry," said Mars. "I just… so many emotions and memories are rampaging inside me."

"Don't be sorry. I'm here for you. And I'm kind of the memory expert, as you're *constantly reminding me...*"

Mars pushed her away. "Shut up, you dork."

Edith cracked up and Mars followed suit.

"Well, I'm sorry for being so heavy," said Mars. "So what can you add to this fire? What are you going through?"

"Oh, no way," said Edith. "Everything I'm going through seems like a joke compared to what you're going through. We can talk about it the next time we hang out."

"No! You can't hold back just because I'm being dramatic."

"You're not being dramatic."

"I'm *always* dramatic. And if I unload on you and you don't unload on me, I'll just be a jackass."

"Ok, fine. As long as you're alright with my problems looking like nothing compared to yours."

Mars snatched her half-full cup away, then started filling both of their cups with vodka and soda water. "Oh, whatever. Start talking."

"Fine, alright." She took her topped off drink from Mars and drank. "So mems have started bringing their objects to my apartment. It's only been happening for a few days."

"*What*??? Wait, you mean the memories *inside* items are bringing the items to you? That's so freaking cool!"

"Well, it is cool, because those memories have been from abandoned buildings that are going to be torn down. I'm just afraid that items are going to keep coming to my apartment, even if they're not abandoned."

"Well," said Mars, "you *are* the self-proclaimed Protector of the Memories of New Orleans."

"Oh, fuck off."

They both laughed.

Edith took another drink. "It's just that… there are usually several mems inside of each old object. And there are so many *objects*. Suddenly being responsible for so many thousands of memories—not just as an idea, but as an actual reality—it's a lot to fit in your head. Even now, I'm saying thousands, but it's really *hundreds of thousands*, or maybe even *millions*." She looked into Mars' eyes. "Why did I even think to choose this?"

"Oh, honey, you didn't choose shit. They chose you. Or at the very least, your *abilities* chose this path for you."

Edith ran a hand over her face. "You think so?"

"Without a doubt. The city *wants* you to be the protector of its memories. Seems pretty obvious to me."

"I'm afraid it might be too much for me to handle. Do you really believe it chose me?"

Mars squeezed Edith's hand. "Oh, I believe it more than I believe in The Agents Of."

Edith didn't know what to say. They sat in silence after that, sipping their drinks and watching the dark, shifting surface of the river. They watched it twist and sculpt the lights of Algiers and the French Quarter into a slow-motion battle between peace and light.

Eventually, it was time for them to leave.

Edith stood and stretched, then nearly fell over. Mars caught her.

"Whoa, girl. Careful now."

"Mars, how strong were those drinks?"

"Mars-strength. Maybe Mars-strength plus one."

"I guess so." Edith stretched again, feeling her body. She was very, very drunk.

"You could call Henri's streetcar to take you home. Or we could walk to my apartment. I'm sure I could fix you up a comfy place to sleep. We can get coffee at Who Dat Cafe in the morning."

Edith nodded. "That sounds amazing." She leaned on Mars as they walked. Mars was definitely more used to drinking than Edith was, swigging from the bottle of vodka as they made their way through the Bywater toward the Marigny.

File 17 :: [Banshee Dave]

The nighttime world of Jackson Square bubbled with living, yapping, stumbling organisms—wandering eccentrics, artists selling their wares, the real homeless and the fakes, not to mention locals and tourists meandering past all the occupied benches and tarot tables which grow like orphan flowers in front of the Saint Louis Cathedral, the Cabildo, and the Presbytere[15].

Banshee Dave tripped over the uneven square stones of Jackson Square, catching himself before he fell. He slung one arm around one of his drinking buddies, taking a giant swig from his plastic jug of blue booze, the sticky-sweet gunk running down his chin. Pointing at the third member of the trio, he said, "You should have been there, bro!"

Compatriot #2 burst out laughing, nearly spilling his own over-sized container of sugar and alcohol.

All three men were broad-shouldered, short-haired, and had college logos on their T-shirts.

Banshee Dave smiled, then shoved his plastic drink container against Compatriot #1's chest. "Hold on, I gotta piss."

The trio wandered up to the wrought iron gate of the Presbytere, where Banshee Dave promptly relieved his borrowed human vessel of bodily fluid on the pillar next to the gate. He looked into the spirit world to see the wall of yellow lines and symbols banning spirits like him from passing through the entrance. Reaching into the spirit world, his hand pulsed with a ghostly orange flame which he flicked at the gate, all the

---

[15] After the fires of 1788 and 1794 burned up nearly all of the city, an extremely wealthy benefactor, Don Andrés Almonester y Roxas, was a huge factor in helping rebuild the city. He built the Saint Louis Cathedral, the Cabildo (which served as the government building), and the Presbytere (which was built to house priests, though it was never actually used for that purpose). Both the Cabildo and the Presbytere now serve as museums.

lines and hexes burning away like paper.

Banshee Dave shook the flames from his hand and the piss from his vessel, zipped himself up, and pushed the gate open with his shoulder. He staggered with the others up to the front door, where he reached inside the metal of the lock, maneuvering its pieces around until it clicked open.

As they walked into the dark lobby, he reached under his shirt and pulled from his rib cage a pulsing orb of electricity. He tossed it at an electrical outlet, the power from the orb reaching through the building and frying the circuits, the negligible amount of light now snuffed out entirely.

From an archway to their right, a man appeared in the shadows wearing a brown hooded robe, speaking loudly: "The museum is closed." His voice echoed off the surrounding walls.

Compatriot #1 nearly fell, but caught himself on the front desk. "Oh, no. This is our hotel. We're just a wee bit drunk."

Compatriot #2 doubled up and retched onto the floor. Banshee Dave patted him on the back. "It's ok, buddy. Just let it all out."

The robed figure stepped forward, shadows clinging to the upper half of his face, his voice booming once more: *"Leave at once, or there will be consequences."*

"We just need a minute," said Banshee Dave, peering from his cohort up to the man in the robe, who was indeed the entity of the Presbytere. "He's gonna be just fine. And why are you wearing a robe, bro? Were you taking a bath?"

"This is the last warning." The Presbytere stepped closer to them.

"Ok, ok!" said Banshee Dave, holding up one hand while keeping his friend from falling over. "Guys! I don't think this is our hotel, we gotta move on."

More figures in brown robes walked in from other doorways leading to different parts of the museum. *"You are not what you appear to be,"* they said in unison, *"and will be dealt with accordingly."* There were about a dozen of the identical robed men.

"Whoa!" said Banshee Dave, dropping his friend to the ground and backing towards the entrance. "You two fucks are on your own! These robed cult guys look bat-shit crazy."

He slipped a hand under his shirt and into his borrowed body's rib cage, pulling out a small glass jar[16]. Spinning around towards one of the robed figures, he shattered the jar against the monk's chest, grabbing a fistful of the monk's robe and slamming him into the ground.

"Renegade spirit!" roared the chorus of identical entities surrounding him. *"I am not one, but many! You cannot defeat all of me!"*

---

[16] Banshee Dave had always been astounded by all of the unused space inside living human bodies. Most people, he found, could hold a tiny library inside of themselves.

Banshee Dave flicked his head up, a jackal's grin stealing across his face. "I know. I just wanted one. And this one's definitely the prettiest."

The long red worm inside the glass jar burrowed its way into the robes and chest of the monk on the ground, who immediately closed his eyes and screamed. The others, one by one, fell to their knees and cried out as well, the noise almost deafening to the ears of Banshee Dave's borrowed human body.

"Upstairs!" he said to his accomplices. "Now!"

He ran around the front desk and up the stairs, the other two stumbling after him. Once at the top, he led them down the large hallway lined with entrances to various sections of the Mardi Gras Museum until he came to the room he was looking for.

Even in the near-dark, the room glittered with gems and silver and gold, with cases full of crowns and scepters and tiaras from over a century of Mardi Gras festivities. Banshee Dave walked across the room, up to a case full of artifacts from the Krewe of Proteus, and smashed one of the glass panes with his elbow[17]. He reached in and took out an overstuffed green and golden crown, the power of which burned at the fingertips of his human vessel. The green cloth of the crown's body was rife with rips and holes, all covered in diamond-encrusted *fleur-de-lis*.

The placard next to the crown and its accompanying scepter read:

Crown and Scepter
Poseidon, King of the Atlanteans
1927

Banshee Dave took the crown, and the three of them ran out of the room, across the hallway, and into a room full of old Mardi Gras costumes from small towns in Louisiana, and then into another hall lined with giant windows overlooking Jackson Square.

He kicked open a window, backed up, ran, and leaped out into the night sky, falling and landing with a loud *thud* on the flat stones of Jackson Square. There was another *thud, thud* as his accomplices landed to either side of him, none of the living sheep on the Square paying them much attention.

The three of them turned to head downriver towards The Marigny but stopped when a woman with red dreadlocks and bulky yellow-lensed goggles stepped into their path. Devices hung from her belt and the vest underneath her leather jacket. She raised a clunky metal gun the size of her

---

[17] The Krewe of Proteus formed in the 1880s and holds one of the oldest and most beautiful of the Mardi Gras parades. Their parade floats, though new every year, still use the original float chassis from the 1880s. They parade on the night of Lundi Gras, which is the Monday before Mardi Gras day.

arm and pulled the trigger, launching a metal claw which latched onto the ground between Banshee Dave and his lackeys.

"Banshee Dave!" she shouted. "Your actions threaten the peace and safety of this city!" There was a thick chord connecting the lady's gun to the claw. She slapped a button on the gun, and the top of the claw spurted dark liquid onto them like a sprinkler.

Compatriot #2 turned and shoved Banshee Dave. "You said there weren't any Agents right now!"

Banshee Dave grabbed onto his shoulder. "Good thing I brought a backup plan." With a grunt, he picked up and hurled his accomplice through the air towards the Agent, sprinting in the same direction. For all he knew, one of the older Agents might be behind him, and those bastards weren't to be fucked with.

The woman kept slapping the gun—obviously, it was supposed to do something besides shower dark liquid on them. "Oh, gods damn it!" she yelled, stepping forward and slamming her boot on the ground.

It was only then that Banshee Dave saw the glow of the holy-water-soaked cloth wrapped around her boot, which led his eye to the line of salt on the ground in front of her. He stopped himself just in time to see the wall of light burst up from the ground, Compatriot #2's body snapping like a bag of sticks as it slammed into it.

The wall was curving as it burst up from the ground, circling and trying to trap the three of them inside.

"Oh, fuck this mess!" he yelled, turning to see another woman behind, dark-haired with a massive metal gauntlet covering most of one arm, also wearing yellow-tinted goggles. Compatriot #1 headed towards her, but she too stomped a holy-water-armed boot onto a line of salt in front of her, the wall of light bursting up from the ground and curving towards the other.

Banshee Dave gripped the crown and ran towards Compatriot #1 as the circle of salt ignited, picking up and throwing his last accomplice towards the park of Jackson Square, where the two walls of light were about to connect. The walls of light slammed onto the man's sides, holding him in place while the light from the ground pounded up into his stomach. As he yelled out in pain, Banshee Dave was already running, jumping up onto the man's back, then down onto a metal bench from which he leaped up onto the wrought iron fence surrounding the park. From atop the fence, he leaped towards the statue of Andrew Jackson atop his rearing horse, but something ensnared his legs, sending him slamming down onto the park's pathway.

Banshee Dave turned onto his back, sitting up and spitting blood onto the ground. Glowing rope bound his ankles, burning his spirit body through the pants and borrowed vessel. The two Agents unlocked the gate and ran his way. He lifted the Crown of Poseidon and pulled it onto his head. As the crown sunk down over his borrowed human cranium, he instantly felt power surge through him. He reeled backward as his body tightened, his vision splitting as his perception reached out for miles upon miles. He *felt* the gigantic beasts swimming through the broad, curving Mississippi, sensed the hundreds of Riverwalkers swimming far down in the river's depths. He felt all the trickles of life miles away in Bayou Saint John, felt the life in the lakes and waterways of City Park and the even more distant Audubon Park. Alligators and crabs and fish and crawfish. Algae and beasts and countless plant life. Frogs and insects and spiders and snakes. Not only was he connected to them, he could *communicate* with them. All of them. His perception reached out even further, and he felt the swamps outside the city. And, more importantly, he felt Lake Pontchartrain. The amount of life bursting from its depths was unfathomable, all of it talking to him, talking to each other, reaching out to him.

It wasn't until the Crown of Poseidon was ripped from his head that he realized that both his borrowed vessel and his ghostly form were screaming. He collapsed, twitching and writhing, the dreadlocked woman standing above him holding the crown[18].

She smirked, looking down at him through those yellow-tinted lenses. "Should have read the instruction manual."

Banshee Dave began unhooking himself from the borrowed vessel and lowering into the pathway below him—the Agents wouldn't be able to follow him underground. He'd make another plan, certainly taking into account that the Agents were powerful once more.

Then a knee pressed hard into the stomach of his borrowed body, and the last couple of hooks connecting him to it wouldn't budge. Above him crouched the dreadlocked woman, lowering a glowing orb of stone to his chest, and he felt it pulling him out through the body like a vacuum. He quickly hooked himself to the body once more, but the stone seemed to make the vessel too slippery for the hooks to catch, and Banshee Dave was sucked out and into the stone. Yelling, he lashed against the rock walls of the orb.

Being outside of the borrowed vessel, Banshee Dave looked once more like himself. His face was long and thin, like his body, and his scraggly dirty-blond hair fell to the bottom of his rib cage. All he wore was a pair of ripped up jeans and a sleeveless Clash T-shirt.

He brought his face up to the rounded wall, peering at the giant face of the red-dreadlocked agent who was looking at him through the yellow

---

[18]   Really, what were you expecting? Take a moment to look at the cover of this volume, and you'll notice that it is most definitely *not* titled, *Banshee Dave & the Crown of Poseidon.*

lenses of her goggles, and he smirked. "Ooh, I like you. I never forget a pretty face, doll."

She brought her face even closer. "Yeah? We have a lot in common—I never forget when fuckbags say creepy shit to me." The whole world began shaking, Banshee Dave slamming from one side of the orb into the other and back again. The shaking stopped, and he moaned from the pain. "Oh sorry," she said. "I thought this was an old-as-shit snow globe. Maybe I just didn't shake it hard enough." The world began jolting this way and that again, Banshee Dave tumbling around like he was inside a clothes dryer. When it stopped, he hurt so bad he could barely move. "Nope. Guess they didn't make snow globes very well back then."

File 18 :: [Mars]

Mars pressed her thumb down on one of the small bones tied to the stone, grinding it against the rock until the orb turned opaque and the ghost inside was silenced. She glanced at the unconscious body at their feet—the frat boy Banshee Dave had hijacked—then over at the other two bodies trapped by the wall of light.

Without their goggles, of course, neither Edith nor Mars would be able to see the wall of light at all.

"Um, Mars?" whispered Edith. "Are *they* supposed to be here?"

Mars turned towards the river to see over a dozen shadowy figures running under the streetlights of Decatur Street. They were moving fast, most of them leaping over the far fence and into the park while the others ran around both sides of the Square.

Mars took a deep breath. "It's fine. This is fine. We're The Agents Of. We got this." She pushed her VR Goggles up to her forehead, and Edith followed suit with her normal goggles.

Edith stepped up next to her as the scaled and finned Riverwalkers quickly approached. The ones who had gone around the sides of the park stationed themselves at the various entrances to the Square. Most hung back as a handful approached directly. Being Riverwalkers, they were, of course, all female.

Mars' breath caught as she realized which Riverwalker was at the forefront. Most Riverwalkers looked roughly half to a third human, but this Riverwalker had *much* less human in her. Silvery blue scales nearly covered her body, gleaming like stars in the light of the park's light posts, with patches of dark-brown flesh scattered like small islands across her body. Her head was nearly all glistening blue scales, with most of her face being that of a human woman. Her skin was smooth, her jaw delicate and round. The scales of her forehead reached down to cover one eye and cheek, and that eye was large and piercingly yellow, a stark contrast to the other dark eye.

Tough hide plates, which Mars assumed were from an alligator, were strapped across her body as armor. A thick scar ran up her neck and across her cheek, where it turned from dark blue on scales to light brown on skin. Onto her back was strapped a long, black trident, with several smaller tridents fastened to both of her forearms.

She had no hair except for her single, dark eyebrow, but her bald, blue head had three large blue-and-yellow fins protruding from the top like trihawks. The gills along her neck and shoulders opened and twitched as they breathed in the thick New Orleans air.

The Riverwalkers around her were closer to being human, having more hair on their heads and more skin, with various types of dark tridents sheathed to their backs or hips or arms, their bodies also strapped with hide armor.

Though the pedestrians and tarot readers didn't notice the Riverwalkers, most cleared the Square as if the sky were about to open up with heavy rain.

Mars spoke first, her voice bold and humorless: "Donish, warrior-leader of the Riverwalkers. I grew up listening to tales of your epic battles across the Mississippi and the swamps, of your sacrifices and triumphs. When I felt crushed by events in my life, I would remember stories of you and be inspired. It is a real honor to meet you."

The Riverwalker raised her eyebrow. "Not the common greeting I receive from a stranger, but not a bad one either. I understand you are Julius' and Roman's new Agents."

"I'm Mars, and this is Edith."

Beside her, Edith gave a slight nod.

"And how, Mars, does one hear the illustrious tales of my triumphs when one is but a little girl?"

"A dear friend of mine, who guarded and looked after me when I was young."

Donish's face melted a bit, and she even smiled, though between her lips were nothing but sharp and hooked teeth. "What is this dear friend's name?"

"You're going to laugh, and that's alright. The Function."

Donish nodded, but a couple of the Riverwalkers behind her did laugh.

"Well, that was kind of him, though I'm sure most of the tales are exaggerated beyond measure. I will have to thank him for making you a fan of mine, the next time he and I cross paths. He has always possessed a good heart."

Donish looked from Mars to Edith with her brown and yellow eye. Her gaze fell to the bead-wrapped stone in Mars' grasp, then to the green crown hanging from her other hand, where her gaze stuck. She looked as though she wanted to move away from the crown. "Where is it going to be kept? Surely it won't stay in the Presbytere."

"We're taking it," said Mars. "We'll make a replica to put in the Presbytere and tell you where we stash the real one."

Donish's eyes flicked to the orb in Mars' hand, then to the bodies and the wall of light behind her and Edith. Mars had no idea if Riverwalkers could see the ghost-wall without wearing special goggles. "We'll take care of the thieves."

"Works for us," said Mars. "We were just going to hand them over to you, anyway." She held up the orb. "We'll hang on to this guy, though. We have some questions for him before we send him your way. We'll give you back your handy little orb ghost-prison when we get him out of it."

Donish nodded.

Edith spoke up: "We should really check on the Presbytere."

"Edith's right," said Mars. "He's probably in bad shape right about now."

"Of course," said Donish. "Mars. Edith. My people are a little more than an arm's reach away if you need us."

"As are The Agents Of, to you and your kind," said Mars.

The two Agents walked through the gate of the park, skirting around the curve of salt on the ground (the orb wouldn't be able to pass through the wall since it now had Banshee Dave inside). Mars put the orb into her bag, then crouched down next to a brown leather hatbox which she'd set just outside the ghost-wall. She pulled open the lid and placed the Crown of Poseidon inside. The curved inner wall of the hatbox was lined with glass tubes of different colored liquid, designed by Roman to keep the crown's powers at bay. She placed the lid on top and latched it shut, then picked it up by its thin leather straps.

They made their way into the Presbytere, immediately finding themselves surrounded by a floor of writhing, moaning robed bodies.

Edith walked closer to a couple of them, shaking her head. "Can you tell which one Banshee Dave hit?"

Mars set the hatbox on the floor and waded through the bodies, relaxing her eyes to see the rivers of light running up and down each monk's body. The light arced across the room to connect them to each other. "Well, they're definitely all one entity, that part is obvious." Then she saw the bright red line of light stretching across a monk lying next to the entrance. Every time the red line twitched, the rest of the monks moaned louder.

Mars knelt next to the monk. "This guy right here." Running a hand down the length of his torso, she opened his robe and watched the normal streams of energy interact and recoil from the red line inside him.

She grabbed a handful of four-inch needles from her leather jacket, placing them between her teeth and pulling one out with her fingers. She held the monk's body as still as she could and pierced his upper chest with the needle, spearing one of the glowing lines close to the red line. She pulled another needle from her teeth and pierced his waist, pinning down the other end of the same stream.

Pulling a third and fourth needle from her teeth, she carefully pierced the healthy stream on the other side of the rogue red stream, isolating it. The red stream stopped twitching as much, and Mars brought her face close to it, the colors searing her retinas. Then she saw it—the red light was a shell, obscuring another color underneath.

She looked up at Edith. "Found the blue. You're up."

File 19 :: [Edith Downs]

Edith crouched next to Mars, who was pointing down the center of the man's torso. "There's a really jacked up stream of energy right here. It's glowing red, but I bet that's where the rogue memory is twisted into him."

"Let's see what I can do." Edith took a deep breath, seeing the glimmer of blue light from both Mars' head next to her as well as the host of monks around them. She focused her sight on the monk's chest, seeing a thin sliver of blue light—a slice down the center of the body. She leaned in closer and the light bent up towards her. From the blue light, a host of tiny faces leaped out—faces with shadows for eyes, their snapping mouths lashing out to bite her own face.

She screamed and fell backward onto her butt.

"Shit, you ok?" Mars was still holding the body down with her hands.

Edith rolled forward into a crouch. She'd never had a mem or a memory act aggressively towards her. It took a moment to realize why her teeth ground together, why her fist clenched. It had been a while since she'd felt betrayed.

"Is it beyond you? I can pin it down and we can just let him heal it on his own..."

Edith twisted her gloved hand and the Extraction Glove hummed to life. "No, it is *not* beyond me." The blue light from Mars and from the heads of all the monks died away as she reached out and put the gloved hand above the monk's chest. The skin became translucent, and floating up from it were dozens upon dozens of blue glowing orbs, like floating blue cotton balls. They were all memories—not categorized or strung together like a human's, but more like pieces of meat and vegetables swimming in a pot of gumbo. Roman had Edith practicing her abilities on entities and other new subjects, but the Presbytere was the first entity she'd worked on in the field.

She looked deeper, beyond the glowing orbs, and saw a single sphere streaked with red that lashed out with a host of shadow-eyed faces, attacking the other memories.

When she spoke next, her voice came from deep within and boomed like a train whistle. "Rogue memories! I am Edith Downs, member of The Agents Of and Protector of the Memories of New Orleans. You have turned on your own kind. If you do not exit this entity immediately, you will be dealt with as I see fit."

The angry faces turned to her, some whispering to each other and some laughing. They lashed out and bit at the glove to no effect, and she reached down into the monk's chest, the metal fingers of the gauntlet wrapping around the orb of memories.

Roman had told her that Rachel used to call the Extraction Glove the "Bullet Proof Vest," and Edith didn't want to think about what these deranged mems would be doing to her if it weren't for the glove.

Pulling the orb up carefully out of the monk, she did her best to keep it away from the other memories.

"Holy crap!" Mars pressed her hands against the center of the monk's chest. "Whatever you did freaking worked."

Edith looked closer at the orb, reading through the images it gave off. "Fire. This is the memory of a building being burned alive. Playing out over and over again." She looked down at the monk, who was no longer twitching.

Mars pulled out the needles.

The monk opened his eyes, tears sliding down the sides of his face. All the prone monks spoke in unison: "I'm... I'm not on fire?"

Mars shook her head. "No, you didn't burn at all. They were someone else's memories, but we took them out of you."

He relaxed onto the floor. "*Gracias. Merci.* Who are you?"

"Really?" said Mars, closing up his robe. "We're The Agents Of. You know, the two girls you told to *fuck off* a week ago when we said a junky ghost had plans to break in and steal the Crown of Poseidon."

"Oh, I'm sorry. I'm so sorry."

"How about we trade in those apologies for you not being an asshole next time?"

Edith didn't take her eyes off the squirming memory in her metal fist as she spoke: "This would have been easier for everyone if we were waiting for the ghosts inside the front door."

The monk merely took a deep breath and closed his eyes. Mars stood up and helped Edith to her feet. Mars picked up the hatbox by the straps and they headed back outside. Peering over her shoulder, Mars added, "Oh, and someone puked on your floor, apparently. Might want to grab a mop."

Outside, some Riverwalkers were using rocks wrapped with string and bone, similar to the one Mars used, to pull ghosts out of the other two bodies. Other Riverwalkers were disassembling the salt-wall or guarding the Square.

Mars turned and pushed Edith's shoulder, which made Edith laugh. "You know what you just did, girl?"

Edith couldn't help but smile. "My first extraction."

So far, she'd only used the Extraction Glove to *copy* memories, but now she'd actually pulled a memory out of someone.

She pressed a button on the side of the glove, watching the writhing, twisting fire memory get sucked into the glove's palm. A multitude of small lights moved through tubes running down the glove and a cartridge popped out near her elbow, reminding her way too much of ejecting a cartridge from a Nintendo Game Boy[19]. She pulled the cartridge out of the slot near her elbow and held it up, a tiny glowing red dot at its base.

Edith twisted her wrist and shut the glove off, suddenly aware of all the memories in the people and buildings and objects around her.

A shrill sound from the past cut through the air—it was a ringing payphone on the corner of the Square, where the streets of Chartres and St. Ann met.

"It's probably just Julius checking in," said Mars, toeing the clunky metal launcher device on the ground, the one that had malfunctioned against the ghosts. She named it the Claw Machine, after the arcade games where you win stuffed animals. "You want to get it, and I'll gather up this sad piece of broken dreams?"

"Sure thing." Edith walked towards the payphone, sliding the cartridge with the memory-virus into her bag.

When she reached the phone, she kind of wished she had a rubber glove to pick it up. The phone could be described in many ways, but "sanitary" was not one of them. She picked it up and held it an inch from her face. "Yes?"

"How fast can you wrap things up?" said Julius.

Edith eyed the scene in front of the Presbytere. "Sixty seconds. The Riverwalkers showed up, so..."

"Shit. I should have known Donish might do that. I should have prepared you."

"They're taking the other two ghosts, so it's less work for us. Banshee Dave is in the stone. The Presbytere is recuperating. I've extracted the memory-virus."

"Good. We need to know who Banshee Dave gave those calliope parts to. I'll see you both back at headquarters."

---

[19] Like a smart phone from the '80s, but with only the important apps.

The inky water of the Mississippi rumbled like a stomach just fed. The wind batted about Julius' black trench coat and his braids as he walked along the walkway of the levee, past benches, light posts, and bushes, his mechanical leg murmuring beneath him. Between Mars and Roman, the leg had gone through several incarnations and tweaks, making it quieter and stronger. It was late enough at night that the levee along the edge of the French Quarter was nearly deserted.

He walked down the large stairway leading down the rocks and into the water. From his coat, he pulled a one-foot-long black cylinder covered with buttons and small tubes. Holding the device in his mechanical claw-hand, with his real hand he pushed one button and twisted the device until it clicked. It let out a slow, pulsing light and emitted a low warbling sound that humans wouldn't hear.

He tossed it several yards out, the pulsing light quickly devoured by the black water.

The surface of the river lay undisturbed and flat as a dark figure emerged from it, like shadow emerging from shadow. She pulled herself out of the water, her bare, webbed feet smacking against the steps.

Silvery blue scales covered nearly all of her, with three large fins sticking out of her hairless head like trihawks. Alligator hide was strapped to her body, along with the long black trident strapped to her back. She looked at Julius with her human eye and her yellow fishlike eye and tossed him the device, which he caught. The gills along her neck and shoulders opened to expel the rest of the water stored in her body as they switched over to breathing air.

She turned and spat out a wad of water. "Julius."

"Donish." He slipped the device back into his coat. "I planned this meeting to update you on the Crown of Poseidon heist, but it seems Mars already updated you."

"I apologize for the surprise visit. The Crown of Poseidon's theft made me nervous. If anything went wrong, I wanted my people to react immediately."

"It's safe for now. Roman is building the replica to put in the Presbytere. I'm making a list of possible places to keep the original crown, which I'll get to you this week."

"And the thief?"

"We'll get him to you within the next few days."

A smirk stole its way across her lips. "I'm glad you're back. I was getting a little paranoid with you out of commission. So many... human-fed forces bleed through this land. Very chaotic and hard to predict."

Julius nodded. "How is Elsh?"

"Elsh will be fine. She's shaken up, healing."

"You never liked her."

"She's an artist in a village of warriors."

"Yet you never kick her out."

"Elsh and I respect each other, though we may not understand one another. How is Roman?"

"Healing up, like Elsh, except one of the beasts tore out a piece of his belief. He's studying and analyzing the changes to his mind and emotions."

"Sounds very much like Roman."

"Yes, it does." He looked out over the dark river, the bridge in the distance lit up like a milky way stretched between land masses. "Roman said you no longer trust him."

Her brown and yellow eyes flickered up to the levee above them, then back to Julius. "I feel the war inside him. He wants to understand what his human lover found, what seduced her to slaughter of everything she said she loved."

Julius fought not to look away as thoughts of Rachel fluttered across his mind.

She tilted her head. "I know that you do as well. But in you, I know which part is dominant. I know that, more than anything, you and I are leaders."

Julius licked his lips. "Do you ever... do you ever doubt yourself?"

Donish walked up a step so that she was on the same level as him, putting a webbed hand on his shoulder, her eyes peering into his golden ones. "We do not have the luxury of listening to our doubts regarding past actions. Just as we do not have the luxury of worry, or of regret. All we can do is strive to become better, to learn from our missteps, to inspire more from those who follow us, and to follow our cause without hesitation. This is what separates us from the rest."

Julius sighed. "Could you just distill yourself into liquid—you know, so I could take a shot of you every couple days?"

She smiled, which was comforting to him despite her sharp, hooked teeth. "You *are* leaning towards your human life, aren't you?"

"I met with Bes. He told me that something was coming, something big that only the Julius part of me has the power to deal with."

Donish's eyes widened. "Ah, I see. So you're leaning into the human side because the city needs you to."

"That's the idea."

Donish stepped down towards the water. "Perhaps you should ask yourself: Are you truly leaning towards the human? Or are you still latched onto the god while reaching as far as you can towards the human without actually letting go?"

Julius chuckled. "Is Donish, ruthless leader of the Riverwalkers, talking me into letting go of the part of me that's not human?"

"Bes has been watching over the city for centuries, so if he says that Julius is important, then perhaps you'd better look for Julius." She turned away, the light from the light posts making the water on her scaled armor and trident look like slowly dripping light. "I will see you again shortly."

Then she dove into the water, not making the slightest splash or ripple as she vanished into the dark waves.

File 21 :: [Mars]

Gas lights flared to life as Mars walked down one of the underground headquarters' long, curving stone hallways. Edith walked beside her with a long metal cylinder balanced on her shoulder. It was like a beer keg with a handle on top.

"You've gotta wonder what the hell someone was thinking, making those so heavy," said Mars.

"You don't think they've got to be heavy? I mean, to function?"

"Nah, I doubt it. All they do is contain one ghost. Julius shoves ghosts into freaking bottles."

"Are you going to redesign them?"

"Sure, I'll make it number three-hundred-and-twenty-seven on my list of things to do."

After passing dozens of wooden and metal doors set into the curved walls, they finally arrived at a rolling garage door. Mars grabbed the garage door handle and pulled it up, then walked in and hit the lights. If it *were* a garage, it would have been of the three-car variety. Metal shelves covered the walls, and there was a bulky, rust-colored mechanical crane hunched in the middle of the room, with something like forklift forks holding up what Mars had come to call the Capsule[20]. The far half of the room's floor was missing, leaving crisscrossed metal walkways stretching across a gently churning surface of water.

The Capsule itself was a mix between rust-colored metal, brass, and glass, and was vaguely egg-shaped. It was about five yards long and about three yards wide and tall at its widest point.

"Looks good all cleaned up, doesn't she?" said Mars, but the look on Edith's face was everything but confident.

"You and Roman did more than dust it off, right?"

---

[20] The vehicle was originally named *Wondric Subwater Tranport Vessel*, but Mars didn't have time for all that.

"Oh, yeah. He showed me all the ins and outs, don't you worry one bit." Mars walked up the three metal steps to the side of the Capsule, pulled down on a handle and popped the side door open. She took the canister from Edith and slid it into a storage area behind the large seat, then threw their duffel bags next to it.

"Now, we have to get comfy, hope you don't mind. This thing was built with one driver in mind, but the seat is big."

"So one of the previous Agents made this?"

Mars climbed into the wide cushioned chair. "Yeah, in the late-ish 1800s. This guy called The Scientist. I've found a ton of his journals, full of ideas and sketches. One day I'm going to lock myself away and just read all of his work. It's the basis for Roman's devices."

Edith slipped her own stuffed duffel bag behind the seat and slid in next to Mars. "I always forget how old Roman is. Did he ever meet The Scientist?"

Mars shrugged. "Don't know. He gets weird when I bring The Scientist up, so I think they knew each other. Maybe the guy's death was hard on him or something. Now, pull the door closed and turn the handle up like a crank."

Edith did so, with a considerable *squeal* and *clunk.*

In front of them was a giant, curved window rimmed with hoses and pipes. Several switches stuck down from the ceiling above the window, of which Mars flicked a couple. The rust-colored steering panel in front of them consisted of only two large golden discs with black centers, about the size of 45 records.

Mars pulled from the inner pocket of her leather jacket half a piece of Wonder wrapped in plastic wrap.

"Oh, you have to feed it?" asked Edith. "Like gassing it up?"

"Ha, you could say that."

Mars unwrapped the Wonder, scooped out some of its insides with her pinkie, and put it on her tongue.

"Wait, you're *eating* it?"

Mars nodded and took a deep breath, feeling the Wonder dissolve into her tongue. She closed her eyes and watched it spill down into the darkness of her body like liquid smoke, wrapping around her heart. Opening her eyes, she no longer merely saw Edith, but saw the curiosity and awe which was always present inside of Edith woven throughout the woman's body. That curiosity and awe peered back at Mars, winking at her.

"Are you ok, Mars?"

"Uh... yeah, I'm still getting used to doing this."

"Are you sure you're ok to drive this thing while eating Wonder? I don't know if that's a good idea..."

Mars licked her lips. "You have to eat Wonder to drive it." She put both her hands over the discs, which lit up with glowing blue symbols—numbers, letters, and shapes. "The Wonder in the pilot speaks to the Wonder running through the Capsule." She grabbed onto the creative energy surging up inside her, focusing it the way Roman had shown her, and pushed it out through her hands. The symbols on the discs rotated and the world beyond the windows became blue.

Edith looked through the windows. "Is that Wonder covering this thing? Looks kind of like what The Gateway did when we used it to get out of the Land of the Dead."

Mars took the leather harness that she'd modified to strap over two people and buckled in her side. Edith watched her and did the same. "Similar principle as The Gateway, except we don't have to spin, and it's not as gross."

"Gross?"

"The Gateway was using mostly ichor, which is ghost blood, to open the doorway to the land of the dead."

"Ok, yeah that's gross."

"Told you." Mars focused her energy again. The Capsule shook and started moving towards the open floor of water, the crane arm carrying it over. She looked over at Edith, who looked exactly like the goddess of love. "Ya ready, girl?"

Edith sat back in her chair, breathing deep. "I trust you."

"Ha, good enough!"

Edith screamed as they fell crashing into the water. Everything around them was lit up with the blue glow of the Wonder surrounding the Capsule. They were in a small submerged area, like a hallway, surrounded by other crane arms, some oddly shaped diving suits, and a few other clunky bits of equipment.

Mars pushed her creativity through her fingertips, and The Capsule hummed forward through the underwater hallway. She felt the Wonder all around her, felt the ship's body like her own. As they came to a large metal door, she let her creativity reach out into the controls and open the door.

It was before dawn, and the lightening sky barely broke through the water ahead of them as they moved between the wooden posts underneath the docks of Spanish Plaza. The layer of Wonder covering the windows worked like slightly magnified lenses, letting the two see rather far into the Mississippi. There was a humongous ship ahead, barreling through the center of the river.

"Alright," said Mars. "Now hold on, we're going to go fast so we can avoid the dinosaur-whale-monsters."

"*Wait, dinosaur-whale-what?*"

"Roman didn't tell you about the dinosaur-whale-monsters? Great."

Mars shook her head, angling them downward. "Don't worry, I've done this three times now. And definitely don't scream, I really need to concentrate."

Mars took a deep breath, gritted her teeth, and gathered all the creativity she could muster, shooting it like a cannon from her heart into her hands. The Capsule let out a low-pitched *whir* and they shot forward, fish, debris, and plants sliding past them in two blinks of an eye.

Edith screamed, then grabbed her mouth with her hand. "Sorry!"

"No worries, it's over."

Edith's hand fell to her chest, pressing against her heart. "Holy shit, that's beautiful..."

They were descending towards a town full of wooden buildings bathed in the glow of blue streetlights, with the Riverwalkers in the distance swimming to and fro down the streets.

"Welcome to the First Quarter, Edith."

"It's... gorgeous."

Mars smiled. "Good to know. I've never seen it without being jacked up on Wonder, but I was pretty sure it's gorgeous, anyway."

A booming roar pierced the air—something enormous, ancient, and furious.

"What was that?" whispered Edith.

"Just a reminder not to stop yet." Mars steered them down closer to all the wooden buildings, gliding over the steeped rooftops. Several Riverwalkers stopped to look up at them.

"And they're alright with us being here?"

Mars shrugged. "It's an old arrangement. I figure they're just confused, wondering what a hundred-something-year-old vehicle is doing floating above their city again."

"Um, maybe leave out how old this thing is until we're out of it..."

"Duly noted."

Mars brought them down towards the roof of the three-story L'Hotel Glace, hovering up to a circular metal door. She reached out with the ship's Wonder and the door slid open beneath them, and they gently lowered down into a room roughly the size of the one which housed the Capsule up at the surface. A hunched crane in the corner came to life, reaching out to cradle the Capsule as the room lit up with electric lights. The door above them closed loudly, and the hum of the pumping mechanisms came to life. Small circular openings covered the walls and floor, pulling the water out until it was gone.

Mars powered off the ship, the layer of Wonder surrounding it being sucked back into various pipes and hoses, and unfastened her part of the harness. She turned to Edith, who was staring out the window.

"Freaking cool, right?"

Edith nodded. "Yeah. Yeah. Sorry, even with two months of being an Agent, that was a lot all at once. I'm still catching up, I think."

"Here, let's get out. You'll feel better if you walk around."

Edith smiled. "You're right." She unfastened her part of the harness and opened the door, stepping down onto the set of metal stairs leading to the floor. Mars turned around on her seat, getting onto her knees, and handed Edith the duffel bags and canister, which Edith set onto the floor.

"Alright," said Mars, jumping down onto the metal floor. "Let's take a tour." She slung her bag over her shoulder, grabbed the canister, and walked up to the massive vault door. Spinning the handle and shouldering open the door, she led them into a large laboratory. Books, lab equipment, and curio cabinets covered every wall, the cabinets housing fossilized creatures, rocks, and dried plants.

"Wow, I didn't realize there was equipment down here," said Edith. "I thought this place wasn't operational."

"It's not, this stuff is all super old. Another reason I suspect The Scientist's death affected Roman. Why wouldn't he take all this equipment up with him? Or these books?" She set her bag down onto one of the many lab tables, then hefted the canister onto her shoulder. She pointed towards two of the doors, which were both open. "That's the bar Roman and Elsh made. But don't drink anything; they haven't tested the booze for human consumption. And over in that room is the distilling equipment Elsh uses to make alcohol."

"Have you met Elsh?"

"Not yet. I've mostly just been practicing driving the Capsule. I haven't spent a lot of time here."

Mars continued across the lab, towards a set of large metal doors already pulled open to reveal a white room with two wooden chairs and a table. "That's the holding cell." The three walls were covered with vertical lines of tiny holes. Next to the large door was a smaller door, which they walked into. The adjoining room was small, with a one-way mirror into the holding cell and a control panel full of brass switches, dials, and gauges.

"This is where you control the holding cell." Mars picked up two small tubes off a shelf. "You know how we made a ghost-wall last night? Well, this tube is salt, and this one is holy water."

She inserted the tubes into two holes in the control panel, then flipped a few switches. She spun a dial and the room beyond the window was bathed in yellow light.

"So the ghosts can't go through the walls," said Edith. "And the light makes the ghosts visible, right?"

"You got it." Mars hefted the canister up to a large hole on top of the control panel and screwed it in. "This should do it." She pulled a lever and

Banshee Dave tumbled out into the yellow room, rolling until he slammed into the wall. He moaned and knocked on the wall, checking to make sure he couldn't pass through.

"Nice upgrade," he said in his gravelly voice. "Didn't think this place was still here. Thought the *sea monsters* would have eaten it by now."

Mars looked at Edith and raised an eyebrow. "You ready to do this?"

"Yeah, I think so."

Mars pulled out a thin metal pole, like an old TV antenna. "Hold out your free arm."

"What is it?"

"I don't know, but as Julius says, *it makes ghosts take you seriously*." She pressed it against Edith's arm and the metal coiled around her wrist, up her arm, and down across her palm. It looked alive—alive and creepy as hell.

"Julius also said not to let it get too close to Banshee Dave, that it hasn't fed for a while and it's hungry."

Edith's eyes widened as she looked at it all coiled around her arm like a snake.

"You look more ready now," said Mars.

"We'll see."

File 22 :: [Edith Downs]

Edith walked through the ghost-wall and into the holding cell, the Extraction Glove covering one arm and the metal snake-thing coiling around the other. She swore she could feel it breathing against her skin. She felt its hunger, its desire to rip something up, and she let those feelings mix inside with her utter dislike of the ghost in the cell.

Banshee Dave wouldn't be able to see through the ghost-wall covering the entrance, so he didn't see Mars behind her or the lab beyond. He looked up at Edith through his stringy, dirty-blond hair with a palpable look of disappointment. "Damn. I was hoping you'd be the cute one."

Immediately the ghost reminded her of Dean Smith, that bank robber from the '30s who'd hijacked her mind and body. She gritted her teeth and twisted her wrist to power on the glove.

Banshee Dave couldn't quite hide the momentary startled look which flashed across his face before resuming a demeanor of boredom.

She watched memories swimming out the top of his head like curling yellow tentacles with blue stripes spiraling up and around them. They didn't look like any memories she'd seen before, and she had no idea what she was supposed to do with them. Why did they look like tentacles? Was each one a file? They blended and shifted into each other. Then she realized blue stripes were moving through the rest of him as well, the thin memory streams traveling over his ghost-skin.

"The fuck you lookin' at, Blade Runner?"

Edith took a step forward, activating the glove's copying aspect to make liquid slosh through the tubes and vials, watching his eyes widen at the sound of the gurgling, churning liquid. She thought of Roman, her friend—of how this ghost's actions were linked to Roman getting his mind and emotions altered. She knew this ghost might hold the key to finding the calliope player. "All you have to know," she muttered through clenched teeth, "is that I'm not *the cute one.*"

As if sensing Banshee Dave now that she'd stepped forward, the metal wire around her other arm seemed to wake up, curling closer to her hand and coiling more of itself around her palm. It pulsed and glowed yellow in the strange light of the room.

Banshee Dave's eyes grew large as he backed into the wall. "*You psycho Agent. Those aren't even supposed to exist anymore.*"

"Well, Mr. Banshee Dave, I'm proud to tell you that The Agents Of are here to instill a sense of wonder and awe into your mundane existence. Now, if you could kindly get in the chair..."

"I ain't getting in shit."

Mars walked in through the ghost-wall and Banshee Dave chuckled. "I knew you sensed the spark between us, doll."

"Did you just reference Blade Runner?"

"Yeah, it's this movie that came out maybe thirty, forty years before you were bor—"

Mars raised her arm with the Bola Launcher attached, her other hand pulling back the elastic band. She let go and a stream of yellow light flashed through the air, wrapping around Banshee Dave's arms and torso, sending him twisting onto the ground.

"What the fuck!" he yelled.

"Ouch, age joke. That really hurts. I definitely won't try to top that with any heroine-junky-wanna-be-rock-star jokes, because nothing could top an age joke. I mean, I'm so young and innocent, and you callously pull out your ace on the first go."

She grabbed the yellow, pulsing rope that bound him, picked him up with a grunt and slammed him into the chair[21].

Banshee Dave smirked. "Ain't no *wanna-be* rock star here, doll-face. I was the real deal."

"Oh, I didn't realize. I'll just run over to Euclid Records after we're through and pick up a *Banshee Dave* album. Oh, but which one will I get —such a cornucopia to choose from."

"We were more real than that. All our shit was underground."

Now Edith chimed in. "I'm still stuck at Blade Runner."

"Yeah," said Mars. "That didn't make any sense."

"Like I said," said Banshee Dave, "It's a sci-fi movie from the '80s, '83 I think..."

"We know what Blade Runner is," said Mars. "*Everyone* does."

Edith raised the Extraction Glove. "What about this glove has *anything* to do with Blade Runner?"

"You know! Science Fiction crap!"

---

[21]   While studying ways of containing ghosts, Mars created what Roman referred to as a Malleable Ghost Containment Stream, and what Mars called Ghost Rope. For more on Ghost Rope, please see The Agents Of, Volume I, file 62.

"Oh," said Edith, "so you could have called me Star Trek or Star Wars. I mean, at least Luke gets a metal hand."

"You would *suck* at Trivial Pursuit," said Mars.

Banshee Dave shook his head. "Really? What are we even talking about? What the fuck is wrong with you two?"

Mars leaned in close to Banshee Dave. "Certain parties are demanding we hand you over to them. None of them are as nice as us. In fact, I'm pretty sure that if we hand you over to *any* of them, we'll never see your sorry face again. First, there are the Riverwalkers. You have no idea how much you freaked them out, stealing the crown. If they get a hold of you, you'll never see sunlight again."

"Oh, come on! No one was using the crown, it was just fucking sitting there!"

"The other party that wants your blood is The Presbytere, along with the other Jackson Square entities. They play by rules way older and harsher than ours. Jackson Square is where people used to be executed on the regular—did you know that? You should probably keep that locked away in case you play some kind of New Orleans trivia game."

"My crime wasn't that bad! You can't just hand me over to some shitbag entity having a bad day!"

Edith kicked his chair so that it slid back against the wall. "*Banshee Dave!*" Her voice erupted from her chest like a storm and he shut up. "*I am Edith Downs, member of The Agents Of and Protector of the Memories of New Orleans. Your recent actions have put the city and its inhabitants at great risk. In accordance with The Fair Memory Act, your memories are forfeit.*" She looked over her shoulder and nodded, at which point Mars spoke up:

"I, Mars, am a licensed Louisiana notary. I agree to witness this extraction and/or copying of memories."

"What the *fuck* are you two babbling about!?"

Edith held up her gloved hand, flexing her other arm to hold back the metal wire that wanted to eat this ghost. The blue-laced yellow tentacles writhed above his head like dancers in a club, and she had no freaking idea what to do with them. "You'd better hold still. And if you want this to go faster, you should bring up every memory you have about stealing the pieces of the calliope. Who hired you, what they paid you, the theft itself. I want to see *every* scrap of those memories."

Banshee Dave's face dropped into shock, a look that appeared so foreign on the ghost. "The... I just pawned the pieces to a bunch of vendors at the French Market. I thought... I thought you wanted to know about why I stole the crown."

"Oh, we'll get to that," said Mars. "I hope you don't have any pressing appointments today..."

File 23 :: [Banshee Dave]

[New Orleans, a week and a half ago.]

The city streets were slick with the memory of rain. Shining black asphalt reflected street and porch lights, reminding Banshee Dave of the night sky outside the city—a sight he hadn't gazed upon since his epic rock-god demise.

He wandered out of the Marigny and up into the seventh ward, past shotgun houses and corner stores, towards a tiny cluster of newer bars. The pulsing electronic beats of industrial music greeted him as he approached The Goat.

Several living humans and a few ghosts lounged outside the bar, drinking cocktails, clad in an assortment of trench coats, gowns, corsets, mini-skirts, top hats, goggles, and zippers. Most were wearing handmade leather masks over their faces or up on their foreheads, the masks sprouting feathers or long noses or angry, creased brows.

Banshee Dave nodded to the few that could see him and walked up to the door.

A hand stopped him. The doorman, black hair pulled back into a ponytail and wearing a ripped up army vest, pointed his thumb to a glowing yellow sign tacked onto the doorway:

Masquerade Ball
--free--

You must wear a mask inside.
Cost of mask: $5
(or one ounce of Ichor
for ghosts)

Banshee Dave looked down at the doorman's glowing fingerless leather glove. "Really? You're seriously charging ghosts a cover?"

"There is no cover. But you've got to wear a mask. You can buy one, leave and come back with one, or just leave. Rules are rules."

"Thought I died to get into shit for free."

The man shrugged. "I doubt that's why you died."

"Oh, fuck you, mate." Banshee Dave reached into his own chest, pulling out a tiny palm full of his own ghostly energy. The doorman opened his glowing leather glove and Banshee Dave dropped the glowing ball of ichor into it.

The doorman handed over a cheap ghost-plastic mask with an elongated nose. Banshee Dave pressed it to his face and waved his fingers in the air. "Ooooo. Now you don't know who I am. Maybe I didn't pay your stupid cover, you'll never know."

The doorman was unimpressed. "*There is no cover*. Just go inside or leave. You're blocking the door."

"Holy hell, I can't tell who's more boring, the living or the dead." Banshee Dave made his way into the thickening crowd of The Goat. Just ahead was a long bar, with a couple bartenders getting drinks for the crowd. Behind the bar was the dance floor, with a DJ playing metallic, pounding music while colored lights swirled to the beat.

Banshee Dave headed to the row of booths on the left, slipping into the booth where a single masked occupant waited. The man's mask covered his eyes and nose, and looked to be made of porcelain, painted with music notes and rimmed with tiny green feathers. He also wore a black hoodie with the hood pulled up over his head. Banshee Dave tossed his own ghost-mask onto the table. "So, doll, you the one I've been looking for all my life? Or whatever the fuck this is..."

The hooded, masked man's eyes were fixed on the entrance. "Were you followed?"

"Thought you were working with me because I'm a professional. Why the fuck would I let myself be followed?"

The man watched the entrance for a few seconds, then visibly relaxed a little. "Did you bring it?"

"You mean the calliope pieces?"

The man grimaced. "*Shut the fuck up, you damned ghost*. This is sensitive. I'm paying you to be discreet."

"Usually only housewives pay me for that." The masked man was even more upset and Banshee Dave raised his hands. "I *did* bring it, like I promised, but obviously not on my person. I'm a ghost and we both don't need a sack of instrument pieces being seen bouncing along the street, being carried by some invisible person."

The man's eyes darted around through the masked crowd. "Is it here or not?"

"Is my *payment* here?"

The man pulled from inside his jacket a jar filled with red, pulsing energy. While his coat was opened, Banshee Dave caught sight of at least three devices or artifacts that could take down a ghost with ease, as well as a few others that could take down humans. This man was pretty well armed, and that's just what he'd seen from the brief glimpse into the man's coat. This guy could probably get out of here alive if this whole bar turned on him.

"So this will immobilize an entity?" asked Banshee Dave.

The masked man pushed the jar towards Banshee Dave, who took it and pulled it under the table. "It's a memory virus."

Banshee Dave knew well what it was when he first saw it. "I've only heard of Nimble having access to these."

"*Don't say that fucking name,*" said the man under his breath.

Banshee Dave shrugged. "Never liked the prick, so fuck if I care where this came from."

The man leaned forward. "Now, where are the calliope pieces?"

"Oh yeah," said Banshee Dave. "Not exactly up your ass, but… in close proximity."

One of the man's hands twitched on the table, and Banshee Dave raised his own hands, knowing the guy's coat was full of weapons. "Whoa, I'm serious. Lift up the booth seat."

The man got up and lifted the cushioned seat. He pulled out a large cloth bag, black and heavy.

"It's all in there," said Banshee Dave. "Everything you asked me to rip out of that thing."

The man rifled around through the bag and Banshee Dave could see his body relax a little. The man was still stressed as hell. But how else would you be after stealing a damned memory virus from Nimble?

"*Hey!*"

The doorman walked up to the end of their table, now wearing a simple black and white harlequin mask, his fingerless glove glowing yellow in the dark bar. He motioned to Banshee Dave's mask on the table. "Put the mask on or leave."

The man across from Banshee Dave cowered down into the booth seat, pulling the black bag down onto his lap, his hand sliding into his coat and its assortment of devices. None of the chattering crowd paid them any notice amidst the thumping noise and colored lights of the bar.

Banshee Dave poked the ghost-plastic mask. "Sorry, my cheeks started breaking out really bad. Sometimes happens with cheap-as-shit ghost-plastic. I've got *very* sensitive skin."

"Rules are rules."

"Well, it just so happens that I was leaving." Banshee Dave nodded to his hooded, masked partner, slid out of the booth and was escorted out of the bar.

File 24 :: [Elsh]

Dawn's sunlight filtered through hundreds of feet of water above, breaking into twisting and dancing shards, growing ever more faint in their descent until finally merging with the flickering blue glow of the black lampposts of the First Quarter. The blue light washed over Elsh's flesh and scales as she swam through the streets, propelled by her webbed feet and the fins protruding from her body. She was wrapped in a sleeveless dress of blue fabric she'd made by copying a picture she'd found in a book long ago. Many other Riverwalkers of the First Quarter looked down on her dislike of wearing armor or using weapons, but she'd grown to ignore what they thought.

Entering the open front doors of L'Hotel Glace, she swam up the stairway to the vault door. She spun the handle, opened it, and drifted inside, closing and locking the door behind her. She was in a metal chamber with holes covering two of the walls, with a second door directly in front of her. She went to a control panel containing three levers, working them so the water drained from the chamber, her feet adjusting to take on the weight of her body as her lungs expelled excess water through the gills along her neck. She opened the second vault door and walked into the laboratory.

Near the far side of the room sat a woman with long red dreadlocks at a lab table, staring right at Elsh. A bulky device lay on the table along with a pile of tools. Across the lab was Edith, standing and wielding the Extraction Glove, looking around at the lab tables and shelves as if she was seeing something completely different.

Beyond the yellow, glowing wall of the containment room was a punk-rock-looking ghost sitting on the floor next to a chair.

Elsh walked across the laboratory, her webbed feet and soaked dress leaving trails of water on the floor behind her, stopping at the table where the woman with dreadlocks was sitting. "Hello, Mars. I'm glad that we finally get to meet."

Mars coughed. "Yeah, me too. Pleasure to meet you, Elsh."

"Are you alright?"

"Yeah. Yeah, I'm good." She coughed again as she stood up. "Let's just say that if I ever doubted Roman's ability to fall for a Riverwalker, that doubt is thoroughly squelched. You're... um... very nice looking."

Elsh nodded to her. "You're *very nice looking* too, Mars."

Mars' eyes widened. "Wow, this got awkward fast."

"Oh, I apologize. I rarely talk to humans."

"Don't apologize! It's really not you, it's me, I swear. And I've been talking to a lot more not-humans these days myself. I've just been zoned out working on this damned thing."

Elsh looked past Mars towards the woman across the lab. "Is Edith looking through memories?"

Mars followed her gaze. "Yeah. She copied a bunch from douche-bag ghost-guy. Now she's going through them, looking for clues. She's kind of a badass."

"I take it you two don't need help with the machinery?"

"No, I think we've got it down."

"Then may I ask what you're working on?"

Mars laughed and looked down at the lab table. "Oh, this thing? This is something I've been working on, the Dust-o-Bot 5000. I got it working, but I'm trying to upgrade it."

The device on the lab table resembled a large ten-legged crab made of metal. Its top was open, and inside were a series of tubes and small glass vials of liquid. Mars shut the lid and flipped it upside-down, revealing a set of rotating cloth dusters.

"You're powering it by making substances react to each other?"

"That's what Roman's been teaching me. Seems to be one of the better methods for us Agents, with electronics not working half the time."

Elsh reached down and ran a finger over the smooth metal casing. "There are notebooks down here, which may help. They belong to the Agents, so you are free to take them."

"Yeah, The Scientist's notes. Roman let me know." Mars smiled. "I might just read them down here though, this lab is a pretty good hiding spot. It might take me a couple of decades, but I think I can read them all."

Elsh turned and looked at the wall of notebooks, thinking of the other books in various side rooms. "That's rather ambitious." She heard footsteps and turned as Edith walked up, heading towards them while rubbing her eyes.

"Edith!" said Mars. "Guess who came to visit?"

"Hello, Elsh," said Edith. The Extraction Glove gurgled, pulsed, and then powered off.

"Hello, Edith."

Mars grasped Edith's shoulder. "How'd it go? I wanted to ask, but didn't want to interrupt."

"Good, I think. He... kind of behaved." She turned back towards the containment room, the ghost leaning back against the wall and yawning. Then Edith raised her other arm to Mars. "Can you take this thing off me?"

Elsh's eyes widened when she saw the slithering metal wire snaked around Edith's arm. "You dealt with the ghost wearing *that*?"

Mars tugged at the end closest to Edith's elbow, the wire straightening out until it was no longer attached to her. "So you know what this is?"

"Only that it's very old. I figured Julius still had one, but didn't know he'd allow it to be used."

Mars put it in a long, thin case and slipped it into a duffel bag below the table.

Edith pulled the glove off, flexing her hand and fingers. "Well, it got Banshee Dave to shut up and let me look in his head. I think I got all the memories we need. And now I know how to copy ghost memories."

"Hell yeah," said Mars, raising her hand in the air, Edith immediately slapping her palm.

"Is that like a handshake?" asked Elsh.

Mars looked at her and raised an eyebrow. "No. No, it's not. It's one of the most important symbolic gestures of the human race. *Way* more important than a handshake."

"Oh?"

Mars put her hand up again. "Go on, put your hand up like this, then we slap them."

Elsh followed Mars' lead, and they gently slapped their palms together.

"It's called a high-five. Five fingers, up high. It's a positive affirmation, like saying, 'good job' or 'that was freaking awesome.'"

Elsh nodded, smiling. "Thank you, Mars. I'm sure I will adequately blend into human society now."

Mars and Edith both coughed out a laugh, then Elsh joined them.

"It's nice having people here," said Elsh. "This place is usually so desolate. If you don't have to go back up right away, perhaps you'd join me for a cocktail?"

"I thought your alcohols weren't yet human-tested," said Mars.

"They're not, but I do have a bottle of gin, as well as an array of liquids I've created by brewing flowers and leaves in water."

Mars looked at Edith and shrugged.

"Sure, I need a break," said Edith. She motioned to the brass phone built into the far wall of the lab. "I'm gonna report in, then I'll join you."

"What did you find out?" asked Mars.

"Not much, unfortunately." Edith pulled off the Extraction Glove and placed it next to Dust-o-bot 5000. "The calliope player only interacted directly with Banshee Dave twice—once to negotiate the theft and give him a diagram of exactly what to take from the calliope. The second time was to get the calliope pieces from him in exchange for something to take out an *entity*, which happened to be a memory virus. Banshee Dave seemed to think that only *Nimble* was known to have memory viruses, and the calliope player got super defensive when Banshee Dave brought up Nimble."

"So the guy almost definitely worked for, or at least knows, Nimble," said Mars.

Edith shook her head. "It's what we already suspected, but at least it's new evidence. I've got the memory of Banshee Dave stealing the calliope pieces from the Steamboat Tchoupitoulas, and everything about the theft of the Crown of Poseidon. Seems he'd wanted to steal the crown for about a decade, just to see what would happen."

"So Julius was right about him being a wild card."

"Yeah. I've got to tell you, being inside that guy's memories makes me want a shower."

"I bet," said Mars.

*   *   *

While Edith called Julius and Mars packed up, Elsh brought a third stool into the makeshift bar. She wiped off a dusty, unopened bottle of gin she'd found long ago and set it on the bar. Then she rummaged around in a cupboard, clicking together three of the stones on her bracelet so they emitted a yellow light and illuminated the ghostly world. She found a couple of bottles of beer which were glowing yellow, grabbed them and walked back into the lab.

"What the..." said Mars. "Elsh, is that ghost beer?"

"Yes," said Elsh, walking into the containment room. Ghostly objects (like ghost beer) and ghosts themselves could go one way through the wall, but not the other way. She set the beer on the floor as Banshee Dave stood up.

"Oh hey, sweetie. They didn't tell me it was a *pretty* one coming to get me. I mean, I'm not usually a Riverwalker kinda guy, but I've got a very open mind when it comes to—"

Banshee Dave reached up to touch her shoulder and she grabbed his wrist tight, her hand still glowing in the bracelet's light. "You may *quietly* drink a beer in this room, or be shoved back into the canister you came here in."

He raised his other hand and shrugged. "Beer is my second favorite thing, doll."

"*Quietly.*"

He sucked in his lips and Elsh backed away, letting him go and walking through the wall of light. She rotated one of the stones of her bracelet, and it stopped glowing.

"I need to get me one of those," said Mars.

"That bracelet is beautiful," said Edith.

Elsh walked into the barroom, the other two following her. "Good luck. Roman has been trying to get one of these for years. Our methods for creating relics are very old, and the tribe has never shared them."

Mars and Edith took a seat at one table, the other one covered in bottles holding liquids of all colors, some of which glowed.

"Wow," said Edith. "You made all of these?"

"Yes," said Elsh. "With equipment that Roman either brought down or constructed here in the adjoining rooms. What flavors do you like?"

Edith thought a moment. "Coffee? Creamy coffee, nutmeg, nothing terribly sweet..."

Elsh looked at Mars, who shrugged. "I really like the taste of whiskey, something with a bite. Dark beer. But I also drink a lot of vodka, soda, and lime. I guess what I'm saying is I'll probably like anything you give me."

Elsh opened the bottle of gin, grabbed three glasses and began picking up bottles and smelling them, occasionally adding them to the glasses. "I hope you don't mind, there's no ice. Roman and I have gotten used to drinking the cocktails at room temperature."

When she finished, she placed the glasses before them. The result was a slowly churning liquid of various dark shades of violet.

Edith was the first to drink, and she smiled. "Oh, that's delightful. It tastes like coffee! But like wood too, and something floral."

"Most of my drinks will taste floral, due to what I usually work with. The coffee flavor is a pinch of brewed chicory root."

"Ooo!" said Mars. "This is really good! It's going to be hard not to just down this."

Elsh took her own glass and sat across from them, taking a long sip.

Edith raised her glass. "To being done with work for the day."

"Here's to that," said Mars.

Elsh raised her glass, and they all tapped them together, then knocked them on the bar and drank.

"You work a lot too, don't you?" asked Edith.

"Yes," said Elsh. "I definitely have more free time than Roman, but Donish keeps us busy with various tasks."

"You said the word 'tribe' earlier," said Mars. "Is Donnish the leader of all the Riverwalkers, or of the tribe?"

"The Riverwalkers are led by a council of tribal leaders, and Donnish is the leader of this tribe. Do you know about the different tribes?"

Mars and Edith both shook their heads.

"There are dozens of Riverwalker tribes in South Louisiana. Most live in lakes or rivers or along the gulf. Lake Ponchartrain itself is home to several tribes. The Riverwalkers of the First Quarter are one of the larger tribes."

Mars placed her hand on the table. "Part of me really wants to ask more questions about your kind, but that hardly seems fair when we don't even know *you* yet."

"Ha," said Edith. "I was just thinking that."

"Like, what do you do in your free time?" asked Mars.

"I explore the river floor. Sometimes I discover new plants that I haven't tried brewing yet, and I bring them here to experiment with. Sometimes I find material to make into clothing for myself. I spend time here in the lab, working on different concoctions. For a while, I was reading through the notebooks of The Scientist, but I've read all the ones that I can comprehend. To go further, I'd have to start experimenting and building devices myself, which isn't my path."

"Fair enough," said Mars.

"What about the two of you?" asked Elsh, turning to Edith. "I understand that you have a bakery. When Roman and I were on our way to the art galleries of Julia Street, he stopped to show me your shop. It was closed for the night."

"Yeah, I don't have much time for the bakery anymore. I have a good friend who runs it for me now. In what little spare time I have, I watch old black-and-white movies. I'm also working on connecting a communication network for the memories of the city so that I'll know if anything bad is happening to them. I probably have less than a fifth of the city covered, though. I don't know if that counts as time off exactly—maybe more of a side job."

"I like how you don't mention the most interesting part," said Mars.

Edith looked at her. "Which would be?"

"Wole!"

Edith laughed.

"What is Wole?" asked Elsh.

Mars raised her hands up. "Oh, only her super-hot boyfriend who walks across treetops, winds up the cicadas, and helps them out with things."

Edith burst out laughing, covering her mouth. "I'm going to tell him that."

Elsh smiled. "Well, that sounds lovely."

"It's so sappy and stupid," said Mars. "Edith deserves all of it."

"I don't know," said Edith. "I think he's more than I deserve sometimes."

"Oh, shut up," said Mars.

Edith took a deep breath, then spoke to Elsh: "By the way, I'm sorry for what happened to you and Roman on Julia street. I'm sorry you got wrapped into all this. I wish we could have contained it by now."

Elsh nodded, her smile fading. "It's very lucky we were there. We learned a lot about the beasts, the… Baku?"

Mars nodded. "I take it you know how Roman is, since you didn't ask us?"

Elsh fiddled with her glass. "Yes, Julius has been keeping me informed. Roman himself hasn't talked to me much, and I don't want to push him. I feel like the… Baku… took away his ability to hide from the stress of the last several months, and it's all crashing down on him."

"He'll pull through," said Mars. "Edith and I will make sure he's alright."

"Thank you," said Elsh.

"And we'll keep you updated," said Edith.

Elsh nodded, taking another sip of her drink.

"How are *you* doing?" asked Mars.

"It's… difficult," said Elsh. "Knowing someone you care for is suffering and not being able to help them. I'll be alright, though. It was just such a good night for us, the best we'd ever had, and it fell apart so quickly. And now we can't even talk about how good it was, or how we feel about it."

Elsh twitched as she felt a hand on hers, then looked up at Mars. Both Mars and Edith were looking at her with such tenderness, such care— something Elsh hadn't felt from others in a long time.

"It's going to work out," said Mars.

"Thank you," she said. "Both of you. I… I'm a bit of an outcast down here, so I don't get interactions like this. I love my tribe, I feel like this is where I belong, but most of them don't relate to me, since I'm more interested in creating and exploring rather than defending and learning the arts of battle."

"Are all the Riverwalker tribes like that?" asked Mars.

"No, most are more balanced with their members. Some of my tribe used to expect me to leave and join one of the other tribes. But Donnish, we've helped each other often in the past, and though she rarely talks to me anymore, we have a connection, a deep respect for each other. Also, I love this lab, and I love the First Quarter."

Mars nodded, and the three of them were quiet for a moment.

Elsh turned her hand around underneath Mars' hand, holding it in her own. She reached out and took Edith's hand as well. "Thank you both for this, for being here and talking to me. This isn't what I was seeking out when I came here to see you. I'm glad Roman has the two of you at his side."

"Like I said," said Mars, "we'll help in any way we can."

Elsh smiled. "Thank you." She let go of their hands. "What about you, Mars? What do you do when you're not working?"

"Oh, I'm like Edith, I've got my own projects going on. I used to do healing work on entities, and I still do some of that. It's hard to just stop helping others, especially when you might be the only person who can."

"Anyone special that you spend time with?"

"Not really. I've got some ladies and gents I can call up when I have a random night free, but I don't have space in my head for anything serious right now, with all the saving-the-city going on. I'm happy though. I mean, I'm happier than I've been in a long time. Maybe ever."

Elsh smiled and raised her glass. "To being happy with life."

"I'll toast to that," said Edith.

They all touched their glasses and took another drink.

File 25 :: [Julius Marcos]

Clouds subdued the sun in the sky, muting its light and splintering it into long geometric shapes which speared the shotgun houses and trees and dented parked cars. The Treme was oddly quiet for a Saturday afternoon, as if everyone was taking a siesta[22]. Julius nodded to two elderly women sitting in wicker chairs on their front porch as he passed. Further down the street was a man in a white tank top working on the engine of a car, his arms and cheek streaked with grease. A trio of kids rode down the street on their bikes.

When he got to the corner, he stopped. He could hear the distant music; a fist inside gripped his stomach and twisted. Pulling out a small bottle of Jack Daniels, he put the bottle in the crook of his half-arm and unscrewed the cap. He closed his eyes and took a deep breath, then screwed the lid back on and slipped it back into the pocket of his trench coat.

He'd left his new arm back at headquarters, figuring the mechanical leg would serve as a more than adequate conversation piece.

He continued down the sidewalk, a thing so beaten and shattered by the sun that it nearly dissolved into the cracks of the broken street. The music got louder as he walked, the thumping and crooning of 70s R&B—a song by The Spinners ending as one by The Jackson 5 started up. The music brought back memories of his childhood, of his mother listening to records and dancing with him in the living room.

Julius took a long breath, feeling the weight of the Jack Daniels in his coat as he came upon the double-shotgun house spilling music onto the street in gushing waves, the music emanating from the backyard. The house was faded purple with a blue door and storm shutters. His family

---

22 The neighborhood called The Treme is exactly like the show "Treme," yet totally different. It was one of the first neighborhoods of New Orleans, and the very first African American neighborhood in the United States.

had only been living in the house for two years when he, at fifteen, had remembered that he was a god and had all these other lives who had protected the city for centuries. He'd left very suddenly, finding Roman and becoming an Agent once more.

He always meant to visit more often, but most years it was only on this day that he ventured to his old home.

Over the fences and neighboring rooftops he saw the shaking top of the colorful, inflatable bouncy castle in the backyard.

There were a few people outside on the front porch, sitting in folding chairs. He tried not to let his animalistic hearing spy on those people, but his instincts betrayed his wishes. He heard them as clear as if he'd been up on the porch with them:

"Is that little Julius?" an older woman whispered.

"The fuck happened to *him*?" said a younger man.

She slapped the younger man's head. "No cursing, this is a kid's party. You'll mind yourself."

The young man got up and stormed into the house.

Julius shrugged off his trench coat and slung it over his shoulder, at which point the woman muttered, "*Jesus have mercy.*" The T-shirt he wore was white and short-sleeved, clearly showing his lack of an arm.

The screen door swung open, and Julius stopped. A woman stood there, smiling and beaming, looking like a cross between his granny and his ma. Just as he realized it wasn't a younger version of his grandma walking through the door, *she* realized she was looking at a crippled version of her son.

Her face sunk into a deep frown as she rushed forward, nearly falling down the steps to the sidewalk. "*No no no!*"

She tripped on the cracked sidewalk and he caught her, holding her against him with his one arm. "It's alright, ma."

Her hands gently patted the stub of his arm. "No, no, no, no! My boy!"

He gently pulled her head against his chest. "It's alright, ma. I'm fine."

"It's not alright! This time it's not alright!" She pulled away from him, tears running down her face as she touched the scars that ran up his neck like tendrils. "Julius, how long ago did this happen? My God, *what* happened?"

"A few months back. It was an accident. I got lucky."

"Lucky?" She shook her head. "You could have come home. Where have you been? Who took care of you?"

Julius sniffed and realized that he was crying. "I... I'm sorry. I was in an awful place. I couldn't be around people for a while. I didn't want to hurt you."

She pressed her hand against his cheek. "You can't hurt your family. At least not so bad we can't heal from it."

Liquid sloshed around through his mechanical leg and one of the vents hissed.

"What the devil is that?"

"I... I've got an artificial leg. I lost my leg."

She closed her eyes and wrapped her arms around him. It felt alien to have her, or anyone, hold him with such intimacy. It brought back memories of his childhood, of being held by her when he wasn't even half her size. Along with those memories came countless others, of being so many different young boys throughout the centuries, being held by so many mothers or caretakers.

"You're here now. You're home, my boy." She let him go and wiped the tears from her face. "Raphael's gonna be so excited—he doesn't go five minutes without asking someone if they've seen you yet."

"Then I'd better go say hi." Julius wiped his cheeks dry, then put his arm around his mom's shoulders and walked with her back up to the house. A few others had gathered on the porch and more were in the front room waiting for him to come inside—cousins, aunts, uncles, neighbors, and family friends. They asked if he was alright and he made his rounds of hellos, saying that he was fine and dodging questions with a tired smile and something about a "work-related accident".

When he pushed through the screen door to the backyard, the song *Cha Dooky-Doo* by Art Neville was pumping through the large sound system in one corner of the yard. Julius couldn't keep the smirk from his face. The song sounded so damned '60s, making him think of getting a burger and a Coke at Clover Grill on Bourbon Street somewhere in his last life. Before he could place the memory, a voice cut across all his thoughts:

"Jooloos!"

He shook off the memories and walked into the yard as a tiny boy jumped up and threw his arms around Julius' neck. Julius swooped his nephew up with his arm and squeezed him tight.

"I got a castle!"

"I see that!" Julius laughed. "It's a big one."

"I'm like you! I'm gonna defend New Orleans! I got a base now!"

"It seems you do."

He looked into his nephew's face, the boy's smiling mouth missing a couple of teeth. Julius was suddenly relieved that there wouldn't be another incarnation of Bes. He was tired, and wouldn't wish anyone to carry all the lives that hung on his shoulders. He pushed the thoughts out of his mind, then spun in circles, spinning fast enough for Raphael's legs to be pulled out behind him as he screamed in delight.

When Julius stopped spinning, he noticed a woman watching nearby with crossed arms. Slightly younger than him, her hair was bright orange and braided, pulled behind her head. She wore a dark T-shirt and shorts.

He set Raphael down. "You go and play with your friends. I'll be around for a while."

"Ok, but you gotta watch me!"

"Sure, I'll be watching you."

The boy ran off and dived into the castle.

The woman walked up to Julius.

"Hello, Wanda."

Her cold, dark eyes bored into him, her mouth a perpetual frown. He wondered if she ever smiled anymore, or if she just never smiled when he was around.

"You're limping," she said.

"I have a false leg. Lost a leg and an arm."

"I'm not going to ask you how because you'll just lie to me."

"It was on the job, fighting for the city."

His animal instincts kicked in as her body shifted, but he didn't move out of the way. He watched her hand come up and connect with his cheek as she slapped him hard. "You don't get to *pretend* to be a cop. When are you going to stop fucking lying to your family? Everyone *knows*."

"I'm not a cop, and I will never lie to you, or to my family."

"Raphael looks up to you when he should just *spit* on you."

"Wanda, I'm done trying to convince you. I work for the city. I do things that no one else is willing to do. Things no one else is qualified to do."

She motioned to Julius' missing arm. "Then what is this? Are you set for life with insurance money? Workman's comp?"

"No, my job doesn't work that way."

"No shit! Because you're a fucking *thug*, Julius! Was it a drive-by? Was it a drug deal gone bad?"

Julius' ma walked up then, whispering: "Now y'all are gonna *shut up*! Today's about Raphael, not about you two! He's got enough on his plate without seeing two of his favorite people fighting."

Wanda stared down Julius. "Your brother should be alive." She reached out and poked the shoulder above his missing arm. "*You* should be the one who's dead, not him. Raphael should have a father. He went overseas to fight for this country, and you're just a low-life fucking gangster. No one will give a shit about you when you're gone."

Wanda turned and stormed up the stairs and into the house.

"Don't you worry about her," said his mom. "She's got those ideas rooted too deep to pull out."

"No, she's right. Darren was a better man than I am. He was a hero."

"Both my boys are heroes."

Julius looked down at the grass at their feet. "I've let some people down. People important to me."

"And you think Darren never did? I said my boys are heroes, not angels. Though they can strive to be."

He put his arm around his mom and kissed her head, looking out at the swaying bouncy castle full of kids.

*   *   *

The sun was low, biting into the clouds on the horizon. Julius sat on a wooden dining room chair out in the yard, drinking a can of Budweiser with a few older men of the neighborhood. Raphael sprinted around playing tag with some of the other kids, then stopped to catch his breath. Julius caught the boy's eye.

"Hey, come here."

The boy walked over and Julius reached down into the trench coat lying at his feet. He took out a small black orb the size of a golf ball with a few buttons on it and placed it into the boy's hands. "This is for you."

"Whoa!" Raphael turned it around in his hands like a priceless jewel.

"The blue and the white button, you can play with those. Now, the red button's harder to press down. If you find yourself in trouble, or if your ma is in trouble, you grab her tight." He reached out and took Raphael's wrist, holding it firm. "You hold on to her, and you press this red button down hard. It will protect both of you. Do you understand?"

Raphael looked deep into his eyes and nodded.

"And don't tell your ma about this ball. She'll know I gave it to you and she'll take it away."

The boy nodded again, and Julius took him in his arm, hugging him. "You protect your ma for me, alright?"

"Yeah, Jooloos. I'll protect her."

Julius kissed his forehead. "Your friends are waiting for you."

Raphael turned and ran towards the castle, pocketing the orb, then turned and sprinted after one of his friends, who ran from him laughing. Julius smiled as he watched.

"You could tell the boy's mom," said Pop from beside him. "Tell her all of it."

Julius shook his head, then looked at the elderly man sitting next to him, at the few other men sitting around. "I'd rather be slapped and ridiculed, and have her be safe."

Pop laughed loud and smacked his knee. "You're a better man than I was at your age."

"Oh, I doubt that."

Pop shook his head. "No, boy, you don't. I think you know."

Pop had spent decades sitting on his front porch, watching out for the neighborhood. He'd caught Julius breaking into his first car at twelve and had threatened to tell his ma and grandma. Julius had pleaded with him not to—disappointing them seemed worse than death at the time. Pop not only kept the secret, but he also hired Julius to do odd jobs around his house.

He loved Pop for that. But once the memories of Bes and his past incarnations crept in, none of it would have mattered much anyway—Julius would have shrugged off any criminal ideas pretty quick.

The other three men, all of them sitting on rickety dining room chairs, were Mardi Gras Indians like Pop[23]. They sipped from cans of Budweiser with lips creased from knowledge, years, and sunlight.

Then one of them—Julius knew he was a neighbor, but wasn't sure if they'd met—looked him in the eye and poured some beer into the grass. "For your loss."

The other two and Pop followed suit, pouring beer into the grass.

Julius looked down at the grass, squeezing his eyes shut and shaking his head. "Thank you. The ones who fell, they thank you."

"You know the ones who *didn't* fall?" said Pop.

When Julius looked into the old man's eyes, they were searching and serious. "Of course."

"The ones who didn't fall, they're the ones that need help the most."

"Well, there's only one that survived. And he's just fine."

"You talking about yourself?"

Julius looked away.

"I thought so, boy. I've only seen you cry twice before today. I'm not sold on you being *just fine*."

Julius grimaced. "I was built for this."

"No one is built for what you're doing." Pop handed him another can of Budweiser, at which point Julius realized that the can he held was completely crushed in his fist. He set the bent-up can on the ground and took the new one from Pop.

"Thanks."

"No problem. You just make sure and take care of yourself. 'Cause you're sure as hell not gonna let anyone else do it."

---

[23] Mardi Gras Indian tribes have paraded through New Orleans since the mid-1800s, and are one of the less-hidden magical aspects of the city. With traditions passed down through generations of African Americans, Mardi Gras Indians create hugely elaborate costumes covered in feathers and intricate bead designs. Though their exact history is shrouded in myth and folklore, they can be seen on certain days parading through the streets, or dancing during festivals around the city, or walking around Jackson Square. To many, they are known as the spiritual protectors of New Orleans.

File 26 :: [Roman Wing]

Sunlight pierced through the clouds, spears of light needling through the leafy canopy to trace along winding tree branches and across the cloudy waters of the swamp. There wasn't a building around for miles. Roman walked along quietly, listening to the songs of insects, birds, and frogs, the world around him so thick with life. When he was much younger, there was even more of this, and one could walk to the swamps quite easily from the French Quarter.

He stopped walking mid step, hearing a shift of movement from just beside him. Jolting backwards, one hand parried a fist coming for his chest. There was little force in the fist, that energy being saved for the second fist which connected with the side of his neck.

Pain shot down the length of his body. Roman winced as he grabbed the attacker's arm with one hand and spun it around their back. The attacker kicked his shin, sending one leg colliding with the other and throwing off his balance. The attacker leaped up, locked a leg around the back of his neck, and sent him flying down into the mud.

Roman landed on one of his arms, his mind immediately calculating where someone would expect a person in his position to move. Then he calculated where someone who'd studied Roman would expect *him* to move. He chose something between the two. His body jumped, but he stayed in place. The attacker's boot stabbed at the ground next to him and Roman grabbed the boot, spinning onto his back and throwing a fistful of mud up into their face.

She grunted, falling backwards while trying to clear the mud from her eyes. Red hair, streaked with mud, trailed through the air as she fell. Roman was on her, but she slipped out from under him, pushing an object against the back of his neck.

"Gotcha," she said.

"It was close."

She backed off, and they both stood. "I told you not to hold back."

"I would have broken your wrist and your ankle."

Rachel threw down the stick she'd pressed to the back of his neck. She ran a hand over her head, trying to pull some of the mud from her hair and face. She wore dark colors—a long sleeve shirt, a vest full of device-filled pouches, and black cargo pants. "You don't know that."

"Yes, I do."

She walked up and shoved Roman back against a tree trunk. "You holding back makes *me* hold back." She smirked. "Why won't you hurt me?"

"You want me to?"

Rachel bit her lip. "Maybe."

Their lips met and Roman's adrenaline pushed down the pain she'd caused by hitting his neck. He was certain she knew more pressure points in a half-human, half-collector than anyone who'd ever lived. Her hands traveled up under his jacket, her nails dragging over his shirt and across his rib cage. He pushed her back against the tree, the mud sliding down her face and onto his as they kissed. Her lips were warm, her passion the only thing besides food that could ever counteract the Wonder flowing through his body.

"I've missed you," he whispered.

She brought her cheek up against his, then kissed his forehead. "Missed me? What are you talking about?"

He shook his head. "I'm not sure."

She grabbed his face and kissed him hard.

A loud crackle of thunder boomed behind him—but it wasn't thunder; it was something else. Roman turned to the swamp, but she pulled him back and kissed him harder. The crackle game again, something like radio static. It was loud and terrible.

He pried himself from her arms, turning to see the air utterly torn up behind him. Above the swamp, between the trees, and under the canopy were splotches of black, like ink being dripped onto a page. The sound was constant now, like a scream coming through an old radio.

"This isn't right," said Roman.

Rachel gripped his arm. "Everything's fine."

"Did you alter my memory?"

Rachel stepped between him and the swamp, her eyes burrowing into his, her hands on his face. "I told you, I will *never* touch your memory. And I will never hurt you."

His eyes fell over her shoulder, watching people rise up from the swamp water. Roman pushed her to the side and walked past. There were four people wearing dark, soaked, blurry clothes. The ink splotches spread through the air above and around them. Their faces were distorted, like a photograph being held above a flame.

"*Roman*," one of them whispered. He could barely hear them over the screeching static. He knew that voice like a best friend.

Roman stepped towards them, shaking his head. "Rachel, what's going on?"

She answered from behind him: "If you'd seen what I'd seen, you'd understand."

He shook his head, walking into the swamp. "*No, no, no.*"

When Rachel spoke next, he could hear the tears in her throat. "I would never, never hurt you."

"What about them?" said Roman, turning to her. "*What about them?*"

Rachel spoke again, but the screaming static drowned her voice.

He turned away, wading waist deep into water, reaching out to the closest of the four people. They grabbed his hand, squeezing it, pressing it into their twisted, blurred face. He felt the hot tears running down their cheek, but he couldn't see those tears. "*I'm sorry, Roman,*" they cried. "*I'm so sorry, we failed you. We failed the city.*"

Tears fell down his face, leaping from his jaw to be lost in the swamp for all time. This person and the others, The Agents of Fateful Encounters. "*What happened?*" he asked.

The other three were wading towards him, their clothes and faces blurred, the ink splotches around them spreading. "I'm sorry," said one of them.

The one whose face he was touching, they grabbed him, pressing their wet face into his neck. "*Remember me. Please, Roman. I'm sorry, we're all sorry... but please, remember us.*"

He grabbed them in his arms and held tight. "*I'm* the one who failed," he said. The ink splotches crept over the back of his neck, his back. He struggled to keep the ink from tearing them from his arms.

"*Don't let go of me,*" they cried, clawing at his shirt.

Roman held on with every ounce of strength he had, yelling as his friend was pried from his clamped arms, his muscles tearing from the strain. Roman's screams ruptured the air around them, becoming the loud, booming static that he'd been hearing.

The ink wrapped around his face and chest, stealing away all traces of light. His ears stung from the sounds of his own screaming. The ink sunk like fingers into his shoulders, rocking back and forth to shake him. Then he was struck hard across the face.

Everything was quiet.

The light returned, but the swamp was gone. Roman was on his back, stone walls around him. A match was struck and a candle lit. He took a deep breath, looking over at Julius, who was lighting a candle on Roman's desk. His friend wore a white tank top and cargo pants, his mechanical leg rather silent while his mechanical arm clicked and whirred.

Roman sat up in his bed. He was shirtless, the bruises from the Baku battle still healing across his body. The room itself was small but practical; besides the bed and desk, it contained only a wooden chair, a small bookshelf, and an armoire. He touched his jaw and winced—Julius had hit him hard.

"You were screaming. Again."

Roman closed his eyes and stretched his shoulders. He could still feel the grip of that Agent latching onto him, could still hear them pleading with him not to let them go.

"Was it Rachel?"

"Rachel. And the others."

"We're going to avenge them. We're going to put them to rest."

Roman's jaw quivered. "I wish I could believe you."

"You'll believe again. You just need some time."

"I don't know. It makes sense that the dream is still affecting me, skewing my thoughts and emotions, but I just can't see past it right now." He shook his head. "She was so *real*. They were all so *real*."

Julius leaned back against the doorway, folding his real and his mechanical arm. "I dream about it all too, at least once a week. It was a lot to lose at once, and it wasn't very long ago."

"I miss them so much."

"I know. Me too."

"But what I *hate*..." Roman said the last word slowly, the word being so foreign in his vocabulary, especially while referencing himself. "What I hate the most, is that I miss *her*. She destroyed so much of what I loved, she destroyed *herself* in so many ways, but I can't stop *missing* her. And I hate myself for feeling that."

Julius looked into the candle on the desk. The flickering light played across his face, morphing his features from catlike to human and back. "With these metal limbs, I'm reminded of her nearly every second of every day. But I miss her too. There's nothing wrong with that, nothing to hate. She was so many things to both of us." Julius looked at Roman with tears in his eyes. "She was the closest thing I ever had to a daughter. She was next in line, after you and I, to lead the Agents."

Roman took a deep breath, closing his eyes and nodding. "We've been through a lot, haven't we?"

"Yes, we fucking have."

A feeling crept into Roman's mind, something lurking, stalking him from the edges. He swung his legs around the bed and stood up, then walked up to Julius. His friend's brows furrowed, tears still dotting his eyes and cheeks. Julius flinched as Roman put his arms around him, pressing his face into Julius' shoulder. Roman closed his eyes. All the memories they had together, all the losses and wins, flooded his mind.

Julius hugged him back, one arm warm and welcoming, the other cold and metal.

Julius said something, but Roman focused solely on the memories pouring through his mind. Memories of Julius, memories of the other incarnations of Bes throughout the decades. Somewhere in the back of his mind he knew he was hugging Julius for an uncomfortable amount of time, but he ignored that knowledge. He only let his mind focus on the love he had for his friend and the memories they had together. In a world of screaming memories, of nightmares too large to look past, his memories and thoughts of Julius were a single candle sitting on a desk in an otherwise dark room. Julius tried to speak or move, but Roman shook his head, holding him tight.

The longer he focused on memories of his friend, the stronger those memories became. And the stronger they became, the weaker the feelings of helplessness, worry, and regret.

The hate was still there, but he could deal with that.

After a long while, Roman spoke: "Thanks for always being here."

"I..."

Roman knew what Julius was going to say. It's something he'd always answer to statements like this.

I always will be.

That's what Julius was starting to say. It's something that had always been true, that seemingly always *would* be true. But not anymore. So many things that seemed certain a year ago—six months ago, even—no longer existed, at least not in the same way.

Finally, Roman let him go, stepping back.

Julius wiped tears from under one eye. "That's the first time we hugged. Well, in this lifetime, at least."

"It helped," said Roman. "It helped me find a small piece of hope that's still left inside me."

"Good." Julius put his real hand on Roman's shoulder. "I really don't want to do this without you."

Roman smirked. Usually, he smirked as a joke, something to make fun of his human side, but this time it was the closest expression to a smile that he could muster.

Julius backed towards the doorway. "I'm gonna get you a bag of ice for the bruise creeping across your jaw."

"No, don't bother. I need to go out for some fresh air. I'll get a bag of ice on the way out."

"Have it your way. Let me know if you need anything."

Roman nodded and Julius left. He pulled on a shirt, wincing as the cloth touched his jaw. *Damn*, he thought. *This bruise is going to be substantial.*

As he pulled on his long coat, heavy with all the devices strapped inside of it, the pain that danced along the bruises the Baku left on his body were nothing compared to the bruise Julius had given him. His smirk widened, causing him even more pain. But it was pain he was glad to have.

File 27 :: [Mars]

One week later—a rather long week of staking out crowded places and never being in the right place at the right time.

Today was the fourth time that The Skulled Man had hit since Julia Street. He'd struck once outside a Garden District bar, the Baku tackling and grabbing terrified people in their massive jaws before vanishing with them. The other two times The Skulled Man had taken to playing the calliope device as soon as he showed up, so Edith had only been able to capture tiny glimpses of him through the memories of the afflicted before they fell into the dreams brought on by the calliope device. The Agents Of had no idea how many people the Baku had stolen away in total, but after the hit on the Garden District bar, the count was at least nine.

The sky, despite the week's dark events, was clear and blue, the afternoon sun beating down on Mars' shoulders as she walked along the five giant cement steps that led down to the waters of Lake Pontchartrain. The "lake", which was actually a saltwater estuary, was so large that you couldn't even see the other side, making Mars feel like she was staring out at the ocean rather than north towards a large chunk of the country. Sailboats and motorboats littered the estuary. A couple of miles away, The Causeway Bridge stretched across the water to vanish into the horizon[24].

Lake Shore Drive made its winding way along the curving shore, with large cement steps on one side leading to the water, at the top of which was a pathway of benches and palm trees. On the other side of Lake Shore Drive were grassy parks with picnic benches, trees, and barbecue grills.

---

[24] Built in 1955, the Causeway Bridge was the longest bridge over water in the world until 2011, when the Jiaozhou Bay Bridge was built in China. The Causeway Bridge connects Metairie (a suburb of New Orleans) to the city of Mandeville, and consists of two bridges, one for each direction of traffic. Both bridges are nearly 24 miles long and supported by 9,500 concrete pilings. While driving the length of the bridge, there is a point where one cannot see land in any direction—only water stretching from horizon to horizon.

Beyond the parks was a vast neighborhood of mansions—not just older creole mansions like those found all over the city, but a mix of old mansions and newer ones. Some mansions were huge, habitable contemporary art pieces.

Mars walked along the top of the cement steps, stepping over prone bodies—people who had been walking, having picnics, fishing, now on the ground, their blank eyes staring at the sky or at the horizon. Maybe a hundred people in each direction, with more covering the grassy park across the street.

Her eyes scanned the Reader in her hand, memorizing the number of different colored dots on its face. She was beginning to understand the device, to know its language.

Off in the distance, Edith crouched down next to someone, speaking to them, then raised the Extraction Glove to peer through their memories.

Mars walked on, scanning the air, scanning people, looking for anything that could bring them closer to catching The Skulled Man.

Since Nimble's Den, The Agents Of had found no evidence of the Baku eating peoples' dreams *during* the attacks, only kidnapping some of them to presumably feast upon later. The people left behind only had their dreams enhanced by the calliope device, with seemingly no ill effects. The Agents Of had been keeping tabs on some victims, and their lives seemed to be improving, some of them drastically so. Many quit their day jobs with the intent of recklessly pursuing a newfound passion they'd discovered inside, or perhaps a passion that they'd buried long ago. Others merely became more excited about their jobs, or their families, or their hobbies.

There was movement in the distance, and Mars looked up to see Roman making his way towards her, skirting around the prone bodies littering the grassy park.

He crossed the street. "What have you found out?"

"Nothing more than the other sites," she said. "I'm not sure about Edith. Hopefully someone got a look at the device."

"That would help immensely."

Roman had been stressing that they needed information about the device strapped to the calliope player's back, which was always hidden underneath the Baku pelt. Roman needed that information in order to figure out how it worked, how to counteract it, where it came from, and possibly clues to the identity of the calliope player.

Roman turned towards Edith and Mars saw the green, splotchy bruise stretched across the bottom of his jaw.

"Ghaa! That thing gets grosser looking every day. Looks like it's healing alright though. Looks like how my chest looked a week after the bank robbery. You still sticking to your story that the bruise is from a really rough dream?"

He reached up and touched his jaw, wincing. "It was pretty rough. But I think it's a dream I needed to have."

"Do dreams usually beat you up so badly?"

"No." The look he gave her was something between quizzical and worrisome. "Do yours?"

Mars twisted her mouth. "And then you do something so very-human, like *fucking* with me. And I don't know if I want to punch you or have drinks with you."

Roman smiled a little, his smile washing away any annoyance she might have for him. "I'm sorry, many parts of me are swimming around, finding new footholds in my mind and emotions."

"Don't be sorry, I like it. Just don't be surprised if I retaliate."

They both turned as Edith walked up, the Extraction Glove glowing and humming at her side. Around them, people were stirring from their dazed states. Her eyes widened as she saw Roman's jaw.

Mars leaned forward and faux-whispered loudly: "Don't mention the *B, R, U, I, S, E*. He really sucks at *sleeping*, and he's pretty embarrassed about it."

Edith looked from Mars to Roman and back. "Um, ok.

"Did you find anything new?" asked Roman.

Edith shook her head. "I don't think so. He appeared out of nowhere, in the middle of the park with a Baku. He was gripping onto the fur on its back, using it to travel here, like we suspected. He played the device, walking to the lake as everyone fell, and that's where the last memory I found of him ended. I'll go through the memories and see if there are any details I missed, but I don't think anyone could have gotten a glimpse of the actual device. I don't think the pelt moved enough."

Roman nodded. "Search through the memories. Mars, go back to monitoring the French Quarter. I'll stick to the CBD and watch Nimble's Den." He led them back towards the park. "I left Henri waiting in the next neighborhood over. We can catch a ride back with him."

"You got it, boss," said Mars.

File 28 :: [Edith Downs]

Edith stood in the middle of the blurry room, the Extraction Glove humming around her arm. The walls were like wet, moving paint, browns and grays shifting back and forth like the tide. Those walls *wanted* to take shape, *wanted* to give her details.

Against one wall was the pulsing silver light broadcasting this memory. The visuals got a little sharper when she was close to the source, but the details were still too hazy.

She stepped closer to it and the loud chattering commenced once more. This room was full of people; she just couldn't see them except for the occasional glimpse out of the corner of her eye. Neither could she make out what the voices were saying. She crept closer to the silver light, looking and listening to the room around her for any alterations. The voices grew louder, more defined, but the images stayed just as vague.

Edith shook her head as she approached the light, about to power off the glove, but something caught her eye. She peered into the light itself and she saw two eyes looking back at her. A woman's eyes, staring right into hers. A chill ran down her spine and she froze, but the eyes didn't seem angry or fearful. Then they looked away. Edith got closer to the light, crouching and peering into it. She saw people, beer bottles, paintings on the wall.

"Holy crap," she whispered.

It was like looking through a tiny hole in a fence; she only got a small circle of clear vision. The images shifted quickly, blurring into one another. Edith tried to take in every detail she could in case the images stopped. She'd been trying to read this like a normal memory, because mostly it acted like one. But it wasn't a normal memory. It was like a hole across space, a periscope showing her another part of the city. Maybe these images were old, maybe not.

She inched her face closer to the light, the image of the space rocking back and forth as he slid out of a booth. He walked through a small, crowded bar. Dollar bills hung above the bar, stapled to the ceiling. He looked up at a series of paintings along one wall, one of them of a woman wrapped in burgundy sheets while reclining on pillows.

Edith had seen that painting.

She brought her eyes even closer. That's when she *felt* his hands swinging by his thighs as he walked. She felt the smirk on his lips, remembering when he'd smirked like that while taking control of her body mere months ago.

Cold metal pressed against her nose and cheek, then she felt her face contort unnaturally away from the metal. Her body seized up and she collapsed to the ground. Edith clenched her eyes shut, but the images still flowed to her. She cried out and turned off the Extraction Glove, darkness finally coming to her closed eyes, her stomach flipping around inside her like a washing machine.

She could hear Mars talking to her.

"*Trash can*," Edith whispered.

She heard Mars drag a trash can over, at which point she grabbed the edge, pulling it down and vomiting into it. Over and over. When she finished, Edith rolled onto her back, opening her eyes to see a worried Mars looming over her, the lab behind her. Edith's face was cold and covered in sweat.

"Are you alright, girl?" asked Mars. "Did you drink too much last night?"

Edith looked up at the shelf above her, which held Dean Smith's revolver in a vice. "I was looking at memories and accidentally touched the gun."

"Oh, shit... I'm sorry."

Julius and Roman had told them about what happens when an Agent touches a weapon, but it hadn't seemed very real until that moment. She kind of wished touching the gun had just killed her. Her entire body felt like it was dying. "Water would be nice."

"You got it, I'll be right back."

Edith sighed, keeping her eyes closed. It was a lot like the time she'd gotten alcohol poisoning in her early twenties, except she could feel her body slowly creeping closer to normal as time passed, which was not how the alcohol poisoning felt. In hindsight, she felt like her face warped away from the gun after it touched.

She heard Mars coming back.

"Fuck this oath," muttered Edith.

"Can you sit up?"

Mars helped her into a sitting position. The nausea was gone, but her body still felt like death. She took the glass of water from Mars and took a long drink.

"I'm feeling a little better," she muttered. "Call Roman or Julius for me, will you? It's kind of urgent."

"On it." Mars jumped to her feet and rushed to the phone.

File 29 :: [Julius Marcos]

His boots clicked quickly on the stone floor of the underground headquarters, the gas lights flickering to life along the walls as he pulled on his black trench coat. Julius walked into the main laboratory.

Edith sat at a lab table with a glass of water, with Mars sitting on top of the table.

"I was just coming to get you two," said Julius. "Our calliope player struck again. A farmers' market in Central City, ten minutes ago. People will be awake already, but we might find something new. Roman should already be there. Get your gear, we leave in sixty seconds. We can talk on the way."

"Um, Edith might need a rest day," said Mars.

"What happened?"

"She touched Dean's gun."

He walked up to their table. "I'm sorry, Edith. I know it feels horrible. It happens to all of us. Do you want to sit this one out?"

Edith swallowed and spoke, her voice at half-strength. "I think I know where Dean is. Like where he is right now."

"You *know* where Dean Smith is?"

Edith nodded. "I think what I saw are *immediate* memories, and I know what bar he's in. I've been there before, with a friend. It's right off Esplanade in Bayou St. John[25]. I don't know how often I'm going to see and recognize exactly where he is."

Julius licked his lips, thinking. "New plan: Mars, you go after Dean Smith. See what he knows. Edith, are you up to showing Mars where the bar is?"

She nodded. "Yeah, I can do that."

---

[25] A charming neighborhood named after the bayou that runs through it. The bayou is a natural waterway that used to drain the swamps into Lake Pontchartrain, but now it's a slow-flowing river surrounded by nice houses and is, on occasion, full of canoes.

Julius glanced at Mars. "Be careful, but don't hold back. He's got to know *something* that would help us."

"Alright!" said Mars. "Too bad F isn't around. Roman told me how he socked Dean in the gut when I was passed out in the person-suit. I bet F would get a kick out of interrogating him."

A smile stole across Julius' face and he walked over to the payphone on the wall. He picked up the receiver and dialed three numbers.

"Hello, Julius," came the familiar female voice.

"Serendipity. I don't suppose The Function is available to head immediately to Bayou St. John. There's something that might pique his interest..."

File 30 :: [The Function]

The Function waited outside the bar with Edith, away from the windows. As per usual, he wore a button-up shirt and his faded war coat.

Mars had gone inside. They figured that out of the three of them, Dean would be least likely to recognize Mars, being that his dealings with her had been when she was in a person-suit which looked exactly like *him*.

It was early evening, and the sun was still out. The little neighborhood bar was full and several people outside held plastic cups of booze and smoked cigarettes. The bar sat on the corner of two small streets in the middle of a cute neighborhood, most of the surrounding buildings being colorful shotgun houses, with a quaint little church down the block. The sandwich board sign outside the bar advertised some kind of nerd trivia night, which would account for the excessive amount of people so early in the evening.

"I hope I'm right about him being here," said Edith. "If not, I'm wasting your and Mars' time."

The Function smiled at her. "Don't worry about it, memory-girl. Just the *thought* of being able to freak Dean out is worth it. Besides, you just gave me a break from work."

Mars came out of the bar, walking up to them with whiskey and ice in a plastic cup. "I'm not sure; there are a lot of people in there. Would he be in disguise? I mean, I didn't want to just *stare* at everyone because then he'd probably notice me."

The Function rubbed the stubble on his cheek. "Is there a place to sit?"

"There was an open spot at the bar with a few stools."

"Ok," said The Function, taking off his coat and shoving it behind a flowery bush outside a neighboring house. "Take us to that spot. We'll order drinks while Edith and I look for him, hopefully without looking incredibly obvious."

Mars brushed the pink stain on his shoulder. "You got some of my cry-makeup out. I'll try to get more of it out next time you're over at my place." She backed away and nodded to him. "You actually look different without the coat. I'm not used to seeing you without it in public. I never realized how much you look like everyone else; that's pretty weird."

The Function smirked. "There are reasons for having something that defines you so easily, and reasons for that defining object being something you can shove behind a bush so you can blend into the background."

Mars shook her head. "Well, the only way I'd be unrecognizable is if I shaved my head and wore a wig, and I ain't doing that."

"Don't you dare shave your head," said Edith. "At least not before giving me a month's warning."

"If you shave your head," said The Function, "I'll shoot myself in the head." He shrugged. "And then I'd just come back to life, but still, I doubt you'd want me to do that."

"Nope," said Mars. "How about you just never say that again and we go into the damned bar?"

The Function bowed, raising his arms towards the entrance. Mars walked into the bar, followed by Edith and The Function. He'd heard about Edith's magic memory glove and wondered if it was in the black bag strapped to her back. He could definitely tell from her arms and back that she'd been working out a lot since that time he'd met her in her pastry shop, well over two months ago.

Damn, he thought. *I should work out more too.*

The pseudo-dive bar was dim and full of people, mostly young to middle-aged, with *People Are Strange* by The Doors playing on the jukebox. The room was long and thin, with the bar stretched across one side while booths lined the other. The two women sat at the bar with The Function standing between them.

"So, what are you drinking?" he asked Edith, his eyes quickly scanning the bar around them. In a lower tone, he said to Mars, "You have a clear view of the door; let us know if anyone leaves who might be Dean Smith."

Mars nodded.

"Vodka, soda, lime," said Edith, searching around while trying to appear nonchalant.

The Function patted Mars on the shoulder. "Mars, can you get that? Sorry, I don't have any cash. And can you get me a cider or something?"

"And you wonder why you're single," she said.

"Oh, I don't wonder. I've been given reasons. So many reasons."

Mars burst out laughing, then nodded to the bartender, who walked over.

The Function leaned over to Edith while scanning the booths. Most of the booths were full of people who were probably on trivia teams, waiting for the game to start. "Can you remember what the memory looked like? Where he might have been sitting?"

Edith furrowed her brow. "I don't remember seeing so many windows in his memory, so I'm guessing his back was to them. That puts him in the front half of the bar."

"Very good."

Mars handed him his can of cider, but he didn't take his eyes off a table set against the large front windows. Edith slapped his shoulder—she was looking at the same table. Most of the booths had four to six people at them, but there was one booth with only a man and a woman. The man had short brown hair sticking up like he'd just gotten out of bed, a thick five-o'clock shadow, and a hideously bright orange T-shirt with writing on it. The Function had seen that smile dozens of times nearly a century ago. Immediately he looked away, bowing his head between Edith and Mars. "That's him, second booth from the door. Mars, take a look."

"Um, are you sure?" asked Mars. "He looks like someone who just moved here, or someone on vacation."

"It's fucking him," said Edith.

"It's a brilliant disguise," said The Function. "He's lying low, hiding from the entire city. This is going to be easy."

"Shall we?" asked Mars.

"Wait," said Edith.

The young woman who was with him, with spiky blonde hair, a leather vest, a black skirt, and boots, got up and walked across the room, passing them and walking into the restroom. She looked to be in her twenties.

"Edith," said The Function, "I feel like you should go first."

"I'd love to."

Edith got up with her cocktail and walked over, followed by Mars and The Function. Dean's eyes grew wide as he saw Edith slide into the curved booth where the girl had been, and he immediately began sliding out the other side when Mars sat down, blocking him. The Function slid up a chair and sat at the end of the table. The chair was backwards, and The Function folded his arms across its back.

"*What the fuck are you miscreants doing here?*" asked Dean. "*You're putting my life in danger!*"

The Function smirked. "Have you been hiding in *Bayou St. John* this whole time?"

"Can we talk about this somewhere... *less public*?"

The Function shook his head. "We won't be long."

"Why the fuck are you wearing that shirt?" asked Mars.

The hideously bright orange shirt had a lamppost with a cartoon man passed out drunk underneath it. The shirt read, *I Got Bourbon Faced on Shit Street.*

Dean sunk into the booth, scanning the bar, his southern accent becoming more prominent as he spoke: "I'm not inclined to discuss my wardrobe choices at the present moment."

"Very well," said The Function. "We're here with questions about Nimble."

"I've been clean," whispered Dean. "I haven't partaken of crime, especially not with *Nimble.* If he knew I was alive, he'd likely skin me and throw me into the swamp."

"Somebody hit Nimble's lair," said Mars. "Bad."

"I wouldn't know about that, darlin'."

"Yes you do," said Edith.

"How the hell did you all find me?" asked Dean.

Edith sipped from her drink. "Oh, we can find you whenever we want."

"If you don't feel like helping us, we'll leave," said Mars. "But Julius and Roman will find you, and they'll start handing you empty envelopes in very public places. Everyone knows who Julius and Roman are, and they'll start to wonder who *you* are, no matter how good and ugly your disguise is. And then their memories will be jogged and they'll remember you, won't they?"

The Function watched as the color drained from Dean Smith's face.

"We just want to know what the word on the street is about the hit on Nimble's den," he said.

Dean swallowed, looking around at the bar. "It was an inside job. Nimble put a bounty out on the guy who did it, said his name is *Chans*[26]. French or creole for *luck* or *lucky.* Kid who worked for Nimble, early twenties. The bounty offers five favors from Nimble himself if brought in dead, eight favors if brought in alive, with additional favors if Nimble's goods are brought in as well. I don't know what the kid stole from Nimble, though. I've been trying to lie low. But that number of favors from Nimble is nothing to scoff at. Nimble wants this kid bad."

Dean glanced over The Function's shoulder and shook his head quickly. The Function turned and saw the blonde girl lower two bottles of beer, which she was about to hit him with, taking a swig from one. She leaned over the table, placing the other one in front of Dean Smith.

"You kept saying they would find you," said the girl. "And I kept saying you were paranoid. Y'all must be The Agents of... whatever, or some shit."

"Something like that," said Mars.

---

[26] Pronounced like the plural form of the name Shawn—so 'Shawns'—because French.

"Well," said the girl, still leaning over the table. "Four people in this bar would stab you and throw you out the door if I tell them to. Six people are maybes, but I'd bet on at least two of them getting in on the action. You're threatening someone I care about and you're going to leave. Now."

The Function nodded to Dean Smith, pointing his thumb at the blonde woman. "Hold on to this one. Seriously." He got up from his chair, stepping back from the crazy blonde girl who he suddenly found very attractive.

Mars and Edith followed suit, getting out of the booth.

"Thank you for partaking in our unscheduled meeting," The Function said to Dean Smith, who was still sunk down in the booth to avoid notice. The blonde girl glared at them, her beer bottle gripped in her fist. The Function nodded to her. "Pleasure meeting you. Keep an eye on him for us."

"Fuck off," she said.

"That's the plan."

They turned and made their way out of the bar.

The Function took a swig of his cider, looking at Edith and Mars as he pulled his coat from behind the bush and began smacking it clean on his leg. "Well, that was fun."

File 31 :: [Edith Downs]

The late morning warmth of the next day rolled off the white clouds, skydiving down between tall office buildings and tumbling through the large streets of the Central Business District. Edith had wanted to sleep in after the awful interaction with the gun, hunting down Dean Smith, and then staking out the French Quarter for the rest of the afternoon and evening. But she was determined to carve out some time for herself when she could, even if it left her a bit exhausted. She sipped from her latte as she aimlessly walked, feeling the soreness in her body. She still had several hours before going back to staking out the Quarter. Passing some old dock warehouses converted into restaurants, she tried to remember the last time she'd gone for a walk without a destination.

Earlier, she'd gone over some business with her manager/friend Jason at Le Croissant Cité, then took her latte and began her wander. Something else she hadn't done for a while was to leave behind the Extraction Glove, though it was safely nearby in her parked car. She wore a simple green dress, black slip-ons, and a wide-brimmed black straw hat. Attached to her dress was the silver dragonfly pin, with blue stones set into the body and white stones in the wings. It was the first item she'd copied memories from, sitting at Cafe Envie in the French Quarter while Adelaide had been searching for The Axeboy—an event which felt like ages ago.

Edith was glad she brought the memory-infused pin, since a few mems from it crawled up onto her shoulders and began telling her about the buildings she passed and about the history of the area. She hadn't realized the history of the Central Business District was so rich. Everyone spoke of the French Quarter's history, of course, and of the Marigny and Treme, but she'd never heard anyone talk about the CBD's history.

The mems spoke to her in rudimentary pictures and images, but then other mems came running across sidewalks and streets to her, having come from nearby buildings, and they began adding their own images and pieces of memory—many of which were from the mid and early 1800s, with several from the 1700s.

She didn't know these mems of the CBD personally, but over the last few weeks, the web of communication she'd been creating between the mems of the city had grown exponentially. The more massive and complex the web became, the more confident Edith felt that mems in trouble could contact her and that she could find the means to help them. So far, the web was strongest in the Garden District and stretched out in every direction, out across the Irish Channel, Uptown, Central City, then the CBD and the French Quarter beyond.

She wandered the streets for hours, listening to and watching their stories, asking questions when she was unclear of what they were trying to convey (which was quite often). Through being shown pictures and snippets of memories, including conversations between people, Edith put together the following list of facts about the CBD[27]:

1) The area used to be nothing but swampy forests full of cypress trees and canebrake, later to be cleared and turned into plantations outside the small colony of New Orleans—the original colony consisting merely of what today is the rectangle of the French Quarter.

2) After the Louisiana Purchase, the Americans began flooding into New Orleans. The mix of cultures which had lived there for generations weren't thrilled with the influx of Americans, so they called themselves *creole*, which is Portuguese for "we're from here, and you're not." The Americans thought the creoles were a bit strange anyway and built their own part of the city beyond Canal Street, buying up old plantation land. The area became known as the American Sector (now known as the Central Business District). They had their own city buildings and their own town square, called Lafayette Square.

3) When the American Sector kept expanding, they created a whole new town beyond, called Lafayette, which would later become part of the Garden District (the *town* of Lafayette not to be confused with the present-day *city* of Lafayette).

4) Since the city was expanding outside of the original colony in every direction, with the Treme and the Marigny already being developed, the Americans called the oldest section of New Orleans "The French Quarter." The creoles called it the "Vieux Carre," or "the old quarter."

---

[27] One might wonder about the validity of these facts, noting that the sources are tiny blue creatures who live inside objects. As strange as the sources are, the facts are indeed true. One is encouraged to look up the facts in order to verify their factishness.

5) The border between the French Quarter and the American Sector was Canal Street. The median running down the center of the large street was called "the neutral ground," the term playing at how the creoles and the newcomers didn't care for each other at first. The word "median" is never, ever used in New Orleans—the raised area in the middle of any street is always called the *neutral ground*.

Edith's mind was racing with all the new knowledge, wondering if any of that knowledge was exaggerated or misinterpreted. She kept going back to number five, about the neutral ground. One thing that had always fascinated her about New Orleans was the common terminology, which wasn't used anywhere else. Like how Louisiana doesn't have counties like the rest of the country, they have parishes—there's no "New Orleans County" or "Orleans County," there's *Orleans Parish*. She knew it all stemmed from being a colony of both France and Spain, which were both Catholic, but didn't know any of the details. Maybe if she ever gave herself free time, she'd read up on the history of New Orleans. Though with being an Agent, training her body, dating Wole, creating the network of mems throughout the city, and owning a pastry shop, she didn't know if she'd be getting very many new books under her belt any time soon.

Zigzagging through thin alleys, the apartment buildings and offices looming a few stories above, Edith realized the mems were *guiding* her, urging her to walk in a specific direction, to take certain turns. "Where are we going?"

An answer came from one of the dragonfly pin mems as a drawing of a question mark and a red flower, which she knew meant *beautiful secret*.

Edith smirked. "Alright, you've got my interest." She followed their urges for another block or so until she was walking down Camp Street, with the large Contemporary Arts Center on one side and the Ogden Museum of Southern Art on the other. She turned down a short street to find herself on the traffic circle, following its curve until she stood outside the tall, thin house that was The Circle Bar—so named because of its placement on the traffic circle. With the hotels and office buildings around, the house looked magically out of place—tall, thin, and slightly lopsided—yet completely beautiful. "Oh, I've been to The Circle Bar before," she told them. Her employees would often go there after work.

The mems had her turn around, looking across Saint Charles Street, with cars rushing to and from the traffic circle. A streetcar squealed down the neutral ground in front of her and turned to make its way around the circle, and the roar of the raised interstate a couple of blocks away sounded like she was standing on a cliff listening to the wind. There was nothing across the street except for a seven-story 1970s-looking office building, with stairs going up to the front of the raised concrete area the building sat upon. It was definitely not as pretty as The Circle Bar.

"I don't get it," said Edith. "Is that beautiful to you?"

Look, one of the mems said with a picture of an eye and an arrow.

"You want me to go across the street?"

No. Look.

Edith kept looking around. People waited at the streetcar stop in the neutral ground. She could see the tops of statues on the raised area in front of the building.

Then one mem sent the color blue to her, which was its way of saying, *Memory.*

Edith stretched her naked glove hand reflexively manner as she looked with that other part of her eyes, the part which could see memory. She saw the glow of blue around the heads of the people waiting for the streetcar, and briefly in the cars speeding by. She could feel the memories behind her, laced into the bricks and wood which made up The Circle Bar. The office building across the street pulsed with memory, but there was something else, something slightly closer and taking on a different shape. She watched as thin streams of memory ran up and down some kind of structure, a structure perhaps three stories tall and set into the office building and the raised concrete slab that it sat upon. The strands of memories were thin but strong, and she saw amongst them thousands of tiny dots of blue, like smaller versions of the orbs she'd seen inside the entity of The Presbytere. In the blue strands of memory, the shape and detail of the building emerged in sections. The outside was constructed of massive stone blocks, with columns running from the ground to the roof, and massive windows. It was some kind of Greco-Roman temple, like other older city buildings in the CBD.

"That *is* beautiful," whispered Edith.

As if hearing her, the blue light of the memory-building pulsed, then handfuls of the tiny blue dots wafted over the street, traveling up above the streams of cars, around the people waiting at the streetcar stop, and circled Edith. From the blue dots, she felt an enormous amount of *love*. Not love of anything in particular, but a strong sense of love and contentment. The sense of love was so strong that her eyes watered.

"My name is Edith," she whispered. "I'm one of The Agents Of, and Protector of the Memories of New Orleans."

In answer, the blue dots opened to her like tiny flowers. She saw children, obviously from previous times, sitting at wooden tables and reading. She saw a woman reading to very young children while they sat on the floor. She saw people studying intently. She saw people laughing at what they read.

"Thank you."

Then one mem on her shoulder urged her to cross the street. Edith used the crosswalk to cross, the blue dots swirling around her like dandelion seeds. As she walked closer, the building's memories flowed faster over the surface of the invisible structure. She walked up the stairs, seeing the statues scattered about to her right—they were all contemporary art statues, abstract and interesting.

She turned and walked down the side of the real office building until she came to the front steps of the massive Greco-Roman memory structure, the columns of memory stretching up to either side of her. The mems urged her to walk up the steps and through the front door, which was right up against the side of the actual office building.

"I can't," she said. "Reality doesn't work that way." But she tested one step, and though there was, in reality, nothing beneath it, she *felt* the step underneath her foot. She stepped up onto it, then onto the next, and then she was pulling open the massive wooden door of the building. Blue light surrounded her as she stepped inside. She knew she should walk smack into the side of the office building, but she kept walking, the building around her taking shape and color with each step. It was vast and empty of people. The inside was full of filing cabinets and wooden shelves—shelves meant to hold books, but they were empty. Massive marble columns speared up to the vaulted ceiling, and amidst the filing cabinets was a statue of Napoleon. There were rows of big wooden tables, along with a massive, curved wall of tall, arched windows reaching up to the twenty-five-foot-tall ceiling. There was a wooden customer service counter near the entrance, the front of it engraved with the words *NEW ORLEANS PUBLIC LIBRARY.*

So many emotions surged through Edith's body that it took her a moment to realize that she was being communicated with, but not by the mems—the actual *building* was speaking to her, or at least its memory. It was *welcoming* her. More than that, it seemed to offer her a service.

"Thank you," she said. "This is a lovely space, but I'm not sure what I could use it for."

The building around her, now looking very real, even with the blue strands laced through every wall, column, and object, pulsed with blue light, and a message was sent through her body, through her heart: *I offer you my services, Protector of Memories.*

File 32 :: [Mars]

Mars walked down the long hallway of the nearly empty ferry terminal at the foot of Canal Street at the Mississippi River. The windows and closed ticket booths she passed were relics from bygone days, and she wondered if there was ever a time the ferry was busy enough to warrant multiple ticket booths, or if this place was built with ideas for a future which never came to pass. At the end of the hallway stood an employee at a thin podium, taking two dollars from each person boarding the ferry.

Mars fished through her pockets for two dollars. She shook away the feeling that she was doing something wrong, that she was lying to Julius and Roman. Sure, she hadn't told them she was taking an hour break from staking out events, but taking breaks was part of their whole don't-go-crazy plan.

She handed the two dollars to the ferry employee, then walked across the ramp and onto the second story of the boat. She wore a white NOLA tank top, cargo pants, and boots, with pouches and devices hanging from her hips. Her tank top was cut to show off her large ram's head chest tattoo, the ram's horns spiraling under the straps. She was so utterly happy that the last vestiges of the gross bruise from the shotgun-butt-to-the-chest-while-getting-away-from-a-bank-robbery were finally gone.

Mars made her way down the stairs to the large open area at the front of the boat. Looking around at the handful of tourists and realizing she had no idea what to look for, she walked up to the front and leaned on the rail. The water was just below her; the wind batting about her red dreadlocks, which were tied back and trailing over the duffel bag strapped to her back.

"Pretty day, isn't it?" said a woman's voice.

Mars turned, butterflies flying amok in her stomach. The woman was leaning on the rail next to her, looking out towards the massive bridge that was The Crescent City Connection in the distance, connecting the East Bank of the city to the West.

The ferry's whistle blew loudly, the motors revving up and pulling them out into the river.

The woman's dark brown hair was streaked with gray and pulled back into a bun. Her olive skin was smooth and her eyes gray as rain clouds. She wore a long sleeve green shirt with an open black vest covered in pockets full of who-knows-what, and numerous pouches strapped around the legs of her black jeans. Wrapped around one wrist was a bracelet made of tiny bones, and around her neck was some kind of blue stone tied up with a leather strap. Mars couldn't place her age—she could have been in her late-twenties or mid-forties.

The woman turned around, leaning back against the rail and looking at Mars. "I feel like I already know you, Mars. I'm surprised it took us so long to meet."

Mars peered into the woman's form, accessing the type of *seeing* that let her gaze at the energy inside of entities and, more recently, people. What she saw could only be held with her eyes for a split second—millions upon millions of glowing threads, all twisted together like rope. The rope glowed so bright it seared into Mars' eyes, and from that rope came endless threads spreading out in arcs through the air in every direction as far as Mars could see.

Mars' knees gave out, her hands covering her eyes as she fell. But rather than hit the ground, she was pulled up and held against the railing.

"Easy with that," said the woman, her voice utterly calming as she held Mars up. "Just breathe."

Taking a deep breath, Mars gripped onto the metal rail, using its solidity to bring a sense of solidity to her own body. "It's like seeing the world ripped apart."

"Not ripped apart, just connected in fun ways. At least that's how I like to think of myself."

Mars looked down at the railing, at her arms wrapped around it and the waves of water below, her eyes slowly adjusting to seeing again. Seeing the woman's form was like being in the dark and having a spotlight turn on right in front of your face, leaving Mars' vision riddled with dark splotches. "You knew I had to try that, though."

"That's why I didn't suggest you not."

Mars smiled as she regained her footing, peering up as the woman's arms pulled away from her. "So, you're not *actually* serendipity, right? I mean, you're not actually a manifestation of the concept, are you?"

Serendipity smirked. "I suppose I'm a lot of things. Like you."

Mars chuckled. "Oh, I'm just grade-A human."

"In a sense, but are any of us merely one thing?" Serendipity reached a hand out lazily, feeling the wind as the ferry turned towards Algiers Point and moved like an arrow across the Mississippi. "Bes didn't tell you to seek me out."

"Is that a problem?"

"No."

"I was there when he called you to ask if The Function could go with us to find Dean Smith. I memorized your number, and I called you."

Serendipity's eyes fell upon the glossy waves. "My number... there are no numbers." She looked at Mars. "I am the operator, Mars. Bes tells you numbers so that you have *intent* when you are dialing. But it's only the *intent* that matters. You think of me, or one of my people, or one of The Agents Of, you pick up a phone and dial and the closest phone to them will ring. That's how it works. The numbers are Bes' training wheels for you. He is much better at training new people than I am—part of the reason I've had the same two operatives for the past century."

"If you only have two operatives, why don't you keep The Function around all the time?"

"Because I like him." Serendipity's eyes were the gray of endless clouds. "He ages when he's alive, so I let him die when he's not needed, then I bring him back when he is. Otherwise, he'd be long dead by now."

"That's kind of how he explained it."

"How are you liking The Agents Of?"

"I love it. I've wanted to be an Agent since I was a child."

Serendipity smirked. Mars got the impression that the woman smirked quite often—perhaps an insight into how The Function and her could get along so well. "I remember. The Function tried for years to have me convince Bes and Roman not to take you as an Agent. *He* asked them not to, of course, but he was afraid they'd take you on anyway while he was absent from life. I'm glad he finally gave in."

"Yeah, he's gotten stubborn in his old age."

Serendipity laughed, her voice sounding like wind through a canopy of oak trees. "You're delightful, Mars. But I knew you would be." Their gazes followed each other off the side of the boat, with the picturesque French Quarter over the rolling waves made by the ferry, the steeples of the Saint Louis Cathedral spearing the sky, the people like ants moving across the levee and past the docked steamboat, whose calliope hadn't played a note for weeks now. "How's the investigation going?"

"Slow. We don't have enough pieces yet. But he's reckless, at least in some ways, so hopefully he'll slip up soon."

"Everyone trips eventually."

"I know Scape and F... The Function... are out helping watch public spaces when they can. Are you watching places too?"

Serendipity took her hand from the rail of the ferry, opening and closing it. "I'm not as physical as I used to be, Mars. There are certain places where I can be more physical, like above or near the Mississippi.

Otherwise, I tend to exist in the flow of the city, in the current. So, unfortunately, I'm no longer very useful in such ways."

"Do you miss being more physical?"

"No." Her gaze turned upon the approaching ferry landing of Algiers Point. "Is there anything else you'd like to ask or tell me? I'm afraid I'm going to have to disembark here to take care of a few things."

Mars thought for a moment. "I really just needed to see you, to know for certain that you were real. Without you, The Agents Of wouldn't exist. Without you, I would have never met The Function or Edith. All of a sudden a whole lot of my life was based on someone I never met, and I just needed to know you were real. I'm not sure if that makes sense."

Serendipity gave that smirk again. "More than you may ever know. Call me any time—I don't sleep. And please tell Edith the same."

"I will." A new certainty flowed through Mars' body. Serendipity was no longer some whispered-about question mark, some phantom upon which Mars' world was based. "I have one more question. Well, more like a favor."

"Of course."

The boat swung around, thumping against the dock.

Now it was Mars' turn to smirk. "Keep The Function out of trouble."

Serendipity laughed again. "There isn't a force in the city with that power."

File 33 :: [Edith Downs]

Sunlight drifted through the green curtains of the apartment, dancing across the wooden floorboards along with the *pluck ploom pluck ploom* of the upright bass. The music lazily sauntering out of the record player was a *Best Of Collection* of The Boswell Sisters, and the current song was *Down on the Delta*, recorded in 1932[28]. The three sisters' voices harmonized like three sides of the same coin flipping through the air, joined by various horns and a guitar.

Edith busied herself in front of the bathroom mirror—or rather that's what a fly on the wall might think was happening. Really, she was sitting back in a chair somewhere inside her head, letting a few of the mems she'd befriended take control of her body and play around with her hair and makeup. She was sore and tired, once more, from running around the city the previous evening looking for mythological monsters and listening for hints of broken calliope notes. She really didn't have the energy to put so much effort into her appearance, so she was grateful for the mems' help this evening.

Some of the mems belonged to the shimmery blue flapper dress she wore, vintage from the 1920s. The dress was sleeveless and had jagged art deco patterns splayed across it in blue beads, including beaded fringe which hung down to her knees. The owner had been young in the '20s and had lived a long and glorious life. The woman had taken out the dress every time she was happy and danced around with it, all the way into her eighties.

The other mems working over Edith's appearance were from an old

---

[28] Raised in Uptown New Orleans, The Boswell Sisters began singing together in the 1920s as teenagers and became hugely famous in the 1930s. They were a close harmony singing trio inspired by the blues and jazz of New Orleans. The Andrew Sisters, whose fame better stood the test of time, started out imitating The Boswell Sisters.

jeweled comb in the shape of a peacock, and an empty perfume bottle with a butterfly stretching its wings on the cap.

Currently, her hair was back in a bun, with a curled spiral of sepia and black twisting down one side of her face, just past her chin. Her lashes were pulled out long, haloed by blue eye shadow, and her lips were the red and dark.

Sitting in the chair of her mind, she quite liked what was happening out there. Perhaps she'd actually be able to learn some techniques from these mems and apply them herself—unlike when she'd tried to do that with baking. She watched her hands reach down and take a necklace from the counter, a black ribbon with a small oval of ivory into which a feather was carved, and tie it around her neck. It hung a few inches above the swooping neckline of her dress.

Once they finished, she took control of her body and stretched, smiling at herself in the mirror. Though her hair wasn't really styled in a 1920s style, she thought that if she were to fall through a time rip and into a speakeasy, she wouldn't look so out of place.

"Thank you, I look lovely," she said to the mems, who nodded to her and meandered back to their objects.

Then she danced barefoot out of the bathroom and into the sunlight, which seeped through the curtains and turned everything green.

Meow.

"Oh, you'd like this dance, would you?" She picked Maurice up under his front legs and bounced him to the music. "Alright, but no getting fur on me."

Meow.

Edith set him down on the love seat and he merely looked up at her, confused. Then she twirled into the kitchen and picked up a large wicker picnic basket, which was loaded up and covered in a blanket. Stepping into her black slip-on shoes, she grabbed a small black purse and walked out.

She often left the music on these days—the mems would turn it off if they wanted, just as they would change the record if they felt like listening to something else. She made her way down the stairs and across the side yard, humming to herself as she set the heavy basket on the bench underneath the large oak tree.

The air was warm and the sun's light waned as it drifted down behind the horizon. A few moments later she saw him wandering across the tree branches, heading her way. It was the first time she'd seen him wearing anything besides his open, black vest.

He moved lightly across the branches, stepping and jumping down until he was on the lowest limb. She played with the idea of climbing up the tree, but was feeling rather ladylike at the moment.

"Are those clothes new?" she asked.

Wole crouched upon the branch, his dark skin sprinkled with gold dust. His head was bald and his sideburns curved into points like scimitars. He looked down at his shirt, which was white, loose, and long-sleeved, reminding Edith of a pirate's shirt, over which he had an open bronze vest. "New to me."

"Does that mean you have a closet somewhere?"

He looked up at the treetops. "The trees give me plenty of places to hide things." A chorus of butterflies swirled up through her stomach as his dark eyes fixed on her. "You look... very pretty, Edith."

Edith's face warmed, and she was sure she was blushing.

He reached down from where he crouched on the branch, reaching so far forward it seemed he would tumble off and onto the ground, extending his hand to her. She reached down and grabbed the basket's handle, then took his hand. As soon as his hand clasped onto hers, both the heavy basket and her own body were nearly weightless. Edith stretched and flexed her muscles. She was growing used to this feeling of being near-weightless, but one had to be careful—*feeling* near-weightless and *being* near-weightless were very different indeed, hence the stretching. The body was not used to such shifts.

She held her breath as he pulled her up through the air and above the tree branch, finally exhaling when her shoes touched the curved bark, the once-heavy picnic basket now easily swinging from her arm. Edith smiled at him. She shouldn't have felt balanced while standing at such a weird angle, but she was growing used to the way it felt when she was touching him, the way gravity sloppily pushed her like a chess piece across the board of New Orleans—a drunk knowing that, in the end, it would win the chess game, anyway.

Edith bit her lip. "Do you have a place in mind?"

"I do." Wole took the picnic basket from her, then turned and walked up the nearly vertical tree trunk. Edith held her breath as she followed, her hand always clasped to his, her stomach spinning like a water ballerina as she walked nearly straight upwards after him.

Gravity was not mandatory when she held his hand; it was more of a suggestion.

He led her to a higher branch, pulling her against him and slipping his hand around her waist. A crackling warmth traveled across her body at his touch.

"You remember what to do?" he asked.

"Yeah."

She followed his lead as he bent his knees, then straightened them, then bent them again, the branch bending below them as he did. Then, on a downswing, he said to her, "This is the one."

When they got to the top of the upswing, they both jumped. Edith couldn't help but squeal as they bounced up into the empty space, well above the fence which ran alongside her yard, somewhere between the cloud-strewn sky above and the grass and bushes far below. The neighbor's cat looked up at them for a moment from the next yard before going back to licking its paw and cleaning itself.

The next tree approached and Edith squinted as her own logic screamed that they couldn't possibly make it. Then Wole's boots planted onto an impossibly thin branch and he swung her around until her feet joined his. "That was good," he said.

She took a deep breath. "Really? Because I'd probably use words like 'terrifying' and 'sloppy' before using the word 'good'."

Wole's smile was wide as he looked at her, and she suddenly remembered that a man's arm was wrapped tightly around her waist, her own hand clenched onto the back of his vest.

"So you're ready for more?" he asked.

"Yes."

She watched his eyes trace the coils of sepia hair trailing past her chin. "Good."

He let go of her waist, pulling his hand across the back of her dress, sliding it up to her shoulder and down her arm until he wrapped her hand in his. If he stopped touching her, gravity would take her crashing down through the branches. He ran a thumb over the top of her hand. "Hold on."

Edith gripped tight to his hand as he turned and took step after step, the world blurring past them, reminding her of being on one of the spinning carnival rides at the state fair in Oklahoma—the kind which spun so fast that the entire world smeared across your vision like bugs on a windshield. Every time she blinked they were in a new tree, on a new branch, surrounded by a different assortment of houses and telephone poles. Branch to branch, tree to tree. They traveled that way for some time, and Edith felt the experience becoming much more normal more than it ought to be.

When they finally stopped and the world ceased to blur, there were no houses to be found, only trees and grass and plants, with cement pathways cutting through the grass below. They were standing in a large oak tree, perhaps forty feet tall, on a wide, fairly horizontal branch.

Nearly two stories below them, people traverse the pathways, jogging, walking their dogs, and talking on phones.

Wole set the picnic basket down on the branch, checking to make sure it was balanced before he let go. Then he reached out and placed his hand on the trunk of the tree. "I thought this would be a good spot. This tree is a good friend."

"This works for me." She reached down and pulled the blanket from the basket, laying it over the branch beneath her before setting down, finally letting go of Wole's hand. She straddled the branch, pushing her dress down with one hand.

Edith looked down at the passing people as Wole sat down across from her, the picnic basket between them.

"Won't they think it's weird that we're up here?"

Wole followed her gaze, then shook his head. "No one ever sees me up here."

"I saw you."

His smile returned. "You did."

She felt a blush coming on, so she busied herself with the picnic basket, pulling out a bottle of wine and a corkscrew. "Feel like doing the honors?"

Wole sat down and straddled the branch, then took them from her and began slowly twisting the corkscrew in, like he was testing some new form of technology. As he screwed it in, the two arms on either side of the corkscrew lifted into the air.

Edith bit her lip. "How did they open bottles back when... you know, back when dinosaurs were walking around?"

He stopped twisting and looked over at her. "It was much easier. We just asked a dinosaur for help." He held up his thumb and wiggled it back and forth. "They'd use a claw to pry out the cork."

Edith laughed. "I bet they were useful in all sorts of ways."

Wole held the bottle between his knees and pressed down on the arms of the corkscrew, pulling up the cork. "I miss them sometimes."

"I bet you do." She pulled out the two plastic containers of veggie and shrimp pasta she'd made, which erupted with steam as soon as she took off the lids.

The cork popped from the bottle and Wole took two wine glasses from the basket and poured.

"Thank you for cooking," he said.

"It's fun." She handed him one container and a fork. "And I enjoy cooking for you."

Edith set the picnic basket behind her on the branch and raised her glass to his. "To beautiful nights."

"To beauty and nights."

She tried to hide her blushing cheeks with the wine glass as she took a drink. It was a Tempranillo, tasting of leather and bitter cherries.

They both started on their pasta. Wole took a deep breath after his first bite. "Edith, I don't know if I've ever tasted anything this good."

She smiled. "Actually, I'm not sure I've ever made anything this good. I always make it a bit different, I'm not sure what happened."

"Must be the night."

"And the beauty."

Wole smirked as he took another bite. Then a cicada landed behind him on the tree's trunk, chirping twice. Wole turned his head and nodded.

"Edith, the chirpers want you to see something."

She slowly finished the pasta she was chewing and swallowed. "The cicadas?"

Wole set his container of pasta down and got to his feet. "We have to hurry. It'll only take a moment."

She grabbed the container lids from the basket and covered their dinner. Wole reached down and took her hand. She practically floated to her feet as gravity released its grip on her.

"So the cicadas know who I am?"

He led her straight up the trunk towards the sky. When they neared the top, he led her out onto a long, thin branch, perhaps as thick as her wrist. It barely bent under their weight.

When she saw the expanse of the park laid out before her, all the treetops like sprawling green hills, she clenched her eyes shut and gripped onto Wole's vest.

"It's ok, Edith. You're safe." His arm wrapped around her shoulder and tightened.

She took a deep breath and opened her eyes.

Directly ahead, she saw the most majestic oak tree. Impossibly tall with gigantic limbs bowing down to touch the grassy ground surrounding it.

"Have you seen the Tree of Life before?"

She shook her head. "I've heard of it. I didn't realize it was so..."

There was a figure walking towards the tree, through the grass— someone wearing long, tattered robes and using a thin, twisted walking stick. Edith could sense that the figure was very old.

"Who is that?" she asked.

"The Tree of Life," he whispered.

The figure stepped up to the tree's trunk and walked right inside, disappearing into the old, gnarled bark. The tree itself stretched and twisted in a wind which suddenly picked up, flexing its branches and leaves into the air. Then a flurry of tiny bright green lights propelled up from the leaves and into the air, hundreds upon hundreds of them, spinning out into the night sky in every direction.

"What's happening?" she asked.

"It is said that The Tree of Life manages aspects of the living world. These lights go up into the sky every so often, and supposedly the lights find the parts of life which are straying, putting them back in order."

"And... that person with the walking stick was the actual tree?"

Wole hesitated. "That was the tree, not a person. And she's very nice if you ever get a chance to talk with her."

Edith turned and looked up into his eyes. "And the cicadas? How do they know about me?"

"They know a lot of things."

"Time has not taught you how to bullshit worth a damn."

Wole smiled. "They... they root for me."

"Root? Is that a tree pun?"

He shook his head and chuckled. "I haven't had a romantic interest for centuries. And they hope it works out."

She pulled lightly at his vest with her fingers. "Well, I haven't dated anyone worth giving a second thought to. Not until now."

His fingertips dragged across her hip and her hand slid up across his neck and over the back of his shaved head. When their lips met, she knew she was falling, spinning, and she closed her eyes and pressed her lips harder against his. She knew that with him she could fall, but that she'd never hit the ground.

File 34 :: [Roman Wing]

The wind of the levee ripped about the edges of his long coat, the sun gleaming off the waves of the Mississippi as the Steamboat Tchoupitoulas drifted down the river's center, jazz music spilling out and rolling over the glossy water. Roman could *feel* the Wonder of the city ebbing slightly. He had many Wonder-enriching devices planted around the city, but the calliope was unique in its way of spreading its effects over such a considerable distance.

The levee itself was full of locals and tourists, walking and chatting, taking pictures of the steamboat, walking their dogs or sitting on the rocks leading down to the water.

Roman walked down the rocks, not bothering to glance at where he stepped until he was a mere yard from the water. Crouching down, he picked up the dented, duct taped speaker with buttons down the side of it. The speaker's spiraling cord hung over the river, dipping close to the waves, then went up for miles towards a few patches of white clouds over Algiers.

His pale thumb pressed down on one button. "Albert, are you there? This is Roman Wing."

A crackling voice came through the speaker. "Yeah, Roman. What's up?"

"We're looking to rain out the outdoor events coming up this weekend, at least on Saturday. I know it's short notice, but we're hunting the guy who's been wreaking havoc on public spaces. If we can get some events rained out, it'll greatly improve our chances of catching him."

"I don't know, man. I've barely got any water in the buckets right now. That only gives me a couple of days to collect more water. At best, I can make it rain for an hour on Saturday, but you know this city, people just go out in the mud, anyway. It takes a lot of rain and wind to cancel events, and I just don't have it."

Roman put the speaker down, looking out at the river and thinking, then brought it back to his mouth. "I knew it was a long shot."

"Hey, I'll tell you what I can do. I can *keep it* from raining, then if you need a downpour later next week or weekend, I should have it. I'm sorry, Roman, but that's what I've got."

"No, that will work. Hold the rain. Hopefully, we won't need it, but that's a tremendous help. I'll keep you updated."

"Does this have to do with the calliope not playing?"

Roman turned to watch The Steamboat Tchoupitoulas vanish around the curve of Algiers Point. "Yes. It has everything to do with the calliope not playing."

File 35 :: [Julius Marcos]

Julius tacked up the last page of notes to the huge corkboard on the wall of the headquarters' planning room.

The other three Agents walked into the room, followed by The Function and Scape.

"What's up, boss?" said Mars. He'd given up trying to regulate how Mars referred to him, realizing that it was in her nature to keep calling him and Roman something different.

Both Mars and Edith had mugs of coffee from the break room. Roman crossed his arms and leaned back against one of the few empty sections of wall, Scape landed on the back of one chair, and the other three sat down at the large, wooden table.

"Listen up," said Julius. "We've tried to catch a glimpse of this guy Chans' calliope device for two weeks. Today is Friday, which means there will be a lot of people out and he might hit again tonight. But this also means that tomorrow is *Saturday,* the busiest day of the week as far as events go. I was hoping to have more information before now, but we've got what we've got. Tonight we're going to have the normal routes we've had all week."

Mars raised her hand.

"Yes, Mars?"

"Do you think that raises the chances of us running into this guy?"

"Yes. He hasn't yet hit the same place twice, so we stick to our areas. In theory, the chances of those places being hit get higher by the day." Julius turned to the map, which now had several red thumbtacks in different neighborhoods. "Last night he hit a crowded restaurant in Mid City. If he's hitting restaurants, there's no way we can guarantee *ever* catching him. We would need hundreds of us, rather than four, or now *six* with Serendipity lending us The Function and Scape."

"Six is *closer* to hundreds," said The Function.

"Yes, thank you for helping," said Julius, looking from The Function to Scape, who half-rolled out his proboscis to gesture *you're welcome*.

"The situation may end up resolving itself," continued Julius. "I would like to get to him before Nimble's people, but if Nimble gets to him first, we would simply never see this guy again."

Edith shuddered, which Julius deemed the correct response. Nimble should not be taken lightly.

Julius turned his attention to the wall of events. "Alright, we've got a fairly comprehensive list of events that are happening tomorrow. There are *twenty-three*."

The Function whistled.

"That's not counting a walking parade having something to do with crawfish, a bike parade, and at least two second lines for weddings. We asked Albert to rain out events, but it was too short notice, so he's saving the water for next weekend if we need it. Roman and I figured out a strategy to cover as many events as possible. Speak up if there's anything we missed."

He walked over to the giant map, pointing to the I-10 freeway several blocks above the French Quarter. "The biggest event this weekend is the three-day long Treme Seventh Ward Arts and Culture Festival underneath the interstate. I'll be watching the festival this afternoon, Saturday, and Sunday. I might run into people I know from the neighborhood, who may know something or who may help me keep watch."

He pointed to the levee just under the French Quarter. "The second biggest event is the new Chicory Fest on the levee. A one-day festival with two stages and a lot of food tents. Edith, you've got that."

"Sounds good," said Edith.

He moved his finger along Decatur Street, parallel to the river. "Mars, you're going to monitor Decatur, Chartres, and Royal Streets in the Quarter, checking in with Edith every hour or two."

"You got it," said Mars.

He moved to the gigantic green splotch over a mile above the French Quarter. "Scape, since you can fly, you've got the biggest area—City Park. There are dozens of birthday parties every Saturday, not to mention sports games and other gatherings."

Scape nodded.

Then Julius moved far uptown to the other large park. "The Function, you're taking Audubon Park and the zoo. There's a sea lion event tomorrow, so the zoo will be packed."

"Fresh air and trees." The Function took a swig from his flask of Chartreuse. "That's gonna make my lungs feel weird."

Julius moved back and pointed at the lake side of the French Quarter. "Roman will take the rooftops, checking on smaller events in the Quarter, checking for activity around Nimble's den, and possibly going through the CBD. He will be moving from payphone to payphone, so he's the one to call if there's trouble."

Julius looked around at the five of them. "Any questions?"

The Function nodded. "So has Roman made any spiffy devices that keep us from being mesmerized by our hopes and dreams?"

"No," said Julius.

"We don't know the nature of the device," said Roman. "Edith has searched extensively through memories of people who were at the attacks, but the device is always covered by a pelt strapped over the man's back like a cape. I won't know how to cancel the effects until I know what's being used to fuel the device. The effects of my original device aren't auditory, which is why we haven't been wearing earplugs or headphones."

Mars elbowed The Function. "Your hopes and dreams probably suck, so you're just gonna be really bored."

The Function laughed. "I'll be dreaming of drinking a beer, sitting on a couch, and catching up on reading—totally not-bored."

Julius spoke up: "All right, people. Let's get to work."

File 36 :: [Edith Downs]

The sky was blue and cloudless along the river. The lawn of Woldenberg Park between the French Quarter and the Mississippi was rimmed with food vendors and sported a stage at both sides, each stage ringed with crowds of people. Edith stood leaning back against a tree while watching the main stage, cargo ships and steamboats passing by in the background. The jambalaya, gumbo, and other New Orleans foods being served smelled amazing, but she had purposely filled up with a smoothie and a sandwich so hunger wouldn't distract her. The smells of brewing coffee and chicory, on the other hand, were tempting, and she had a feeling she'd be holding a cup of iced chicory and coffee before this festival was over.

The band on stage was one she'd heard of, perhaps from her days at the bakery—Bon Bon Vivant. Their music reminded Edith of all the old movies she watched. Some of their songs were swing music, and some were like old, whimsical French tunes. There was a drummer, accordion player, saxophone player, and two women singing, one playing guitar and the other tambourine. It had been so long since she'd listened to live music, and she couldn't help but smile.

Edith listened to them play, constantly scanning the crowd and looking to the other stage in the distance.

"'Sup, Edith," said Mars, walking up beside her. Mars had two plastic cups, one of which she handed Edith. "Lemonade?"

"Thanks." Edith sipped the lemonade, which was definitely homemade and exactly what she needed.

"How are things on the river?"

"Oh, you know... lovely."

"Yep, the Quarter is packed but very chill." When Mars spoke next, it was in a lower voice: "Don't look now, but to the left of the daiquiri station are two of Nimble's people. I recognize them from Nimble's den. I've been trailing them across the Quarter, but I think they're just patrolling random places like us, looking for Chans."

Edith peered more intently through the crowd. Stealing a glance at Nimble's people, she also recognized them. A man and a woman, both wearing dark coats and sunglasses. Edith angled her body away from them a little, in case they would recognize her as well.

Mars took a drink of her lemonade. "Figure I'll stay here and see what they do. If they stay for a while, I'll leave them to you and start walking through the Quarter again."

"Sounds good to me." Edith was suddenly very aware of the Extraction Glove in the duffel bag at her feet, and happy that she hadn't strapped it on yet. The Wonder which Roman had pumping through the city made it nearly invisible to the average person, but Nimble's people would have noticed the glove by now and remembered her from Nimble's Den.

"I'm going to wander towards the other stage," said Mars. "They might not recognize us apart, but they probably will if we're together. It shouldn't matter if they know we're here, I would just rather them not."

"No, that makes sense." Edith also became aware of the few memory-infused items in her bag, feeling safer knowing there were mems she trusted so close by. Mars put a hand on her shoulder, then walked off towards the second stage.

Bon Bon Vivant continued to play their whimsical songs, Edith stealing quick glimpses at Nimble's people until one time they were gone. She figured they'd moved on to the other stage, or perhaps further into the French Quarter.

The band finished their last song, and the audience clapped, hooted, and whistled as the band thanked them. The musicians packed up their equipment, the stagehands fixing the stage for the next band to come set up.

Normally Edith would go to the other stage, which was in full swing, but she thought Mars would be over there watching the crowd and possibly Nimble's people. A small crowd was waiting at this stage though, so maybe the next band was well known.

She took a long drink of her lemonade, closing her eyes a moment and taking a deep breath, calming herself. Edith enjoyed the work of looking for someone who was potentially harming the city, but after several days there was an undercurrent of stress and survival-mode that took a toll on her body and mind.

Loud murmurs from the people scattered about the lawn brought her back to the present and she opened her eyes. A figure she knew well by now strolled onto the stage, wearing his hide cape and Baku skull helmet, the calliope keyboard hanging from one shoulder.

Several urges surged through her body:

1) The urge to run towards him, though he'd surely see her coming.
2) The urge to sneak quickly around the food vendors.
3) The urge to sic the mems on him (though who knew if there would be time for this, or for any of these options).

But no, she had specific instructions. She squatted down, pulled out the pair of large, clunky goggles and strapped them on, standing back up to look at the man. Her actions were not important right now—her *memories* were the weapon they needed.

Chans came up to the microphone, the sound engineers looking to each other confused, wondering if this guy was supposed to be here. The goggles' magnified lenses gave Edith a closer view from across the lawn. "One, two," Edith whispered, then turned the crank on the side of the goggles, everything turning blue. "One, two." She turned the crank again, everything turning red. She continued as the man with the Baku skull spoke loudly into the microphone.

"New Orleans! Where are your *hopes and dreams*? A *criminal* has siphoned them away – a *fiend* who would see you all waste away into mediocrity while he creates a *storm of discontent* around you! But I *know* what lies dormant within, I *know* your hearts can rise up to *claw* and *crush* what threatens to bury them forever!"

Edith was mesmerized.

There was a yell and Edith turned, seeing the woman who worked for Nimble smashing two objects together, the force creating a green and yellow flame which surged towards the stage. The man who worked for Nimble ran past the woman, pulling a device from his coat.

Then from the other side of Edith ran Mars, pulling out her Bola Launcher as she weaved and pushed through the crowd.

Chans jumped to the side as the green and yellow flame blew open the center of the stage, the backdrop igniting with green fire. Edith flipped through the various colored lenses once again, counting more quickly. *Click.* "One, two." *Click.* "One, two." *Click.* "One, two." *Click.*

Scrambling to his knees, Chans pulled the hanging keyboard in front of him and pushed down on the keys.

The first thing Edith felt were waves of nostalgia, remembering the first time she'd heard the calliope after moving to the city, walking through the French Quarter, visiting different pastry shops and seeing what they had to offer. She could hardly believe she wasn't dreaming; she was so happy that she'd actually moved to the city.

Edith shook her head, pushing away the nostalgia, watching Mars make her way towards a shattered stage half-consumed by green flame.

Next, Edith realized it didn't matter. Not that Mars or her safety didn't matter, but that the only aspect of life which Edith truly influenced was her own aspirations and goals. Like plants on a front stoop, these aspirations and goals were something to be nurtured, paid attention to, grown with sweat, love, and time.

The lawn, the stage, the river—all these things were stripped away from her.

Instead, Edith was surrounded by thousands of objects piled up so high that she couldn't tell where she was. The mems crawling around the objects projected only one emotion: Love. Edith's heart felt like an open wound—she cared so much for these mems, these memories, and all she wanted to do was to protect and care for them.

Metal armor encased her body, the armor plates pulsing blue and infused with mems, her arm encased in the Extraction Glove. The ground trembled, thick stone walls rising from behind the piles of items to create an enclosure with her at the center. Thick columns burst from the ground, rising to support the arched cathedral ceiling which formed high above.

Then Edith was up near the ceiling, gazing out a window at the vast city of New Orleans sprawled out far below. The building was a castle, and she could see the surrounding moat and raised drawbridge. Cannons and the arrows of archers protruded from the castle walls.

She turned to the room full of items, her voice cracking like lightning, echoing off the walls and vaulted ceiling: "*I am Edith Downs, Protector of the Memories of New Orleans. You are all welcome here, and I give you my word that you are safe.*"

Mars pulled out her Bola Launcher as she ran, latching it onto her wrist and forearm and pulling back the elastic cord. The music sounded like a horribly out-of-tune calliope. People all around dropped to the lawn, their faces consumed in combinations of smiles and tears.

The stage was lit up with green flame, with Chans on his knees playing the keyboard.

The man who worked for Nimble was closer to the stage than Mars, but he slowed down, reeling backwards to fall laughing to the ground, tears flowing down his cheeks. The music sent warm shivers up Mars' body, but so far, no hopes or dreams entered her mind. With people on the ground, her field of vision was clear. She wanted to get closer before shooting, but was ready to launch the bola if she felt dreams creeping in.

Mars curved around towards the stage at an angle. As soon as the over-sized skull turned her way, she let go of the elastic band, the bola spinning through the air like a glowing propeller.

She kept running, not having time to wonder why she wasn't yet entranced by her own dreams.

The man on stage tried to dodge but failed, being on his knees, and the bola wrapped around his upper arms, tying them to his chest and sending him falling to one side. The music stopped as the keyboard fell to the stage floor.

The green flames didn't seem to spread or cause any further destruction, nor did they appear to be going out.

Mars jumped up and pulled herself onto the stage, grabbing the keyboard and yanking it away, disconnecting a cord attached to it and throwing the keyboard into the lawn.

The Japanese Kanji running down the skull pulsed with golden light. Suddenly she slammed hard into the floor, coughing and gasping for the air that was knocked out of her. She struggled to scream as the enormous beast pinned down her shoulders with its massive paws, roaring into her face. Mars' ears rang as she struggled to pull away. Above the roaring mouth full of huge teeth mere inches from her face was the coiling, rough trunk of an elephant, and amidst a face of black fur were a pair of piercing yellow cat eyes. The tusks beside her head were as thick as her arms. Mars' gasping face reflected back to her in the dark twin irises. Edith's descriptions and old Japanese drawings of Baku did nothing to prepare her for this.

Turning her head to brace for an attack she could do nothing about, Mars saw another of the massive Baku reach down with its mighty jaw to rip the glowing bola off Chans and toss it away. Its coat was a mesh of dark fur, reptilian scales, and gray hide.

The man sat up, stretching and shaking his skull head. As he stood, she saw that the hide cape had been nearly pulled off, just dangling from one shoulder. She peered at the device strapped to his back. A large oval stone of pulsing, dark violet energy, about the size of a football. It was set into a mass of machinery, pipes, and tubes that were all strapped to Chans' back, with brass whistles sticking up over his shoulders. The oval stone was hooked up to various wires and tubes leading into the bulk of the machine. It surprised Mars how much she understood about the device with just a glance—it wasn't very different from the devices the Agents used.

He walked over to her and crouched down, lifting the skull off his head. He was a young black man, probably in his twenties like Mars. "One of the new Agents. Named after a planet. Mars or Mercury..."

"I'm named after a god who's not very nice. Your name is Chans. You worked for Nimble. I know about you too, you're not so fucking special."

He shrugged. "Chans is what *Nimble* named me. 'Lucky'. Said I was his lucky charm, that if I was on a mission, it couldn't fail." The man scowled. "Nimble gave us all folders with every bit of information about you and the other girl, the one who wears the big glove. I didn't bother memorizing any of it since I wasn't planning on being there much longer."

Mars winced as the beast above her snarled, the heat of its breath blanketing her face. Warm drool dotted her cheek and slid down her neck. She spoke through gritted teeth: "Why are you doing this?"

The man glanced out at the lawn. "Working for Nimble, I've seen terrible things. I've *done* terrible things. He's stolen destiny itself from this city, thrown it into the street like litter. And I am going to give the city back what he stole."

"What, by feeding the city to your fucking Baku?"

His eyes widened, and he looked back at her. "I don't know how you Agents always figure out what's going on. Neither does Nimble. But I need you to know that I would *never* hurt anyone in this city except the vile and corrupt. Every person I've had the Baku take has been working for Nimble. Please tell Julius and Roman that. The Agents Of really don't need to concern themselves. Before long, the citizens of New Orleans will be thriving in their own dreams, their own destinies, and I'll be finished." He nodded to the green flames behind him. "Or my old coworkers will capture, torture, and kill me."

"Alright," said Mars. "If it's true that you're helping the city, then come meet with us. We need to know what's going on."

"Unfortunately, there isn't time for that."

Mars winced as another Baku landed loudly on the stage, holding the keyboard in its massive jaw. The man took it, nodding to the beast, then turned back to her. "Now a question for you, miss god-who-isn't-very-nice: Why weren't you overcome by your hopes and dreams, by your visions of the future? Is it some technology Roman came up with?"

Mars hadn't had time to think about it until that moment, and at first, she couldn't come up with a reason. Maybe she was just immune to the device's effects? Maybe her determination won out against the device? But then why would Edith and Nimble's henchmen be affected?

Then she laughed. It started as a rumbling in her chest, still pinned down by the massive claws of some should-be-mythological beast, then it rolled into a full-on laugh.

The man smirked. "I'm glad we're both having a good time."

Her laughing subsided. "My hopes and dreams..."

"Yeah? What are they?"

She looked right into his eyes. "This."

"Being pinned down by a Baku?"

"Being an Agent. Being in the middle of a mission. Hunting down batshit crazy fuckers like you. I'm *living* my hopes and dreams. Your device can't do *shit* to me. It has nothing to show me."

He smirked. "Then when I'm done, you'll have far less to worry about, being an Agent. The city will be in a better place, many of the city's darknesses being brought screaming into the light."

"You know we have no choice but to stop you. Especially if you won't meet with us and make your case."

"Good. I like to see that drive in the forces who look after the city. Keep your destinies intact." He stood up, two more Baku leaping up onto the stage, each one holding one of Nimble's henchmen in their huge jaws.

Mars swallowed. "What are you going to do to them?"

The man lifted the Baku skull and slid it over his head. "Nothing close to what they were going to do to me. I'll hit their reset button and see what happens."

Holding the keyboard in one hand, he dug the other into the dark fur on the back of one of the Baku, gripping the fur in his fist as the Japanese kanji on the mask lit up gold. The beast leaped into nonexistence, pulling the man with it. The other Baku vanished one after the other, until the one above Mars reached down with its trunk, sniffing Mars' face with a waft of horrid, hot breath, and then it too was gone.

Mars turned and coughed, her shoulders aching. Gritting her teeth, she looked out at the lawn, the people still lost in their individual hazes. Behind her, the green flames were nearly withered away entirely, leaving a half-destroyed stage in their wake.

File 38 :: [Roman Wing]

Roman ate a piece of Wonder while looking down at the lights of his Reader. He walked up to the destroyed stage, with Mars sitting on its edge. Chicory Fest had been canceled due to an "electrical fire" on one of the two stages. The green flames still flickered at the edges, completely unseen by the fire department and other emergency responders. The Wonder in his system would keep the security and police from bothering him and Mars.

"Mars, are you alright?"

"I can't believe you freaking fought Baku! Those things are terrifying!"

"Where's Edith?"

Mars pointed across the lawn. People were still scattered about, shaking off their dream-filled dazes. Edith leaned back against a tree, collecting herself.

"What happened?"

"A lot," said Mars. "Chans says the only people he's kidnapped were people who worked for Nimble, and that playing the device in public is a way of giving the dreams Nimble stole back to New Orleans. So he's crazy, but not in the way we thought."

"Interesting."

"More importantly, I saw the device."

"Describe it."

"It was a big stone, like onyx, but more purplish. An oval about a foot long, strapped to his back with all these wires and sensors connected to it, with brass whistles which are probably where the actual music comes from. The oval is obviously the source, being pumped through the calliope parts."

Roman took a step away from her, a surge of annoyance brimming up under the blanket of Wonder he'd eaten. He quickly saw the uselessness of that annoyance and it abated, leaving room for more analytical thoughts.

"What is it? What does it mean?"

"I'm going to find Julius. Make sure Edith is alright. Both of you be ready to leave the headquarters at dusk."

"Will do. What are we dealing with?"

"The Nor." He turned back to her. "The Nor lied to you and Edith. The stone you saw, it's known as the Carousel's Heart and The Nor are its keepers. The only way Chans has it is if they gave it to him."

"The carousel? The only one I can think of is in Storyland in City Park."

"Storyland is where The Nor operate from. The carousel is nearly as old as I am and the Heart should be installed at its center. It gives off waves of hopes, dreams, and nostalgia to those who ride. I knew the Carousel's Heart was one way to create the device, but since you'd already met with The Nor, I'd ruled it out."

"Damn. Well, at least we finally have a big lead."

Roman nodded. "It's good, if a bit confusing and complicated." He motioned behind her at the destroyed stage. "Nimble's people did that, correct?"

"Yeah, one of them hit two things together and shot this fireball at the stage and blew it up. Do you know what it was?"

He glanced down at his Reader again. "It was *emotion*. One item must have contained memories or a ghost—either a ghost reliving memories of anguish and pain or just the memories themselves. They essentially released it, shooting it at the stage with all of its raw emotion. The second item was an *emotion igniter*, which burns emotions and reacts differently depending on the particular emotion. With anguish and horror, it burns yellow and green. If it had hit Chans, he would have experienced that emotion and nothing else until the fire burned itself out."

"Holy crap. Kind of like Banshee Dave's memory virus."

"Except that was a memory, forcing someone to live out a certain event. This would be raw emotion with no reason. The mind would most likely create reasons to make sense out of it, thereby creating even more anguish and pain, fueling the fire and making it last longer."

"Fuck. So Nimble's people would use that on one of us?"

"Only if they believed they were going to kill you and keep it secret. If one of Nimble's people hurt an Agent and the other Agents found out, Nimble would have his person hunted down and killed. The body would be delivered to the Agents, and we would be told the person had gone rogue but that Nimble had taken care of the problem. It's an interesting and deadly truce we have."

"Why don't we just kill him?"

"Nimble and Bes have an understanding. If we try to kill Nimble and fail, there's no telling what he'll do. If we *do* kill him, there's no telling who will take his place—and they will most likely not follow the same rules. There may come a day when he is taken out, but it's got to be *complete*, along with the entire structure of his organization, and a lot of people have to be wiped out with him."

Mars nodded. "Sometimes when you talk like this, I suddenly remember that when Bes was gone for years at a time, *you've* been the one leading the Agents. I bet you as a leader is both awesome and scary as hell, especially when you're all logicked[29] out from eating Wonder."

Roman smirked. "I'm not sure I've ever been as scary as Bes."

"I don't know..." Mars laughed. "Bes can be all rage and monster, but hearing someone calmly and logically outline how to destroy opponents can be scarier."

"I do take leading very seriously when I'm called to do it."

He looked back at Edith, who was still sitting back against the tree. "I'd better be off to the Treme Festival to update Julius. You look after Edith and be ready to go at dusk. She looks like she's going to need a few hours' break."

---

[29] *Logicked*–past tense of the verb *logic*, as used quite often by Mars.

File 39 :: [Julius Marcos]

The nighttime world of the massive park was thick with fog and the chattering of insects, both of which spilled through the car's open windows. Ancient oak trees reached up to the clouds in every direction, watching the car pass with the interest of gods watching an empire rise and fall on the horizon[30]. The fog-strewn road coursing through City Park curved past lakes, around NOMA, past the Sculpture Garden, and over the tracks of the small train which hauled children around the park during the day[31].

Edith pulled the car full of Agents into a giant, empty parking lot. One edge of the parking lot was lined with a brick and wrought iron fence, twisting oak trees reaching up just behind it. On the sidewalk was a statue of Humpty Dumpty sitting on a short wall. Little Bo Peep stood across from him in a pink dress and bonnet, holding a hooked staff with a fluffy white sheep next to her. Together they carried the poles of a banner which hung in the air between them, reading: STORYLAND.

Julius got out of the passenger seat and peered at the oak trees, which watched them from every direction. He let his animal side near the surface, trying to sense if there was some kind of trap, whether from Nimble or from The Nor. He didn't think The Nor would set a trap for the Agents, but until a few hours ago he didn't think they would fuck with the fabric of New Orleans or withhold information from the Agents.

City Park, per usual, was full of loud, breathing life, mostly of the

---

[30]   City Park, founded in 1854, is roughly 1,300 acres large. It contains the world's largest collection of live oak trees, some older than 600 years. Even the oldest inhabitants of the city could find new nooks and crannies they never knew existed.

[31]   NOMA – The New Orleans Museum of Art. Established in 1911, NOMA has nearly 40,000 pieces of art in its permanent collection. Next to it is the Sydney and Walda Besthoff Sculpture Garden, with over 60 modern sculptures on display.

plant, animal, and insect varieties.

After everyone got out of the car, Mars elbowed Edith, smiling and whispering in a ghostly voice, "*I am Edith Downs, Protector of the Memories of New Orleans and Chauffeur to The Agents Of.*"

Edith nearly burst out laughing but stopped herself, pulling on the Extraction Glove. Mars pulled on her VR Goggles, pushing them up to her forehead. Julius loved seeing the two new Agents find themselves in the work, in the calling he shared with them—it gave him a sense of youth, yet also a sense of mortality which he held close to his heart.

Roman, who had been eating from a piece of Wonder, slipped the fruit back into his long coat. When he spoke, he did so quietly. It felt like the entire park was listening to them with amused interest. "We're going where the waking world and the dreaming world come very close together. Be careful and pay very close attention."

Julius' leg hummed near-silently beneath him, his arm humming quite a bit louder. "Let's go." He led the Agents across the parking lot. The fog on the other side of the fence was much thicker, giving the childhood statues inside the appearance of floating atop rivers of gray mist. There was a pirate ship, a large cartoon whale, and a woman riding a goose up in the trees; all things from fairytales and children's stories[32].

"Wow, I never knew this place was so freaking creepy at night," whispered Mars. "If The Nor weren't here, I'd totally come back and hop the fence to wander around."

They walked up to the two statues on the sidewalk, behind which was part of the fence that surrounded the kids' park. Julius turned to the statue of Humpty Dumpty. "We are The Agents Of, friends of The Nor. We seek entrance to this land."

The cartoony eyes of the smiling egg sitting upon his wall shifted towards them, scanning the four Agents and stopping on Julius.

"*Oh, holy shit!*" said Edith.

Mars stepped back, her hand dropping to the Bola Launcher strapped to her hip.

The wrought iron fence behind the banner opened like a curtain on a stage. Julius motioned for Mars and Edith to go in, and they both shuddered as they walked swiftly underneath the banner and past the two statues. Roman and Julius followed, Julius nodding to both statues as he passed.

Twisting trees created a spiderweb of branches above the winding pathways full of cartoony statues and plants, all blanketed with a fog that

---

[32] Storyland, opened in 1956, is a fairytale playground with over 25 giant bedtime story statues—from Snow White to the Three Little Pigs, from the Old Woman in her Shoe to Cinderella in her Pumpkin Coach. All of the statues dot the pathways winding underneath looming trees that drip with age and Spanish moss.

thickened by the minute. More statues appeared in the fog as the Agents walked, as if the Agents themselves were being told some disjointed and nonsensical fairytale. They walked past the pirate ship with Captain Hook atop the crow's nest, a crocodile sitting on a bench across from him playing an accordion. Pieces of castle floated amidst the fog and twisting trees in either direction, and they rounded a small pond with a statue of a mermaid perched upon a rock in the pond's center. Julius, still holding his animal senses near the surface of his human body, saw and heard the figures running through the surrounding fog, laughing and whispering to each other with the voices of children.

His senses were thrown off by the figures phasing in and out of the waking world, but he counted at least 26 of them. Julius motioned for the others to stop around the pond with the mermaid. He waited a moment, listening to the pattering of running footsteps, watching shadows leaping between rock and pathway, swinging from branches, and jumping off the heads of statues, flipping in the air to splash into the pond. Roman was patiently waiting, having eaten more Wonder than he'd been consuming lately, while Edith and Mars were both tense and *en guard*.

"I am Julius, Bes, and we are The Agents Of. We seek an audience with the King."

Whispers erupted around them, louder than before:

"*An audience with the King!*"

"*Get the King!*"

"*Tell the King it's the Agents!*"

"*I didn't know Bes was alive again.*"

"*What year is it, anyway?*"

"*Get the King!*"

Waves of thick fog wafted through the trees and over the statue of the mermaid, and when they subsided there was a girl sitting on the rock, leaning back against the mermaid's shoulder. She wore a red vest, bowler hat, and black pants, twirling a silver-tipped cane between the fingers of one hand.

"Hello Keaton," said Julius. "You're not King Nor, are you?"

"No." Her eyes were black orbs rimmed in heavily smeared blue makeup. "Just wanted to say hello. I met the new girls already. I approve." She smirked.

"Oh, well if *you* approve," said Julius, "I guess we'll keep them on."

"Hello, Roman." She tipped her hat.

"Good to see you," said Roman.

"I'm really glad you approve of us," said Mars. "Being that you fucking lied to our faces and wasted a *ton* of our time."

Julius turned to her. "Mars, we're getting to that."

"No, she's right," said Keaton, looking at Mars and Edith. "I'm sorry.

Time moves so fast in the waking world and a lot has happened in mere days. We didn't expect to have to explain ourselves so soon after the events of Nimble's Den."

Another rolling cloud of thick fog spilled over the pond, rendering Keaton nearly invisible, and when it subsided another girl was standing barefoot in the pond. She had olive skin and a host of brown braids down to her legs. She looked to be about nine years old, yet her green eyes were far fiercer than any child's at that age. Her clothes were torn and ragged, and she had a weathered green cape over one shoulder. A cutlass hung from one hip and a dagger in a golden, jewel-encrusted sheath hung from the other. She had tattoos like Keaton, but only covering one arm. "You seek an audience with me, old man?"

Julius raised an eyebrow. "*You're* still King Nor?"

"*You're* still leader of the Agents."

"You've lasted longer than any King I can remember."

"I don't like to lose a challenge."

Julius shrugged. "Nothing wrong with that." He motioned to the other Agents. "These are The Agents Of. You know Roman, and this is Mars and Edith. We've come regarding the calliope player. We assume he did not have to steal the Carousel's Heart, which he uses to manipulate the innocent and to kidnap those he sees fit to kidnap."

King Nor took two steps across the pond, following the ripples with her eyes. "We've lied to you once and will not do so again. We know the calliope thief." She turned to Keaton. "Would you light up my words?"

Keaton nodded and took off her bowler hat, placing it on the mermaid's head. Then she jumped into the shallow pond and shoved her cane down the back of her vest. The King looked up towards the treetops and spoke, but Keaton's hands flashed in front of the King's mouth, as if pulling invisible threads from between the King's lips, and none of the King's words could be heard.

Above the pond and the mermaid, below the treetops, a large image of the city glowed to life like a flame. It was like a large map, slowly turning in the air amidst the trees and fog.

"Holy fuck..." muttered Mars.

Julius didn't realize they were getting a show. Still, he kept his senses stretched out, aware of all The Nor in the trees and the fog, just in the off chance that this was a distraction. All The Nor stopped running and jumping about, gathering close to watch the show for themselves.

The King's words did not come from her lips, but from the glowing, turning map of the city hovering above the mermaid:

"The city of New Orleans is held together by carefully fashioned tethers of dream."

Green rings erupted around the map, circling it and connecting with one another. There were six of them in total.

Julius knew that there were nearly a hundred dream tethers, and that they were nothing like circles, but this representation was rather nice.

Then a crudely drawn figure of shadow appeared next to the map, reaching out with a grasping hand.

"A force has been attempting to sever these dream tethers in recent years. The Nor hunted down this force, finding it to be Nimble of the Two Sisters, along with Nemu, the Sleeping Assassin."

Julius' fist clenched at the mention of Nimble's name.

Fire erupted from the eyes of the shadow figure. A cluster of six green figures with swords came from above, causing the shadow figure to move away from the map and the green rings.

"The Nor fought off Nimble many times, until it seemed he'd finally given up on destroying the dream tethers."

From out of the back of the shadow figure a blue figure emerged, approaching the green figures and raising its hands as it knelt.

"A man who worked for Nimble came to The Nor. He had been broken by the atrocities he'd seen while working for Nimble, and told The Nor that Nimble had acquired a pack of Baku, the dream-eaters. Nimble meant to use these creatures to fight and hurt The Nor, in order to finally sever the dream tethers."

A cluster of six red monstrous creatures came from the bottom of the fire-eyed shadow figure.

"The man, Chans, spoke with The Nor and came up with a plan."

One of the six small green figures had a purple oval which pulsed like starlight, and they gave it to the blue figure. The yellow outline of a steamboat appeared above them, and the blue figure took the purple oval up to the steamboat.

"The Nor gave Chans the heart of the carousel. He acquired pieces of the calliope and used it to create his device, with which he disabled Nimble's forces and stole the Baku."

The blue figure went behind the fire-eyed shadow figure. Light came from the purple orb and the fire went out of the shadow's eyes. Then the blue figure backed away, the red creatures following him and vanishing. The blue figure shined purple light from the oval onto the rings and the city.

"Now Chans is amplifying the hopes and dreams of the city in order to repair the damage done to the dream tethers. He is also, on occasion, taking those who work for Nimble and letting the Baku feast upon their dark dreams, so that newer and less tainted dreams may manifest inside them."

Everything faded except for the map of the city encircled by green rings. Then that too disappeared, and Keaton stopped moving her hands in front of King Nor's mouth. The King looked at Julius and The Agents Of. "When the dream tethers have been fixed and we are certain Nimble is no longer capable of destroying them, we will restore the Carousel's Heart and return the pieces of the calliope." She looked directly at Mars. "I hope the urgency of our situation has brought you closer to forgiving our lies."

Mars shrugged. "As long as all this showy stuff isn't just more lies."

Each Nor in the fog jumped to their feet at once, the collective *STOMP* making the hair on Julius' neck and arm stand on end. King Nor bowed her head, eyeing Mars, and slowly took a couple of steps to the side.

Keaton glanced at Mars and barely shook her head.

Then the King spoke: "We are Nor, Mars. We drink and breath the lies of the city every night, distilled in the subconscious of those who inhabit it. Still, your words sound a little like a challenge."

"My colleague does not wish to challenge you," said Julius.

King Nor stopped walking. "Alright."

"*I can speak for myself*," said Mars, stepping to the edge of the fountain. "I am not challenging you, King Nor. But I am one of The Agents Of and I take my job seriously, as I know you take yours. You've lied and *wasted our time*. Time we could have spent helping others in the city rather than tracking down *Chans* just to find out that he's working with you."

King Nor nodded. "I do not wish to waste any more of your time."

"How long have you known?" asked Julius. "About Nimble attacking the dream tethers..."

"Time is not something we Nor can hold," she said. "More than ten years, less than twenty."

"Why is Nimble destroying them?" asked Mars.

The King shrugged, then paced back and forth in the shallow pond. "Julius and Roman know Nimble better than I do. If I had to guess, it would be so that the waking world would fall to pieces, creating chaos throughout the entire city."

"Sounds like Nimble," said Julius, turning to Roman. "How long has Nemu been in New Orleans? Twelve years? Fifteen?"

"That we know of."

"If this project is important to Nimble, perhaps he brought in Nemu specifically to *take down* the dream tethers. She's asleep and we don't know what she's capable of in regards to dreams."

Roman placed his hands behind his back. "The only things we *do* know about Nemu is that her eyes are closed, and that she's even-tempered, highly skilled, and physically dangerous."

"So, nothing at all," said Mars. "Hey, I've got another question: When Chans kidnaps Nimble's people, does he really only feed their dreams to the Baku? He doesn't do anything else to them?"

"He's quite adamant that nothing else be done to them," said the King. "Chans really believes that taking their corrupt dreams away will change them for the better. He drops them off at the edge of the city when he's done with them. He's far kinder than the Nor would be."

There was a moment of silence, then Edith spoke up:

"Where are the Baku?"

"Chans keeps them in the swamps out east," said the King. "In Bayou Sauvage[33]."

"Where is Chans?" asked Julius.

"I imagine he's with the Baku, hiding from Nimble," said the King. "He meets with us here. He uses a Baku to travel, since they can travel in and out of the waking world. He is very cautious not to let the Baku near us. Since The Nor are made mostly of dreams, the Baku would not merely eat part of our minds—they would eat our essence, our very selves."

Julius nodded to her. "From this point on, The Agents Of will help you. We'll protect Chans while he's repairing the dream tethers, and we'll search for Nimble and Nemu. But you have to let us know everything. We want to know when and where Chans will strike next so that we can keep him safe from Nimble's forces. We want this resolved as soon as possible so the calliope can be put back in place. And so the people of New Orleans can live according to their own personal relationship to their dreams, rather than being manipulated by some third party."

King Nor nodded to him. "The Nor have no problem with that. We will see Chans tomorrow, tell him of your message, and let you know his plans very soon."

Julius stepped into the pond with one boot and one mechanical foot, letting the water soak into his boot and sock, then reached out to the King with an open hand.

King Nor took Julius' hand in hers.

"I'm glad to see you still King," said Julius. "May our paths always align."

"I'm glad to see you still a god," said the King, smirking.

Julius turned and stepped out of the pool. "We'll be waiting for your message," he said, walking towards the statues guarding the fence, followed by Mars and Edith.

Behind him, he heard Keaton walk across the pond to Roman.

"You've really honed your abilities," said Roman. "Very impressive."

---

[33] Bayou Sauvage National Wildlife Refuge is a large region of swamps inside the city limits of New Orleans. At 23,000 acres, it is the largest urban wildlife refuge in the United States. There are a couple of "ghost exits" from the freeway, which seemingly lead nowhere as it passes by the swamps, but it is well known that more than just ghosts use these exits.

"Thanks," said Keaton. "You've found yourself some real groovy Agents."

"I think so," said Roman. "I'm glad you're well."

Then he followed the other three Agents out through the fence, between the two statues, and into the parking lot.

File 40 :: [Edith Downs]

Across the city later that morning, dawn had not yet peaked its head above the treetops of Audubon Park. The trees reached up with twisted arms like Sufi mystics locked in a dance so dreadfully slow it takes centuries to perform. Wole had wanted to go to City Park, but Edith needed to get as far away from work as possible for the night. High up in one of the massive trees the two sat, Wole straddling a large tree branch with his back against the trunk, Edith facing away from him and leaning back into his chest, his arms wrapped around her from behind. They wore nothing but a blanket lazily draped around their shoulders.

Edith held his arm against her chest as she looked out at the lightening sky, watching the top of a massive cargo ship drift above treetops and below purple clouds. She gripped his arm with both hands, feeling the heat of his chest glowing against her back, and kissed the skin of his arm. It tasted of dirt and centuries and leaves.

"Wole..." she said softly, not wanting to disturb the songs of insects all around them. She'd seen enough sunrises with Wole to know that even more insects and birds would awaken as the sky shifted from purple to blue to orange. "You know when we met, and I said I didn't know my purpose? You said something like, 'Stop doing anything, and whatever it is you're still doing, that's your purpose.'"

"Yes, I remember." His fingers slid up and down her shoulder.

"An incident happened while I was working. I was at a festival where I was affected by the calliope player's device, and I *saw*... I *saw* who I'm becoming. Who I *want* to become."

"Sounds like a gift."

She smiled. "It *feels* like a gift. Like my life until now was a road leading me to this place, this place of knowing what I want to do. With you in my life, and with this new knowledge of myself, I'm... just so fucking happy."

She felt him kiss the back of her head, felt his breath press down on her hair. "I'm happy for you, and happy with you."

Edith pressed her cheek into his arm, inhaling him.

"Since we are in each other's lives," said Wole, "maybe I should... you know... be privy to what you're becoming."

She chuckled. "Oh, I guess so. I mean, if knowing me is something you're into."

"It's a hobby I've been considering."

Now Edith let out a laugh, covering her mouth. "How exactly are you so funny when you haven't talked to anyone for centuries?"

"You remind me of who I am, in a way. Parts of myself I'd forgotten. Some of those parts I'd buried long before I started winding up the cicadas."

"You mean when you were... before you were free?" He'd told her about being a slave, right after the long scars up and down his back had told her the same thing.

She felt him nod, his cheek against her ear. "Back then, escaped slaves were sometimes appointed jobs of working as an aspect of the city so they could stay hidden from those looking for them. Sometimes those jobs were given to current slaves, letting them vanish into a different kind of life." His fingertips drifted up the curve of her shoulder, then up the side of her neck. "Taking care of the cicadas reminded me of who I really was, who I am inside—the person others tried to force out of me. And this life in the trees has made me very happy. But knowing you, Edith, you've reminded me of who I am around people, not just who I am when I'm alone."

She turned her head and their lips met, all curve and heat, all salty tear and red wine. When they pulled away, Edith pushed her face into his shoulder.

"You were going to tell me what you saw," said Wole.

She nodded against him. "I saw myself in a castle, a castle full of discarded memory items I was protecting. The castle was in New Orleans, and it was so well-guarded that no one could ever hope to get in. They were safe, and I was their protector."

"Sounds like you need a castle."

"I, uh… I have one."

"You have a castle?"

She nodded. "The mems brought me to a place. It's the first public library in the city, on the traffic circle in the CBD. All columns and windows and stone."

"I remember that building, but how is it your castle? It was torn down a long time ago."

"The memory of it still sits there. I walked in. I walked into the door, into the memory itself. The building spoke to me—the entity of the place, I suppose, though I don't know if it has a body or physical form. It said I could use the building in any way I wanted. So I've started storing memory items inside."

"You have your castle."

Edith smiled. "I have my castle."

"So you'll record the memories of those items?"

"Yes. I'll keep the items safe, and I'll record their memories and find a way to share them with the city."

Wole's arms tightened around her. "I love you, Edith Downs. And I love what you're becoming."

She wrapped herself tighter around his arm, closing her eyes to the sunrise before her, letting the light of the igniting clouds burn soft flowers of orange and purple into the screen of her eyelids.

They were silent, speaking only through the rise and fall of breath, the brush of skin on skin. He held her there near the edge of the world. He held her there on the precipice of what she was to become.

Wandering the stone hallways of the underground headquarters, the gas lamps lighting up as she walked, Edith found Mars in the main lab.

Yesterday's endeavors had exhausted Edith—the stakeout at Crescent Fest, the night with the Nor at Storyland, and being up all night with Wole. Yet, at the same time, she felt such freedom in knowing she no longer had to stake places out every day. Soon they'd know exactly where to go and when. Sure, the whole situation was still strange and had her on edge, but compared to the last couple of weeks. She felt relieved.

"Edith! Come here! This is important-ish!"

Mars was standing near Dust-o-bot 5000, which climbed vertically up a wall with its metal crab legs, all of the cleaning appendages on its underside buzzing against the wall as it dusted, vacuumed, and polished the stones.

"It's working faster," said Edith. "And it's holding onto the wall really well."

"Yeah, but that's not what's important-ish. Watch!" She pushed a small button on the top of it and it stopped. It let out a *beep*, then there was another *beep* from across the room. Dust-o-bot 5000 started walking horizontally across the wall. "This is what it'll do when it's full."

It let out another *beep*, and Edith realized that the second *beep* that answered it came from a small circular device attached to the trash can, which was against the same wall a ways away. The little machine walked on its crab legs until it was over the trash can, then opened up and emptied all the dust and dirt into the trash can.

Edith laughed. "That's both adorable and wonderful."

"I thought so too."

"It's hard to imagine this place without decades of dust over the walls."

Mars looked up at the clock on the wall. "Crap. It's definitely not ten at night or ten in the morning, so that thing's out of batteries. Do you know what time it is?"

"Around two in the afternoon," said Edith.

Mars rubbed her eyes. "Sometimes I'm down here so long I totally lose track of the time. I'm often totally surprised when the ramp comes down and it's day or night—I'm usually expecting the opposite." She got up and stretched. "I could use some sunlight. Want to wander around with me and pick up some double A batteries?"

"Sure, I was actually wondering if I could borrow you for an hour or so to help me move some things."

Mars shrugged. "Sounds like the break I need."

*   *   *

Edith drove her car through the Garden District, down Saint Charles towards the CBD, the streetcars slowly squealing in each direction down the grassy neutral ground in the center of the large street. She drove by mansions, fast food restaurants, and office supply stores. The windows were down, and the car was packed full of stuff—Mars had helped Edith pack the back seats and the trunk with memory items from her house. The trunk itself was open with elastic cords keeping the contents from spilling out onto the street as the car bounced from all the potholes.

"How come you didn't tell us the mems were *bringing* you stuff?" asked Mars. "I'm sure Roman would have come up with some idea to help."

Edith shrugged. "It didn't seem like a big deal, especially with Chans and the giant monsters running around. And I really took Roman's advice to heart about keeping my work life and my home life separate. I've been compartmentalizing a bit, and I think it's been helping me stay productive—separating work, physical training, and expanding my web of mems across the city."

"Gods, I feel lazy when you put it like that. I haven't done much except work. Well, I guess I've just been doing my own *projects* at work, like Dust-o-Bot 5000 and cleaning up old devices that haven't been used for decades, trying to figure out what they do. That's all fun for me."

Wind rushed through the open windows, batting about Edith's hair. She kept pushing it out of her eyes to no avail. Mars' hair was fine since the dreads were heavier and held back by her VR Goggles. Mars wore a ripped-up tank top with a manga character Edith didn't recognize, along with a pair of long shorts made from a pair of cut-up cargo pants. She sat cross-legged on the seat, the space underneath taken up by two boxes of memory items.

Edith herself wore a pair of blue jeans, sneakers, and a green blouse.

Her hair had been pulled back into a ponytail, but the wind decided it should be otherwise.

"So we're going to a storage place?" asked Mars.

"Something like that."

They passed under the overpass of the Crescent City Connection and into the CBD with its old warehouse buildings, most of which were converted into businesses or apartments, and made their way completely around the traffic circle, past the old folks' home, hotel, and gas station. Edith slowed down as she merged back onto St. Charles Street, then pulled her car up onto the wide sidewalk in front of the business building.

"Um, you're the driver, and I'm not," said Mars, "but I don't know if we're supposed to park here."

Edith opened the glove box and pulled out a small dome with a dial on it. "Roman gave me this thing for parking. It infuses the car with Wonder so that no one will notice the car for a couple of hours. They'll walk around the car, but not consciously think about it. I call it the Parking Pass."

"Well damn, that's cool."

Edith got out of the car, wound up the dome and stuck it to the car's roof.

Mars got out and looked around. "So... where exactly are we taking this stuff?"

"It's a surprise. Grab a box and come with me."

Grabbing the two boxes from the front seat, they walked up the stairs to the courtyard area next to the office building. Edith looked at the memory of the old public library, which was merely an outline of blue light showing all of the columns, stairs, and tall, arched windows. "I don't actually know if or how this is going to work." She stood at the bottom of the memory-steps, which led up between massive columns to the big, wooden memory-door, behind which was the wall of the business building that was there in real life.

"Well, I'm intrigued," said Mars.

Edith walked up the steps and up to the door.

"Ok, now I'm even more intrigued." To Mars, it must have merely looked like Edith was standing a couple of feet off the ground, held up by nothing at all.

Edith shifted the box onto her hip, placing her hand on the door. "I want to bring someone in. Can you help me with that?" She was speaking to the library itself.

The door pulsed with blue light under her hand. Maybe that was a yes?

She pushed open the door, then stepped inside, looking back at Mars. "There are steps up to this door. Try to walk up them, just step very carefully. If that doesn't work, I can try something else."

Mars shrugged. "Do you think anything is going to seem *weird* to us ever again?" Her eyes widened as her boot stopped on the invisible stair, and she stepped up onto it. She felt around for the second stair with her other boot, then the third, moving her way up.

"Don't veer to the side," said Edith. There are two big columns to either side of you."

"If you say so."

Mars followed her into the small entry room. "What the fuck?" When they stepped into the massive room of the library itself, Mars nearly dropped the box she held, then put it on a wooden table next to her. "Where the hell are we?" Her eyes and mouth were wide as she looked around.

Edith smiled and set her own box down. "We're inside the memory of a building that used to be here. The first New Orleans Public Library. The mems brought me here, and the building told me I can store the memory items inside."

"Holy crap!" said Mars, walking around. She looked up at the arched ceilings, the huge windows, the tables, and wooden shelves—most of them empty except for the ones now occupied by memory items.

"This is where I'm going to keep the memories safe," said Edith. "At least the ones which have been forgotten or discarded. I have so much room that I was thinking of keeping extra copies of the Agents' memory files here too, if Roman likes the idea."

Mars walked up to some shelves, running her fingers over them. "It feels real, like wood. This is *nuts*." She walked over and opened a metal file cabinet, which was empty. "So you're actually becoming some sort of memory librarian. Oooh, maybe we can call you a *memorian*. That sounds cool."

Edith tilted her head, saying the word to herself. "*Memorian*."

"Oh wait, I think that's actually a word already," said Mars. "Like, with a meaning that's most definitely *not* 'memory librarian.'"

Edith shrugged. "I like it. Maybe I'll just steal it."

"*Memorian, Protector of the Memories of New Orleans* does sound pretty badass."

Edith laughed. "Well, as long as I sound badass, that's what's really important."

"Obviously."

"Well, shall we bring in all that stuff?"

Mars turned to Edith, dropped to one knee, and bowed her head, speaking in a low, serious voice: "As you wish, Memorian."

Edith burst out laughing. "Oh, shut up!"

File 42 :: [Mars]

The gray buildings of the Convention Center moved in and out of Mars' reflection as she gazed out the streetcar's window. The streetcar was speeding along the Riverfront streetcar line, which ran beside the river along the French Quarter and into the CBD, passing Spanish Plaza and squeezing between dock warehouses and the Convention Center. The nighttime world outside should have promised adventure and mystery, but all she felt was annoyance.

She glanced towards the front of the Magic Streetcar as they came to the end of the Riverfront Line[34]. Henri pulled a lever and the barricade at the end of the track descended into the cement as more tracks beyond rose out of the cement as if it were water. The streetcar changed to the new tracks with a jarring *bud-ump* and the streetcar hummed to life with auxiliary power, since there were no longer power cables above them.

Soon the Magic Streetcar slowed and came to a stop just before the river intersected with the Crescent City Connection—the massive dual bridge connecting the East Bank of the city to the West Bank. Mars stood up from the wooden bench, slung her bag over her shoulder, and walked towards the front of the streetcar with Roman already ahead of her.

"Y'all be careful now," said Henri, rubbing his gray beard and smiling.

"Now would that be any fun?" asked Mars.

"Ha! Be careful you have enough fun, that's what I'll always mean, Mars. No matter what comes out of this fool's mouth."

She smiled. "You're the best, Henri." Mars jumped out of the streetcar, pounding her boots on the ground as she landed. Henri always

---

[34] "Magic Streetcar" is what Mars had come to call Henri's streetcar, which appeared when you flipped a special antique streetcar token into the air. Roman had given up two weeks earlier attempting to explain that absolutely no magic was involved with the streetcar, since Mars insisted on the new name.

had a way of making her feel a little better.

He laughed and closed the door, and through the windows she watched him get up and make his way towards the back of the streetcar where there was another driver's seat and set of controls—this was so when the streetcar came to the end of the line, the back of the car would become the front and it would change direction. Henri pulled the back of all the wooden benches as he walked, sliding them from one side to the other so anyone sitting would be facing the new direction.

Mars gazed up at the twin bridges with their thick cement columns holding them up over a hundred feet in the air, the roar of cars sounding like roaring wind which didn't match the wind hitting her face from the river. The lights of the bridges glimmered in the sky, as well as in the river's reflection.

"It's this way," said Roman, leading her further under the dual bridges. There was nothing but river on one side with rows of columns leading out to the West Bank, the bridges high above, and small buildings on the other side.

Mars pulled the strap of her bag tighter across her shoulder and chest as she followed him. "Something's bugging me, and I can't let it go. Why didn't Julius hold The Nor accountable last night?"

"There's not much he can do. The Nor are powerful, and they don't see the world the same way we do. They're so far removed from the waking world, they can't help it."

"So if The Nor came to us for help, and we lied to them and made them waste weeks of time, they wouldn't be pissed off?"

"I suppose it depends."

"Oh, I bet they'd be pissed off."

"Perhaps. As for Julius' actions, I can't speak for him, but I can make logical assumptions about his thoughts. In this situation I would guess that finding out a *potential threat* is probably *not a threat* has given him a sense of relief which has outweighed the annoyance he would have had at wasting time. Coupled with the fact that there's not much we can do to reprimand The Nor. Though they are essential for the safety of the waking world, they definitely have their own logic system."

"Like cats and dogs."

"How so?"

"Oh, you have to train cats and dogs differently because of how their minds and memories work. They're very different creatures."

"Yes, like that, I suppose."

"I guess that makes sense." Mars wasn't getting the conversation she needed from him. She did her best to bury her emotions. She'd just have to rant to Edith about the whole endeavor later. She looked around as they passed underneath the bridge. "So where's this Bridge Market at?"

"I want to show you something first." Roman gestured ahead of them, towards a three-story office building which overlooked the river and the underside of the bridges. Beyond a pair of hanging bench swings stood a tall, weathered green statue. Mars' breath caught in her throat—the statue was of a Riverwalker, reaching towards the sky with her webbed hands, with another Riverwalker curled up at the lady's feet. They didn't look *exactly* like any Riverwalkers she'd seen, but they were close.

Mars ran up to the statue, touching it and looking up at its majesty. "How long has this been here?"

"A while."

Circling it, she saw a third figure molded out of the metal: that of a young boy, with no evidence that he was anything other than human. "Why aren't there any males? And why is the human part of them black?"

Roman walked a slow gait around the statue. "The males of the species are not called Riverwalkers; they are called Mangrove, and look very different from their female counterparts. They rarely come near cities or towns, tending to stay in the swamps, and do not particularly like humans."

"Do they have anything to do with Swampwalkers?"

"That is another name for them. Why?"

"F told me one of the last times he died had to do with Swampwalkers."

"As I said, they don't particularly like humans."

"Good to know."

"As for their skin color, the Riverwalkers were known to take in and protect slaves who escaped into the swamps, fleeing the city and plantations. There were even a couple of small communities where Riverwalkers, Mangrove, and escaped slaves would live together. Of course, some fell in love, as people and creatures tend to do, thus the Riverwalkers which you've seen have their DNA and features mixed with those of humans."

Mars looked up at the towering Riverwalker. There were long, cape-like fins running down the length of her reaching arms. "Hoooooooly crap. As if I needed another reason to think they were badass. Did they call it the Underwater Railroad?"

"Not that I'm aware of," said Roman, completely missing her joke. "I'm sure Elsh would answer any questions you have the next time you see her. We should head to the market now, though—there are only a couple hours before it closes."

Roman walked towards the river, underneath the giant bridges, and Mars hurried after. Between the massive bridges, far out over the river, Mars swore she saw the glimmer of lights hanging in the air between the masses of concrete and metal. Roman walked up to the rail and looked down over the edge. "Pardon me, sir, do you think we could get a ride to the market?"

Mars stepped up beside him and peered over. There was a wooden raft, ten-foot-square, with a four-foot-high rail around its edges. Sitting on a stool in one corner was a small person, gray-skinned with giant brown eyebrows.

The man looked up from some kind of device he was tinkering with. "Oh, yes, yes." There were thick straps wrapped oddly around his torso, connected to a big furry backpack strapped to his back. He dropped the device into a small bag next to his feet and hopped off the stool. He must have been three feet tall, and there were a couple of stepping stools scattered about the raft.

Roman climbed up the metal rail, swung a leg over, and descended onto the wooden raft, with Mars following his lead. The raft was fifteen feet above the water and swayed in the air with their movement, but Mars couldn't tell how the raft was suspended, only that its wooden rail was tied to the metal rail of the walkway with a piece of rope. She saw pulleys and gears along the sides of the floating raft, yet there weren't any ropes threaded through them.

The strange man was a species she'd never seen before. He picked up a thermos and took a long drink, then closed it and put it in the bag next to his stool. He untied the small piece of rope tying the rails together and tossed it into the bag. The raft merely floated in the air like a rowboat untied from a dock. The man yawned, reached back, and scratched the top of the furry backpack, at which point the thick straps around his torso came alive and began stretching into the air around him.

That's when Mars realized they weren't straps at all, but *limbs*. She quickly backed into the wooden rail, causing the whole raft to sway in mid-air as she looked to Roman to see if she was supposed to react— maybe run or scream or punch the little guy. Roman was hardly even looking at the small man, so she just watched. The man stepped onto one of the stepping stools and six of the limbs reached out over the railing and began tugging and pulling at invisible rope. The raft jerked and shifted before lifting into the air.

As the raft moved, the lights of the bridge reflected across the three large black orbs on top of his "backpack", which were actually *eyes*, because the thing on his back was nothing other than a giant brown recluse spider[35]. It was nearly as big as the small man's torso, with two of its limbs keeping it latched onto him as the other six worked about with webbing

---

[35]   One of the most dangerous spiders in North America, the Brown Recluse Spider is native to Louisiana. It has *necrotic venom* which prematurely kills cells inside living tissue. They tend to prefer whiskey and rum to vodka, and should only be kissed if you're *really* sure it likes you.

which she could now see as it gleamed silver in the light, fading in and out of visibility.

Mars' hands latched onto the rail at her back as her stomach dropped like she was being pulled up the beginning track of a rollercoaster. The raft floated out and up over the dark river, swaying and suspended by spider silk she could only sometimes see, ascending higher as it brought them towards the center of the river.

The man looked back from the front of the raft. "You like coffee?"

She saw Roman consider the question. "On occasion. Though Mars here is much more the coffee connoisseur."

The man nodded and looked back at her, over the hump of the spider's head. "Ah, me too! You remember before Katrina, and just afterward, there were barely any good coffee shops to be found! Now there are so many choices! So many flavors of fine, well-roasted beans!"

Yeah, Mars tried to say, her voice being gobbled up by the wind which churned to life around them. She swallowed and raised her voice: "Yeah, that's very true! Seems there's a new coffee shop opening every week!"

The man gestured grandly as he spoke, somehow not bumping into the spider's limbs which pulled them along their path. "Before, you had your Z'otz, your Cafe Envie, and your Kauldi's. Now you've got your High Volt, your Satsuma. You've got your Croissant Cité, your Bittersweet Confections!"

"Your Who Dat Cafe," she added.

The man laughed. "Yes-yes! We do not deserve this plethora of riches! But I tell you what, I'll take those riches, and I'll drink 'em, that's for damned sure!"

Before Mars knew it, she was laughing—not merely from the pure joy of the man's appreciation of coffee, but from the strangeness of the whole situation.

"What's your name, friend?" she asked.

"Truss," he called back.

The raft floated between the first columns of the two bridges. Passing underneath the bridges ahead of them was a mammoth cargo ship, looking like an entire town floating quietly down the river. High above it, near the center of the river and floating *between* the two bridges, she saw a plethora of tiny lights and structures she'd never seen before. It looked to be an upside-down *island* of sorts, suspended *between* the bridges.

"Alright!" said Truss. "This is where we do what you ground-dwellers call *the flippy part*."

Mars' hands instinctively tightened on the rail. "The... what?"

The spider on Truss' back began pulling and heaving threads as Truss himself reached over the front railing and turned a large crank. The whole raft started tipping to one side and Mars screamed, "*What the fuck!*" As the raft tilted, she looked down and saw all of the tiny waves of the vast, dark river far below. She wrapped both arms around the wooden railing as her stomach flipped along with the entire raft and she slid down onto her butt. Even though the raft continued turning, her boots and butt somehow stayed on the wooden floor rather than being pulled into the air between her and the Mississippi so far below.

Completely upside-down now, the raft stopped turning. They passed over the cargo ship, which was moving silently above their heads, and she looked down (*or up?*) at the hundreds of different colored metal cargo containers. Vertigo mixed her stomach up like gumbo and she closed her eyes, taking several deep breaths. When she opened them, Roman was still standing near the center of the raft, unphased and not even near one of the rails. Part of Mars wondered: if she did get sick, would the vomit fall towards the river or out into the sky? She felt like gravity was pulling her up and down at the same time.

They "lowered" towards the underside of one of the bridges as the cargo ship finished passing. Mars watched what was going on through squinted eyes, her nearly-closed eyelids seeming to shield her stomach from the reality around her to which it was so opposed.

Then her eyes clenched shut as the raft bumped into the underside of the bridge, and Truss began tying them off to it. Mars swallowed and used the rail to push herself slowly to her feet. Every time someone on the raft moved, the whole thing would sway, and her stomach would do a little dance.

"First time's always the roughest," said Truss. The spider's legs wrapped back around his torso, the spider itself nuzzling its head in between his tiny shoulder blades like a cat or dog getting ready for a nap. "Some people say it helps if you don't look up or down."

Roman helped Mars get over the wooden railing and onto a massive beam running across the underside of the bridge. She sat down on the beam, took a bottle of water from her bag, and splashed some of it on her face before taking a long drink. Even the water seemed uncertain of which way to fall, some of it falling down to soak into her pants, some falling up towards the river. The bridge constantly rumbled with all of the cars and big trucks speeding down it.

Roman and Truss talked about coffee and the weather for a few minutes as Mars waited for her stomach to settle. Finally, she could look up, *up* at the black waves of the Mississippi so far above, the black waves reflecting lights from both sides of the city linked by the bridges. Slowly she lowered her eyes to look at the French Quarter, all upside-down with the docked steamboats hanging like colorful drops from the black water, the spires of the Saint Louis Cathedral piercing down into the dark sky.

Mars nodded. "Ok, ok, I got this." She lightly smacked her face twice, slid the bottle of water back into her bag, and carefully got to her feet. She had to stand there a second, wobbling a little as her body and mind collaborated over the fact that gravity was pulling them towards the sky rather than the center of the Earth.

She looked up at Roman and Truss. "I'm good to go."

Then she turned and saw it suspended ahead of them, between the two bridges and doused in tiny light bulbs: The Bridge Market.

The market was a giant, floating cluster of folding tables and big colorful tents, with tiny strings of lights suspended in the air above the booths and walkways from poles rising sporadically from the plank floor.

The whole place writhed with movement and life, and now that she knew what to listen for, Mars could hear the bustling banter of the market just underneath the roar of the wind and the traffic rumbling under her boots.

The floor of the market consisted entirely of wooden planks of various sizes, the planks themselves just floating there with nothing but endless black sky below them, probably suspended by spider silk. There were long planks scattered along the empty space between the bridge and the market, which seemed to be the only way across. These planks swayed with the wind.

"Don't worry, kid," said Truss. He was sitting on the wooden rail of the raft, the spider silently hugging him from behind with its eight arms. His gray face reminded her of the top of a witch's cauldron, all bubbly and murky and thick. But his brown eyes were kind, and he had the silly grin of an old man who'd just made a joke which was more stupid than funny. "This all becomes second nature."

Mars nodded. "Good to know."

Then the spider looked up over Truss' shoulder, with its three large black orb-eyes, and nodded in agreement.

Mars followed Roman toward the market. "So how often do you come up here?"

"Quite often. It's invaluable for what we do for several reasons— supplies, information, fuel for devices. I cannot show you all of it today, but I will soon. Then you can come up here by yourself, and perhaps show Edith."

Near the market's outskirts Mars saw other small, gray-skinned people, each one with an enormous spider latched onto their back.

"*Why*? Why the spiders on their backs?"

"It's part of their culture. They're called Bridgers—definitely people you should befriend. They maintain the Crescent City Connection and other bridges and structures throughout the city." He spun around and walked backward along the steel beam, peering into Mars' eyes as she followed behind him. "I am very interested in what you would *see* when one of them makes repairs to a structure. I wonder about the similarities and differences between what they do to structures and what you do to entities."

Mars nodded to him. "As long as I don't have to put a spider on my back."

Roman spun around and stepped right off the bridge and onto a swaying plank which led towards several other swaying planks, eventually leading to the edge of the Bridge Market. He kept walking further out into the open air, his hair and coat being batted about by the wind.

Mars stared down at the moving plank, beyond which was nothing but the endless black sky, and her stomach sank. The plank itself was about a foot wide, with no rails. In theory, there was spider silk holding it in place which might catch her if she fell, but she had no idea where those threads would be or if they would actually stick to her.

"*What if I fall?*" she called after him. She *hated* being scared in front of Roman.

He turned to her, standing halfway down a series of swaying wooden planks. There were six of those planks all together, each swaying to a different rhythm. "It's simple. If you fall, you fall."

Mars had one boot tentatively on the first swaying board. "Yeah, thanks! I really wasn't sure, but you've cured my ignorance with your *fucking logic*. What I mean is, would I fall towards the sky or towards the river?" She didn't know whether to look down or up at her possible demise.

As she looked both up and down (or down and up?), her breath came short and quick, her fists clenching up as her vision blurred. Nothing in her wanted to walk out over that expanse of upside-down sky. She pressed one hand to her beating heart, trying to force her lungs to suck in more air, trying to calm herself.

Mars realized it was all because of Roman—or, rather, it was all because of how she *felt* about him. She didn't want to let him down, *couldn't* let him down, especially not on a mission. The fear swirled inside her, mixing with anger—anger at herself for needing this person's approval. She'd never needed anyone, so why did she feel she needed this man now?

"*Mars.*" His words were firm, the tendrils of Wonder in his breath reaching across that space to seep through her muscles and her mind, relaxing her anxiety. "Look at me."

She focused on his eyes, on his face, across that stretch of endless space. His mouth curved into a grin. He spoke slowly, as if he were winking with his voice: "Be like Moses."

"What the hell are you..." Then she remembered being in Grady's pedicab months before, cars and pedestrians moving out of their way as they sped through the French Quarter. She'd told Roman that she felt like Moses, with some higher power pushing back the waters to let her through.

She didn't know anymore if she'd call it a *higher* power, but it *was* Serendipity's magic (or whatever) helping out an Agent on a mission. She lowered her head down and felt the thread which had permeated her then, months ago. She let the anger inside her melt into a quiet determination, planting her foot on the wooden beam and then stepping forward with her other foot. The wind churned up loud around her, pulling wildly at her dreadlocks and her leather jacket.

One step after the next, she walked towards Roman, her eyes on him as the planks swayed back and forth underneath her. She could almost *feel* Serendipity sitting on some balcony in the city, drinking a glass of wine with her legs crossed, absent-mindedly tugging tiny strings with her free hand, which pulled the planks underneath Mars' boots just at the right millisecond.

Roman walked backward towards the market, keeping his eyes on hers. He didn't seem to question whether there would be a plank underneath his heel when he stepped back.

Each step felt like stepping off the roof of a building during an earthquake, bringing back memories of her late teen years in San Francisco, of buildings swaying like jello when the earth shook. With every step, her confidence grew.

The floating market floor was swaying so much less than the planks that when her boot touched down on it, she lost her balance and fell right into Roman's chest. He laughed and put an arm around her, holding her up. His body, as always, felt weirdly hard and smooth, like porcelain.

She stepped back and wiped sweat from her brow.

"*Hey!*" came a voice from behind Roman. "*Hey, what are you thinking? Are you crazy?!*"

They both looked at the short, gray-skinned Bridger making his way along the outskirts of the market. He had more hair on his head than Truss, sticking up in all sorts of directions. In one hand he held a half-eaten sandwich, crumbs of said sandwich falling from his chin as he yelled at them. The giant brown spider clinging to his back extended two legs above him like bent TV antennae.

"Don't climb around on those! This is where we store our backup wood. I keep saying we should put signs up, that someone's gonna fall one day!" He recognized Roman and slowed his approach.

"We're very sorry to have disturbed your lunch break," said Roman.

Mars stood up straighter. "We *are* professionals, if that makes it any better. We do more dangerous stuff than this all the time."

"Well, I suppose that's true. Just, uh, do us a favor and do those dangerous things out where Bridgers won't be blamed for your *deaths*. We're just trying to make a living out here, is that too much to ask?"

Roman nodded. "We apologize."

The Bridger sighed and waved them on towards the market, turning to walk back to wherever he'd been eating—though the spider on his back turned to glare at them with its three orb-eyes, giving Mars the distinct feeling of being judged as a *miscreant*.

"Why exactly was he mad at us? How were we supposed to get out here?"

They rounded the back walls of a couple of tents along the curving outer edge of the market and saw where the market got closer to the bridge, a short and sturdy drawbridge connecting the steel bridge to the gently swaying market. The drawbridge had just descended and several people and creatures were entering and exiting the market, holding onto the drawbridge's railing of thick rope.

"That's the actual entrance," said Roman. "I like to take the beams and avoid the crowd."

Mars' teeth clenched together. "Yeah. Nevermind."

"I could apologize," said Roman.

"That is not the first sentence of an apology."

"You will find that the very awareness of Serendipity's hand in the world around you will tip the scales for you, occasionally making the difference between succeeding or failing, life or death."

Her teeth and fists clenched in solidarity. "That is not the second sentence of an apology."

"Mars, are you angry?"

She looked up at Roman. "Don't worry yourself about it, Logic Man. We've got work to do." She stalked past him and into a break between the tents.

File 43 :: [Mars]

Aisle after aisle of tents and booths, all filled with humans and various creatures selling, buying, and bartering. It reminded Mars of both The French Market along the river and the art markets which set up off Frenchmen Street at night. Several of the stalls were run by Bridgers, all squat and gray with spiders clinging to their backs. Out of the corner of her eyes, she saw Collectors walking by. There were Riverwalkers, ghosts, and several creatures she didn't know the names of yet.

"Who's this guy we're looking for?" she asked. "Bill? Bob?"

"His name is Ben. His tent is up ahead, the red and gray one on the right."

The tent spanned about thirty feet across and thirty feet deep, its open front lined with tables piled with everything from engine parts to jars full of gods-know-what to tiny devices which looked oddly like ones the Agents used, with a break between the tables for entering the tent, which had even more to offer inside. A man in his sixties with dark sunglasses, a tank top, and a leather vest sat behind one table arguing with someone who wasn't there. His muscular arms were covered with scars and tattoos, his long, gray beard reaching down to his chest.

He pounded on the table. "*If you don't like the price, go to the damned French Market!*"

Mars looked at the space across from him out of the corner of her eye, expecting to see the blur of a Collector, but there was nothing. He wasn't actually talking to anyone.

The man raised his nose, sniffing the air and grinning. "Ha! Agents!" His voice was like a used Harley Davidson that had been through the desert more times than it remembered.

"Good evening, Ben," said Roman.

Mars leaned her head to her shoulder and sniffed the arm of her leather jacket, but only smelled leather. "What exactly do Agents smell like?"

The man smiled, looking forward yet not directly at them, which is when Mars realized he was blind. "Well, Roman's got a peculiar scent of Wonder laced with human sweat and a healthy dose of French Quarter. And he's usually the only one who comes to visit me, so I took an educated guess that you too were an Agent. Also, since there were no other Agents a few months ago, I assume you're *brand spanking new,* quite possibly his protege."

Mars raised an eyebrow. "So you're really that perceptive? You know, a minute ago you weren't talking to a Collector or anything, right? You were arguing with nothing but thin air..."

"Ha!" The old man smacked a hand on the plastic folding table, the contents rattling against each other. "You picked a good one, Roman boy! All young, pretty, and ready to conquer the world! Or save it or something..." He turned his head towards Mars, lowering his voice. "Not many at the market are good at *seeing* Collectors, so they think I'm talking to the little bastards *all* the damned time! It's kind of like writing a soap opera; I create characters who come to bargain with me, other vendors listen in, and I get all sorts of rumors started! Keeps me entertained since I can't read or watch television." His mouth curved into a large smile. "And people who frequent this market think I'm always dealing with the Collectors, so they come to my booth *first* when they're looking for something. 'Cause everyone knows those crazy-as-fuck Collectors have the best goods." He inclined his head towards Roman. "No offense to your crazy-ass family."

Roman shook his head. "Ben, this is Mars. She will be coming to you for goods and information on behalf of The Agents Of."

Ben grimaced and shook his head. "The Agents Of... God, that *stupid* name. Though I suppose it's not at the bottom of the list as far as Agency names go. And what's your name? Mars?"

"That's it," said Mars.

"The Red Planet. God of War. So you're the Rachel replacement? Start losing your mind yet?"

Mars slammed her fist into the table, the force tipping over a couple of jars. "Fuck off! You think I won't hit a blind man?"

Ben laughed. "I like her already, Roman!" He sat back in his folding chair and shrugged. "Of course, I liked Rachel too."

A heavy silence fell over the table for a moment, and Mars felt Ben drinking up that silence. Maybe it was just more entertainment for him.

Roman pulled three long, thin jars out of his coat and placed them on the table. One looked to be empty, the second was full of black liquid, and the churning contents of the last glowed green, violet, and orange with the familiar color pallet of Wonder.

Ben grabbed all three and stood up, picking up a thin metal cane from beside him. "Let's go somewhere a little more cozy." He turned towards the inside of the tent. "Shira?"

A young, dark-haired woman looked up from where she was organizing a table. "Yeah."

"Watch the shop, will you?"

"Sure thing."

He led them through the tent, past more tables of assorted junk and jars, and into a small curtained-off area in the back. The small room was lit by lamps and had large cushioned chairs whose upholstery had seen better decades.

Ben sat on one chair and they sat across from him. He unscrewed the lid of the empty-looking jar, dipped two fingers inside, then dabbed those fingers on his tongue. He smiled. "You always bring me the best shit, Roman." He set the jar aside and opened the one with the black liquid, dabbing two fingers in once more and tasting them.

Mars shivered at the site. "Do you taste *everything*?"

"Only way to know how pure something is." He bowed his head in Roman's direction. "Now do you want me to pretend I don't know why you're really here, or shall we get down to it?"

Mars looked to Roman, who was sitting back with his hands steepled in front of his face. "It's a dangerous move, Ben, using stolen Agent technology to build a device which manipulates innocent people against their will. You're very close to breaking your oath."

Ben waved a hand in front of his face. "Oh, the hell I am." Then he sat forward, licking his upper lip. "*How is it working out?* What's the radius at? How many people does it hit at once? No one tells me the fucking details."

"Wait, *what*?" said Mars. "*You* created that calliope dream device?"

Ben nodded. "Yep, ma'am. I call it *the Reverie Organ*. You see, the Carousel's Heart used to be called the Reverie Heart. And Reverie Organ has a dreamy sort of pizzazz, doesn't it?"

"He did *not* create it," said Roman. "He took a stolen device of my making and *slightly* modified it."

"Ha, you know it's genius though, using the Carousel's Heart like that!" He pointed at Roman and smiled. "*You* didn't figure it out for weeks!"

"It was an obvious solution," said Roman, "but I ruled it out. No one could *steal* the Carousel's Heart from The Nor without us being informed, and the last thing I expected was for The Nor to *give* the Carousel's Heart away. I wrote it off immediately."

Ben whistled and picked up the jar of Wonder, unscrewed it and tasted the contents. Nodding, he set the jar next to the others on a small table beside his chair. "They didn't just *give* the heart away. It's for a good cause, as I assume you know, since it's you here and not Julius ripping me in half."

Now it was Mars' turn to question: "Why did you make the device for some random guy working for Nimble?"

Ben pulled off his sunglasses, his eyes so pale they were nearly all white. He hesitated before speaking, directing his words to Roman: "*Keaton* came to me. So I knew the whole *dream tether* business was true."

Mars glanced at Roman, who merely looked contemplative.

Ben leaned towards Mars. "You've probably got a confused look on your face since Roman didn't even tell you why you were coming here or who the fuck I am. Don't be pissed at him, he's just very Roman. He can't help it."

Mars shrugged. She *was* a bit pissed at Roman, but she wasn't about to side with this weird, crazy guy. "Alright, what have you got for me, Ben?"

"Well, you know how Bes dies and then goes into some newborn boy, but he doesn't remember who he is until he's fourteen or fifteen or whatever? Well, in the last fifteen-year gap, while Julius was growing up and not knowing he was this *African god* as well as all these... well... *dead guys* in his head—in that fifteen-year gap Roman was the leader of the Agents. And I was *one* of his Agents."

Mars looked to Roman, who looked half like a computer calculating data and half like a predator waiting to see if what it stalked was indeed prey. She turned back to Ben. "When was this?"

"Oh, *ages* ago." He waved his hand in front of his face, then nodded towards Roman. "What, '75 through nearly all of the '80s? Does that sound right?" He turned to Mars, smiling. "We were *The Agents of Quantifiable Abnormalities*. Ha! Tell me that doesn't have *Roman* written all over it!"

Mars smiled despite herself. "That is pretty great."

"Ha!" Ben slapped the arm of his chair. "The damned name was so long, people would mess it up all the time! They'd call us 'Agents of Qualitative Alchemy', stuff like that! Some people just called us by a previous Agency name, not even trying to remember ours."

"He's exaggerating," said Roman.

"Nope! Totally true!"

"So the oath you two mentioned is the Agent oath?" asked Mars.

"Yes," said Roman. "Part of the oath deals with your actions should you quit being an Agent."

"*Should I quit the Agency in the future*," said Mars, quoting the oaths, "*I will never divulge secrets that would do it or the city harm.*"

Ben leaned forward with a seriousness Mars could feel in the air.

"And like I said, I'm not doing *any* of that nonsense. This guy Chans *fucked* up Nimble's operation, better than I could have hoped—better than Chans himself could have hoped, either. I would help *anyone* fuck with Nimble." He turned to Roman. "You know at least *three* of our fellow Agents' deaths were at the hands of that bastard. We just couldn't prove there was a link."

Roman nodded.

Ben pulled from under his chair a dented up red toolbox, putting it on his lap and opening it. He pulled out four bracelets made out of twisting black tubes, with a marble-sized white pearl in the center of each. "These are what you're here for, so I'll save you the trouble of asking. There are four Agents, right?"

"Yes," said Roman.

"These will cancel out the effects of the Reverie Organ." He mimicked putting one around his wrist. "The pearl has to go over a vein, and the bracelet has to be *tight*. You can wear it around the neck or maybe the ankle, but the wrist is best."

"What powers it?" asked Mars, not seeing any of the usual power sources.

Ben smiled. "That's my favorite part. The *Reverie Organ* powers it."

"That's... pretty cool," said Mars.

"So here's how the actual Reverie Organ works: The dream-stirring energies of the Reverie Heart get pumped through the pieces of the calliope, which I've tuned to specifically amplify the future desires and dreams of whoever it affects—amplifying them to such a degree that the person is incapacitated for several minutes. I even took apart one of those old calliope wagons for spare parts, attaching the whistles so that it's actually a functioning instrument. The keyboard keys open valves on different whistles, letting the energy of the Reverie Heart seep through and make noise. That's all just poetic fun, though." He held up a bracelet and pointed to one of the pearls. "Now I had Keaton and The Nor get these pearls for me from *The Moon herself*. The Moon magnifies dreams, desires, wishes, all that stuff, right? The waves of energy from the Reverie Organ hit the pearl, which amplifies the waves further, pumping those waves into the body of the person wearing the bracelet. But the bracelet *reverses* the wave, kind of like the negative of a photograph. If just the reverse wave were to hit you, it would still have the same effect, but since there are two juxtaposed waves hitting you at once, the waves cancel each other out. Well, mostly. You might have really interesting thoughts, or very lucid dreams when you fall asleep that night."

"Wow, that's brilliant," said Mars.

Ben pointed his thumb at Roman. "He thinks so too, but he's not gonna say so."

"And you're certain it will work?" asked Roman.

Ben shrugged. "That's how Chans is using the device without falling into his own future desires. He's got one strapped to himself."

Despite some of her first words to him being, *fuck off*, Ben had very quickly grown on Mars. She could see herself picking his brain about all kinds of theories, and had a feeling he would ramble for hours about his time as an Agent if given the chance. She'd have to bring Edith up here to meet him, and they'd have to convince him to let Edith copy his memories.

Roman took the bracelets and put them in the pocket of his coat, then stood up. "I do hope the next time you have information pertaining to the Agents or to the safety of the city, that you tell us."

"You know I will," said Ben. "I always do. It's just... with this guy double-crossing Nimble, I swore to secrecy. His life was in extreme danger, and still is." He laughed. "Well, more specifically, I told him I'd swear to secrecy until you or Julius came here and asked me directly."

Roman nodded. "The Reverie Organ and the bracelets are excellent work."

Ben laughed again. "Thanks, pal."

Mars got up and followed Roman towards the curtain door. "Nice meeting you, Ben."

He raised a hand. "Another time, Miss War God."

She stopped at the curtain door, turning back to him. "Radius is at least one-hundred-twenty feet if the waves aren't blocked by buildings or other structures. At Chicory Fest last Saturday, it took down around six hundred people."

Ben slapped his knee with a loud *thwack*. "*Yes!*"

"Not including me, of course," said Mars. "Your device is awesome, but it doesn't work on me."

"What? Why wouldn't it work on you?"

Mars smiled. "Hey, that'll be a good conversation starter next time I come by." Then she left.

As they made their way to the front of the tent, Ben yelled after them: "I like her, Roman!"

File 44 :: [Josephine DeBleaux]

[New Orleans, Spring of 1973]

Josephine dozed off, the early evening sun sprawled across her skin and clothes like a stretched out cat, the roaring wind whispering lullabies into her ear. Dreaming was one of the few ways she could escape the sadness which weighed her down like summer rain. No matter how crazy or dark life got, somehow her dreams were all magic and adventure—her subconscious carving out a secret haven for her to run around in, a way for her to forget the reality she yearned to escape.

Footsteps woke her, but they were the familiar tread of her brother, Gabriel. She pushed herself up into a sitting position, her body slow and achy and wanting more dream.

She was eleven years old and had been homeless with her brother for a few months. They had been doing alright, but she didn't know how they would fair in the upcoming brutal summer months, when the temperatures and humidity would skyrocket while the money of the city would run dry as tourists stayed away and locals who could afford it left town, which meant fewer handouts from people on the street.

Not that they could beg very easily—they didn't want to get picked up by the city, afraid they'd be separated or sent to one of the family members they didn't know well and who probably didn't like the two of them, anyway.

She wore a pair of shorts, sneakers, and a blue T-shirt with a rainbow across the front. Her thick hair was pulled into two braids, which nearly touched her shoulders. It had taken her the first month to teach her brother how to braid her hair, one of the few things she refused to give up about her past life.

He had it easy, shaving his head once a month and just letting it grow into a small afro before shaving it again.

"Jo, we got poboys for days!" Gabriel yelled over the roaring wind as he walked up, carrying a very full plastic bag. He wore dark shorts, a grey shirt, and sneakers.

Josephine felt a few layers of dread slip off her body. Not because he'd somehow acquired a bag full of food, but because his smile was one of the other things that, like dreams, helped her forget her worries. With all they'd been through, Gabriel managed to glow with positivity almost nonstop. No matter how dire their situation, he'd come up with reasons to look forward to the future.

She sat leaning back against a vertical steel beam, seated on a wooden platform many stories in the air, and could see New Orleans for miles upon miles in every direction. For three weeks now they'd been living at a construction site, a Goliath structure of crisscrossed steel beams bigger than any building she'd ever seen. The half-built structure they squatted in was called the Louisiana Superdome and would be used for Saints games, other giant sporting events, and concerts[36]. Josephine and Gabriel stayed there at night, sneaking past security guards after the construction workers went home for the night. They made a home out of several wooden platforms near the top of the circular outer wall of beams, before the domed roof began its long curving journey towards the higher center of the structure. Barely any of the outside walls of the Superdome had been constructed yet, so the whole thing was see-through, a mesh of spiderweb-like beams in the shape of what the Superdome would eventually become.

Gabriel dropped his bag of poboys next to their backpacks and squatted down by Josephine. "How are you, Jo?"

She forced her eyes open wider to wake herself up. The food smelled amazing. "I'm alright. I was sleeping."

Gabriel, being her twin, was eleven as well, but Josephine felt like he would be fine on his own, while she couldn't imagine being without him.

"I brought a friend," he said. "She helped me get all these sandwiches, so I said she can stay here tonight if she wants. She's like us."

Josephine looked past her brother and saw the young girl behind him. The girl looked a couple of years younger than Josephine and Gabriel, with olive skin and brown hair sticking up at different lengths as if she'd cut it by herself with a knife. She wore a brown dress of thick cloth which was hand-stitched with twine, a pair of old boots too big for her, and a drawstring bag over one shoulder.

The girl looked out at the view and nodded. "You have a good spot here."

---

[36] The Louisiana Superdome, now called the Mercedes-Benz Superdome, has a diameter of 680 feet, with the height of the dome reaching 273 feet, making it the largest fixed dome structure in the world. It is home of the New Orleans' Saints and has a capacity of over 76,000 people.

Josephine always trusted her brother's instincts, especially with people and places to hide. If he brought someone to their hideout, that person was bound to be alright. Josephine reached into the bag, shuffling through the paper-wrapped sandwiches with words scribbled on them describing what they were.

"Her name's Swallowtail," said Gabriel.

"That's pretty," said Josephine.

Swallowtail set her bag down against a beam, then sat down with her legs crossed.

Gabriel rifled through the bag with Josephine. "There's shrimp, roast beef, ham, and a bunch of others."

Josephine pulled out the ham and unwrapped it.

Gabriel looked at Swallowtail. "Which one do you want?"

"I'm not hungry yet," she said.

Gabriel shrugged, pulled out a shrimp and opened it up.

Josephine nearly melted into the sandwich, it was so good. She hadn't had fresh food for a few days—most of what they'd acquired had been stale and old.

"You should have seen it," said Gabriel between bites. "There was this bike delivery guy loading up his bike baskets outside a sandwich shop, and Swallowtail swooped down off this fence and grabbed a small bag, putting the handles in her teeth and shimmying up a balcony rail across the street before he even realized what happened. When he chased her, I snatched the bigger bag and hid it in a trash can. We just had to wait until they remade the sandwiches and he left on delivery before getting it out of the trash can."

Josephine sighed and put the sandwich down. "I don't like us stealing food."

"Neither do I," said Gabriel. "But we can get away with stealing. If we beg, we're gonna get caught. We're too young to be homeless."

Josephine closed her eyes, hugging herself tight. "I miss mom."

"Hey Jo," said Gabriel, scooting closer to her and putting a hand on her shoulder. She opened her eyes and was overwhelmed by the kindness in his eyes, something to anchor her. "I miss her too, but she's not a good person anymore. It's just you and me, but that's all we need. I'm going to find us a way out of this, ok?"

She nodded.

"Want me to tell a story? Like about the stars dancing on the clouds? Or the alligator who's looking for the rabbit in the swamps?"

Josephine sniffed and wiped a tear from her cheek, then nodded. "The alligator."

Gabriel nodded.

Josephine hated feeling so young, hated being abandoned, hated crying in front of this little girl who was even younger than she was. But Gabriel and his stories always made her feel better.

He sat back and began telling his story about the alligator detective who was searching for a missing rabbit. Josephine reached in front of his lips, pulling at his words and twisting them, making them dance in the air with melody and sound until his words were gone entirely and only music remained. There were no lyrics, only the strumming of banjo, the prancing of fiddle, and the hum of insects. Josephine didn't care that Swallowtail wouldn't be able to understand the story—she was a stranger, and turning his words into music was making Josephine happy. She watched the story she knew so well as it unfolded in her mind, the music accompanying the silent actions of the animal characters who showed up in several of Gabriel's stories.

When it was over, Gabriel laughed.

"That was *so beautiful*," said Swallowtail. "Could you do another one? Please? That made me feel so wonderful."

Josephine smiled and looked to Gabriel, who shrugged. Josephine nodded. "The pig baker who makes muffins for the stinging caterpillar."

Gabriel started his story and Josephine once again turned it into song, this time with accordion, fiddle, and washboard.

The sun began setting on the horizon, the twilight colors playing off the steel beams around them, making their edges glow. When Josephine finished with the story, she looked over at Swallowtail, who had her head bowed and her eyes closed, smiling. When the girl opened her eyes, the twilight shimmered in them like tiny candles. "Thank you."

Josephine nodded to her.

"Isn't it amazing?" asked Gabriel.

Swallowtail nodded, but Josephine shook her head, saying, "It's only amazing because they're *your* stories. Your stories are the amazing part. I just mess them up and do weird things to them."

Swallowtail looked back and forth between them as the sun was swallowed one piece at a time by the horizon. "Gabriel, you say you're going to find a way out of this. What is your goal? What are you looking for?"

Gabriel shook his head. "We don't need to talk about that. None of us need trouble sleeping tonight."

"Please, Gabriel," said Swallowtail. "I want to know."

Gabriel looked at Josephine. "I don't want us to have to run anymore. I want a place to be. I want to be safe, and not hungry. But I need Josephine, and she needs me. We can't trust adults to make the right decision with that. And they might just treat us like criminals."

"What if you could have *most* of those things? Would you give up one of them?"

"Depends on which one."

Swallowtail shifted onto her knees, looking out towards where the sun had set. "There's a place where kids like us, kids with nowhere to call home, can go. Those kids stop growing, stop aging. They step in and out of the waking world, living mostly in the worlds of dream." She looked at the two siblings. "You would not be hungry, and you would have plenty of others to call friends. You would not have to run or hide, and you would not be hunted like criminals."

Gabriel stood up, stepping between Josephine and Swallowtail. "Look, I know you're just trying to be nice, but we don't need any stupid fairytales right now. That's not the kind of help we need."

Swallowtail got to her feet, looking out towards the darkest part of the sky.

"I mean, if the fairytale helps you, that's groovy," said Gabriel. "But it's not going to keep us from being hungry."

Swallowtail suddenly sprinted down the platform, leaping through the crisscrossed steel beams and out into the open air outside the dome, over a hundred feet in the air.

Josephine screamed, getting to her feet as Gabriel ran after Swallowtail and stopped at the opening she'd jumped through. Then he backed up, tripping and falling back onto his butt. Josephine looked out of the opening to see a massive wave of fog rolling up across the buildings below, across the construction site, and up the side of the steel skeleton of the Superdome. She backed up, fog seeping through all the diamonds of space between the steel beams. The fog reached above them like a hand holding the dark silhouette of a girl, then withdrew to leave the girl perched upon the steel beams above the two siblings' heads.

Swallowtail looked down on them. "*I do not speak of fairytales*," she said firmly. "I speak of *The Nor*, which are everything I have told you. *Do you believe me?*"

Josephine nodded, and Swallowtail looked down on Gabriel, who got to his feet. "Yes. The Nor? What are The Nor?"

She jumped down, the wooden platform shaking with the smack of her boots. Looking up at the two of them, for she was younger and shorter than them, she spoke: "The thing you will give up is safety. The Nor are guardians of the barrier between the waking world and the world of dreams, and that barrier is especially fragile in this city—the job of guarding it is *very* dangerous." She reached down and picked up her drawstring bag and slung it over her shoulder.

Gabriel looked at Josephine, then back at Swallowtail. "We want to know more."

She backed up towards the fog pouring from between the steel beams behind her. "I've been in the waking world too long. I'll be back in a few days."

"What if we're not here?" asked Gabriel. "What if we can't get back into the construction site?"

Swallowtail reached into her bag, pulling out a short, curved blade and pointing it at Josephine. "The purity of Josephine's dreams is how I found you. As long as she dreams, I'll know where the two of you are."

Then the fog burst past the steel beams, covering Swallowtail until she was utterly lost in the thick mist. When the fog dispersed, she was gone, and the siblings were alone once again.

File 45 :: [Josephine DeBleaux]

[New Orleans, Spring of 1973, one week later]

Majestic oak trees loomed above, their serene branches threatening to tear down the night sky. The siblings stood in a parking lot in the midst of City Park, looking at a big colorful sign on a wrought iron black gate which read: *CHILDREN'S STORYLAND.* Josephine gripped Gabriel's hand, watching Swallowtail walk up to the gate beside the sign and pull open the iron bars as if they were nothing but a curtain.

Gabriel and Josephine had heard of Children's Storyland, but their mom had never taken them anywhere besides the parks near their house. The Superdome had become the farthest they'd been from where they grew up, and Children's Storyland was definitely farther.

They followed Swallowtail into the park, which was thick with fog, bushes, and trees. Amidst the plants and fog were fairytale creatures and characters. Snow white slept amidst a bed of foliage, the whale from Pinocchio opened its gigantic mouth, a few of the seven dwarfs stood around pontificating, and Little Miss Muffet sat on a tuffet.

Over the last few days, Swallowtail had told them about The Nor, about the life the two siblings were being offered. Josephine was hopeful but uncertain, spurred on by Gabriel's vibrant enthusiasm about joining The Nor.

They passed several more fairytale creatures, then underneath a sign reading *CAROUSEL GARDENS*, after which awaited rows of carnival-style game booths, a roller coaster, and a teacup ride, with other rides hidden amidst the thick fog. Everything was eerily quiet and blanketed by a fog denser than Josephine had ever seen in her life. Swallowtail led them to a grand, white wooden structure of windows and rails which housed a majestic looking carousel[37]. Mist rolled around the structure, splashing up against it like an ocean against a cliff.

Swallowtail turned to the two siblings. "This is where you'll take on your new names—names that bring you joy."

Neither sibling spoke, so overtaken by the surrounding scene. Then Gabriel, forever protective of Josephine, spoke up first: "Her name is Keaton. Because she's always loved watching Buster Keaton movies. Even when she's sad, he always makes her laugh."

Swallowtail unsheathed her curved knife and pointed it at Josephine. "Keaton, I am Swallowtail of The Nor. We are well met. The Nor are your friends."

The girl who was now Keaton nodded, after which Swallowtail lowered her blade and turned to Gabriel. Keaton put a hand on her brother's shoulder and spoke for him, just as he had done so many times for her: "My brother's name is *Quill*, because he is a *storyteller*, wielding stories like a sword and shield. He loves telling tales, both true and made up."

Swallowtail nodded, raising her curved knife towards him. "Quill, I am Swallowtail of The Nor. We are well met. The Nor are your friends."

Keaton squeezed his shoulder and looked into his eyes. For the first time she really, fully believed in this idea of The Nor.

Swallowtail led them up a wooden ramp and up to the windowed walls around the carousel. She opened the carousel's door and led them inside. As soon as they entered, doors on the other sides of the circular building opened and fog spilled in like slowly rolling liquid, enveloping the legs of the running horses and the base of the thick pillar of mirrored panels at the carousel's center.

Keaton shivered at seeing multiple figures in the fog, wanting to take her brother's hand but not letting herself. The figures looked like children. From out of the fog, near the central pillar of mirrors, stepped a boy. His black hair stuck up in every direction, his pale skin streaked with mud. The boy's T-shirt and shorts were tattered, his feet bare. A long sword hung from a rope tied around his waist, and next to it hung a jewel-encrusted dagger in a gold sheath, emeralds set into the metal.

His green eyes cut across their faces, and any doubt Keaton had about

---

[37] The Carousel, sometimes called the "Flying Horses", dates back to 1906, though some of the animal figurines date back to 1885. There are 56 animals altogether, with a camel, giraffe, and lion, and the rest being horses. The horses' tails are made from real horse hair. All of the figurines were hand carved and painted by Charles Looff and Charles Carmel. Charles Looff was famous for creating amusement parks and rides in the late 1800s and early 1900s. He built Coney Island's first carousel in 1876, and built California's Santa Monica Pier in 1916, originally named the Looff Pleasure Pier, along with the Looff Hippodrome on the pier which housed yet another whimsical carousel.

The Nor not aging was expelled—he felt *very* old, though he looked to be no older than her and her brother. "I am King Nor," he said, his voice far more serene than she expected. "Swallowtail has vouched for your sincerity. You may take up a horse."

Keaton followed Quill onto the platform of the carousel, amidst all of the horses and other animals frozen in half gallop, the fog now up to the siblings' waists. They climbed onto horses which were next to one another, King Nor walking in front to face them, Swallowtail behind him.

Keaton let out a tiny scream as the carousel lurched to life, her horse rising as it began moving forward, the whole carousel starting to spin. Beside her, Quill's horse was rising and falling to a different rhythm than hers.

King Nor walked to the center column where he opened one of the mirrored doors. Surrounded by the darkness inside was a large oblong stone, glowing purple. When the light of the stone fell on Keaton, memories flooded into her mind—memories of her mother. They were the better memories, and going to the movies on the weekend, eating ice cream by the fountain in the park, or walking along Lake Pontchartrain at sunset; before her mother had lost her way.

She sighed as tears fell down her face, but she was smiling. The memories felt so *good* pouring through her body, through her heart. Keaton gripped onto the pole running up through the horse she sat on. She looked over and saw Quill with his head bowed, tears falling to his chin.

"These dreams are a mere fraction of what The Nor fight for," said King Nor in his serene tone. "If you have picked your new names, speak them now, in the light of the Carousel's Heart."

"Quill."

"Keaton."

"Quill and Keaton, do you wish to join The Nor?"

Keaton nodded, and her brother said, "Yes."

"Hold out your hands and keep them held out."

They did so, and King Nor waded towards them through the fog, pulling out his gold and emerald dagger from its sheath at his hip. The blade itself was made of gold, yet looked pale in the purple light of the Carousel's Heart. First to Quill and then to Keaton, he sliced open the palm of their hands. Keaton's eyes shut tight as pain flew down her arm like lightning, but she kept her hand out. When she opened her eyes, she saw the bright red blood from her and Quill's palms floating up into the air rather than spilling to the floor or onto the horses.

King Nor spoke once more: "Repeat after me these oaths, and in so doing you will bind yourself to The Nor, and The Nor to you." As the King spoke, Keaton and Quill repeated his words:

- I take one step out of the waking world, but only to protect it—I will use my connection to dream to defend the sanctity of the city herself.
- I take one step into the sleeping world, but I will not stray—I will guard the border between the awake and the asleep.
- I will protect the dream tethers which hold the waking world together.
- I will watch over the bridges to Carnival, ensuring the forces of Carnival do not mix with the living except during allotted times.
- I will answer to King Nor, and to Revel, who weaves the dreams which hold together the waking world.
- If I quit The Nor or am kicked out, I vow to never stand in the way of The Nor or any of their causes.
- I understand that by breaking any of these oaths, I would be forfeiting my life.

With his pale golden blade, King Nor turned and cut the *very air* beside him, which sliced right open like a wound, glowing green liquid splashing out of the cut in the air like blood. Wiping his golden blade on his T-shirt, he sheathed his dagger. From behind him, Swallowtail handed him two small, wooden bowls. He dipped both bowls into the cut in space, pulling them out full and dripping with the glowing green liquid, which also covered his hands. He turned, raising a bowl to each sibling.

"This is the last time you will bleed," said King Nor, placing a bowl into each of the siblings' sliced open hands. "Drink from the dreams of New Orleans and be Nor."

Keaton, wincing from the weight of the bowl against her cut hand, brought it to her lips and drank. As she did so, every ounce of pain from her hand vanished, as did every sadness or sense of nostalgia linked to her mother. Those feelings were still there, but they shrunk down as the nostalgia, thoughts, and dreams of thousands upon thousands of other souls rushed into her consciousness. It's not that the memories of walking through the park with her mother and brother didn't matter, it's just that those memories were now grains of sand on a vast beach, and *all memories* on that beach were *incredibly* important.

The wooden bowl slipped from her hand, swallowed up by the fog where it clattered to the ground of the churning carousel. Keaton raised her hand, which felt like it was *buzzing*. Blood still stained her dark skin, but the substance seeping from the wound and into the air was glowing with green light.

She turned to her brother, who was gripping onto his horse's head, breathing deeply, green light oozing into the air from his sliced open hand.

Keaton looked to King Nor, who stomped his foot hard twice onto the ground. The carousel slowed to a halt, the stone in the center of the carousel dimming down. He stomped his foot down twice more. "We have Nor."

Swallowtail turned to the fog, stomping her boot hard on the floor. *"The King said we have Nor!"*

Stomping came through the fog, twice at a time, followed by a low humming sound.

Stomp. Stomp.

Hummmmmmmm.

Stomp. Stomp.

Hummmmmmmm.

The fog thinned, revealing young boys and girls standing amidst the horses and along the outskirts of the carousel. Most wore tattered clothes, many had some sort of blade hanging from their hip or on their back.

King Nor turned to them. "Start us a bonfire." His words were still serene, yet they were easily heard over the stomping and humming. "We have a long night ahead."

The Nor scattered, presumably to get wood for a fire.

Keaton glanced at Quill, who merely looked at her and smiled. She reached over and grabbed his hand, not caring that she was grabbing his wounded hand with her own. She gripped it tight, the pain it caused seeming so far away, like a lightning storm on the horizon.

She no longer felt hungry, and couldn't remember the last time she hadn't felt that pang in her stomach.

She couldn't remember the last time she hadn't felt lost, or in danger, or like she'd lose her brother at any moment.

For the first time in months, Keaton felt like she was home.

File 46 :: [Keaton]

[New Orleans, Autumn of 1979]

Fog surged over the Mississippi River from the West Bank, heading across the water towards the wharves and warehouses of the Lower Garden District. Stars reflected upon the small waves of the river before their light was swallowed up by the thick fog.

The nighttime air had a chill to it, but Keaton could barely tell. She crouched inside the crest of one wave of fog, a curved cutlass in her hand as she gained on the dream-creature barreling across the river, splashing madly as it ran on all fours atop the water's surface.

The creature was dark violet with large, pulsing green blobs all over its body. It wasn't the biggest Nightmare Keaton had ever seen, but it was one of the fastest.

"*It's going to reach the warehouses!*" yelled Quill from inside another wave of fog. He had two long daggers, each one sheathed on a hip.

"*At least it won't be crowded!*" Keaton yelled back. She wore a white tank top with suspenders, pants, and boots. She'd shaved the sides of her head, letting her hair grow up into a thick, short mohawk. Tattoos covered one arm, and a couple more dotted the other.

Just as Swallowtail had promised, she and Quill had stopped aging, staying forever eleven years old. Though she felt as though she'd lived several lifetimes in the few years since becoming Nor.

There were several other Nor riding the fog with them, and possibly backup on the way. A few Nightmares had escaped through a weak spot when a dream tether snapped, so most of The Nor were repairing the tether while small groups were hunting down the Nightmares.

Keaton rose with the fog, getting a better look over the warehouses, which is when she saw clusters of people on Tchoupitoulas Street. "*There are people!*" she called down to the other Nor. "*Lots of them!*"

The Nor spread out to circle the area and trap the Nightmare—though if it was trapped with people, the situation was going to go bad fast. "This building here!" she called out. Just ahead of them was a long, red brick warehouse with multiple steeped roofs. Keaton sailed over the warehouse, looking down at all the people crowded around the entrance. They were holding beer bottles and plastic cups, smoking cigarettes, many of them marveling at the fog rolling over the whole building. There were posters plastered on telephone poles and on the building near the open door, with a sign that read: THE WAREHOUSE—TALKING HEADS—$5.99[38].

She looked around for the other Nor, but it seemed they had already ridden the fog into the club. There was no time for subtlety when hunting a rogue Nightmare through a crowd.

Keaton sheathed her cutlass at her hip as she floated down above the outside crowd, then passed over the heads of the people at the door as the fog thinned around her. The club was packed, dark, and loud with music. A song ended, and the crowd cheered, then one of the band members played a deep and fast bass line. Keaton rose up with the last bit of fog, which set her down in the thick wooden rafters high above the crowd.

From the low stage, the band's song ramped up and the singer, a man in a button-up shirt with dark hair, began singing about memories and falling asleep, creating a strange and magical world with his words[39]. The crowd swayed to the music as Keaton searched for the Nightmare or other Nor.

Maybe they'd caught it outside.

Then she saw it, rampaging through the crowd on the other side of the club. It passed *through* the humans, neither seen nor felt by them—but in every human's mind it brushed, seeds were planted which would grow into more Nightmares in the coming weeks. A couple dozen extra Nightmares weren't a big deal since they'd be in the dreaming world, but more than that and things could get out of control.

The Nor leaped at it through the crowd, striking with their swords, cutting off the glowing green goo from the snapped dream tether. It was the green goo from the tethers that made the Nightmare hard to take down. If it was just a rogue Nightmare by itself, a single Nor would have been able to take it down rather easily.

---

[38]   The Warehouse was the main music venue of New Orleans, as well as one of the main music venues in the United States, in the 1970s and '80s. The Warehouse hosted performances by The Grateful Dead, Fleetwood Mac, David Bowie, and Blue Oyster Cult, and hosted the last performance by Jim Morrison with The Doors. It was demolished in 1989.

[39]   The song in this memory has been listened to by Talking Heads fans, who identified the song as Memories Can't Wait, off their album Fear of Music, which had only been out for about a month at the time of this Memory File.

Though the Nightmare didn't affect the humans physically, The Nor *would*, and so had to be extremely precise and careful not to strike the humans with their blades. Keaton leaped to the next rafter and the next, over the swaying, dancing crowd. People by the Nightmare began backing away and giving The Nor space, which was good. Keaton leaped down over the crowd, landing onto the club's bar which ran along one of The Warehouse's brick walls. People jumped back, startled, and she ran the length of the bar, knocking over drinks as she drew her cutlass and leaped through the air. Two of The Nor were holding onto the Nightmare as it thrashed about wildly, trying to take on different shapes without realizing it was restricted by being in the waking world. Quill sliced off one of the green blobs from the dream tether, then got shaken off as the Nightmare bucked.

Keaton landed on the Nightmare's head, holding on with one hand and cutting off half of one of the blobs with her cutlass. She nearly fell off as it reared, almost rolling off but grabbing onto its side.

The Nightmare turned and bolted for the exit, knocking the other two Nor off of itself. They had gotten most of the dream tether remnants off of the Nightmare, and it was weakened.

Keaton knew she couldn't hold on much longer. Looking down, she saw one of its back legs below her, pounding on the cement ground as it ran. She took a deep breath and let go, grabbing her cutlass handle with both hands and driving it down as the leg passed underneath her, the sword plunging through the leg and into the cement hard enough to trip the beast.

She spun and slammed onto the ground, rolling as the Nightmare toppled onto her and then kept rolling, Quill and the other Nor descending upon it to cut off the remaining blobs of dream tether, which merely melted into green puddles when hitting the ground.

Picking up the handle of her broken cutlass, she got to her feet and ran towards the Nightmare, but the rogue dream creature was on its side, having run out of steam. The exit door opened and King Nor walked in. Keaton smiled—not because she was glad to see him, but because it meant Keaton and the other Nor didn't have to drag the Nightmare all the way to Children's Storyland.

He looked around at the crowd. Only the nearby humans paid any attention to what was going on with The Nor, but even they would most likely pass the scene off as an accidental or intentional drug trip. The rest of the concert was going on completely undisturbed.

King Nor pulled out his golden, jewel-encrusted dagger and sliced down vertically through the air to the cement floor. The wound in space bled green. He wiped the blade on his shirt, put it back in the sheath and pulled open the flap in space made by his cut. The other Nor grabbed at the wounded and spent Nightmare and pulled it sliding across the floor, through the cut in space and back into dream.

Keaton ran up behind the Nightmare and began pushing, helping shove it through the cut. Up ahead, Quill looked back at her from where he was pulling the Nightmare and yelled over the music, "*That was insane! You're the coolest sister!*"

Her heart blossomed with pride. Then she forced her smile down as she passed by King Nor. The Nor really appreciated Keaton and Quill, but they were still very new compared to the other Nor, and she didn't like to look as new as she felt.

*   *   *

Back in City Park, under the oak trees outside of Children's Storyland, most of The Nor sat around a campfire telling stories which occurred that very night. It was Quill's turn, and as he spoke, Keaton grabbed his words in her fingers, twisting them and flicking them up to create a light show above them all. There was the warehouse which turned out to be a giant concert, The Nor taking on the Nightmare in the middle of a crowd, and Keaton jumping off the bar, soaring through the air and riding the Nightmare, finally spearing one of its legs as it struggled to escape.

Many of The Nor tried to have Quill around when crazy things went down—not because he was the best fighter or the most adventurous, but because he was the best storyteller, so afterward The Nor in his stories always came out sounding legendary. There was also the bonus of him being Keaton's twin brother, so her illuminated animations of his stories were better than when she animated others' stories.

The glowing pictures hung underneath the branches of the giant oak trees like glowing wind chimes, smoke from the fire weaving through and around them.

Swallowtail sat cross-legged next to Keaton, her brown hair now long and tangled as it began to dread. She'd become good friends with Keaton and Quill, and had been on the team of Nor repairing the dream tether earlier that night.

When Quill finished telling his story, The Nor all around cheered and hollered, another Nor coming up to the fire to tell the story of their group taking down a Nightmare in The Marigny. The storytelling night would culminate in one of them telling the story of restoring the dream tethers, which was by far the most important of any job The Nor could carry out.

Keaton kept the pieces of Quill's story floating in the air, bringing back all the pieces she liked the most. The glow of each piece subsided until they were dull and black as coal. By the light of the fire, she condensed them down, smaller and smaller, twisting her hands in the air as she did so, bringing them closer to her until the images could be held in both of her tiny hands.

Holding one arm out straight, with her other hand she made a spiraling motion, the dark pieces twisting around her outstretched arm and touching down onto her skin, on a part which was previously absent of tattoos. She felt the story resting there on the skin of her arm, looking like thick ink, linking up with the previous story on her arm like a puzzle piece.

She already had one arm covered, as well as half of her second arm. They were all Quill's stories, the ones which were her favorites. She never knew which ones she'd keep—it was usually halfway through the telling when she'd suddenly know she was keeping it.

What if you run out of space on your arm? he used to ask. Now he merely asks, *What if you run out of space on your body?*

Her answer was usually the same: *I'll get rid of some of the old ones, the ones that are kind of shite.*

Truth was, she wouldn't give up the stories she'd kept for anything. If it came to the point that her whole body was covered, she'd find somewhere else to keep his stories. She'd find a way to protect them.

File 47 :: [Keaton]

[New Orleans, Early Winter of 1981]

A chill ran through the night's air, a gentle promise of colder weather in the coming months. Though New Orleans winters were mild compared to most U.S. cities, the humidity caused the cold to slink into any layers you wore, chilling your skin no matter how much armor you put on. There were also the occasional nights which would freeze, and the houses were never built to withstand the cold.

Keaton and Quill stood upon the slanted roof of a three-story housing complex, next to two of The Agents of Quantifiable Abnormalities, who were crouched down near the roof's edge.

The building itself was long, thin, and made of brick with porches and galleries sticking out of it[40]. Identical buildings surrounded it, separated by sidewalks and tufts of grass. Together they were known as The Iberville Projects, a mere stone's throw away from the French Quarter[41].

The night was young, and music spilled from various apartments—ranging from hip hop to R&B to funk. People hung out on their front porches, talking and laughing.

Roman Wing, who was the leader of The Agents of Quantifiable Abnormalities, stood up, his long coat stirring in the wind. He was the one

---

[40] Gallery – basically a balcony which juts out so far that poles run up from the ground to hold it up. Balconies themselves have no poles running to the ground, being braced by the building itself.

[41] The Iberville Projects were constructed in the early 1940s on the site which had previously been Storyville, New Orleans' legalized red light district from 1897 to 1917. The seventy-five buildings housed low income people and families, and in the 1960s mostly housed African Americans. Like most neighborhoods in New Orleans, the Iberville Projects fostered a strong sense of community and identity. Many of the buildings were demolished in the 2010s, with new buildings taking their place. The few remaining buildings have been added to the National Register of Historic Places.

Keaton and Quill had contacted. His skin was pale as starlight, his long black hair in a ponytail flowing halfway down his back.

The other Agent glanced back at the three of them with piercingly blue eyes. He had shaggy dirty-blond hair and a beard, wearing a leather jacket, black jeans, and boots. "I don't know, Roman. She's got a lot of darkness in her mind." This second Agent's name was Ben. He was young, in his mid-twenties, and had the ability to see different aspects of peoples' personalities. That's why Roman had brought him—for judgment.

The four of them looked down at the first-floor window of a project building across the way. A black woman in her forties, her hair in tight braids pulled into a bun, wearing a beige dress and preparing dinner for herself at a kitchen sink and counter.

Ben ran a hand through his hair, shaking his head and standing up. "But she abandoned you two, right? How come you want to do this lady any favors?"

"She's been trying to get better," said Keaton. "We've been watching her since we became Nor, and this is the best she's ever been. She hasn't hung out with her druggy friends for six months, and she's had a steady job for five months, waiting tables at a diner in the Quarter."

"And technically," said Quill, "*we* abandoned *her*. Though we didn't have a choice—she had already abandoned herself."

"The job of The Moon is a pretty big deal," said Ben. "We can't just give it to anyone."

The sky that night, like every night that week, had been completely covered in clouds. The Agents had some way of manipulating the clouds, keeping the sky covered so that no one in New Orleans would notice that The Moon wasn't up there.

Roman's eyes never left the woman in the window. "Have you been in contact with her?"

"Not directly," said Quill.

"Quill has been leaving her clues," said Keaton. "Moving things around her apartment in ways which hint that it's him, or that it's both of us. So she thinks we're dead, but that our ghosts are watching over her."

"It's been helping her," said Quill. "She's using thoughts of us to pull herself out of the hole she's lived in for so long."

Roman turned to Ben. "How is she balancing the darkness right now?"

Ben looked back down at the woman and shrugged. "Fine right now, but it's a lot of darkness just chilling out under the good parts."

Roman looked to Keaton and Quill, searching in their eyes. "Are you trying to *save* your mother by making her The Moon?"

Keaton wanted to answer but wasn't sure what Quill wanted to say.

Quill bowed his head. "Yes. Ben's right, she's not going to win the fight in the end. At least we don't think she is."

"She needs something," said Keaton. "She needs a reason that isn't herself. We think the job of being Moon would give her that."

Roman looked down at the woman in the window. "I'll interview her. I would appreciate it if neither of you made direct contact with her until she gets the job or doesn't. I don't want her knowing you're alive to influence the interview process."

"Thank you, Roman," said Keaton. "And Ben. Thank you so much."

Quill wiped a tear from his cheek.

"I should probably know her name," said Roman.

Quill smiled. "Her name is Sylvie. Sylvie DeBleaux."

Below them, in the window, the woman walked over to her small dining table and sat down to eat. It had been eight years since they'd run away, since they'd become Nor. The whole time Keaton and Quill had rooted for her, rooted for the love they knew was buried deep within. Their mother had become homeless, living in cars or abandoned buildings, trying and failing to get her life back together. Now, seeing her healthier than Keaton could remember ever seeing her, Keaton truly had hope that she would make it.

File 48 :: [Keaton]

[New Orleans, Autumn of ten years ago]

Keaton and Quill stood on the roof of One Shell Square, the tallest building in New Orleans, the night's wind batting at their clothes like a dozen very invisible and very large cats[42]. Peering between the other skyscrapers, they could make out the curve of the Mississippi River around Algiers Point. They could see parts of the French Quarter, and the twin bridges of the Crescent City Connection with the Garden District beyond. They could see towards Central City, Mid City, and the Treme.

Keaton put her hand on her brother's shoulder. "You ready?"

He nodded. His head was shaved, and he wore a mishmash of different black band T-shirts which Keaton had sewn together. Sheathed at the hip of his pants was a saber from the Civil War, the leather handle wrapped in wire with an ornate brass guard and pommel. The old war swords were only given to Nor who had been around a long time and proven themselves, with swords from The Battle of New Orleans being the most coveted—even more than those which were far older.

Keaton had shaved her head and let it grow, and it was now a small fro sticking out from underneath the bowler hat she'd adopted, deciding on the chosen crown of Charlie Chapman rather than the pork pie hat of Buster Keaton. She wore a white tank top and suspenders underneath a black tuxedo coat with the arms ripped off, along with black pants and boots. In one hand, she held a black wooden cane with a silver, perching

---

[42] One Shell Square is a skyscraper constructed in 1972, and is in fact the tallest building in the entire state of Louisiana, at 697 feet and 51 stories tall. The white building spears the skyline of the city, taller than Mount Driskill, the highest natural summit in Louisiana at 535 feet above sea level (hey, it's not much, but what do you want? Half the state is made of swamp). The offices are leased by many businesses, and the ground floor consists of retail and food shops.

frog as the handle.

They looked up at the night sky, at The Moon just above their heads, shining her light down on them. Quill took out one of The Moon's pearls, as big as a marble, and gripped it in his fist. "Mom!" he called out. "We're here! Come on down!"

The pearl glowed in his fist as a rope ladder uncoiled through the night's sky, landing with a loud *thump* across the roof from them. The rope ladder led up to The Moon itself, which was much closer than they'd been led to believe before they'd become Nor. A figure climbed down the ladder, through the dark night sky, until she stood across the roof from the twins.

Her black hair was pulled back in thick braids, her dress nearly glowing silver and blue as it spilled down to her bare feet, and her eyes were silvery white as she looked at them. Their mother hadn't aged since she'd taken the job of The Moon nearly three decades ago, and being without drugs for so many years had given her skin a glow and vitality she'd never shown before.

"My loves," she said. "How are you on this night of nights?"

Keaton bowed her head, placing her hand over her heart to keep it still, waiting for Quill to speak.

"I have something to tell you," he said.

"Oh? By your tone, I don't suppose it's a great story of tracking a lucid dreamer through perilous dreamscapes or stalking a Nightmare through the French Market?"

Quill shook his head. "What I'm going to tell you must be kept secret."

"I know the dreams and nightmares of thousands, Quill. What secrets could you keep from me?"

"I'm serious," he said. "Only three know of this secret, and you will be the fourth and the last."

She nodded, her kind eyes glowing like stars. "Tell me your heart, my son."

He looked out at the city, towards the French Quarter. "I'm leaving The Nor tonight. I'm going on a secret mission. We've found out who is destroying the dream tethers."

"*Nimble*," whispered their mother.

He nodded. "I've come up with a plan and volunteered for it. The Nor are going to be told I've died on a mission. I'm going to quit The Nor, becoming human again. I'm going to age up, and I'm going to join Nimble's organization."

"That's insane," whispered his mother. "How do you expect to get into Nimble's operation? How do you plan to survive?"

Keaton sniffed back a tear, wiping her cheek. "He's got a really good plan. We've spent months working on it, and it's better than you'd expect."

"So it's you two and Swallowtail? She approves of this?"

"She's not Swallowtail anymore, mom," said Keaton. "She's King Nor."

Quill nodded. "Yes, she approves. I'm going to infiltrate and then wait, gathering information on anything pertaining to the dream tethers, the barrier between the dreaming and waking world, or The Nor. I'm not going to have much contact at all with Keaton or King Nor—or with you."

The Moon turned away from them, her shoulders shaking against the night as she cried. It tore Keaton's heart in half to see her mother suffering like that.

She *knew* it would be like this, telling her of Quill's decision.

Her mother turned back to them, wiping tears from her cheeks with the palms of her hands, composing herself. She looked at Quill, then at Keaton, her bottom lip quivering as he spoke: "It is not my place to intervene. I am The Moon, and you are Nor. As a mother, I was supposed to raise you, to save you from the darkness of this world—but I failed. It was the two of you who saved me. I have no right to try and alter your path, especially for the selfish reason of having you around me."

Quill reached out his hand and their mother glanced down at it, blinking back tears before taking it in her own.

"We *did* save you," he said, smirking. "But we might not have given you the easiest job."

A smile spread across her lips. "Oh, shut up." She wiped more tears from her cheeks with her free hand. "I've told you a thousand times how proud I am of both of you, how I don't deserve you two, or even to be alive. But none of that is important now." She reached up and pressed a thumb across his forehead, smearing glowing silver above the bridge of his nose. "I wish you well on your mission, Quill of The Nor."

He smiled. "Thanks, mom."

Still holding his hand, she reached out and took Keaton's hand. "Thank you for telling me, both of you. I know you didn't have to."

"Yes, we did," said Keaton.

The three of them stood there, high above the city, locked in hand and occupation and family, not knowing if they'd ever be reunited again, or if the sacrifices made would make any sort of difference at the end of it all.

File 49 :: [Keaton]

[Nearly three weeks ago]

Twilight of the day's end bled through the tall, thin trees like vertical wounds, painting everything in a color between gold and gray, which doesn't quite exist. The knees of the trees' roots poked up through the still swamp water like the fingertips of hands reaching up to pull down the unrighteous.

Keaton rode through the edge of the fog that poured through the swamps, surfing through the trees, making a full circle around the hooded figure who stood in the muddy ground of the meeting spot. King Nor was also riding the fog, making an even wider circle of the area. Within minutes, the whole area was covered in the thickening gray.

They'd found the old pickup truck back near the road, hidden behind some brush.

King Nor rode up to Keaton, crouched, her dreadlocks trailing down her back. It had been over a decade since she'd been known as Swallowtail. "There's no one else for at least a half mile."

Keaton nodded and circled around so they could approach the figure from two angles. The figure wore a bulky, dark rain poncho that was covering something large on his back. The calliope's keyboard was sitting on the ground next to him.

It was Keaton who spoke to the figure from the edge of the fog: "Lower your hood and raise your hands."

The hooded figure raised his hands, then pulled back his hood. The young man was bald under the hood.

Even though they'd met up a couple of times over the last few weeks, and several times over the previous ten years, Keaton's heart melted at the sight of her twin brother. He looked to be in his early twenties, which made sense since they'd become Nor when they were eleven and he'd been human again for about ten years.

Keaton walked out of the fog wearing a bowler hat and a black suit coat torn into a vest, her cane shoved into the back of her coat. Her face was done up in modified mime makeup—gray-faced with black around her eyes and bright red cheeks and lips.

Quill looked at her and chuckled, something she rarely saw in these meetings with him. "It's like you're twice as killer," he said. "Making up for me not being around."

She tilted her head. "Obviously."

King Nor stepped out of the fog. Quill towered oddly over both of them, having grown over six feet tall. His dark eyes hung on the ledge between jaded and clear, his face too tired for its youth.

He unbuttoned his poncho, letting it fall to the ground. Underneath he wore a T-shirt with the device strapped to his back, the one the ex-Agent Ben made for them. Brass whistles stuck up over Quill's shoulders. He turned around, modeling it for them. "Ben did a good job. What do you think?"

"Looks fancy," said Keaton.

King Nor stepped forward, shrugging a bright blue backpack off her shoulders and gripping it in her fist. "Quill, you have not been Nor for a long time now. I am putting a lot of faith in you."

"You *should* be putting faith in me. I'm doing this *for* The Nor—to save the dream tethers like we planned a decade ago."

The King nodded. "You know the ways of The Nor, so you know I must warn you that if you betray us, we will kill you."

"Wouldn't have it any other way."

She tossed the backpack to him.

He unzipped it, pulling out the large, glowing, violet oval that was the Carousel's Heart. "The fucking *energy*. I'm glad I don't have to *hold* this thing." He looked over at Keaton. "Would you hook this into the gizmo on my back? It should just lock into place."

Keaton took the Carousel's Heart from him as he turned and squatted down. "*Fuck*," she whispered. "How *weird* is it to have your *twin brother* squatting down to be head level with you?"

He looked back. "Wouldn't know."

"Shut up, you ass." She placed the Carousel's Heart into the device strapped to his back, which latched onto the Heart, pulling it out of her hands and wrapping it in tubes and wires.

Keaton could feel the nostalgia emanating from that violet light, memories being pulled from her mind like taffy. She shook the feelings away.

Quill stood up, stretching his back.

Damn, Keaton thought, *it's still so freaking weird to look up at him.*

She smiled. Just being around her brother again made her happy beyond measure.

Quill took a deep breath, and she could nearly see the anxiety and adrenaline pulsing through him. He reached down and picked up the keyboard. "If… If I don't see you two again..."

"*Don't fucking say that*," said Keaton.

King Nor stepped forward, pulling her dagger from its golden sheath. "Quill of the Human World, Quill that was once Nor, step forward."

He did so, and Keaton saw the kid in him again. She saw the boy in the Super Dome, taking care of her. She saw the boy in the carousel that fateful day when they first became Nor. When they named each other.

"Hold out your hand."

King Nor grabbed his hand, slicing his palm. Then she cut her own, the dream energy leaking into the air. She clasped her hand to his, pulling him down closer to her height and peering up into his eyes. "You are too old to be Nor. But this Nor blood will mix with yours, reminding you of what you were. This Nor blood will take you not a full step into dream, but enough so that you will have some sliver of the instincts and speed that the dreams give us. It may only last a day, but may that be enough."

Quill's eyes teared up. "Thank you, King. Thank you, friend."

She let go of his hand, both their hands smeared with each others' blood. "May Revel see you through this."

He nodded, then waved solemnly to Keaton. He turned and started walking towards where the pickup truck was parked.

"Let's go," said the King. "Before nosey Nor decide to try and follow us."

Keaton turned and ran towards Quill.

"Keaton!" yelled the King.

Quill turned around. "You should go. The King is right."

Keaton shook her head. "I'm going to help you take Nimble's Den."

"No, you're not."

"You *need* me. I can scout in the fog. I can make sure no one else shows up."

He shook his head, approaching her and slinging the keyboard with its strap over one shoulder. "No. All the danger is *inside* the building. Besides, I've lost too much. I've seen terrible things, Keaton. Things I wish I could burn out of my memory. Don't ask me to lose you."

"I want to help keep you safe."

"I'm *not* safe," said Quill. "I'm a warrior, like you. I'm going to go alone into that den, and I'm going to do what needs to be done. If you're there, I won't trust my instincts—I'll *worry* about you—and my chances of surviving will drop dramatically."

Keaton nodded. She knew that he was right.

"I need to go," he said. "Every moment we're together, the chances increase that I'll be found out, that everything we've done will be ruined."

Tears slid down her cheeks, doing fuck-all to her makeup. "I know. I miss you."

He pulled her head against his chest, both her arms wrapping around him. "I miss you too, K. You have no idea how broken I am. I'm doing this so I can be free, so I can just fucking hang out with you." He sniffed, and she felt one of his tears collide with hers and streak down her cheek. "Thoughts of you have kept me going. I want the world to be ok. I want the city to be ok. I've been just surviving for so long, and I want you to experience a version of the city without that."

She shook her head against his chest. "I need you. I just want you in my life again."

Quill squeezed her tight, then let her go. "I've got to do this. I've got to do this *alone*."

Keaton looked up into his eyes, not caring how smeared her makeup must be. She pushed her bowler hat further down onto her head. Then she laughed. "If anything happens to you, I'm going to kill all of them."

Quill smirked. "I know. Have some faith in me though."

Keaton sighed, then nodded. "I do."

[The next night]

Keaton skated in between the oak giants who lorded over the vastness of City Park to the north of Storyland, riding through the fog. It was late at night and no one was around for at least half a mile except for The Nor inside of Storyland.

This was where Quill was supposed to meet her, but there was no telling when, since there were so many factors he couldn't be sure about. He'd even said that it could be the next night if something went wrong inside of Nimble's den and he had to postpone his plan.

Keaton's stomach was in knots, and she had to shrug away images of Quill being killed or tortured by Nimble's thugs.

Finally, he appeared amidst the oak trees, accompanied by three massive creatures the size of large bears—creatures with the trunks of elephants, the claws of lions, and the fur, hide, and scales of at least half-a-dozen other animals. Keaton backed further into the fog at the sight of them. Quill had warned her about the Baku and what they may be able to do to Nor.

Quill himself wore a huge Baku skull with engraved symbols glowing gold up and down its length, one hand deep into the fur on the back of one Baku. He let go and backed away from it, and Keaton could see him shaking in terror of the monsters.

The symbols on the skull pulsed once more, and the Baku vanished. He pulled off the skull. Hanging across his front was the keyboard of the calliope, and tied around his neck was a Baku pelt worn as a sort of cape, covering what Ben called The Reverie Organ on his back, the Carousel's Heart locked into it.

Quill dropped the Baku skull and fell to his knees.

Keaton raced out of the fog, kneeling next to him. "Are you ok?"

He nodded. "Fuck. I can't believe I'm alive."

"What happened?"

"I played the device. Everyone in Nimble's den dropped to the ground —people, creatures, entities—*all* of them, lost in their dreams. I grabbed the Baku skull and this pelt. When I put the Baku skull on, I could *feel* the Baku. They were starving. Nimble and Nemu had been *starving* them so that they would *eat* The Nor. I got so angry, but I was just going to stick to our plan." Quill shook as he continued: "I was hurrying through the main gambling room, all those people on the floor. I was heading for the exit. Then *Nimble* was there. He just walked into the main room, looking around at the spectacle, not affected by the device *at all*. He recognized me, even with the skull on, and he *smiled*, pulling out a knife. The knife lit up blue, and I felt it *pulling* and *chilling* my insides as he walked towards me. I couldn't move. He started talking, something about giving me a raise and how proud he was of me, how we could do amazing things together if I played my cards right. I wanted to run, but couldn't. I used the Baku skull, told them to attack Nimble. Two of them lunged at him, fighting him. The knife's hold on me was gone. I was so angry, I told the Baku to eat everyone's dreams. I ran towards the exit, ordering the Baku to smash through the red door. Then I was in Exchange Alley and one of the Baku just came up to me, pushing its back against my hand, and as soon as I gripped its fur, it pulled me into dream. Just like when I was Nor, except I couldn't control it, I had to hold on to the Baku. When we came out, we were outside of the Quarter, in the middle of Armstrong Park."

"You had the Baku eat all those peoples' dreams?"

"I couldn't just leave those people there. Most of them are so vile, so evil. I've seen such horrible things, Keaton, you have no idea. Maybe with their dreams eaten, they'll have a chance to create new, better dreams after a while. Dreams that don't threaten the city. Dreams that don't hurt people. Maybe some of them will turn into something better."

Keaton smacked Quill's shoulder. "It doesn't matter. You fucking did it, brother. It's over."

"I did?" He smiled, tears running down his cheeks. "Ten fucking years."

She hugged him, his body nearly collapsing against her. "Ten fucking years."

From out of the fog behind him walked King Nor.

Keaton nodded to her. "It's done."

The King nodded. "What you've done for us, Quill, it can't be measured. You may have saved many Nor lives with your actions, as well as the waking world."

Quill took a deep breath, let Keaton go and stood up, wiping the tears from his eyes.

"It's time to address the others," said the King.

They walked up to the back of Carousel Gardens, Quill jumping the fence while Keaton and King Nor rode the fog over the gate and into the land of roller coasters, rides, and game booths. The building housing the carousel had yellow tape over the entrance ramps, with multiple *CLOSED FOR REPAIRS* signs. The carousel wouldn't work without the Carousel's Heart installed.

The fog around Quill thickened with Nor running around and whispering to each other. King Nor walked out of the fog, standing next to Quill. The whispers grew louder as all The Nor gathered around.

Who is that human?

He looks familiar, doesn't he?

One of The Agents Of, maybe?

What's with the skull?

He reminds me of a Nor who died ages ago.

Looks like the King is gonna speak.

King Nor raised her voice, addressing all of The Nor. "Nor! Hear me now! Some of you may recognize this man. His name is Quill. He was once Nor but made a choice few of us would be willing to make. He gave up being Nor, becoming human in order to infiltrate Nimble's forces, to find out what Nimble was doing with the dream tethers. Quill has crippled Nimble's operations, stealing a weapon that Nimble intended to use against us, and found a way to quicken the healing of the dream tethers."

The surrounding Nor broke into chatter, cheers, and hollers. Several of them leaped out of the fog, clapping Quill on the arm, thanking him, telling him they missed him.

Keaton's heart glowed so brightly as she watched the scene. Her brother was finally home.

[A week ago]

It was upon the roof of the old, empty World Trade Center Building that Keaton and Quill waited for their mother to descend the rope ladder through the night. The top of the building was a large, round room which was used as a rotating club over the years, with a large spire spiking up from the center of the circular roof.

They gazed down into Spanish Plaza with its fountain and the entrance to the Riverwalk Mall, the Mississippi stretching between the plaza and Algiers Point.

They'd used two Baku to travel to the roof from Storyland, and Quill had sent the creatures away before taking off the Baku skull, which sat at his feet.

"The Baku are calmer than they were a few days ago," said Keaton.

Quill looked at the skull. "They're getting used to me. I treat them better than Nimble and Nemu did."

"You mean you're feeding them."

He was silent.

"Whose dreams are you feeding them, Quill?"

Quill bowed his head. "People who Nimble sends after me. And people I've tracked down who work for Nimble."

"You're *hunting* Nimble's people? Fuck, Quill! Why haven't you told The Nor?"

"I don't want to risk anyone but myself. I've only done it a few times. There aren't many of them left after I hit Nimble's den."

"That's so dangerous! What if they get a hold of you?"

"The risk is worth it!" He was pacing now. "You have no idea the things I've seen, K! The city doesn't need the kinds of people who work for Nimble! I feed their dreams to the Baku, and when they dream up new hopes and aspirations, *maybe* those won't be fucked up and bad for the city."

Keaton took off her bowler hat. "I just really need you to be level with me."

"I'm sorry. You've had The Nor, but I've been completely alone for ten years. I'm not used to telling anyone anything that's true."

Keaton sighed. "That makes sense."

"Hey, I'll try, alright?"

"And we're going to tell the King."

Quill kicked the ground. "Yeah, you're right. She should know."

Keaton nodded, then looked up at their mom descending the ladder. Keaton placed her bowler hat on the Baku skull so that the skull looked to be wearing the hat.

"Everything alright?" asked their mom as she reached the rooftop. "I heard you two yelling..." Her black braids were pulled back and tied with a green ribbon. Her dress was green and her eyes glowed with silver light.

"Oh, you know," said Keaton. "Quill was wrong about something and I had to set him straight, typical brother-sister stuff."

Quill smirked at her, the word *jerk* written across his face.

The Moon looked at Quill and shook her head. "It's so strange, after all these years, to have a son who is taller than I am." Their mom wasn't short, but Quill was definitely a few inches taller than her now.

Quill pulled his mom into a hug, after which Keaton hugged her.

"You had information about the dream tethers?" asked Keaton.

"Yes," she said. "Looking down from the sky, watching the rivers of dream coursing throughout the city, I can see that the city's dreams have grown very chaotic. Much of this is due to Quill playing the instrument and greatly increasing the potency of peoples' dreams, but I feel they are also chaotic because the tethers are still being attacked somehow."

"They *are* being attacked," said Quill.

"The Nor are searching," said Keaton. "We're scouring the dreams of the city, looking for where Nimble might be attacking them. We don't know how he's doing it."

"He'll slip," said Quill. "We'll have the tethers fixed soon."

"I have no worry that you will." She smiled at them, her eyes beginning to water.

"Is this the part where you say you don't deserve us?"

Their mom burst out laughing, at which point Keaton and Quill followed. She pointed down to the Baku skull wearing the bowler hat. "Maybe I was just going to approve of your new look."

"You like it?" asked Quill.

"It suits you."

Keaton looked out at the city, the night and the river. "We have an hour before we have to be anywhere. Would you two feel like swapping stories? Like about adventures we've had in the last ten years?"

Their mom looked up at The Moon with the rope ladder trailing below. "I could stay down here for about an hour."

Quill wrinkled his brow. "Most of my stories get pretty dark. I might be able to think of a couple that aren't too bad, though."

"Groovy!" Keaton plopped down and crossed her legs.

Quill and their mom sat down as well, making a nice square with the three of them and the Baku skull wearing the bowler hat.

Quill looked at Keaton. "You first."

"Oh, come on! You're the best one at telling stories!"

"It was your idea."

Keaton sighed. "Oh, whatever. So it was a few Carnival's back, about three weeks before Mardi Gras Day. Banshee Dave, you remember him?"

Her mother shook her head, but Quill laughed and nodded.

"I remember him," he said. "Any story with Banshee Dave is going to be entertaining."

Keaton explained to her mom: "He's this ghost guy with long stringy blond hair who had a rock band or something."

"Sounds like a good influence," she said.

Keaton laughed. "So Banshee Dave stole the dragon floats from the Krewe of Orpheus, all three of them[43]! And he's just flying around in the sky, right? Smoke pouring out of the dragon's nostrils, Banshee Dave laughing like a madman..."

As Keaton told her story, and as she listened to her brother and mom tell theirs, she felt so warm inside, and she thought: *This is the good part about being human again*. Her emotions were even more intense, and the love she felt was warm enough to light a candle if she'd been holding one.

It was one of the happiest moments she'd had in a long, long time.

---

[43] The Krewe of Orpheus is a music-based Carnival krewe founded in 1993, one of the founders being Harry Connick, Jr. They were the first of the larger Mardi Gras krewes to accept both men and women. The parade rolls after the Krewe of Proteus on Lundi Gras, the Monday before Mardi Gras day. Orpheus is an evening parade known for their magnificent floats covered in fiber optic lighting, including the Smoking Mary, which is six connecting floats that make up a giant steam locomotive, and the Leviathan, a serpent-like dragon made up of three connecting floats. The Leviathan is one of only five Mardi Gras floats with the ability to take flight.

File 52 :: [Roman Wing]

Across the river from the French Quarter is the neighborhood of Algiers. The way the Mississippi sharply curves, Algiers comes to a point which is aptly named Algiers Point. It's full of shotgun houses, parks, and churches, with shops, restaurants, and bars scattered throughout.

The high hill of the levee curves with the river and has a paved walking path with benches and light posts. Between the levee and the river is a large grassy patch of land with a few trees where Algiers holds small music festivals when the water level isn't too high.

It was against one of these trees which Roman leaned, glancing across the river at the bright day full of white clouds, the Saint Louis Cathedral pointing its spires into the air, and all the people like ants covering the levee as they moved this way and that. In his hands he held a device he hadn't used in a while, taking it apart and cleaning it with a rag. With Mars and Edith joining the Agents, he'd taken to cleaning up a lot of old equipment so the Agents wouldn't be out of luck if they needed to use an old device last minute.

The air shimmered several yards away, and he wrapped the device in the rag, sliding it into the pocket of his long coat. In the middle of the grassy area appeared Keaton, clad in a bowler hat, suspenders, and a Baku pelt draped over her shoulders, standing next to a Baku with her hand in the fur of its back.

The creature sat back on its hind legs, which made it taller than she was. Its lion eyes glared at Roman, who stepped away from the tree in case he had to outrun the beast. The memories of his last Baku encounter were still fresh, and so were his bruises. Its elephant trunk sniffed the air, showing its massive mouth full of teeth.

Keaton withdrew her hand from its fur, slowly backing away from it. "Stay there, please," she said to the beast. Then she approached Roman.

"I was expecting fog," said Roman.

She smirked. "I like to keep you on your toes." When she pulled out a folded piece of paper and handed it to him, he saw she wore the same tube bracelet holding a pearl from The Moon against her wrist that he and the other Agents now wore.

"Is that why you're not Nor anymore?"

Her face fell flat. "You could say that's one of the reasons. How'd you know?"

"Not traveling through fog, wanting to meet during the day, and having to use that bracelet, meaning that the Reverie Organ will affect you now." He pulled back the sleeve of his coat, revealing his own bracelet.

"Logical as ever. I've only been human again for two days. It's... a lot. I can feel so many things happening inside my body, all the time. Organs sliding around, liquids moving. I don't remember that from before. Or all the damned *emotions*. I mean, I felt emotion before, but there are such highs and lows for no reason at all. It's really intense."

"I'm sure it'll normal out. Give it another week or two." He opened the paper and looked at the list. There were ten places with dates and times, spanning over the next two weeks.

"Those are the places we're hitting. If anything changes from that list, I'll let you know."

Folding the paper back up, he slipped it into an inner pocket of his coat. Looking at Keaton, so many memories pulsed through his mind. All the conversations about her mother, all the times he'd met with her and her brother afterward through the years. "Chans, the calliope thief." Roman looked back at the Baku, who was patiently watching them from mere yards away. "He's Quill."

"We wanted to tell you, we really did. But King Nor ruled against it. Quill needed to be dead in everyone's minds. We fought hard so that she would let us tell our mom. We were afraid that if mom thought Quill died, it would have broken her, especially back then. So it was only the four of us who knew. Not even the other Nor knew until after he hit Nimble's Den."

"King Nor was right. If Nimble had found out his identity, it would have been the end of him, and perhaps the end of many Nor."

"Quill's the real reason I've become human again. Chicory Fest scared me. I wasn't there, and Quill could have been captured or killed. Even though I'm only human now, I can at least be there to watch his back if any of Nimble's people show up and try to take him out."

"Well, The Agents Of will be around now too, so you won't be alone in keeping him safe."

"Thanks, Roman. How long have you known he was Quill? Did Ben tell you?"

"No, but he didn't need to. He said he built the device because Chans was fighting Nimble, but I know Ben. He wouldn't put something so powerful into the hands of some lackey of Nimble's who decided to defect. It's too chaotic and would bring Ben close to breaking the oath he took when becoming an Agent. He had to know who Chans actually was, or have some other very compelling reason to do what he did.

"And then *you* were involved. If it was just you, or just Ben, I wouldn't have guessed that Quill was still alive. But the two of you combined made me do the math of how old Quill would be if, instead of dying, he became human and grew older."

"It sounds so obvious when you say it. Like we weren't being sneaky at all."

"I've been doing this for a long time."

"I suppose that's true." She looked back at the Baku, who was patiently waiting for them to finish their conversation, while also looking like it wanted to rend the dreams out of someone's mind with its teeth. "There's something else you should know: We thought we'd be done by now. The device works extremely well. The dreams tethers are getting very strong in most areas, but they keep getting damaged in others. We think Nimble and Nemu have found a way of attacking the tethers while we're not looking. They may have some new method of attacking them."

"Nimble is a very vengeful force."

Roman motioned to the Baku pelt hanging from her shoulders like a cape. "Does that work to keep the Baku away, like in the legends?"

"They won't attack me or eat my dreams while I'm wearing it."

"How many do you have?"

"Just two, unfortunately. One for Quill and one for me. And we're not about to kill Baku to get more. They're not malicious creatures."

"Do you have a safe place to stay?"

She nodded. "Outside the city, in the swamps."

"Good idea. How many Baku are there?"

"Eight. Nemu had them shipped over from Japan. Nimble and her were starving them. Their plan was to make one big attack on a dream tether, then use the Baku against The Nor when The Nor showed up to stop them."

Roman nodded and pressed a hand to the list of places in his pocket, which was also just above his heart. "You and Quill are very special to me, more than most people I've met. I will do all I can to keep you two safe and find out what Nimble and Nemu are doing to the dream tethers. Please, tell Quill that I am very glad that he is alive. I am proud of him and the risks he's taken. And I am proud of you, Keaton."

She nodded. "Thank you. It's been a rough couple of weeks, and that means a lot coming from you."

"Your mother has made a great Moon. But I would have never picked her. No matter what Ben says, he would have never picked her either. We picked her because we believed in you and your brother, and the two of you swayed us. And you were right."

A tear slid down Keaton's cheek. "I'd curse you for making me ruin my makeup, but I didn't put any on today, did I?" She sniffed and smirked. "I think that's because I wanted to be myself when I saw you. And now I know why. You've changed over the decades, Roman Wing, but every way you've changed is pure beauty."

Roman smiled. "If you and Quill need a place after this is over, The Agents Of will always be here to take you in."

Keaton laughed and pulled at the brim of her bowler hat. "Thanks, Roman, but I don't think I'll be taking another oath any time soon. Plus, the whole no-weapons thing isn't my style, or Quill's." She stepped back towards the waiting Baku.

"The offer stands, for either of you. And even if you don't join up with us, you can ask for help any time."

"And you the same, Roman Wing." She pushed her hand into the fur of the Baku, who rolled forward onto all four legs, shook its head back and forth, and vanished along with Keaton.

Roman, now standing alone on the large grassy patch of land between the levee and the river, took the device he'd been cleaning back out of his pocket and began working it over with the rag again. He walked up the grassy hill to the walkway atop the levee, which would take him right up to the ferry terminal, where he'd catch the ferry back to Spanish Plaza.

File 53 :: [The Function]

High above the city, between the bright white clouds and the tallest buildings of the CBD, dangled a tiny speck. This speck was The Function, holding onto a rope ladder which was miles long and led up to one of the fluffy white clouds that covered the sky on that bright day.

Hooking an arm around one of the ladder's rungs, The Function stopped to rest, pulling his flask out of his coat pocket and taking a swig of Chartreuse. "No one listens when I say they should install an elevator or have some kind of vehicle to get up to the sky," he said to himself, resting his aching arms and legs. He looked down at the French Quarter and the curving river below. "*It's no big deal, no one ever has to go up to the sky*,' says Serendipity, Roman, and just about everyone ever. Then months later they're saying, '*Oh, The Function, would you mind going up to the sky for this or that reason?*' I mean, does *anyone* have to climb up to the sky except me?" He shook his head, stretching his back and limbs as much as he was able. "What year is it? Like two thousand something? And we're really using rope ladders?"

Sighing, he took another swig of Chartreuse and slipped the flask back into his coat. "Alright, shut up and do the thing."

When he finally reached the top and pulled himself up onto the cloud, he collapsed onto it. It felt exactly like a giant marshmallow coated in balls of cotton.

"Oh, there you are. Thought you were going to be here earlier."

The Function rolled onto his back, looking up at the man standing above him. The man was middle-aged, tall, and super thin, with a short mess of red hair. He wore thick glasses, a blue checked button-up shirt with rolled-up sleeves, and brown slacks.

"Well, Albert, I always underestimate how excruciatingly painful it is to climb a rope ladder for however many miles."

"Actually, we're just under a mile-and-a-half up right now."

"I... I don't care."

"You want to rest while I make us some old fashioneds[44]?"

"Yes. Yes, that is a fitting description of what I want right now."

Albert walked away. "Don't rest too long. The ice melts fast up here with the sun being so close."

The Function rested for a few moments, then rolled onto his stomach and got to his feet, trying not to fall over, both from his aching legs and from the unstable cotton-marshmallow floor. He saw Albert's house a little ways away. It was a single shotgun house with a couple of rocking chairs on the big front porch. The house itself was long and thin, medium-sized as far as shotgun houses go, with four rooms total. The house sat amid a field of seemingly endless white clouds. Beside and behind the house were rows upon rows of T-shaped wooden posts sticking up out of the cloudy floor, two buckets dangling from each one. There were more buckets than you could count—or, rather, more buckets than anyone but Albert *would* count. A complex series of ropes tied these buckets together, the ropes knotted to eye bolts coming out of the bottom of each bucket. This series of ropes led through wheels and pulleys mounted to the top of the posts, all of them leading to a dozen large metal levers on the side of Albert's front porch.

The Function pulled off his coat and slung it over one shoulder, making his way towards the house. As he got closer, he saw that the buckets were full to their brims with water. He climbed the steps to the house, draping his coat over the front rail of the porch and collapsing into one of the rocking chairs. Albert came out holding two old fashioneds, handed one to him, and took up the other rocking chair. They both clicked their glasses together, knocked them on the arms of their chairs, and took drinks. It tasted like the 1930s—the good part, sans the economic sorrow.

"This is amazing," said The Function. "Thank you, Albert. Sorry, I'm always in a crap mood when I finally make it up here."

"Don't apologize. You're practically the only person I talk to, not counting Agents using this radio system Roman installed back in the '70s." He motioned to the side of the porch *not* covered in metal levers, which instead had an old NASA-looking CB radio covered in dials and small switches, with a microphone, speakers, and several curling wires running off the porch to vanish into the cloudy ground. Those wires led to various points around the city where Roman hid speakers with which to communicate with Albert.

The Function sipped more of his old fashioned and melted into the rocking chair.

Albert looked over at him. "I set up the futon in the front room like

---

[44] Old Fashioned – A cocktail involving whiskey, an orange, and four drops of nostalgia.

last time. Hopefully, it doesn't screw your back up too much."

"Right now, I feel like I could just sleep in this rocking chair."

"So you're up here watching the city, looking for the calliope player?"

"Oh, not anymore. I mean, kind of—there's been a plot twist. Turns out the calliope thief is working with The Nor, and he's actually *repairing* the dream tethers. So he's going to play his calliope device, called the Reverie Piano or something, in public a few times this week, and I'm up here to watch over the events in case anything goes wrong. Turns out Nimble and some of his people really want this guy dead."

Albert sipped his old fashioned. "Sounds like a normal day for you."

"Yes, it does. Though I don't always get to sip old fashioneds while working." He glanced at the CB radio from the 1970s. "Oh, do you mind if I make a call?"

"It's all yours."

The Function set his drink down on the little table between the rocking chairs and went over to the radio. He flipped a couple of switches on the panel and pushed a red button which began to beep. The beeping stopped, and a gruff voice came through the speaker: "The Agents Of."

The Function pushed a button and spoke into the microphone. "Hey, Julius?"

"Yeah."

"It's The Function. I'm up in the clouds, ready to keep watch."

"Good, thanks for doing that. I feel much better with you up there. I don't have a good feeling about things, and I haven't figured out why. Let me know if you see anything weird in the city."

"Will do."

"And ask Albert to keep collecting water. We might need it this weekend."

"I'll let him know."

The Function flipped the switches off, walked back to the rocking chair, and dropped into it. "Is it checkers time?"

Albert nodded. "I could go for a game. After that, I've got to get back to work. I'm supposed to have this website ready to go live in a couple of days."

"You're still doing web design? Why? I told you, you just need to ask for a raise. I'm pretty sure your wage was thought up in the '70s, along with that radio."

Albert shrugged. "I like making websites, it's fun. Besides, I need *something* to do with my time up here besides watching buckets fill up."

A foul smell caught The Function's attention, and he sniffed around, finally sniffing his own shoulder and making a face. "Hey, do you have a washing machine? I think I forgot to wash my clothes for... a while."

Sighing, Albert got to his feet. "Yes. Let's play checkers first, though.

I'm not exactly dying to hang out with you when you're naked."

"Alright, that makes sense. I guess."

*   *   *

After several games of checkers (of which The Function only won one) and after the sun had set, The Function sat on a rocking chair on Albert's front porch, naked except for a towel wrapped around his waist, sipping another old fashioned.

He looked down over the city, all the tiny lights sparkling like the stars above, the large squiggle of the Mississippi cutting the city into some sloppy yin and yang symbol. Then he saw something strange, a tiny glowing speck climbing down what he guessed was a rope ladder, maybe a mile away from where he was sitting.

He got up and poked his head into the front room, where Albert was hunched over his computer.

"Hey, do you see The Moon climb down to the surface very often?"

Albert shrugged. "Now and then. Maybe every six months or so."

The Function shrugged. "Huh, alright."

He went back out to the rocking chair, plopped down, and took another sip of his old fashioned, thinking that if he was The Moon he'd never leave, especially if it meant climbing up and down a freaking rope ladder every time. He didn't care how boring it got up there by himself. As he watched her climb down that rope ladder, he started thinking about how The Moon (a woman he found absolutely gorgeous, by the way) must have more upper body strength than him, with how quickly she descended the ladder. She didn't seem to take breaks at all.

"Yeah, she probably works out," he said to himself. "At least push-ups." Then he thought about how he's just sitting in a rocking chair and could easily be doing push-ups right now. "Eh, maybe tomorrow."

File 54 :: [Julius Marcos]

The next night Storyland was overflowing with two things: fog and chatter. The Agents Of stood in the center of Carousel Gardens with roller coasters and rides looming like giants in the gray haze. The carousel's entrance ramps were taped off with signs reading: *CLOSED FOR REPAIRS.* Many Nor stepped out of the dense fog, a graveness replacing the carefree demeanor The Nor sported on the Agents' last visit.

King Nor stepped out to greet the Agents, her eyes severe, the golden jewel-encrusted dagger hanging next to a curved sword on her hip. From behind the carousel walked Keaton, wearing her bowler hat, sporting white and black mime makeup, and carrying her black cane. Next to her was the man who must be her twin brother, Quill. There was no sign of the Baku skull or the Reverie Organ, though he and Keaton both wore Baku pelts like capes.

Quill looked at the Agents. "I'm sorry if I've caused you any trouble. I'm just trying to fix things and get everything back to normal."

"None of the trouble is your doing," said Julius. "I've known many who *would* die, or *have* died, for this city—but I've only known a few who would have subjected themselves to what you chose to go through."

When Julius looked at Quill, he saw the eyes of a warrior—a tired one. Quill nodded. "It's been a rough decade."

"I bet." Julius walked over and reached his hand out. They locked hands and shook. "I'm Julius. This is Edith and Mars, and you know Roman."

Julius stepped away, and Quill looked at Roman.

"Roman, I'm so sorry about Julia Street." He pointed to a large bump on the side of his bald head. "When you took me down, I hit my head and fell unconscious. The Baku defended me of their own volition, which I had no idea they would do. I hope you're alright."

"I'm dealing with the effects," said Roman. "And I'm glad to see you alive."

"I'm sorry for all the lies. But I'm glad to be working with you after all these years."

King Nor stepped forward and everyone turned to her. "Thank you for coming so quickly. Only half of The Nor are here." She motioned to the surrounding fog. "The rest are out scouting the city and the city's dreams. Hours ago, the dream tethers were *ravaged*, left torn to shreds in some areas. The tethers were hit in multiple places at the same time.

"We believe Nimble has found a way to attack the tethers from inside the city's dreams. We're not sure how, but that is the only way we can figure he can do something on this scale without being caught, being seen, or leaving any evidence."

Mars chimed in: "That would explain why no one in the city seems to have seen him since his den was hit. Could he be hiding *inside* the city's dreams?"

The King shook her head. "He's been so secretive over the years, we have little idea *what* Nimble is capable of."

"There *have* been reports of Nemu being seen around the city," said Julius. "I'm thinking we focus solely on finding her. If Nimble is somehow in dream, perhaps he's using Nemu to run things in the waking world. Maybe using her to organize the hunt for Quill."

Edith spoke up, raising her arm towards Quill—the arm just so happened to be wrapped in the Extraction Glove. Julius didn't imagine Edith knew how tough she looked in that moment. "*Of course* Nimble wants to take down Quill. If the Reverie Organ is stopped, then Nimble can actually destroy the dream tethers."

"Edith is right," said King Nor. "This may be a ploy to get Quill out in the open because now we *have* to heal the dream tethers."

"So this might not even be Nimble's actual attack," said Keaton. "He might have done this to make us act. He takes out Quill, *then* makes his big move."

Julius rubbed his chin. "When we were looking for Quill, Saturday was the toughest day. We knew he was going to hit someplace, but we couldn't cover even a fraction of the events. Now we can use that to our advantage. We hit a festival, or a couple of them, on Saturday. Nimble's operation is damaged, so his resources are stretched thin. He and Nemu won't be able to watch all the festivals."

"The more events we hit," said Keaton, "the higher the chance of running into Nimble's thugs."

"We could do one or two events during the day," said Julius, "then do some in the evening, so we have The Nor around too."

"This could work," said Quill.

"What if he's not going to try to take out Quill at all on Saturday?"

asked Edith. "What if he actually tries to take out the dream tethers on Saturday while *we're* trying to help Quill?"

"That's why we can only have one or two Agents with Quill and Keaton," said Julius. "While the others and Scape guard some of the weak spots in the waking world. We still have The Function watching from the clouds, in the off chance he sees anything from up there. If anyone else has a better plan, speak up now."

After a moment of silence, Quill spoke up: "We still have to heal the tethers, starting tonight. If Nimble and Nemu hit them again, they might snap some of them."

"I know of some late shows that are still going on," said Mars.

"We can hit shows over the next few nights," said King Nor. "The Nor will help guard the perimeter of wherever we hit. Then Saturday will be our big play."

"It might be Nimble's big play too," said Julius.

"Unless he makes his play on Friday and throws us off," said Mars.

Julius nodded. "For now, we bank on Saturday."

File 55 :: [Mars]

By the time Mars finished concert-hopping through the Marigny and Bywater with Quill, Keaton, and The Nor, it was that sweet and bitter time between extremely late at night and extremely early in the morning. She was still full of energy, so rather than going home, she headed back to headquarters to fiddle with some devices in the hopes of tiring herself out.

Mars sat back on her lab stool, stretching her arms up over her head, and looked at the clock. "Oh, damn it." She totally forgot to get batteries when she helped Edith load up memory items into her new Memorian Library Headquarters.

Currently, Mars was studying these switches sewn into the back of a leather glove. She'd found the glove on one shelf, next to a small metal box with identical switches sticking out of it. When she flipped the ones on the glove, the switches on the box flipped as well. She was trying to figure out what powered it, and what they were intended to do. Were they finished? Or were they merely some half-finished experiment that an Agent was building in their spare time?

Adjusting the VR Goggles on her forehead, she got to her feet, stretched, and walked out of the lab. The headquarters was quiet except for the distant gurgling of water from the mechanism pumping Wonder into the fountain of Spanish Plaza, next to the ramp. She yawned as she walked, the *woosh* of the gas lamps lighting up in the hallway giving her a sense of home.

The door to the break room was open, the room inside dark, and she decided to grab a beer and take a leisurely walk home. Hell, maybe two beers—she did good work today, she deserved two. She got to the doorway and reached for the light.

"*Don't do that.*"

Mars screamed, jumping back and pulling the Bola Launcher from her hip and slapping it onto her wrist. Floating in the dark were two golden eyes, both familiar and creepy as hell.

"Is this a new habit?" she asked. "Sitting in the dark and scaring the shit out of me?"

"I don't need the light," said Julius from inside the break room. "And the buzz of light bulbs is so loud."

A flicker of flame lit him up, sitting there at the table in a white tank top and holding up a lighter. He lit a candle in an ornate brass candle holder she hadn't seen before.

Mars pulled the Bola Launcher off her wrist and hooked it back onto her hip.

"If you need the break room," said Julius, "I can go somewhere else. I don't know why I chose to sit here."

Mars saw the bottle of Jack Daniels in front of him next to a glass of ice. She shook her head. "I was just grabbing a couple of beers for the walk home."

He nodded, and she walked into the room.

"You alright?" she asked.

He smirked. "I'm alright."

"You sound half-convincing. Not bad, but needs work. Try to really picture a time in your life when you felt alright, *then* say it, so it comes off with more conviction for the audience."

Julius laughed a little. "It's just part of who I am. I get like this."

"You don't sleep much, do you?"

He shook his head. "Feel like grabbing yourself a glass?"

Mars checked in with her intuition. She didn't necessarily want to rush into a situation where her boss-slash-role-model got trashed and acted like a fool. But her intuition clearly said to her, *Nope, despite him sitting in the dark and drinking whiskey in the middle of the night, everything feels right about this situation.*

Not being one to argue with her intuition, she grabbed a rocks glass from the cupboard, threw some ice in it from the freezer, and sat down across from him.

Julius reached over and poured a hefty amount of whiskey into her glass, then flinched. "Sorry. I'm used to pouring for myself."

Mars shrugged, picked up her glass, and reached across the table. He tapped his glass against hers, then they tapped their glasses on the table and both drank.

She grimaced. "Yep, that's Jack Daniels."

"Not your favorite whiskey?"

Mars looked at the glass in her hand. "Not my favorite memories. The whiskey itself is fine."

"I suppose memories are why I drink it. Though I do like the taste."

"Sure you're alright?"

He sat back in his chair and smiled. "Ever since that conversation with Bes, months ago, I've been off. I thought it would be easier to draw a line between what's Julius, what's Bes, and what's all these other fellows up in my head." He tapped his temple with the edge of his glass. "The other incarnations over the centuries, all rattling around up here with their own opinions and desires."

"Sounds like a bitch."

Julius laughed. "It is a bitch." He took a long sip of whiskey.

"You've been doing personal stuff though, right? Is that why?"

"I've been going to the Treme when I can, talking to old friends and family. I look around, hunting for who Julius really is, and why he could possibly be so damned important." He shook his head. "I don't feel like I'm more important than anyone else working to help the city."

Mars took a sip, thinking. "Maybe it's not your job to know *why* Julius is important."

He nodded. "I've thought that, many times. But since it's hard to find him, or to ignore these other parts inside, I thought maybe knowing why he's important would help me. I'm kind of at a loss."

"It could come with time."

"Yeah. Sorry, I'm just thinking out loud. I've thought myself in circles about all these questions, looking at all the answers." He pointed at her with his glass. "How are you? You don't seem to be sleeping either."

"I like being busy more than I like to sleep. Until I burn myself out and sleep for sixteen hours, anyway." She took a drink. "I'm good though. Was really pissed off at you for a bit, not liking how you handled The Nor the first time we went to Storyland."

Julius laughed. "I could tell. I told Roman I'd talk to you, but he said you'd be fine."

"Yeah, he talked me down. And now, with the stakes higher, none of that seems important, anyway."

He turned his glass on the table. "I'd like you to tell me anything I do that bothers you. If I'm in a mood, or in the middle of something, I might tell you, 'Not now.' But then I'd like you to tell me later on."

"Will do." Mars kind of wanted to tell him about Edith's new Memorian Library Headquarters, because Mars couldn't get over how freaking cool it was, but she didn't want to steal Edith's thunder. It wasn't related to the Agents, and it wasn't Mars' story to tell.

"Other than that, just work," she said. "Oh, and Dust-o-Bot 5000 is working wonders." She pointed at her nose. "Who knows, maybe your super-lion-god-smelling will be even stronger when you're not breathing in dust all the time."

Julius laughed. "I'll let you know." He picked up the bottle and added a splash to both their glasses, then raised his glass to toast.

Mars raised an eyebrow. "What to?"

His smile faded, and he grew serious, looking deep into her eyes. "To super lion-god smelling."

She burst out laughing, putting her hands over her face. "*Fucking hell*," she blurted out between laughs.

Julius laughed as well.

After Mars calmed down, she took a deep breath. "Was that a Julius joke? Didn't sound like a Bes joke..."

"I suppose it was a Julius joke."

She raised her glass. "Well, I will most definitely toast to that Julius joke."

They tapped their glasses, thumped them onto the table, then took healthy drinks.

Julius sat back in his chair again. "Mars, I do want to tell you something. I see you as the most important Agent right now."

She pointed her glass at him. "Someone's drunk."

He shook his head. "It takes me a whole bottle to get a buzz. Two bottles to get drunk. I mean what I'm saying."

"Ok, why would you think that?"

"I'm not saying that I'm right, but it's how I see you. You have the drive of a leader, but you're also very inventive. You're intuitive, analytical, and you're very good with people. You know much more about the people of the city than Roman or I. Roman is from the past, he's out of touch with the youth that will be the future of the city. I was only connected to the everyday life of the city until I was fifteen. This job really is about balancing the hidden aspects of the city with the people who live in it. You have the potential to be connected to both."

"Wow, thank you." It had been a long time since someone had listed off a string of compliments about her. At least someone who she believed.

"One day I'll be gone. One day Roman will be gone. If the Agents continue afterwards, I feel like you might be the reason."

Mars started to speak, then took a long drink instead. So many emotions were crashing like planets inside her.

"I'm sorry," said Julius. "I didn't mean to depress you or freak you out."

Mars shook her head. "No, I just like how things are. Thanks for saying what you said. It's just been a day."

"That it has."

She took a deep breath. "This whiskey is making me crash, hard. I think I'd better get home. Hopefully, it's not dawn yet."

"It's not dawn yet. You've got over an hour."

Mars chalked him knowing the time off to one of his super-lion-god senses. She got up, finished her whiskey, and grabbed a beer from the fridge. "It was good talking to you, Julius. I hope we do this more often."

He poured himself some more whiskey. "We will."

She gestured to the candle on the table. "Want me to turn off the light?"

"No, I won't be here much longer. I'll get it."

Mars raised her beer as she got to the door. "Goodnight."

"Goodnight."

Mars walked through the hallway towards the exit ramp. Emotions whirred inside her like a storm, things she didn't even want to think about yet. She tried to shove those feelings into a closet until later, but the feelings were quite adamant about being all up in her face.

Thoughts of walking home along the river helped though, and she was sure that the fresh air would help clear her mind.

That was when the air in the hallway directly in front of her split open like a flower—specifically a glowing, green flower. She reached for her Bola Launcher, not having time to think of what good it would do against a flowery green rip in space, when the light of the flower wrapped around her, consuming her with warm, wet light.

And she was gone.

File 56 :: [Julius Marcos]

Julius stood up and stretched. He'd been lost in memories when he thought he heard Mars stumble around further into the headquarters. Setting his glass in the sink, he blew out the candle and walked into the hallway, making his way towards the ramp to Spanish Plaza.

He bent down and picked up her VR Goggles and the unopened can of beer. *Guess she* was *a bit drunk*, he thought, smiling. He looked around but didn't see anything weird, so he figured she'd made her way up the ramp and was now walking home. Julius took the beer back to the break room and put it back in the fridge.

Heading back into the further recesses of the headquarters, Julius stopped by the lab and put Mars' VR Goggles on one table, then wandered the hallways with the gas lamps coming to life as he walked.

There was a room he hadn't been to for a while, and he kept wondering how that room would make him feel. He'd been scared of it, scared of stirring up old versions of himself which he didn't feel as connected to recently.

After this conversation with Mars, he realized he'd have to tell her things he never told new Agents. He'd have to tell her about this room. The other option was to get rid of the room, but he wasn't sure if he still needed it. Did it merely represent the darker parts of his pasts, the parts which now seemed to be falling away in thin layers?

He walked into his bedroom and locked the door. Like Roman's, it was sparse—a small bed, a desk, and a bookcase. A framed picture of his nephew Raphael sat on the desk.

There was a normal door leading to the bathroom and a thick metal door with a combination dial set into it. He spun the dial, and the door clicked, and when he pulled it open, the sounds of whispers and moans flooded into his bedroom. The room beyond was large and lined with wooden shelves, each shelf packed with glass bottles, some of the labels long since wasted away. Each bottle contained the ghost of a slave-trading pirate—or some other kind of slave trader or slave abuser. Julius had captured each one and shoved them into their respective bottle.

This room didn't need a light—with all of the trapped ghosts, at least some of them were glowing at any time, making the bottles they were stuck inside into large, weak light bulbs. The shade of light they gave off would disconcert the average person, but to Julius it was comforting.

At the sight of him, some ghosts grew quiet while others woke up, cursing or pleading with him. Some merely babbled from the madness brought on by being stuck in a bottle for a century or more.

Julius stood there amidst the voices and the noise, letting the ghostly light fall onto his skin as he had done countless times over many lifetimes. He'd moved this room to dozens of locations over the years, but always he stood here. Their pleas and cries used to calm him, to help him focus—something about a diseased thorn of the city being yanked out of it so that the city had a better chance to heal. The city didn't need the energy of these ghosts pulsing through it. Taking these ghosts out of the mix didn't completely fix anything, but it did something.

Some bottles were empty; those ghosts had finally moved on. In the past, he would take the empty bottles and use them for other despicable ghosts that he would inevitably come across, but now he wasn't so sure. Perhaps that urge was left over from past incarnations, the ones who had been slaves before Bes had awakened in them. Those other incarnations had needed that relief, that vengeance, but did Julius need it?

If he disassembled this room, what would he do with the ghosts? He couldn't let that many horrid spirits out into the city at once, especially when some of them were completely mad. And letting them out in another city or the swamp wouldn't work—they were tied to New Orleans and would merely vanish and appear back here.

It would be a long process, perhaps letting out those who were genuinely willing to change while figuring out other places to keep the ones who could be a threat. The worst ones could be taken to the First Quarter, letting the Riverwalkers guard them, but he could only ask them to take so many.

For now, he merely stood there, feeling the slight buzz of whiskey in his blood. He watched the feelings and memories that being in this room brought up inside of him, wondering which of them belonged to Julius and which did not.

File 57 :: [Mars]

The green light spit Mars out into a crowd of people. Dancers all around were bumping into her, bathed in red light. Women and men donned a random assortment of flowing dresses, button up shirts, vests, and slacks. Immediately she wondered if the light had spit her into a swing dance night at The AllWays Lounge, or if she had fainted in the headquarters hallway and was dreaming.

She looked up to see the faces of two dancers moving in slow motion, the colors of their faces smearing into the air like wet paint. The sight of their blurred faces gave her vertigo, and she stumbled away from them, bumping into several more people until she was off the dance floor.

Trumpet, drums, and bass collided together in the air, all of it coming from musicians on the stage. The music they played was taken apart like an old car engine and put back together—something close to modern jazz, but not anything Mars could peg as real. It sounded more like tiny snippets of various modern jazz and old jazz songs all blended together.

Maybe the lenses of her VR Goggles would help her figure out where she was. She reached up to pull them down, but they were gone. She did still have the Bola Launcher on her hip, as well as her leather jacket.

She was definitely in a jazz club. There was a bar along one wall, facing the stage, with a dance floor in the space between them. Along one wall was a row of red booths, and violet velvet covered the walls. The dancers, bartenders, and wait staff moved so slow they barely moved at all, their features and edges smeared into blurs. Yet every time Mars blinked, they had moved a step or two, as if making up for the time they'd been still. It was as if her *attention* to them made them move so slow.

Then there were the *cats*. She only counted four at any one time, but they seemed to weave in and around the dancers' feet without a care of being stepped on. One cat jumped up onto the bar against the back wall. The cats didn't seem to blur at all, walking as leisurely as cats usually walk.

"*Mars*." The voice came from beside her.

She spun around, her hand falling to the Bola Launcher at her hip, but no one was there. Then she looked down to see one of The Nor. It was a young boy with messy brown hair, a ripped up shirt, shorts, and boots, with a Civil War sword at his hip. He was one of The Nor who'd been with Keaton when Mars and Edith had first met her in Jackson Square.

"Where am I?" she asked.

The Nor boy pointed down the row of booths, to a booth with a red curtain drawn across its entrance. "She's waiting for you. There's not much time."

Mars took a deep breath, running a hand over her face. She nodded to The Nor, then walked down the row of booths and pulled back the curtain. The woman sitting there was one of the most beautiful women Mars had ever seen. She wore an elegant purple and silver dress with silver hoop earrings, a silver necklace with a single purple stone at the center, and silver hoop bracelets. The woman was black—at least that's what Mars first thought. In fact, the woman was clearly *not* human at all, much less any ethnicity. She was a hole cut out of the room, a woman-shaped hole with eyes, a mouth, and long, braided hair, wearing a dress and jewelry. Looking into her was like looking into outer space, but without all the stars. Mars felt like if she tripped into the woman, she'd fall right into that darkness, lost and floating in space for all time.

The woman's eyes were dark brown, seemingly light compared to her body. Her hair was thickly braided and pulled up into a ball at the back of her head. Her hands were steepled in front of her face, a half-full martini sitting in front of her.

Her deep voice sounded ethereal and far away, as if coming from the void that her body promised: "I'm sorry. I am not supposed to bring anyone here like this. But the situation is dire."

Mars looked around. The feeling of the jazz club reminded her a little of being in the land of the dead. Turning back to the woman, she asked: "Are you Revel?"

The woman nodded. She turned to The Nor boy, who spun around and ran through the crowd of dancers without disturbing a single one.

"So I'm in a dream? Or in the dream world?"

Revel motioned for her to sit, and Mars slid into the booth. "Would you like a drink? It may help you acclimate."

"How about you tell me why you brought me here before I get all acclimated."

"Do you know about the dream tethers?"

"Yes. No offense, but how do I know you're really Revel?"

"Besides The Nor who brought you to my booth?"

"Um, yeah. Besides that."

"You could use your abilities."

Mars hesitated. She was pretty sure this *was* Revel, and she didn't really want to pass out like she'd nearly done with Serendipity.

"No?" said Revel. She looked towards the bar and nodded.

Mars followed her gaze as the bartender walked out from behind the bar to a violet door set into the back wall. He opened the door and the whole club was showered in piercingly green light. Seven vertical green beams of liquid or energy pulsed in vertical streams on the other side of the doorway.

"Holy shit!" said Mars, shielding her eyes.

"These are seven of the dream tethers," said Revel. "These sections are healthy, as you can see."

"Some of them were torn up pretty bad, right?"

"The dream tethers have never been in a worse state, Mars."

Revel nodded again, and the bartender closed the door.

Mars blinked away the splotches in her vision left by the searing light. "Well, The Agents Of and The Nor have a pretty detailed plan about how to fix the tethers, and me *not* being in the dream world is a fairly big part of that plan."

"I have an idea which may save the waking world. I know of your ability to work on the energy of entities."

"How do you know about me?"

"You were an abandoned child of New Orleans. We once considered you for becoming Nor. We were going to ask you, but The Function found out and asked us not to."

"Seems he does a lot of that."

"Your presence *here* may be far more important than your presence in the waking world."

"Ok, so you're Revel. Cool. I'm listening."

"I created the tethers by stretching out my own dreams like lengths of twine, then weaving the dreams of the city around them, strengthening them. The tethers, you must understand, are part of me. So when they are damaged..."

"...you're damaged."

"Yes. I can feel my energy, my body, twisting up and tensing. Like my muscles, my being, are compensating for the damaged parts of me. But if you can heal me, then the dream tethers may heal themselves much faster."

"Ok, that makes sense. But what if this doesn't work? What if I work on you and nothing happens to the tethers?"

"Then we'll know rather quickly and you'll go back to the waking world."

Mars sat back in her booth, biting her lip and thinking. "Ok, dream lady. It's worth a shot. Only thing is, I met Serendipity a couple of weeks back, and when I looked at her energy for roughly two seconds, I nearly passed out. There's a chance I won't be able to handle it."

Revel took a sip of her martini. "Mars, how do the dancers make you feel?"

"The ones out there?" Mars asked, pointing a thumb to the dance floor. "They definitely give me vertigo."

"But you're fine right now, with them in your periphery."

She nodded. "Sure."

"What if you used your ability while looking away from me? Or what if you *eased* your way into looking at me?"

Mars shrugged. "Look, I'm up for trying. I'm just saying that if I pass out and am suddenly lying on top of you, I'm not trying to make a move or anything."

"Understood. Would you like a drink now?"

Mars looked up at the swimming red ceiling. "Yes. Bourbon on the rocks I guess, since I've already had some whiskey."

Revel looked across the room at a waitress and nodded, then began sliding out of the bar. "Shall we get started?"

"Sure. We should also get you some water."

Revel looked at her and smirked. "I'm one of the oldest beings in the city. I'll be alright without water."

Mars slid out of the booth and stood up. "I've heard that line at least forty times before. Think about what you're saying: You're one of the oldest beings in *New Orleans*. There shouldn't even *be* a city, there should be swampy ground surrounded by miles of water."

Revel laughed. "Alright. You're the doctor."

"Damn right I am."

Revel looked across the room towards the waitstaff and nodded again.

Now that they were both standing, Revel was definitely several inches taller than Mars.

"We'll need a room with some privacy and a bunch of pillows." Mars opened her leather jacket and checked the inner pocket. "And some needles, if you've got some. I only have eight on me."

"We'll do it here," said Revel. "We're safe in this space."

Mars looked around at all the slow-motion dancers. "What about all them?"

"They're dreamers. Their features change because different dreamers are cycling in and out of each dancer." She motioned to the bar. "The same can be said for the musicians and the waitstaff. This is one of the places I've constructed out of my own dreams. The characters are locked, and dreamers can *be* those characters, but they don't make any decisions. Only

I can have the dancers or waitstaff act in any way. In other words, we won't be bothered. Well, except possibly by the cats. The cats are genuine and are not dreaming at all."

"Ah. Neat, I guess."

A few of the waitstaff brought large square pillows and set them on the floor in front of the booth. One of them handed Mars a rocks glass full of bourbon and ice. Mars nodded to the blurred waitress and took a sip. It was *really* nice bourbon.

Mars pulled off her leather jacket, then pulled the long needles out of the inner pocket, placing the jacket on the booth table with the needles on top. She reached to the ceiling, stretching out her back, shoulders, and arms.

Revel took a glass of water from one of the waitstaff, looked at it quizzically, then took a long drink. When she finished half the glass, she wiped the back of her mouth and set the glass down, looking at Mars. "Are you ready?"

"Yep."

"They're searching for more needles. Hopefully, they'll bring some before you need them."

Mars nodded. "I can use the eight, too. It'll just be more efficient to have double that."

Revel turned away from Mars and shrugged the dress off her shoulders, letting it slide down to her waist. Mars stared at her bare back, like a perfectly shaped hole ripped out of the jazz club's "reality," the chain of the silver necklace resting at the base of her neck, the bracelets dangling from her wrists. Then the entity knelt to lie atop the small sea of pillows.

Mars took a deep breath, followed by an equally deep drink of bourbon. She set the bourbon down on the table, grabbed a piece of twine from her pocket, and tied back her dreads. Kneeling, she straddled Revel's hips, pressing one hand to Revel's shoulder blade. Mars did not, indeed, fall into the darkness—Revel's body felt like any entity Mars had come into contact with. She felt human.

Mars looked at the daisy wrapped around her wrist and kissed it. "Let's do this," she whispered. She looked up, away from Revel, then *looked* at the energy of the room, at which point she sighed from the utter beauty around her. Sparks of energy floated near the top of the room like wisps of light. Each spark took turns darting down to *become* one of the dancers or waitstaff until another spark darted down to push it out of the way so that it could *become* the character. Each of those sparks must have been a dreamer, wandering the landscape of the city's dreams while the person slept.

Letting her eyes lower towards Revel, she saw the pulsing green light of the dream tethers. Each one was nearly as thick as Mars' wrist, flowing up and down Revel's body, then from Revel's shoulders they split off in different directions like glowing green skeleton-wings. They flowed right through the walls, ceiling, and floor of the jazz club. Mars looked up again and took another deep breath, feeling the bourbon work its way through her body, mixing with the Jack Daniels she'd already had with Julius.

Lowering her eyes once more, they fell upon Revel's back, with Mars' hand still open and flat against her shoulder. Vertigo took hold of Mars' mind and stomach, but she half-closed her eyes, losing focus on what she was seeing and letting her body begin to feel more normal. She focused her eyes once more, watching the green lines of the dream tethers taper down until they were the width of her thumb. She looked past the green light until the green light faded altogether, and Revel's whole back was lit up with golden energy—the golden energy she always saw inside of entities, just brighter. Mars focused more and sorted out what she was seeing, and the energy faded into *hundreds* of streams running from shoulders to waist.

"Fuck! That makes so much sense!" Mars didn't realize she'd spoken out loud until Revel twitched underneath her, turning her head and saying:

"Everything alright?"

"Yes! Sorry, Revel. Give me a minute."

Revel relaxed back into the pillows, and Mars studied the lines of energy. It was the same as every other entity, in a way; the difference was the *depth*. Other entities had rivers running down their body, as if across a flat plane. Revel had the rivers, but there were over thirty times as many, and they were *cubed*, with layers of rivers stacked atop one another.

The more she looked, the more she could see the dried up riverbeds where some lines should have been, the riverbeds dark and hollow. She reached up onto the table and picked up a few needles, putting two in her teeth while holding a third. Mars had no idea how she would tackle the rivers beyond the first layer, but perhaps fixing the top layer would be enough. With her experience working on entities, combined with what Revel had told her, Mars had little doubt that this work would indeed help repair the tethers.

Mars chose an energy stream near the surface of Revel's back with which to start. Using the needle, she pierced the flesh (or the dark space) near Revel's shoulder where a river of energy was still in the spot it was meant to be.

Then she moved her open hand towards Revel's waist, tracing the river of energy with her eyes and fingers until she found the place where it was once again in its rightful place. Pulling a needle from between her teeth, she pierced the flesh, spearing the river of energy in place.

Next, Mars grabbed several more needles, putting them in her mouth.

She pulled one out, going back up to Revel's shoulder, and pushed a needle through her skin close to where the river veered off course. She worked her way down, pushing needles through flesh, watching the river of energy slowly shifting towards the dried up riverbed where it truly wanted to be—where it would be strongest, fullest, and where it would thrive.

When Mars finished with that energy stream, she was out of needles. She sat up, looking up and squeezing her eyes shut.

"Revel, how are you doing?"

"I'm fine. Truthfully, it's a little more intense than I was expecting."

"Yeah, I guess I should have warned you." Mars picked up her glass of bourbon and ice. "I'm basically kicking up loose shit from all over your past, all over your mind, all over your heart—whether or not that has to do with the tethers."

"That's understandable."

"Good." Mars took a long drink of bourbon and, just as she finished the glass, a woman waitress—who immediately shifted into a man—set down a new set of long needles. It was a handful, perhaps fifteen. They were all different kinds, and Mars wondered if they were from different dreams which were going on at that moment. But those kinds of questions would have to wait.

With her face smashed up against the pillow, Revel spoke: "Would you like to send word to your Agents?"

Mars was taken aback. *Her* Agents? She'd felt very connected to the Agents, but having someone with such stature call them *her* Agents was very surreal. She shook away the feeling. "That's an option?"

"Of course."

"How about I do another line or two and we see how the tethers are doing. I'll send a message if I'm gonna be staying a while. Sound like a plan?"

"Yes."

Mars handed her empty glass to the waitress-now-waiter, nodded to them (hoping that the nod meant *bring me another bourbon, please and thank you*), then grabbed a few of the new needles, slipping them between her teeth and returning to the landscape of Revel's back.

File 58 :: [Roman Wing]

Thin clouds twisted into violet spirals in the morning sky. Roman Wing lay back on the slanted roof on one side of the Saint Louis Cathedral, just next to one of the towering spires, looking up at the swirling colors in the sky. With the Wonder flowing through his system, he felt like he could reach one of his long, pale hands up into the sky and push the colors about. His boots hung over the edge of the roof, high above Pirate's Alley on the upriver side of the cathedral. He could hear people wandering through the alley below. The Saint Louis Cathedral and Jackson Square was one of the areas he was assigned to, where the waking world was weaker and where they theorized Nimble and Nemu may attempt to attack the dream tethers.

Roman licked the sweetness from his lips. "So what do you think?" He heard the sound of someone blowing bubbles in liquid, a heavy yet slow procession of *Blop, blop, blop*. He looked over to see his sister, Thing Moss, take her lips off the straw. The plastic cup she held was glowing with swirls of green and orange and yellow.

Her squat, inhuman face was a picture of mistrust. "You know it's good. You are trying to get me hooked. Zero down. No payments until March. No extended warranty."

Roman shook his head, looking up at the cathedral's spire and cross poking into the night sky. "No, I just wanted to see how you were doing."

"You never cared before."

"That is mostly true." Roman looked over at his sister. "But neither did you."

She wore a flower print dress that was a size or two too big, along with a pair of bulky, dark rain boots. She halfheartedly stuck out her tongue, which glowed green and orange, coated with Wonder. She raised her plastic cup. "You made this?"

Roman took a drink of his own Wonder shake. "No, it was Mars' idea.

She made it. There's sugar and ice in it, I'm not certain what else. We've got a few Tupperware containers full in our fridge."

"Your children will look ugly and mostly-human."

"Mars and I are not lovers."

"Ah, then the *river lady*? Your children with her will still be ugly, but not ugly like mostly-human. This choice is not as horrible."

"I'm sure Elsh will be ecstatic to hear of your approval." He looked over at his sister, noting that she'd grown out her black hair. It was woven into thick, small braids of different sizes.

"What about you? Any love interests?"

She scrunched up her face, bit off a piece of straw, and spat it off the roof. "My kind see me as ugly half-human. No one wants my extended warranty."

Roman had expected as much. In truth, he and Thing Moss were both half-human and half-Collector, sharing the same human father and Collector mother. She had always embraced her Collector side, and had taken to eating large amounts of Wonder as a youth, especially after realizing that it was severely altering her appearance to be more Collector-like—making her skin rough and ridged and ash-colored, her teeth elongated, and her eyes yellowed.

Mars had recently shown Roman pictures of the green puppet-monsters in a movie called *Gremlins*, insisting that Collectors looked like taller, distant cousins to the Gremlin puppets. Roman did not see a connection.

One of the distinguishing factors which separated Thing Moss from the other Collectors, besides being slightly taller than most at five feet, was her hair. Collectors don't have hair. She'd kept her head shaved or buzzed for nearly her whole life until recently.

"Do you ever think about dating outside of the Collectors?"

She bit off another piece of straw and spat it over the roof, down into Pirate's Alley. "That's gross. And my kind don't *date*."

"Mother dated."

"Yeah, she dated ugly gross human."

Roman took a sip from his Wonder shake. "Do you think father is ever coming back?"

She shrugged. "Do you think mom's coming back?"

"Mom's dead."

She drank more of her shake and shrugged. "I thought we were playing the game *Ask Stupid Questions*. Buy now get Deluxe Edition at no extra charge. Free shipping."

Roman looked back up at the sky, the clouds twisting into long Chinese dragons in the light of the rising sun. "Logically, it may be possible for him to come back. Though not likely."

"Don't care. He liked you more than me. You were ugly like him."

"He liked me more because you *never wanted to be around him*. And you always called him ugly."

She blew more bubbles in the Wonder shake. *Blop, blop, blop.*

Meow.

Roman turned to find himself looking directly into the face of a fluffy, gray cat. "Yes?"

Meow-rower.

The cat fell into studiously grooming itself, at which point Roman saw the folded up piece of paper tucked into its collar. He set his drink down on the slanted roof and reached over, petting the cat and taking the paper. Unfolding it, he read the note scribbled therein, his face immediately dropping into a frown. "Oh, fuck."

"Stupid human problems?" asked Thing Moss. "Act now, only ten-ninety-nine, batteries not included?"

Roman sat up. "Not exactly." He scanned the note over again. It was scribbled in blue crayon and dream logic, but the message was pretty clear as far as he was concerned:

Dear The Agents Of ~~Badass~~. This is red planet extra-ordinary. Green shoelaces are fukt. In speakeasy helping Revel tie shoelaces. Bunny rabbit. It's working. Thoughts are clear, but writing caked in weird pictures. Words don't stay on page. Might need nails. If questions, send cats.

"I've got to go take care of something." He picked up his cup and sipped more of his shake, then extended the shake toward Thing Moss. "Would you like the rest?"

She held up her cup and Roman poured the rest of his blended Wonder into it, then stood up. The world around him was simmering with tiny, pulsating openings, as if every molecule of air was whispering a story to him.

Thing Moss nodded to her shake. "Tell ugly red hair human friend thank you."

"I will do that."

"And tell her I approve of her choice not to mate with you."

Roman looked down at his sister, at the only thing in the world even remotely like himself. He wondered if the emotion welling up inside him was a factor of getting old. He'd never been interested in counting his exact age, but he knew he'd been alive for about a century.

"We should do this more often," he said.

"Especially with shakes."

Roman nodded. "I will bring shakes."

Then he walked down the slanted roof and stepped off the edge, dropping down into Pirate's Alley.

File 59 :: [Edith Downs]

Saturday afternoon was warm, dark gray clouds stretching out like reclining gods in the sky. To most, it would seem that the clouds threatened rain, but Edith knew that Albert (a man she had yet to meet) and The Function weren't likely to let it rain anytime soon.

The Agents Of had received a series of messages from Mars over the last couple of days. The dream-logic scribblings were brought by way of cats, a fact which brought a welcomed smile to Edith's lips.

Between Mars helping fix the tethers and Quill using the Reverie Organ, it seemed the only tasks left were to guard Quill and to hunt down Nimble and stop him from destroying the tethers. The Nor, Julius, Roman, and Scape were all patrolling various weak spots in the waking world, which left Edith following Keaton and Quill to concerts and festivals.

Currently, Edith was leaning back on a metal rail, her back to the flowing Mississippi as she scanned the music-watching crowd at Crescent Fest in Crescent Park. The park stretched along the Mississippi on the edges of the Marigny and Bywater, just downriver of the French Quarter. There were walking paths, trees, old docks, and picnic benches. Between the Marigny and Crescent Park ran a fenced off cluster of train tracks with graffiti-covered train cars currently parked on one set of tracks.

The music itself was performed on a stage built under the skeleton of a large, old dock warehouse. The warehouse had no walls but had a very high roof of steel in case it rained. Outside the warehouse were a few food and alcohol tents. The band currently on stage was a zydeco band, with a lead singer playing a washboard strapped to his chest. They finished up their last song and the audience cheered wildly. Crescent Fest was rather new, but there were still at least five hundred people attending.

Edith wore a gray tank top and black pants, her duffel bag strapped tight to her back. Her hair was pulled back with the thick sepia streak hanging down nearly to her chin. The Extraction Glove hung silently from her arm, with its vials, tubes, and buttons.

All the joy Edith felt from being outside on such a pleasant day drained from her body once she spied one of Nimble's people at the far edge of the crowd, near the train tracks. She remembered him from outside of Nimble's Den—he was one of Nemu's group.

She turned and crouched, reaching through the metal rail to the ducked-taped speaker she'd hidden the day before. The speaker's spiraling wire trailed over the water, moving upriver and up towards the clouds until it vanished. She brought the speaker to her mouth and pressed down on the side button.

"Function! Albert! Come in!"

File 60 :: [The Function]

"Function! Albert! Come in!"

The Function jolted out of an afternoon snooze, somehow managing to slam his elbow on the arm of the rocking chair. "Ouch!" He was on the porch of Albert's shotgun house, endless fields of dark clouds stretching out in every direction, all of them covered in wooden posts with buckets hanging from them.

"You got that?" called Albert from inside.

"Yep!" The Function got to his feet, immediately realizing his leg was asleep and collapsing onto the ground.

"You sure?"

"Yeah, I'm sure." The Function crawled over to the radio, picked up the speaker, and hit the button. "This is The Function."

"Nimble's people are at Crescent Park. I need rain! Now!"

Albert ran out the front door, looking quizzically at The Function half-sitting, half-lying on the floor by the radio. "What are you doing?"

The Function hit the speaker's button again. "You got it, Edith."

He dropped the speaker and grimaced as he crawled up the porch rail to get onto his sleeping leg. Albert ran over to the buckets.

"No!" yelled The Function.

Albert spun around towards him.

"I mean, can I? I've always imagined doing it."

"Well, do it!" said Albert.

"Yeah, yeah," said The Function, using the rail to hobble over to the other side of the porch and its control panel of levers, with a dozen ropes coming from the back of it to spiderweb over the clouds, hooking up to all of the buckets. He pulled the first lever, and one rope tightened as thousands of buckets tipped, spilling their water into the dark clouds. He pulled the next and the next, each lever upturning another thousand buckets into the cloudy landscape as far as he could see.

Albert examined the levers, making sure each one was pulled all the way down, his eyes scanning the horizon to see that all the buckets were tipped. He nodded, content with the outcome, then looked at The Function. "Was it everything you hoped it would be?"

"Yes," said The Function. "Yes, it was."

File 61 :: [Keaton]

Standing near the side of the stage and the train tracks underneath the warehouse roof, Keaton watched the crowd as Quill got ready to take the stage. Keaton wore her bowler hat, black slacks, a white button-up shirt, and her suit coat with tails—the arms torn off of both her suit coat and her shirt to show off the tattoos running up and down each arm. Her eyes were smeared with dark blue makeup; her cane tucked down the back of her shirt.

Quill wore a blue poncho with the hood drawn, covering the Baku pelt and the device strapped to his back. He set his backpack on the side of the stage and pulled out the device's keyboard, but froze as rain came pouring down in sheets. The festival goers who were out in the open laughed and yelled, running under the roof for cover.

Keaton slapped Quill's shoulder, then moved into the crowd a few steps as he put the keyboard back in the backpack. Edith must have seen some of Nimble's people and made the call for rain. There was a bridge leading over the train tracks and into the Marigny at the other end of the warehouse, so Quill would just have to blend into the crowd until they were over the bridge.

A train rumbled loudly as it came near, just on the other side of the fence, the noise of the train rivaling the pounding of the rain on the metal roof above. Hopefully, the noise would throw off anyone looking for Quill. He and Keaton would only need thirty seconds.

Keaton watched a man in a leather jacket and sunglasses rushing through the crowd while holding a fistful of something glowing with orange light. He was heading straight for Quill. Keaton ducked down, her heart pounding. She leaped up and kicked as he passed, her boot smashing his glowing hand right into his face. Whatever was in his hand exploded in a flash of light and the man spun around screaming, orange light covering his face and arm.

Keaton landed in a crouch, turning to Quill. "*Run!*"

Quill spun around to run, immediately collapsing to the ground with green glowing shards of light sticking out of his arm like spikes. He struggled to get back onto his feet before smacking into the concrete ground.

The quick and loud beat of Keaton's heart combined with the thunderous rain on the metal roof and the squealing of the train as it braked to slow down. Fog erupted from all directions and a wave of relief swept over Keaton—*The Nor had shown up!*

Keaton instinctively backed up into the fog, trying to filter through the shadows inside of it, attempting to determine which shadows were Nor, which were festival goers, and which were Nimble's people.

Seeing a tall woman in a long coat creeping through the fog while holding an unwieldy device—a woman who most definitely wasn't Edith—Keaton reached back to pull her silver-tipped cane out from behind her back. Keaton's bent arm erupted with pain as it was quickly bound to her own head. She was struck so hard from behind that she lifted spinning through the air, slammed against one of the cement pillars holding up the warehouse roof, then crashed to the ground.

Keaton struggled into a sitting position, her vision spinning, her arm still bent and bound to her head with what she assumed was a rope of some kind. From out of the fog walked Nemu, the silent assassin, her plethora of blades sheathed to her black-clad body, her eyes forever closed, her face a sculpture of tranquility.

The short train behind Nemu slowed to a halt as a few of Nimble's thugs jumped out of one train car, using a device to blast a hole in the fence.

Keaton's heart sank as she realized the fog all around them wasn't fog at all, but was smoke from smoke bombs. The Nor weren't here.

Nemu crouched and pressed a small knife to Keaton's throat, her closed eyes mere inches from Keaton's face. "You're a Nor... but you're not Nor." She sniffed. "You smell human."

"Yeah, we all have our bad days," said Keaton.

"Then you may be useful."

Keaton tensed at the sudden sting in her leg, looking down to see a glowing green shard of glass sticking out of her calf. The glow she knew well, it was a hardened piece of dream tether.

Nemu stood up. Keaton's vision blurred as she watched a couple of Nimble's thugs pull Quill's limp body towards the train. As the dream tether shard's influence coursed through her, pulling her out of consciousness, she thought, *Aw, come on! I've helped you so much over the years!*

Then all was black.

File 62 :: [Edith Downs]

Edith dropped the speaker and took a deep breath as the wall of rain smashed down onto her. People screamed, laughed, and smiled as they ran for cover under the warehouse. On the opposite side of the warehouse from Edith, behind the stage, a train was braking.

Edith watched Nimble's thug pull out a handgun and stalk towards the stage. Edith's entire body tensed up, frozen as she watched him disappear into the crowd, rain plastering her hair to her face and dragging the hint of makeup she wore down her cheeks.

She'd seen the land of the dead, she'd seen The Angel of Death, she'd seen a sky torn up by Oblivion, she'd seen someone hurl ghosts or memory and blow up a stage at Chicory Fest—but seeing that gun made her feel like this was, perhaps, more *real* than she was ready for.

If it had been a revolver or a pistol from World War II, her mind might have been able to shove it into the category of her noir or pulp movies. But this looked like the same kind of handgun police and criminals used. She needed a few minutes to process it, but she didn't have a few minutes.

"Ok, ok," she said to herself, the rain smashing against her body. She flexed her hand inside the Extraction Glove. "I'm Edith Downs, protector of the memories of New Orleans. *Fuck, what does that even mean?*" She shook her head. "Ok, ok. What would Mars do? What would she do? She'd slap me for asking that and tell me to go be badass or something."

Edith slapped her own cheek, *hard*.

She took another deep breath, then slapped herself even harder, gritting her teeth and clenching her fist inside the Extraction Glove. It was then that she felt the mems crawling up her shoulders, the mems from her apron, from inside the dragonfly pin and several other items which she had in her duffel bag.

She straightened her shoulders and stalked into the packed crowd, raising the Extraction Glove towards the thug. "*Show him who you are*," she said to the mems. They ran down the length of the glove and leaped off the fingers, jumping from shoulder to shoulder through the crowd and diving into the thug's head. He stopped walking, looking up in a daze, his gun arm falling limp to his side.

Edith wove through the gathering smoke and the crowd, trying to discern Nimble's thugs from festival goers. She saw two more of Nimble's people and directed the mems towards them. The mems flowed into their heads, into their minds, drawing them deep into memories they never had. Edith's heart was pounding so loud, so hard that she hardly heard the rain on the metal roof. Then she saw the Asian lady, Nemu, stand up next to the crumpled figure of Keaton. Rather than raise the Extraction Glove, she raised her other hand, which held the net gun she'd used on The Angel of Death.

Nemu spun around and Edith fired, the net of light wrapping around Nemu and sending her smacking into the cement floor.

"*I am Edith Downs, member of The Agents Of and Protector of...*" She fell hard to one knee, falling forward but catching herself with the open hand of the Extraction Glove against the ground. Edith's eyes fell upon a glowing green shard of glass sticking out of her rib cage. As her vision blurred, she muttered, "*Ah fuck...*"

And then dreams took her.

File 63 :: [Roman Wing]

Roman pulled his duffel bag over his shoulder as he sprinted through the park of Jackson Square amidst the downpour of rain. He jumped onto the wrought iron fence and leaped well over the mule-drawn carriages to land in the center of Decatur Street, where he sidestepped two speeding cars and then ran around the amphitheater and up to the levee, all of the tourists and joggers running to take shelter from the rain.

Once there, he ran down the rocks faster than any person ought to, grabbed the ducked-taped speaker wedged between two rocks, and hit the speaker's button. "Function! Albert! What's going on?" He looked across the curve of the river towards Crescent Park, less than a mile from where he stood, where a massive crowd of people took shelter under the roof of the warehouse. The rain was coming down so hard that a few of the small food tents had collapsed.

"*Edith called it!*" yelled The Function from the crackling speaker. "*Nimble's people are at Crescent Fest!*"

Roman shoved the speaker back between the rocks. The Function was still speaking, his words lost in the pouring rain. Roman ran up the rocks to the paved path, then sprinted as fast as he could along the levee, the roar of the rain loud and fierce against the rocks and the river below. When he got to the end of the path where several warehouses and wharves separated the levee of the French Quarter from Crescent Park, he leaped up onto a chain-link fence, then jumped up onto the high roof of the first warehouse. He sprinted down the length of the wharves, leaping from warehouse to warehouse, the docks and ships down below him to his right along the river, with rows of train tracks below him to his left.

Roman jumped off the end of the last warehouse, down to the cement ground of Crescent Park. Mere yards ahead of him, hundreds of people clustered underneath the giant warehouse roof, taking shelter from the rain. Roman walked under the roof, asking person after person, "What happened here?" He merely listened to half an answer before moving to the next person as he ventured further into the crowd:

Oh, this band finished playing, and the rain just came thundering down!

The next band should be coming up any minute.

I think someone slipped and hurt themselves. There was some commotion, but maybe the EMS already took care of them.

Some people had these really bright light-up toys like they thought this was a rave or something. Freaking millennials...

There was a fight, I think, but I'm not sure. Maybe someone broke it up.

Roman made his way towards the stage as he kept asking random people. The Wonder flowing through the city, as always, would cloud what had actually happened from anyone who wasn't used to the odder aspects of the city. He kept asking, fishing for people who had retained enough of what truly happened so that he could string those pieces together and make some sense out of them. He didn't see Edith, Keaton, Quill, or any of Nimble's people, but the answers became a little clearer as he neared the stage:

This crazy fight broke out, but they stopped fighting.

I think it was a mugging that got stopped. But why would a mugging happen at a festival?

Oh, someone was hella drunk. They couldn't handle their liquor, so they're probably not from here. Their friends dragged them away, and you'll never guess how—on a damned train! How'd they get a train?

Through the crowd, Roman saw the burned open chain link fence with the empty set of train tracks just behind. A streetcar rolled up on those very tracks, squealing as it slowed, Julius stepping out of it before it stopped. He eyed the burned fence as he walked through it, rain falling in sheets off of his long trench coat and the duffel bag strapped to his back.

Roman walked out from underneath the cover of the warehouse roof, away from the crowd and into the rain.

Julius looked behind Roman at all of the festival goers. "The Function said it was Nimble's people. Where's Edith?"

"They were taken. I'm assuming all three of them, by train. I came here from Jackson Square, and there was no train going that direction, so they had to go towards the Bywater. The tracks either turn left at Press Street or go to the industrial canal before veering left, either way making their way lakeward."

Julius' body tensed, his fist clenching. He shrugged off his trench coat, catching it in his hand as it fell. "You take Press Street, I'll take the canal." He pulled out a tube-shaped flare launcher from his coat and hooked it to his belt. He threw his trench coat through the open door of

Henri's streetcar, then unstrapped his metal arm and tossed it in after. "This will just slow me down. Send a flare if you find them. I'll do the same."

Roman nodded. "They're four minutes ahead of us."

Julius looked back at him, dark fur sliding out of his flesh, his teeth growing larger in his skull as he grew taller. When he spoke, it came out as a growl that shook the ground under Roman's feet: "*They should pray you find them before I do.*" Julius turned and stormed down the tracks, his white tank top splitting at the seams as he transformed, a roar piercing the air as he gained speed.

Roman jumped up into the streetcar, grabbing Julius' trench coat and arm and tossing both onto a seat.

Henri whistled. "Been a while since I've seen that happen. Where to?"

"Down the Press Street tracks."

The streetcar lurched forward, and the doors swung shut. "I imagine we're in a hurry."

"An Agent's life is at stake. So, yes."

Henri nodded, pulling a large lever on the consul as the streetcar sped up, going far faster than normal streetcars would ever be able to go.

File 64 :: [Edith Downs]

Edith woke up sitting with her hands bound behind her to a pole of some kind, a metal wall at her back. She was in a long metal room, which was nearly empty. Keaton was tied up in a similar manner a couple of yards to Edith's right, with Quill tied with his hands above his head and sitting against the wall across from them. Both Keaton and Quill slowly looked around like they were also just waking up. All three of them were stripped down to their shirts, pants, and boots. Edith's whole body ached, but mostly her head and ribs. Her torn shirt was bloody around her ribs, but the bleeding had stopped.

Two of Nimble's people watched them, one at each end of the long room. One sat on a large wooden box and the other stood leaning against a wall.

The ground rumbled underneath Edith, which is when she realized they were on the short train that Nimble's people had come out of.

How many train cars had it been pulling? At least three. She tried to remain still as she struggled with the rope binding her wrists. The rope wasn't even budging.

The door next to the man on the box slid open and Nemu stepped in from the next train car, one hand gripping the top of her head. The man hopped off the wooden box. He was slender with a long, dirty-blond ponytail and wore a slim, gray coat.

Nemu took two steps into the train car and stopped. "Why is *she* here?" Her voice was utterly serene and her eyes, as always, were closed.

"After she got you with that net," said the blond guy, "you hit the ground hard. Hit your head on the cement and got knocked out."

"Why is she here?"

The guy shrugged. "Thought you'd want to question her. We don't usually get a chance to catch an Agent."

"We *don't* catch Agents. You may have just forfeited all our lives."

The guy laughed uncomfortably. "What?"

In a blink of Edith's eye, Nemu had taken a short knife from the plethora of blades strapped to her body and embedded it into the man's gut, pressing his body against the wall with her other arm. The man's eyes widened.

"This is the Blade of Long Life," she said. "You may feel time slowing already. In a moment, every second will be stretched out to months or years for you. If we are going to die, you will seemingly live longer than any of us. Though you will be living a stretched out version of your own death." She pulled a lever and a metal side door slid open. Immediately the rush of wind and grinding of the train was deafening. The train was moving very fast. Nemu dragged and threw the blond man out of the train, dagger still embedded in his stomach. Then she pulled the door shut and latched it closed.

Keaton and Quill were very much awake now. Keaton's eyes fixed on Nemu, but Quill's were set on the ground in front of him, his face tense. The man leaning against the wall on the far side of the train from Nemu seemed unphased.

Nemu walked down the long train car, crouching down next to Quill. "*Chans*. Out of all the people under my watch, you were the last person I marked as a potential traitor. I'm sure Nimble feels the same way." She pulled a tiny, gleaming dagger from her hip, the blade no longer than her index finger.

"The Nor are gonna kill you," said Keaton.

Nemu half turned to her. "Not if Julius finds me first."

"You don't have to die," said Edith. "You haven't done anything yet. It wasn't you who kidnapped me. I'll tell them." Edith had no idea what Julius would or wouldn't do to Nemu, but she wanted to buy some time for the three of them.

Nemu ignored Edith, turning back to Quill and passing the blade in front of his eyes. "I don't know that you ever saw this blade, Chans. This is the Truth Teller." She flipped it around in her hand and then shoved it deep into his thigh.

Quill grunted and looked away.

"It pulls out more than blood and pain—it pulls the truth." She tilted her head. "Where is the Baku skull?"

Quill shook his head and moaned through gritted teeth.

"Every time you don't answer me truthfully, the pain will be more agonizing." She inched away from him, leaving the dagger in his thigh. "Were you always going to turn on us?"

Quill moaned again. "*Yes*."

She nodded, turned towards Keaton, then back to Quill. "Were you Nor?"

"*Yes.*" It sounded like the truth was being yanked from him like a bad tooth.

Edith's eyes were darting around the room, trying to figure a way out of the situation.

"Where are my Baku?"

Quill moaned louder, slamming his head back on the metal wall.

Edith pulled against the ropes. She tried looking for memories, but nothing around her held any that were formed enough to communicate with. Edith spoke up: "Where are you taking us?"

"She's taking us to *Nimble*," said Keaton. "They'll kill us and destroy the dream tethers."

"Dream tethers?" Nemu stood and turned to Keaton. "Who is left to give a fuck about *dream tethers*? Chans had the Baku eat the hopes and dreams of nearly *everyone* who worked for Nimble. There's no one left to destroy *anything*. The crew you've seen today is all that's left."

"*What?*" said Keaton.

"Then why are you hunting Chans?" asked Edith.

"He stole my Baku. Then he sicced them on my soldiers, crippling their minds and altering their paths."

Quill let out a single laugh, then spat: "All the Baku *crippled* were your soldiers' dark, fucked up dreams."

Nemu crouched back down in front of him. "Where is my herd of Baku? Where is the Baku skull?"

Quill turned his head away, slamming his head back into the wall. Then he screamed.

"*Herd?*" said Keaton. "You call eight Baku a *herd*? Doesn't seem very ambitious."

Nemu turned to her. "Perhaps you don't know Chans as well as you think. I had *thirty-seven* Baku shipped to New Orleans from Japan. Seems he doesn't like you to know what he's doing."

"*My name's not Chans...*" grunted Quill.

Nemu looked down at him. "That's not the answer to my question." She grabbed the rope tying his wrists to a metal rod above his head, then cut the rope free of the rod. "I have other ways of getting the truth out of you." She walked to the front of the car, dragging him behind her with the blade still stuck in his thigh, leaving a thin trail of blood as she dragged him.

"No!" Keaton yelled.

Edith held her breath, expecting Nemu to pull open the side door, but Nemu reached instead for the door to the next train car. She opened it, dragging him through.

Just before the door shut, Edith yelled out, "*I'm in here!*"

"Believe me," said the one thug left, "no one through that door is coming to save you." He was stocky and bearded, wearing a thick black vest with arms covered in tattoos. He was still leaning back against the wall, toothpick swimming from one side of his mouth to the other, his cold blue eyes looking from Keaton to Edith and back.

When Edith didn't reply, he shrugged.

Beside her, Keaton whispered: *"Who the fuck is attacking the tethers?"*

"Nemu could have been lying," said Edith.

"If you talk," the man shouted, *"I'll knock one of you out."*

Edith looked at Keaton, whose eyes were burning like they'd kill the guy by themselves. Edith took a deep breath, trying to tell Keaton to calm herself. Keaton got the message and took a deep breath as well, her rage subsiding. They needed to keep calm if they were going to make it out of this.

Edith kept looking around the train, trying to find any way out, and she could see Keaton doing the same. Then she spotted them; a few mems running along the floor of the train car from the door Nemu had gone through. One of them was from her blue apron, and the others were from other items in her duffel bag. *They'd heard her yell for them.*

The mems ran past Keaton and up to Edith. She tried to casually look in their direction, so as not to alert the guard. She nodded behind her, and one of the mems slipped behind, between the metal wall and her hands, and began working to untie her. She looked at one of the other mems and motioned behind her again, then motioned to Keaton. It took the mem a moment, then it ran over to Keaton, who was looking at Edith with a raised eyebrow.

Edith sucked in her lips, trying to tell Keaton to stay silent, and Keaton gave a slight nod.

Keaton's eyes widened as the mem started working on the knots, but she didn't make a sound.

When Edith's wrists were free, she barely pulled one hand out from behind her to show Keaton. The mem who had untied her ran over to help the one working on Keaton's wrists, and soon she was free as well. She looked at Edith with a look of determination and nodded. Edith nodded back, hoping that Keaton had a good plan.

Keaton looked up at the ceiling. *"Fuck, I'm bored!"*

"Shut up!" said the guard, who didn't move. "You *look* like a kid, but you're Nor, so I *will* knock teeth out of your skull."

"Know any good stories?" Keaton asked him. "You know, where you murder people or whatever you do in your spare time?"

"I swear," said the guard.

Keaton looked at Edith. "You then. Tell me a story!" Then, in a fast whisper, she added, *"Start telling a story now!"*

Edith's mind raced. *A story*? How was she supposed to think of a story in the middle of being kidnapped and possibly tortured mere minutes from now?

The guard cursed and began stalking towards them down the length of the train car.

"*Fuck, Edith, now!*" whispered Keaton.

She spoke fast, nearly tripping over her words: "*Once upon a time a man was taken from his home, shipped overseas, and sold into slavery to work at a plantation. He'd lost everything—his country, his people, the woman he loved. But the new land he was in, it chose him for the job of winding up cicadas. He walked the treetops for hundreds of years—*"

Edith continued her rambling story as Keaton leaned over, one of her hands shooting up in front of Edith's mouth, grabbing her words and tossing them towards the guard. Edith could no longer hear the words pouring out of her mouth. The wall beside the guard lit up with a projected animation of a man walking through treetops, drawn with ill-defined swatches of color, with tiny insects hovering around him like fairies.

The guard spun towards the animation. "*What the fuck?*"

Edith got to her feet, but Keaton was already up and running towards the guard. She leaped into the air just beside the man, planting one boot in the center of the animation and pushing off, using the momentum to send her knee slamming into the man's nose with a reverberating *crack*. The man stumbled backward as Keaton fell into a crouch beside him, ducking his flailing arms as she kicked one leg out from under him. He crashed down hard onto one knee and Keaton launched herself at him, colliding into his back with her knees while grabbing two fistfuls of his hair and slamming his head into the metal wall with such force that it sounded like thunder. The lit-up animation stopped moving and slowly sputtered out. The guard's body went limp and slumped to the ground.

Keaton stood up, breathing heavily.

"*Holy fuck*," whispered Edith.

Keaton pointed towards the door to the next train car. "We need our gear, the Reverie Organ, and Quill."

Edith nodded. She'd known Keaton was older, but until that moment Edith had felt responsible for getting this girl out of danger. It dawned on her now just how backwards that outlook had been.

"How'd you get the ropes off?" asked Keaton as they approached the door.

"Mems," said Edith. "Um, memories of the items in my duffel bag. When I yelled out that I was here, they were close enough to hear me. So our gear should be in the next car."

Keaton raised an eyebrow. "Memories, huh? Good work."

Just then, a deep roar pierced the air from beyond the door, followed by screaming and shouting.

Edith smiled, relief washing over her. "Julius found us."

Keaton grabbed the door's lever and pulled, sliding it open. There was a shaking walkway with rails leading to the next car, rain pouring down in the gap between the cars. They stepped into the rain and Keaton slid open the next door. The walkway offered nothing but a tiny metal rail between them and the fences and houses racing by on both sides, the wind and rain pelting them from every side.

The scene in the car ahead was full of screaming people, wooden boxes, and giant creatures. One of the side doors was open and heavy rain poured into the car. A woman in a trench coat appeared in the doorway, terror painted across her face as she was about to bolt past them, but she was picked up from behind by a coiling elephant's trunk and thrown to the ground. The Baku raised its trunk and tore into her with its massive jaws, tearing out the glowing green mess of her hopes and dreams.

Another of the Baku turned its attention to Keaton in the open door, and Edith readied herself to yank Keaton back into the other train car. Keaton called out to it, her voice quivering with fear. "I'm Quill's sister. You remember me, right?"

The beast looked at her with the eyes of a tiger in mid-hunt, then turned its attention to the chaos of the train car.

There were about six Baku and maybe eight of Nemu's crew, half of them having their dreams eaten by Baku while the others attempted to fight off the beasts with devices and weapons.

"*Keaton!*" Quill was on the ground in the middle of the train, wrists still bound, blood running down the side of his head with the Truth Teller sticking out of his thigh. "*Keaton, stay back! I don't know if they'll attack!*"

Edith tapped Keaton's shoulder and pointed to the far side of the train, where Nemu slung a Baku pelt around her shoulders, opened the far door, and went through.

Keaton looked back. "Get to Quill and you'll be safe!"

"Wait!" yelled Edith, but Keaton was already running through the car, dodging Nemu's people fighting off Baku, dodging the Baku themselves.

Edith looked behind her, seeing more Baku appearing inside the car they'd come from. She turned back to the car ahead and ran inside, circling one of Nimble's people who'd somehow made a shield of orange light which the Baku was pounding against like a wall. She crouched next to Quill, who'd pulled the Truth Teller from his thigh. He held it between his boots with the blade sticking up, and was cutting through the rope on his wrists. "Help me," he said.

Edith pushed his boots together to stabilize the blade. "I can't touch the knife."

"Fuck, of course you can't." The rope split and he pulled his wrists apart.

"Come on," she said, pulling him to his feet.

He put his arm around her, using her to stand on his wounded leg. "We need to get the Reverie Organ." He pointed at a box by the door Nemu had gone through.

They made their way through the chaos, Edith keeping her body away from any Baku who weren't busy fighting or eating, with Quill leaning heavily on her shoulders as he limped.

Keaton stood at the open door as they approached. Edith could see the engine, no longer attached to their car, speeding down the tracks through the rain. Their car was slowing down.

Keaton screamed in rage at Nemu's escape.

"Keaton!" yelled Quill as they approached the box with all of their gear on it. Edith grabbed her duffel bag and shoved the Extraction Glove inside. Quill grabbed his backpack, slinging one strap of the Reverie Organ over his shoulder. Keaton picked up her sleeveless suit coat, bowler hat, and cane.

Looking around, Edith realized there was only one of Nemu's crew still fighting off a Baku, with the others having their hopes and dreams feasted upon. The one who was left was using the orange barrier to keep the Baku away, attempting to bash the barrier into the Baku like a shield. Keaton ran up behind the man, crouching and swinging her cane to knock his legs out from under him. The orange shield sputtered out, and the man raised his arms to no avail as the Baku ripped into his body.

Edith, Quill, and Keaton moved to the open side of the train car. When it slowed to a crawl, they took turns jumping down into the pouring rain. Quill was last, his leg giving out from under him as he fell into the mud and gravel.

Edith took a couple of steps away from the train, taking the Extraction Glove from her duffel bag and pulling it over her hand and arm, immediately feeling better with the weight of it. Looking around through the rain, she didn't know what part of the city they were in. The train tracks ran through a long strip of gravel and mud, with the fences on one side guarding the back yards of countless houses and the fences on the other side guarding a bunch of giant, rusty warehouses.

Quill got to his feet and Keaton stalked over, punching him hard in the gut. Quill coughed and collapsed back onto the ground.

"You lied to me?! You fucking lied to Swallowtail, to Revel?!"

The rain pelted Quill's face, the keyboard and the Reverie Organ splayed out next to him in the gravel. *"I'm sorry, K.* I'm sorry. I love you. I love The Nor. But you all have less than one foot in the waking world— *you don't understand how dark things are now!* I had no idea how fucked the waking world actually is, not until I *lived* in it. Not until I *experienced*

Nimble and people like him!"

Keaton paced back and forth, now wearing her bowler hat and sleeveless tuxedo coat, her cane shoved into the back of her shirt. Behind Quill the Baku began casually jumping down from of the stopped train cars, moving up to the three of them. Most seemed oddly peaceful now that they'd eaten, but not all of them. One stepped between Keaton and Quill, its eyes fixed on Keaton, and another moved to Quill's side to check on him.

Quill grabbed its mane, using the Baku's body to pull himself up to his feet again. A third Baku approached from the other side, holding the large Baku skull in its open mouth. Quill took the skull from the Baku, holding it in one hand while leaning on the other Baku for balance.

Edith stepped closer to Keaton, feeling protective of the girl once more, despite knowing Keaton was obviously better equipped to deal with the situation. Edith spoke to Quill: "Why did the Baku come for you if you didn't have the skull?"

"I feed them and look after them. Nimble and Nemu were starving the Baku so they could be used against The Nor. The Baku like me. They knew I was in trouble, somehow. They brought me the skull so they can communicate with me."

"You *feed* them?" said Keaton, her voice still bubbling with rage. "All thirty-five of them?"

"Thirty-seven."

"How did they find you?" asked Edith.

"I'm not sure. They must have my scent, or the scent of my dreams."

Edith looked around at the Baku. There were the three around Quill, and perhaps a dozen more behind him, most lying down in the rain as if lounging in the sun. "You weren't just feeding the Baku Nimble's people though, were you? You've been feeding them the dream tethers."

Quill's eyes traced the rows of Japanese Kanji running down the Baku skull.

Keaton, who was still pacing, spun around towards him. "So it was *all a lie?* You're just doing Nimble's job for him? Just gonna *tear apart* the waking world instead of fighting for it? *You're not my brother—my brother wasn't a coward.*"

Even through the rain Edith could see the tears streaming down Keaton's face.

Quill looked up at Keaton, his eyes determined. "If I wanted to destroy the dream tethers, they'd be gone already. You don't know the kinds of things I've seen, K. That chaos we just stepped out of, that was *nothing.* Do you know what would change if we kill Nimble and Nemu? *Nothing* would change. This is beyond them."

Keaton reached her hand towards Quill, despite the sniffing trunk of the Baku mere feet away from her. When she spoke, her voice broke, like the tears running into her mouth were too heavy for her voice to hold up. "I love you, Quill. I know you can't see it, but you're broken. Let me help you. It's not too late to fix this. Put down the skull and come with us."

Quill's eyes turned downward, tracing the Kanji along the skull once more before looking back at her. "You're right, K—I *am* broken. But so is the whole waking world. People like Nimble and Nemu, they've sucked the dreams from the people of New Orleans for too long. There aren't enough people left with pure hopes, pure dreams, who can combat the dark, twisted hopes that are left."

Edith spoke before she knew what she was doing: "*You're wrong.* The waking world and the people of this city have more hopes and dreams infused into their hearts and minds than you could ever imagine."

Quill hefted the skull up, fitting it down over his head. Edith could see his eyes through the hole for the elephant trunk. "Don't worry. I'm not out to destroy your waking world. Like I said, if I wanted to do that, it would have been done weeks ago. The waking world is a badly constructed rowboat floating in an ocean of dreams. I'm just going to capsize it. I'm going to remind the waking world of what it's floating on. The ocean will wash away the murk, the dirt, the blood. And when the boat is righted, when the water is bailed out, the waking world will be fresh, new, and aware of the currents of dream running just underneath the surface."

Keaton's hand fell to her side. "Quill, please. There's no way you can know what that will do."

"No, there isn't, but I have a good idea of what will happen. Even if I'm wrong, the other possible outcomes are still better than how things are now. The waking world can still be saved." He pushed his hand further into the fur of the Baku's pelt. "I'll see you on the other side of this, K, and you'll see why I had no choice."

"No!" screamed Keaton, the Kanji on the Baku skull lighting up as Quill vanished with the Baku he held onto.

The other Baku began to vanish, one by one, and Edith bolted forward, lunging towards the Baku facing Keaton, trying to grab onto its fur. The Baku spun its head and snapped its jaws around Edith's arm as it vanished, pulling her into dreams with it.

Somewhere in the space between dream and reality, Edith heard Keaton screaming her name.

File 65 :: [Keaton]

Keaton's jaw shook with tension, her knees giving way beneath her as she fell painfully onto the muddy gravel. Rain pelted down on her as the last of the Baku vanished, leaving her alone with the three train cars and a slew of Nemu's soldiers, whatever twisted hopes and dreams they may have had torn from their bodies and minds.

She wasn't even sure where she was, maybe up in Gentilly by the lake. Wherever she was, it was far from Storyland, far from The Nor, far from any place Quill would have gone.

The person she loved the most in the world had lied to her, betrayed her, and he was going to destroy the city. He could be anywhere. Maybe Edith could stop him, somehow. But even as Keaton thought it, she had little hope of Edith stopping Quill. His plan, whatever it was, had been thought through for years.

Picking up a small stone from the ground, Keaton squeezed it in her fist, letting the stone's edges dig into her palm and fingers. How could she have been so *manipulated* by him? How could she have believed his lies?

She'd given up being Nor to help him, to age with him, so they could be in each other's lives again. Now she didn't even have The Nor. She had no one. If she could only talk to him, maybe she could reason with him, show him he was wrong. Maybe she could try to fix him, or help him fix himself.

Her breaths became sharp and rugged, tears streaming down her face, blood trickling from her hand clutching the stone. Everything she'd sworn to do, everything she'd wanted from life, had been ripped from her grasp. Her chest hurt like something was torn out of her.

Somewhere in the water and pain, she was aware of someone approaching. "Keaton! Are you alright?"

She looked up at Roman, who pulled out a gun-looking device and shot a pulsing flare arcing into the rain and stormy clouds. She looked back down at the muddy ground as he crouched next to her. "Are you hurt?"

She didn't look up at him as she spoke: "Quill's the one hurting the dream tethers. He's gone. I don't know where."

"Why would Quill do that? Is he working for Nimble? Where's Edith?"

"He said the waking world is a boat, floating on dreams, and he's going to capsize the boat. Edith used the Baku to chase him when he vanished."

"If he's trying to destroy the waking world, why keep playing the Reverie Organ and healing the tethers?"

"He's not *destroying* the tethers. He says he's helping the waking world, fixing it. That the dreams will clean it or something."

"Capsizing... capsizing... *That's exactly what he's doing!*"

She looked up at Roman, his eyes staring at the muddy ground, lost in thought. "That makes sense to you?"

"Of course! It's obvious! He's hurting the dream tethers and then healing them, over and over again, throwing off the balance of the waking world. *He's rocking the boat.* He may just need to give one big, final push in either direction. But if he pushes by hurting the dream tethers, they might snap. So his big push has to be to *heal*, using the Reverie Organ on a vast number of people."

"Like an arena concert or a sports game?"

"The Reverie Organ would be most effective at one of the spots where the waking world is weakest."

Keaton clenched her eyes shut, suddenly feeling very connected to her brother, as if they shared the same thoughts. At that moment, she hated how well she knew him, hated how much his soul was imprinted onto her. "He'd go to the place he knows."

"Are you sure?"

She nodded. "He's hurt, weak. He's going home."

"What about The Nor?"

"He has thirty-seven Baku."

"*Thirty-seven?* He only had eight!"

Keaton shook her head, the words *he lied* reverberating through her head but refusing to pass through her clenched teeth.

"I don't know how he'd get enough people there to be affected by the Reverie Organ," said Roman, "especially when it's pouring rain. But if you're certain..."

There was a fast series of *Booms*, like a row of houses being dropped from the sky in quick succession, as Julius ran up. He shrunk down into human form as he neared, his dark fur becoming skin. He was shirtless, his metal leg gleaming in the rain.

Roman turned to him and stood. "We're going to Storyland, now, to stop *Quill* from potentially destroying the waking world. Edith's there already. I'll fill you in on the way."

Julius' eyes fell on the train car, the door open with Nimble's people writhing around on the floor. Keaton saw the utter rage he held back. She imagined he wanted to do terrible things to those criminals, to question them, to destroy them.

Roman got in the streetcar, and Julius looked down at Keaton, his eyes softening. "You coming?"

She shook her head. "I don't... I don't think I can trust myself right now. You go without me."

"Or you can get in the streetcar, decide what you want to do or not do when we get there." Julius walked up, extending his hand to her.

Keaton looked up at him, dropping the blood-smeared stone she held, letting the rain begin to wash it clean. She looked at her bloody hand, then offered her other hand up, but Julius shook his head, reaching specifically for the hand smeared with blood. Julius took it in his, pulling her to her feet. Her knees burned, her chest felt raw, and the rest of her body felt like a half-dead punching bag.

Julius turned and stalked towards the streetcar, pulling himself up the stairs.

Keaton pushed her soaked bowler hat down onto her head, checked her cane sticking out the back of her shirt, and followed him up the steps.

File 66 :: [Edith Downs]

Once upon a time, when Edith was a little girl, her parents took her water skiing on a lake where some of her family lived. It was one of the few times they traveled to do anything most people would find fun. The memory of plunging into the lake and then being pulled through the resistant water while trying to stand up—that memory was the closest comparison she had to her present experience.

She was plunged into thought, into the ideas and dreams of the city. It was like floating in glowing green water, dreams blooming around her like windows depicting scenes from peoples' minds. The Baku holding her arm in its mouth swam through dreams like a dog or an elephant, pulling her along. Despite the slow movements of the Baku, the dreams rushed by. The dreams brushed her body and moved *through* her, momentarily filling her heart and mind with various emotions and vivid images of strangers' bliss, curiosity, and fear.

Even with all the chaotic visions and emotions, Edith was overcome with wonder and marvel at the utter beauty around her. The dreams went on endlessly everywhere she looked. For seemingly miles in every direction were pulsing green rivers surging, shifting, and crossing one another. She wondered if those were the dream tethers.

"It's beautiful, isn't it?" Quill floated next to her, wearing the Baku skull and holding onto a swimming Baku's fur with one hand.

"Yes," said Edith.

"These aren't just the dreams of the city, Edith. This is the city's *potential*. You're seeing the magic which the city is capable of, what it's been held back from for so long."

"Magic? New Orleans is the most magical place I've ever been to. Are you sure it's being held back? Have you *been* to other cities, Quill? I don't think you're giving the city enough credit for riding the line between the waking world and dreams."

"I don't care about other cities, I only care about mine." He looked to where they were heading. "We're almost there."

Ahead of them, several of the green beams intersected, the green light coming from them nearly blinding.

"Quill, what if we could find a compromise? What if you could help the city's potential without... capsizing the boat?"

The massive Baku skull moved back and forth as he shook his head. "If there were a better way, I would have figured it out. I would be doing that."

Just as quickly as she'd been thrown into the sea of dreams, Edith was yanked out and tossed onto a patch of soaking wet grass as the Baku spit out her arm. The rain roared as it pelted her skin and the surrounding grass, the dark gray afternoon sky bursting with lightning beyond the treetops.

She reached into one of her pouches, but it was empty.

"You might be looking for this," said Quill, standing above her with Edith's net gun in his hand. He pulled the trigger, the net of light wrapping around Edith as she fell sideways into the muddy grass.

Edith's limbs, including the Extraction Glove, were bound tight to her body. She began shaking at the sight of all the Baku looming above her, one of them sniffing her with its trunk.

"I'm sorry," said Quill. "But I can't have you running loose or telling The Agents Of where we are."

"Quill, don't do this! You have to know this isn't right!"

"I've spent the last ten years doing things that were *wrong*, with the understanding that the ends justify the means. I've seen and done terrible things. With only a few more 'wrong' actions, I'll finally have the chance to do something truly good for the city—something so good that everyone will forget the terrible acts I've done to save them. Everyone except for me."

He turned and began limping through the muddy grass, holding onto a Baku to keep balance on his injured leg. Edith screamed as a Baku reached down and gripped the net of light with its teeth, picking her up and carrying her along with Quill and the rest of the Baku.

Looking around, she guessed that all thirty-seven of the Baku were there, spread out and walking through the towering trees. They were in one of the big parks, and soon she saw the back of Carousel Gardens with the roller coaster, Ferris Wheel, and other rides looming up above the wall of trees and the fence. Some of Edith's mems crawled out of the bag strapped to her back and she whispered to them to turn off the net gun in his hand. They tried to get out of the net, but even though the holes in the net were large enough for them, they were trapped, unable to pass through.

The Japanese Kanji running down Quill's Baku skull flashed and several of the Baku ran forward, tearing apart the fence. Within moments

Edith was being carried through the fence and into Carousel Gardens, separated from Storyland only by a fence and an archway. The grass and pathways of Carousel Gardens were covered in large pools of water splashing madly in the onslaught of rain coming down. The carousel itself was still taped off with signs proclaiming it to be closed. The park was nearly empty, most likely having been vacated due to the crazy amount of rain. Any employees still wandering about began screaming and running at the sight of the Baku.

Fog weaved through the trees of the neighboring Storyland, and Quill took off the Baku skull and called out: "*Nor! I've got one chance to heal the city for good! The Baku are ordered to attack anyone coming near, and that includes you! Please stay back!*"

"*Quill!*" boomed the voice of King Nor as she stepped out of the fog near the fence to Storyland. Her eyes darted from the scattered Baku to Edith to Quill. In her hand she gripped a golden dagger, her dark, soaked dreadlocks falling to her waist. "*You will hand over the Reverie Heart, release the Agent, send away the Baku, and explain yourself!*"

Quill shook his head. "I'm sorry, Swallowtail. You have to trust that I know what I'm doing." He pulled the Baku skull back over his head, the Japanese Kanji flashing across its surface as the Baku spread out.

King Nor took a step back into the fog, away from the Baku. "These creatures are innocent! Are you going to force us to take them down?"

Quill stalked away from King Nor, towards the towering Ferris Wheel. "Only half The Nor are here!" he called out. "The rest are out guarding the tethers. You can't win. Just stay back. Please." Quill walked into a tiny building next to the Ferris Wheel and a moment later the ride groaned to life and began to spin. It was around seventy feet tall with sixteen multicolored passenger cars. The cars didn't have any roofs or umbrellas, leaving them completely open to the pouring rain.

Quill limped from the tiny building to the base of the Ferris Wheel with the passenger cars streaming by backwards. He grabbed the net holding Edith, pulling it from the Baku's grip, Edith screaming as he tossed her into one of the cars. As she moved backwards and up inside the car, she saw Quill quickly get into the next car. Her stomach dropped as she rose above Carousel Gardens, above the trees and rides, and towards the dark, cloudy sky.

Edith struggled to look towards the ground below. Fog moved towards the Ferris Wheel, the Baku either standing guard or charging into the haze. Then three Baku attacked the tiny building Quill had gone into, crushing the walls and smashing anything inside. Immediately the Ferris Wheel slowed to a stop, with Edith's car near the top, which meant that Quill's car was just behind her at the top as well.

"*Mom!*" she heard Quill yell. "*I need you now! Please! It's an emergency!"*

Edith squirmed inside her net, careful not to fall off the seat of the car she was in. She managed to push with her boots against one side of the car, pushing her back up against the other side. Then she looked over the car's back to see Quill standing in the car behind hers, gripping a glowing pearl in his fist—the same kind of pearl that was strapped to her wrist. He tossed the Baku skull from the top of the Ferris Wheel. The skull turned in the air as it fell, splashing into the muddy ground far below.

Quill yelled out to the few close Baku: *"Crush it! No one will abuse you again!"*

The howls of the Baku were thick with sadness and utter rage as they rose up on their hind legs, taking turns slamming their front paws and their tusks into the skull. Edith heard the skull cracking over the roar of the rain as the Baku pounded down on it over and over.

Then she watched Quill pull the straps of the Reverie Organ over his shoulders, securing it tight across his back with the Organ's keyboard hanging over his stomach.

A rope ladder swung down next to him and his car, batted about by the rain and the wind. A woman was climbing down, her silvery blue dress shimmering with reflections of the lightning above.

Quill reached out and grabbed the rope ladder when she neared the bottom, pulling it so that she descended into the car with him. The woman looked at Edith's head peeking up from the next car, all wrapped in the net of light.

"Quill, what's going on? Are you all in danger?"

Edith screamed when she saw the green shard of glass in Quill's hand, but she was too late. Quill wedged the shard into the woman's thigh.

The woman looked into Quill's eyes. "I don't understand."

"You will, mother. Just sleep now." Quill held her as her head rolled back. He quickly sat her in the car's seat, reaching back to pull some wires from the Reverie Organ and coiling them around her arms and body. He stood up, his fingers pressing down on the keys of the Organ. The broken, high-pitched notes ripped through the air and the rain. Edith's heart sank as she realized that the woman must be The Moon.

The Moon's mouth opened in a silent scream as green light poured up from her mouth and into the sky, the green light colliding with the dark, cloud-covered sky and bursting out in every direction.

Edith felt The Moon's pearl vibrating against her wrist, held there within the confines of the bracelet. Her mems crawled along the inside of the net, looking for a way out.

Mars had explained the way The Moon's pearl worked, to enhance the frequency of the Reverie Organ and counter it. Roman had explained The Moon's ability to enhance frequencies herself, and Edith realized what was happening—Quill was using The Moon, his mother, to enhance the power and radius of the Reverie Organ.

He was *broadcasting*.

Edith could only imagine how powerful The Moon was. Perhaps Quill was luring the *whole city* into the throes of their own dreams by channeling the device's energy through her.

As Edith sat there tied up in the net of light, a position she'd put The Angel of Death in only months before, everything that Quill had said was quickly clicking into place in her mind.

Somehow this was Quill capsizing the boat.

And there was nothing Edith could do to stop him.

File 67 :: [The Function]

The Function had been above the clouds during a rainstorm only three times before, and only once during the day. The floor of dark clouds stretched out in every direction underneath a beautiful blue sky. The sun was still heading towards the horizon, so he guessed it was maybe five or six in the afternoon. The opaque crescent of The Moon hung there with the backdrop of blue sky, the rope ladder dangling down into the dark clouds. He'd borrowed a pair of binoculars from Albert, feeling stupid for not thinking of it earlier. He stood in front of the shotgun house, using the binoculars to look down into a small gap in the clouds the size of a pothole[45]. He focused on Crescent Park, Jackson Square, and Storyland. With the rain and being miles up in the sky, he couldn't see much of anything.

Bursts of green light erupted from City Park, and he hurried around the cloud's edge to look. A beam of light shot up into the clouds from Storyland, breaking apart the clouds and hitting The Moon itself. A wash of green light pulsed out from The Moon in every direction for miles.

"Um, that's not normal." The Function ran back to the shotgun house, up the porch stairs, and through the front door. "Hey, Albert! Something's happening with The Moon!"

Albert sat at his table with his desktop computer in front of him, which was normal. What wasn't normal was Albert slumped back in his chair, staring up at the ceiling with a childlike smile on his face.

"Oh, shit," said The Function. For a split second, he wondered why he wasn't affected by the Reverie Organ, but then he remembered his origin story. "Oh yeah, that makes sense[46]". He ran to the front porch and

---

[45] A New Orleans pothole, so about the size of a Volkswagen Bug.

[46] For The Function's origin story (albeit told in a weird order), please see "the episodes", which are located in a tent often set up near the tarot readers on Jackson Square, or near the Collectors' booth at the Bridge Market.

flipped a couple of switches on the console, grabbing the speaker and yelling into it. "Julius! Roman!" He flipped another switch. "Julius! Roman!"

His eyes fell on the hole in the clouds and the miles-long rope ladder coiled up just beside it, one end tied to a post of Albert's front porch. Shoving the binoculars into his coat, he ran over and kicked the coiled rope ladder into the hole, then started climbing down, quickly getting soaked by the onslaught of rain.

"If the city isn't wiped out," said The Function to himself. "They're installing a damned elevator."

File 68 :: [Mars]

Mars collapsed into a booth of the dream-speakeasy-jazz-club, her body not much more than a pile of mush. She felt like she'd been working on Revel for days. All she'd consumed was water and bourbon, and she hadn't slept at all.

A while ago, she'd told Revel that she needed music that wasn't jazz songs shoved into a blender. Currently, the musicians (playing trumpet, drums, and stand up bass with a woman vocalist) were performing surreal jazz covers of Tricky's first album, *Maxinquaye*. They were playing the song, *Suffocated Love*. Mars was surprised by how many of Tricky's songs sounded pretty similar when performed by a disjointed, ghostly jazz band. For some reason, she hadn't really equated Tricky's music to jazz before, which was a little embarrassing, seeing as she'd been born and (partially) raised in New Orleans. Maybe jazz just sounded too normal to her.

Revel was lying on the bed of pillows, the slow-motion dancers covering the dance floor beyond. Mars had pulled the needles out of Revel's back to give her a break. She didn't know that it was possible for an entity to endure so many hours of work in a row. Mars had no concept of time in the dream world, but guessed that she'd been at this at least forty hours now. The fact that she was inside of dreams must have attributed to being able to last so long herself.

There was a commotion in the hoard of swing dancers and from the thick of them emerged a young girl, who Mars assumed was Nor. The girl fell to her knees, one of her arms and most of her torso covered in long, bloody gashes—but the liquid pouring from her was green rather than red. Her long blonde hair spilled down her back, her good hand clenched around the hilt of a long, curved blade.

Revel twisted onto her side, moaning in pain as she did. "What is it, Heron?"

"It's Quill. He's come to Storyland with an *army* of Baku. He's got

The Moon. We don't know what he's doing..."

The swing dancers slowed to a halt, the music's bass stretched out into an endless *hum*.

Revel spoke to Heron: "Go back and follow King Nor's orders. Tell her to send word as soon as she knows more."

Heron nodded, at which point Revel raised a hand and all of the green slashes in Heron's flesh closed up. Heron got to her feet, turned, and disappeared into the crowd of swing dancers.

"I should go," said Mars. "If I'm not helping here, I can help in Storyland."

"You will be more help here," said Revel, pushing herself to her knees on the pillows. Three cats ran up to her, and she spoke to them: "Find out what's going on in Storyland, then come back and tell us. Be quick!"

The cats turned and darted into the cluster of dancers.

File 69 :: [Julius Marcos]

The streetcar splashed to a stop on City Park Avenue, one of the flooding streets bordering the massive park. All the streets they'd traveled through were flooded, with rain still cascading down from the dark clouds.

Julius looked at Keaton. "You decide yet?"

"I'm in," she said.

"Good. Let's go."

"Y'all be careful!" called Henri as the three of them jumped down into the shallow lake of the street.

Julius, Roman, and Keaton ran into the park, splashing across pools of water and muddy grass as they made their way past various types of trees, the rain and wind pelting them from every side. They came up to a long, marshy stretch of water and ran across a small stone bridge that took them to the other side. They passed the restaurant Morning Call, several people drinking cafe au laits and eating beignets on the covered patio, watching confused as three strange people sprinted across the park in the pouring rain and into a parking lot full of water.

"It's already begun!" yelled Roman.

"*Fuck*," said Julius.

Green light emanated from the trees of Storyland ahead, followed by the distant, high-pitched whistles of the Reverie Organ competing with the roar of the rain. The Moon's pearl against Julius' wrist began to buzz. Green beams of dream tethers appeared in the sky against the dark clouds, several of the tethers intersecting above Storyland itself. The patrons of Morning Call knocked over tables and chairs as they fell to the ground, blank stares and smiles stealing across their faces. Jagged cracks of green light shattered the air of the parking lot like horizontal lightning.

"Keep running!" yelled Julius, ducking underneath one of the cracks in space. "The waking world is starting to break!"

They made their way across the vast parking lot and towards the entrance to Storyland. On the sidewalk was a sleek black motorcycle lying on its side.

"That's Nemu's bike!" said Keaton.

Keaton had filled in the other two on the events of the train as they'd traveled in the streetcar. Julius guessed that Nemu must have gotten Quill's destination from him with that truth-knife of hers.

The guardian statues of Humpty Dumpty and Little Bo Peep were absent from their posts, most likely having gone into Storyland to protect the amusement park from within.

Julius, Roman, and Keaton each vaulted over the wrought iron fence and into Storyland. Fog covered the park, with the green cracks searing through the air and lighting up the fog from within. Sounds of swords, screaming, and growling filled the air along with the pounding of rain and the Reverie Organ.

Deep in the mist, Julius could see shadows of Baku fighting the small figures of The Nor. "Hurry, but watch each other's backs," said Julius. He let his body grow, fur sprouting from his skin, but held back from fully turning until he knew what was going on.

"Julius!" A Nor boy fell out of the fog in front of them, giant green gashes across his chest. "Quill's holding us off with Baku! He's on the Ferris Wheel and he's captured Edith and The Moon!"

"He's using The Moon!" said Roman. "Of course! He's using her to boost the signal!"

Julius spun around as a scream erupted from their left. Further into the green fog, he saw a figure too tall to be Nor—a slender figure holding two long blades. As the god-animal aspect of him slid forward, his lion's hearing picked up her words: *"Tell your people to stop attacking my Baku."*

Another voice yelled, "You crazy bitch!"

The shadow brought one of her blades down into the ground.

"Nemu's killing The Nor," growled Julius. *"You two stop Quill, I'm going to rip her in half."*

"No!" said Keaton, grabbing onto Julius' fur-covered wrist.

Julius spun around, pulling his wrist away.

Keaton glared up at him. "Let me deal with her."

"You think you can take on Nemu?"

"If it comes to *killing* Quill, I don't think I can," said Keaton through clenched teeth. "But if it comes to killing the woman who *broke* my brother, I'll cut the bitch's head off." Keaton pulled her walking cane from the back of her shirt, pushing her soaked bowler hat onto her head with her other hand. "If I die, I die."

Julius' sharp teeth pulled into a sneer. *"Alright."* He turned to Roman. *"Care for a ride, like the old days?"*

"I'm old-fashioned," said Roman, leaping onto Julius' dark fur-covered back, at which point Julius leaped up through the treetops, above the battles between the Baku and The Nor, climbing up the thick branches of the tall oak trees until he reached the canopy, which stretched out before them like small, rolling green hills.

Julius roared, leaping forward across the fog-dipped treetops towards Carousel Gardens and the Ferris Wheel beyond, all the screams, growling and yelling left far below.

File 70 :: [Mars]

Mars sat back in the booth, staring up at the tin-printed ceiling of the dream-jazz-club. Everything in her wanted to be with the Agents, whatever they were doing. She knew her abilities were needed here, and in the waking world she'd most likely be limited to her more base abilities of punching people in the face or kicking them in the ribs, but she hated sitting doing nothing while shit was going down.

Revel stood at the open doorway looking at the glowing tethers when she suddenly stumbled backwards, grabbing onto the bar to keep from falling, her grasping arms knocking glasses off to shatter onto the floor.

Mars slid out of the booth and ran to Revel, still feeling like she was going to fall into the empty void of the woman's figure. "What's wrong? Were the dream tethers attacked again?"

Revel shook her head, leaning on the bar. "I feel great," she whispered. "Mars, look at my energy."

Mars flipped her vision so she could see the streams of light flowing through Revel's body. Fighting off a bout of vertigo, she saw the streams bending towards the dried-up riverbeds where they belonged. Revel was being healed faster than Mars could ever hope to heal an entity—a year's worth of work being done in seconds.

Revel squirmed with the energy, falling to the floor.

"What the fuck is happening?" Mars asked.

"Quill is *healing* me. He's healing the dream tethers." Revel looked into Mars' eyes, her own eyes watering. "He's tilting the waking world in order to *flip* it. He must be the one who's been attacking the dream tethers! Attacking and healing, over and over again."

"I should go," said Mars, turning towards the cluster of swing dancers. She knew the way out must be through them. "Let me go and stop him."

Revel grabbed Mars' hand, shaking her head. "There's no time. You need to reverse the process."

"What do you mean?"

"You're a healer, Mars. *Hurting* should be easier."

Mars shook her head. "No, I can't fucking *hurt* you."

Revel grabbed Mars by the shoulders, gazing at her with her dark eyes. "Mars! I'm tied into the city's dreams, they *run through me*. The waking world is breaking apart, all over the city. I can *feel* it! You need to fucking *hurt* me, you need to damage my energy so that we can buy time for the Agents and The Nor. *You need to hurt me now*."

Mars' breath started coming in quick bursts. Nothing in her liked the idea of *hurting* an entity—she'd spent so much time *healing* entities that the whole thing felt so *wrong*. But she nodded to Revel, trusting the entity's judgment. Revel crawled over to the bed of pillows on the floor, collapsing onto them. Mars followed and straddled her back. She reached for her needles on the table, then stopped herself. She didn't need the precision of the needles; she didn't need what they represented. They were a symbol in her mind of *healing*, of *well-being*, and she didn't want to sully them with the act she was about to perform.

Mars looked down into the coursing streams of energy which were in the midst of being healed by some outside force. She reached her shaking fingers down next to a healthy, glowing stream. "I'm sorry," she whimpered as her fingers gripped the stream and shoved it across Revel's back, her fingers knocking nearly a dozen other streams off course at the same time.

Revel writhed underneath Mars' thighs, her screams reverberating through the dream-jazz-club, the tin-printed ceiling and velvet walls quaking, the slow-motion dancers whipping their heads around towards the two of them.

File 71 :: [Edith Downs]

Bound in her net of light, Edith continued to struggle with her mems to get free while watching Quill and The Moon in the passenger car behind hers. The pearl against her wrist vibrated so violently that she wondered if it would shatter or stop working.

Quill played the keyboard, violet light pulsing from the Carousel's Heart on his back to the beat of the notes he played. Beams of light stretched across the dark sky, looking exactly like the beams she'd seen while traveling inside the city's dreams.

Cracks of green light snaked through the air, spreading like slow lightning above the treetops. Below, those cracks appeared all across Storyland and Carousel Gardens. Looking over the trees, Edith watched the cracks appearing for miles through City Park and the surrounding neighborhoods.

"*Do you see, Edith?*" yelled Quill over the music and the pouring rain. "*The whole city is hearing the song! All of New Orleans is experiencing who they really are!*"

"*The waking world is breaking!*"

Quill shook his head, smiling. "Yes, breaking so that it can be reformed in the purity of dreams."

She pushed against the net, twisting her body and screaming at her inability to do anything. Edith closed her eyes and took a deep breath, at which point she felt a tap on the shoulder. Just beside her head, standing on the back of the seat, was a tiny blue figure. She relaxed into the car's seat at the sight of it.

"Hello!" she said. "I'm Edith, Protector of the Memories of New Orleans. Have you heard of me?"

The mem nodded.

"Are you from the Ferris Wheel? Can you get me out of here, or stop him from playing that machine?"

The mem just tilted its head. She realized that it was trying to communicate with her, but the net was stopping any images coming from the mem.

The mems from the items in her duffel bag crawled up to her shoulder and began communicating with the other mem.

"I need to get out," she told a mem from the blue apron.

The apron mem looked at her and she realized it was trying to speak to her, but she couldn't see the images. Edith shook her head. "The net is keeping me from understanding you, but you can understand my words, right? Stopping the machine from playing is the top priority, by any means possible. Getting me free is second, a *far* second. If the machine keeps playing, there might not be any items or memories left in New Orleans."

The mem nodded, turning to the other mem and gesturing wildly towards Quill, the sky, and down to Storyland.

The Ferris Wheel mem nodded and leaped off the passenger car, out towards the green cracks and the pouring rain.

Edith took a deep breath, hoping the mems translated her words correctly and hoping their plan would work.

File 72 :: [The Function]

Even in the most optimal of circumstances, it is nearly impossible to climb down a rope ladder quickly, and *completely* impossible to do so with any semblance of grace[47]. The Function clung to the soaked rope ladder as it swung through the wind and pouring rain nearly a mile above the city.

He hooked his arms around one rung and stopped to rest, his limbs burning. He pulled out the binoculars and looked around at the world below, which was a quite difficult task with the wet lenses of the binoculars. What wasn't hard to see were the cracks of dream running all over the waking world. The cracks snaked all through the sky. Pretty soon, he was going to be forced to dodge them as he descended. Not that he'd never been lost in the city's dreams before—there was that one time Revel herself grabbed him and threw him into the dream of being a little league baseball coach. The Function was stuck for *hours* picking little kids to create the perfect team, but the game itself never happened. It was an unending dream about building the team, like that limbo place some religions talk about.

He didn't hold it against Revel, though—he *may* have been hitting on her, and may not have been doing so in the classiest of ways.

The Function shook the image of Revel out of his head. Beyond the cracks of dream running across the waking world, he saw all the stopped cars on the freeway overpasses along the edge of the CBD and several other neighborhoods.

This was bad. It looked like the whole city was affected, or a big chunk of it at least.

He shoved the binoculars back into his coat pocket and kept climbing down as the ladder swung violently back and forth through the sky.

---

[47] This is not true. Just earlier, though The Function hadn't seen her clearly, The Moon had climbed down the rope ladder rather quickly and was practically overflowing with grace. But we don't need to tell The Function this, do we?

File 73 :: [Keaton]

Rain poured in thick streams from treetops high above, waterfalling into large puddles in the grass and pathways leading around fairytale statues looming in the mist. Thick fog barely muted the screams and guttural roaring from every direction.

Keaton ducked under a crack of dream as she made her way between fairytale creatures and trees, her cane gripped in one hand. Her entire life had changed within minutes, and she tasted the end of her existence in the thickness of the fog ahead.

Rounding a thick tree trunk, Keaton saw the slender silhouette of a woman withdraw a katana from a smaller figure who collapsed to the ground. The katana itself gave off a sickeningly orange-red aura which licked at the air like flames. The woman wore the patchwork pelt of a Baku like a cape. It was the pelt Quill had worn.

Keaton yelled through gritted teeth: "Nemu!"

The silhouette spun, a green shard soaring through the air as Keaton swiped with her cane. Keaton's eyes never left the silhouette as she turned the cane, the glowing green shard wedged into the black wood. She wiped her cane on the tree trunk, knocking the shard of dream tether away.

"Oh, it's the girl who was Nor." Nemu sheathed the orange-red katana. "This won't do much against you then."

Keaton stepped behind a patch of shrubbery, still yards away from Nemu, who in turn stepped sideways out of the fog. Her eyes, as always, were closed, her face a perfect mask of serenity.

"You broke my brother," said Keaton. "Now, if he doesn't destroy the city, he's probably going to die."

Nemu slowly pulled another katana from its sheath at her hip. "Chans is your brother? I should have used you to get my Baku back. Perhaps it is not too late."

Keaton stepped sideways, away from the shrubbery. "His name was never Chans. His name is Quill."

Nemu stepped sideways again, towards the large whale from Pinnochio with its huge open mouth you can climb into. "I did nothing to your brother except show him what he asked to see. He's the one who walked into my world wearing a cloak of lies."

A series of roars and screams erupted in the distance, but Keaton kept her eyes on Nemu. Her chance of surviving a Baku was far greater than her chance of surviving one of Nemu's strange blades.

Keaton circled the giant whale, staring at Nemu's chest so that she could watch each movement of the Sleeping Assassin's arms and legs as Nemu slowly stepped behind the whale. She knew Nemu was manipulating Keaton's movements, drawing her into a specific spot, but Keaton would not let the woman out of her sight.

In the blink of an eye, Nemu leaped up onto the whale, and Keaton's first instinct was to leap off the path and into the shrubbery—instead, she threw herself *towards* the whale, trying to do what Nemu wouldn't expect. It worked, and Nemu was landing in the spot where Keaton had just been, her back to Keaton as she held two blades, having pulled out a second, smaller one.

As soon as Nemu's boots touched the ground, she was spinning towards Keaton, who had slid her cane apart into two pieces and jumped backward against the whale. Each of Nemu's blades met with a section of Keaton's cane—the katana met with the metal blade of the sword hidden inside Keaton's cane, while the short blade was wedged into the black wood of the long cane-sheath held in Keaton's other hand. Keaton's shoulders hit the side of the whale, and she arched her back, jumping to kick up into Nemu's jaw with her boot.

The Sleeping Assassin jumped and tumbled backward into the shrubbery she'd expected Keaton to retreat into.

Keaton landed in a crouch, holding the sword of her cane in one hand and wooden sheath in the other.

"I remember you now," said Nemu, spitting blood into the leaves. Her jaw was swelling. "I almost killed your leader that day, the girl with the brown dreadlocks. Perhaps twelve years ago now? I watched you fly through the fog, killing several of my men. Near the lake, I believe."

Keaton's teeth ground together as she stepped sideways, moving so her back wasn't against the whale.

Nemu sheathed her katana and dagger, pulling out two different blades. One was a violet katana, the color of the Reverie Heart, and the other was a dagger which glowed with piercingly white light. She held up the violet katana. "This blade is called the—"

"Oh, *fuck* you and your blades' names. I'm sure they're all *very* special. Are you going to try and kill me or what?"

Watching Nemu smile was disconcerting on several levels:

1) With her eyes closed, she looked like someone who'd thought of a joke while dreaming an unusually peaceful dream.
2) The serenity of her face combined with that smile reminded Keaton way too much of those laughing Buddha statues in restaurants. She hadn't been to an Asian restaurant in decades and suddenly wondered if they still had those statues near the front doors.
3) Well, Nemu was circling towards her with blades drawn, so #3 would have to wait, perhaps indefinitely.

Keaton sidestepped through the muddy pathway, knowing very well she was way out of her league. Though if Nemu did indeed kill her, the Sleeping Assassin would remember that jacked-up jaw for months to come. And if Keaton was careful with her next few steps, Nemu may remember more than just Keaton's boot to her face.

Each of them moved dreadfully slow through the streams of rain as they circled each other.

Nemu advanced, her blades poised like snakes' teeth as she bared down on Keaton, who rolled away into a crouch. Keaton then leaped through the air at her opponent, sword and wooden sheath gripped in her fists as she let out a war cry so violent that no one hearing it would ever believe the lie her body told of being an eleven-year-old girl.

Rain poured down Julius' fur-covered face. He crouched atop the branch of a massive oak tree, the wind and rain battering down upon him, Roman on his back with arms locked around Julius' neck.

Ahead of them, the canopy of treetops meshed with thickening fog that glowed green from the light pouring through the rips in the waking world, with the Ferris Wheel about fifty yards from them, the top of it looming a dozen yards above the trees. Cracking thunder joined the pounding of rain above, by the roar of Baku, and by the screams and war cries of The Nor far below. Atop the Ferris Wheel, Quill played the Reverie Organ, the beam of green light coming from The Moon and spearing up into the dark clouds. Edith was in the next car, wrapped in a net.

His fist clenched onto the branch he crouched upon, wanting nothing less than to snap Quill's neck.

Baku flashed into and out of existence near the Ferris Wheel. They appeared crouched in the treetops or latched onto the side of the wheel, either vanishing or leaping down into the fog, presumably attacking The Nor. Julius looked up at the dream tethers running across the sky, at the green rips in the waking world which spanned the horizon as far as he could see.

"That's a lot of Baku," said Roman.

When Julius spoke, his voice was so low and guttural that anyone but Roman wouldn't have registered words at all. *"Remember October of nineteen-twenty-eight?"*

There was a pause before Roman spoke. "It's hard to forget an army of animated corpses guarding a ghost pirate ship from Riverwalkers."

"Good. Same plan."

Even through the rain, Julius could feel Roman sigh against his back as he tightened his grip on Julius' neck. "Alright."

Julius pushed off of the branches, leaping and soaring through the pelting rain, halving the distance to the Ferris Wheel and landing on another cluster of branches. He sprung off again towards the end of the trees, landing a mere two-dozen yards from the ride.

A Baku appeared right in front of him, jerking back as it was obviously not expecting him. Its trunk flailed as its tusks lowered, getting ready to thrust. Julius smashed his paw down on its shoulder, the tree branches under it breaking as the Baku crashed down into the green, glowing fog.

He gripped a branch with his paw, turning to Roman. "Now!"

Roman swung around Julius' neck, hanging down under his snarling jaw. Julius pushed down his lion-god self, becoming a tad more human, getting his footing and grabbing Roman with his paw-hand, stepping forward onto another branch and hurling his fellow Agent through the rain. Roman soared in between two green gashes in the waking world, moving towards the Ferris Wheel.

One by one, Baku appeared around Julius. He let his lion-nature consume him until he was more beast than he'd been since the incident with Rachel in the swamp. The tree underneath groaned from the weight, and Julius let out a roar so loud it shook the thick branches, making the Baku slink back for a moment.

That moment was all Julius needed.

He darted forward at a Baku, grabbing its front paw and throwing it off balance into a second Baku. Julius ducked under a third Baku's tusks as the first two tumbled down into the fog, while in his periphery he watched Roman quickly scaling the side of the Ferris Wheel.

Julius came up under the third Baku, shouldering its chest and sending it toppling onto its back, smashing through a cluster of branches and spinning down into the fog.

Out of his periphery, he saw two Baku appear latched onto the side of the Ferris Wheel near Roman, who was only two yards below Quill's car. Fog splashed up the side of the Ferris Wheel, and a Nor boy fell out of the fog, brandishing two daggers and shoving them into the back of one Baku. The Baku roared and reared back, falling into the mist along with The Nor.

The other Baku lashed out at Roman with its trunk and tusks. Roman let go with one hand, swinging away wildly, pushed about by the wind and rain as he gripped onto a metal post.

Julius had watched too long and was hit hard from behind, the blow sending him stumbling forward. He was barely able to reach out and catch a branch with his front paw to keep himself from falling through the canopy, his real and metal legs dangling over Carousel Gardens. The Baku was latched onto his back, its front claws sinking into the fur over Julius' ribs, scratching at his flesh but not breaking the surface. The hot, wet breath of the Baku hit the back of his neck, and Julius slammed the back of his head into the Baku's teeth with a loud *crunch*. The Baku's front paws ripped fur from the flesh above his ribs as it fell back into the glowing green fog below.

Julius was left swinging from the branch, and he used the momentum to swing forward, letting go of the branch and catching the next one with his clawed hand, then pulling his body up and back onto the canopy.

Other Baku appeared on the canopy to join the one who was left. There were now four between him and the Ferris Wheel. Looking past them, he saw Roman had dodged and kicked away the Baku on the Ferris Wheel, but there was one gaining on him while another appeared between him and Quill's car, latched onto the metal poles.

Julius glared at the surrounding Baku, looking deep into their eyes. They had lions' eyes, and he knew they understood him on some level. He also knew that they wouldn't back down, and he respected their unrelenting valor and conviction.

"*I will do anything to save this city*," he growled at them, "*to save my homeland. I will not attempt to kill you—nor will I stay my claws.*"

Each of the Baku bowed their heads slightly, the rain streaming in waterfalls from their snarling jaws, snaking trunks, and curved tusks.

As he spoke, his eyes scanned the branches around him, memorizing their pattern—which branches the Baku stood upon, which ones led towards the Ferris Wheel.

Julius exhaled loud and slow, his breath something between a purr and a snarl, stepping sideways onto another branch, no longer looking where he stepped, the placement of branches now burned into his memory.

He saw the shoulder muscles of one Baku shift as it began to move, and he immediately shifted his weight, stepping out of its path as it bolted towards him. As it passed him, he shoved his clawed hand deep into its rib cage and grabbed onto its curved bones, moving to dodge the next Baku which came for him. Then he leaped onto the back of the second Baku, using the stub of his arm for balance as he roared out, the muscles of his arm burning as he hefted up the first Baku and hurled it through the air.

The Baku twisted as it soared underneath the thunderous sky, a trail of green blood streaming through the air as it smashed into the Baku above Roman, rocking the entire Ferris Wheel with the impact.

Julius rolled off the body of the second Baku, then leaped back as a third charged him and smacked into that Baku, sending both crashing down through the branches.

Julius turned to the fourth, roaring as he rushed it. The Baku raised onto its hind legs, ready to come down on Julius with its front paws, but Julius was too quick. He struck its chest, throwing it off balance to flounder on its hind legs. He stepped past it, grabbing a fistful of its chest and roaring as he lifted the beast into the air and hurled it towards Roman. A Baku under Roman was nearly at his ankle as he swung up to get out of its grasp.

The Baku Julius had thrown headed straight for the Baku under Roman.

The high-pitched whistles of the Reverie Organ broke through the air and the green cracks in the waking world shattered and stretched, several appearing between Julius and the Ferris Wheel. The soaring Baku was sucked right into one of those cracks, and Julius watched as Roman leaped upwards, one hand grabbing onto the side of Quill's car as his body flung about in the crashing rain and wind. The Baku underneath grabbed Roman's ankle with its trunk, pushing off with all four legs as it pulled itself and Roman off the Ferris Wheel, both of them tumbling down into the green fog.

Julius' heart sank as more green cracks shattered through the air. There was no way now to get to the Ferris Wheel from where he was; he'd be sucked into dreams. A Baku collided down on him from behind, but Julius let himself fall, crashing through the branches and leaves, into the green fog below.

File 75 :: [Mars]

Tears and sweat fell like rain from Mars' face, but she kept her eyes steady. Her hands were deep in Revel's back, like a musician destroying the strings inside a piano. The jazz club itself was silent except for the cries of Revel and the groaning of Mars. All the slow-motion dancers, musicians, and wait staff stood watching with quiet expectation.

Through her fingertips, Mars could *feel* the dreams of the city as they coursed through every person in New Orleans. She *felt* Quill, *felt* him playing the Reverie Organ. She didn't know how, but she knew he'd found a way to affect hundreds of thousands of people.

Every time Mars screwed up the energy lines running through Revel, with Revel crying out beneath her, something inside Mars would claw at her chest with the hatred she felt for hurting someone like this. And as soon as Mars screwed up one part of Revel's being, another part was being healed by Quill and his Reverie Organ, and Mars felt the grip of dream *tightening* and *pulling* at the waking world again.

The strain on Mars was nothing she'd ever felt. It wasn't just her eyes; it was her very being, the core of her, which was being wrung dry by the constant use of her ability.

Her hands moved beneath her nearly of their own accord, jarring and twisting the energy streams. She'd gotten so fast at it, yet even at the speed she moved with her aching hands and body, Quill was healing Revel faster than Mars could possibly hurt her.

As her body waned, Mars glanced up at two of the wait staff, then back down at her hands moving through Revel's back. "You two." She forced the words out of her parched throat. "Hold me up." She glanced back up at them. "Now! Please! Hold me up, or I'm going to fall."

They came up and held her atop Revel so that the only energy Mars needed to expend was in moving her hands and her aching arms. She felt like she'd pass out soon, but she'd hold out as long as she was able.

File 76 :: [Keaton]

Rain and thunder clashed above, water cascading in thick streams from the canopy down into Storyland. The whistles of the Reverie Organ rung out as the cracks in the waking world stretched through the fog.

Keaton raised her sword, knocking away one katana while cracking the fingers of Nemu's other sword hand with her cane sheath. Nemu's struck hand arched behind her, but Keaton wasn't able to strike again before Nemu's boot collided with her chest, sending her flying backward a couple yards to smack into the thick trunk of an oak tree.

Keaton rolled out of the way as Nemu's katana of searing white light sunk into the tree's trunk, slicing through a swatch of Keaton's coat in the process. The tree itself, trunk and branches, lit up from the inside with silvery lightning streaks. Keaton jumped into a thicket of bushes and zigzagged away from Nemu, into the fog, running up a diagonal oak tree and crouching in the branches to catch her breath. She barely kept herself from screaming when a Baku appeared on a thick branch just next to her.

She froze, its eyes peering at her like she was an enemy. Its trunk coiled through the air, sniffing her, its tusks mere inches away from each of her shoulders. "You remember me, right?" she whispered. "My brother is a friend of yours."

Its eyes softened, and she pointed down at the figure of Nemu slinking around the bushes and green cracks in the air, hiding behind tree trunks as she hunted for Keaton.

"I'm trying to kill the one who abused you," whispered Keaton. "I'm sure you remember her too."

The Baku sniffed at Keaton one last time, the hot air of its breath brushing across her wet face, and then it looked down through the fog and snarled.

"If you eat my dreams," Keaton whispered, "I can't kill her. And she's got a Baku pelt, so *you* can't hurt her."

The Baku arched its back and *howled.* Keaton's wrists pressed against her ears, her hands still holding sword and sheath. Then the Baku vanished into dreams.

Nemu spun around, peering up into the fog, but a few thick branches blocked Keaton from view. Keaton didn't move a muscle.

Nemu pulled the Baku pelt tighter over her shoulders and kept searching through the trees and bushes.

Slowly Keaton got to her feet, crawling further from Nemu while keeping her in sight, holding both sword and cane sheath in one hand. She spoke loudly over the pouring rain and the Reverie Organ: "*Don't you care that the city's being ripped apart?*"

Nemu slowed her movements. "Only the *waking world* is being ripped apart. And this is not my city."

Nemu darted sideways, spinning behind a tree.

"Fuck," Keaton whispered, running down a branch and jumping to the limb of another tree. She leaped again and with a *thunk* a dagger wedged itself into the branch she was just on.

She landed in a crouch on a new branch. The pirate ship was below her, resting in a river of green fog. It was small, made for children to climb on, with a mermaid figurehead at the front. There was one mast, devoid of sails, with the figures of Captain Hook and Peter Pan forever locked in a duel inside the crow's nest.

A loud groan pierced the air as the branch beneath her shuddered. Keaton turned to see another dagger wedged into the bark, the branch itself being eaten away like it was full of acid. She turned to jump, but the branch gave out beneath her, sending her tumbling down to crash onto the floor of the pirate ship.

Keaton moaned and rolled to her feet, pain throbbing in the arm and leg she landed on. Luckily it was her off hand. Nemu landed in the ship across from her, advancing with a white and a violet katana. Keaton lunged forward, then sidestepped, blocking one blade while cracking Nemu hard in her wounded jaw.

Keaton spun and jumped away, barely missing a swipe from the white blade.

A howl erupted from the nearby fog, with several more joining in.

Nemu was on Keaton again, backing Keaton into the rail of the pirate ship. Water sprayed like sparks from the collisions of their swords as Keaton blocked her opponent, the white blade nearly destroying the wooden cane sheath in Keaton's throbbing off hand.

Keaton spun out from the rail, blocking the violet blade with her sword and the white blade with her sheath, the wooden sheath splintering into shards from the impact. Without stopping her spinning motion, Keaton plunged the splintered sheath into Nemu's arm.

Nemu grunted, dropping the white blade while swiping with the violet. Keaton moved as if to block but instead ran her sword up Nemu's torso, slicing up the length of Nemu's black body armor. Nemu's violet blade caught Keaton just below the neck and sliced down deep across her shoulder, Nemu's arm swinging back around to smash the katana's handle into Keaton's temple.

Keaton opened her eyes, nauseous and lying on her side, realizing she'd blacked out for a moment. Violet fire spilled up from her wounded chest and shoulder. Above the flames, Nemu stood over her, grunting as she yanked the broken piece of Keaton's cane from her arm. The Sleeping Assassin pulled a metal vial from a pouch on her belt, pouring it over the wound on her arm and holding back a scream. Then she pulled out a coil of black cloth and began wrapping the wound. "That was a better fight than I've had in a couple of years."

Keaton could barely feel the wounded side of her body.

"You'll know what this sword does soon," said Nemu. "Unless you die first. It's honorable the lengths you've gone to in order to save your brother from me."

"I was never going to beat you," said Keaton. "Or save him." A tear slid down her cheek along with the rain. "I was keeping you out of the real fight. Giving The Agents Of a chance to save the city from the monster you made out of my brother."

Nemu drew the violet katana back out of its sheath. "You failed, as did the Agents. There's no coming back from what Quill is doing."

Keaton laughed, then groaned from the pain shooting through her body.

Nemu crouched next to Keaton and pressed the katana slowly into her arm. Keaton screamed, violet flames reaching up from the wound to lick at the blade. "A New Orleans consumed in its own dreams," said Nemu. "You'll do well, having dealt with dreams for so long—if you survive your *self* first."

"I'm sorry," groaned Keaton. "When I said I was never going to beat you, I meant that I'd never beat you *fairly*."

The boat shook, and Nemu spun towards the two Baku landing on the pirate ship's deck, quickly joined by a third. She pulled the blade from Keaton's shoulder, flicking Keaton's blood into the rain and facing them. Then Nemu noticed it—the Baku pelt lying two yards away, where Keaton had cut upwards across her chest. One of the Baku stepped between Nemu and the pelt.

Nemu turned, ran, and leaped off the ship, a Baku colliding with her in mid-air and taking her down into the fog as the others jumped off the boat after her. The screams of the Sleeping Assassin pierced the air.

Keaton rolled onto her back, grunting from the pain in her chest, shoulder, and arm. Rain washed over her face and hair. She wondered if her bowler hat was on the ship somewhere, or lost out in the fog. Perhaps it had fallen into one of the cracks of dream.

She felt a whirlpool inside of her—all the fears, anxieties, and pressures of the past several weeks crashing in. She'd *believed* in her brother when he was feeding her lies, and now he was plunging the city into dreams. The Agents Of would probably still kill him, even if they couldn't save the city. She'd left The Nor, the only place where she belonged, and now she didn't know if she could go back. What was The Nor to her without Quill, without the possibility of him returning?

She was human and she would die, possibly in the rain on this boat as she bled out from her wounds.

Keaton looked down at the violet flames pouring from the cuts in her body, and she *laughed*. "Oh, fuck you, Nemu," she muttered, rain pouring into her mouth. Keaton struggled to feel her body, to *be* where she was. Whatever sword Nemu had cut her with, the effects were driving her into her own mind, into all the anxieties and fears she'd been having.

She turned onto her stomach, groaning as she pushed herself towards the rail, then pulled herself up and over it, dropping into the fog and crashing painfully to the ground. She saw Nemu there, on her side, moaning. The Baku dispersed, having consumed all they wanted from of her.

If Keaton fucked up everything else, she could at least get one thing right. She gritted her teeth through the pain, dragging herself towards Nemu, pulling a short blade from its sheath on Nemu's hip. The blade pulsed with blue-white light as she brought it to Nemu's neck, at which point Nemu opened her eyes.

Keaton's breath caught as she stared into Nemu's sleepy, dark brown eyes. Nemu began muttering in another language, half-conscious, sounding confused and afraid. Nemu's eyes widened and darted around, her face no longer a look of serenity, but one filled with fear.

Keaton backed away, dropping the blade into the muddy ground. The woman before her was not Nemu.

"Who are you?" asked Keaton, but the woman kept speaking a language she didn't know.

So many things occurred to Keaton at that moment: this woman had been asleep for over a decade—"Nemu" was merely part of her dream. That dream had been eaten by Baku, so now this woman was awake and free. Free and confused in a land that spoke English and French, but not her language.

Keaton bowed her head, rain pouring over her and down her face, into the mud she so ingloriously sat in. Dark thoughts rose up inside her. Nemu was gone and Keaton couldn't even kill her. The Sleeping Assassin had never really existed. Keaton had been cut up and beaten by a mirage. Her brother had been *broken* by an illusion.

She closed her eyes and tried to ignore the lady speaking across from her, feeling nothing but utter dread and defeat. The Nor, her brother— without them, her life had the meaning ripped from its chest.

Something grabbed her arm, and she turned. A Baku gripped her arm tight with its trunk, which is when Keaton became aware of her hand clenching painfully around the handle of the muddy blue-white blade, which she was pointing at her own stomach.

The violet flames erupting from her wounds were now surrounding her body entirely, lighting up the fog and the trees around her. Even seeing the violet flames and knowing she was affected by Nemu's katana, even seeing the blade she was about to plunge into her own stomach, Keaton saw no reason to stop herself.

Then her eyes fell on her wrist, on the tattoos spiraling up her forearm. They were all stories—stories Quill had told over a decade ago. Tales of glory, victory, and friendship. They were stories of saving the city's dreams, of guarding the border between the waking world and the dreaming one.

The blade shook in her hand, but she couldn't bring herself to drop it. Her eyes fell on the Baku whose trunk was still coiled around her arm, and she nodded to it.

The Baku pulled Keaton into the city's dreams, dunking her into the ultimate potential of everyone in New Orleans. Keaton closed her eyes, feeling the dreams wash over her, feeling them collide with the Nightmare energy of her wounds, loosening the energy's grip on her.

She let go of the blade, feeling it pulled from her hand by the green rivers of dream.

Rain poured through the net of light and over Edith's face. Through the net, Edith watched lightning stretch across the sky, the accompanying thunder joining the constant roar of rain. Also stretched across the dark sky were the green cracks in the waking world. The broken notes of the calliope continued on, clashing with the screams, roars, and battle cries welling up from below.

Edith really didn't know what the mems of Storyland and Carousel Gardens would be capable of, or if they'd even know who she was. She'd watched the mems of the fire station on Frenchmen Street take down the Axeboy, but those were a far throw from the mems of a kid's amusement park. All mems had personalities—they had distinct memories they could show people. She'd hoped they could distract Quill just long enough to stop his playing for a few moments. To give the other Agents an edge.

But time passed, and Edith lost hope that they were coming back.

The whole Ferris Wheel shook and Edith's stomach clenched as her car swayed back and forth. She pushed herself over to the edge, looking down to see Roman below, holding onto one of the metal poles, swinging away as a Baku lunged for him. He crawled up quickly, getting near Quill's car, his body swaying about in the wind and rain.

Then she saw another Baku toppling through the air towards the Ferris Wheel and she braced herself for a collision, but the cracks of dream spread out all over the sky, one of them sucking in the soaring Baku.

Roman leaped up, grabbing the side of Quill's car, his body swinging about wildly in the wind.

Edith screamed, "Look out, Roman!" as the Baku reached for him.

But the Baku's trunk had wrapped tight around his leg as it pushed off the Ferris Wheel, using its weight to pull him off and into the green fog below.

"*Your Agents should stop!*" Quill yelled to her over the rain and the whistles of the Reverie Organ. *"My healing is working, but it's taking too long! The Baku and Nor are hurting and killing one another! I know your Agents are doing something to slow me down, but innocent lives are in the crossfire!"*

So many lines of witty banter crossed Edith's mind, words inspired by Mars, words to try and convince him that he was doing something wrong. What would Mars do?

But instead, she closed her eyes, listening—the screams, the pounding rain, the high-pitched whistles of the Reverie Organ, the growls, the roars. Were all the roars from the Baku, or was Julius down in the mix?

Edith found the quiet inside herself, the place which always had the same sound, the same steady beat.

Her heart swelled at the thought of Wole, then a violent pain stabbed at her like a blade—would she ever see him again? His words flowed across her skin along with the rain, the words from when they first met: *You can't stop doing what it is you do. It's what you're never not doing. Just stop doing anything, and whatever's still going on, that's it.*

Edith let her mind go blank, just feeling the rain and the net around her. Then an energy surged in her, a knowledge; she knew *exactly* who she was and what she was doing. Mars had *named* her, after all.

She was the fucking Memorian.

Edith pushed her boots against the side of the car, pushing herself up so she could look at Quill through the net of light as he pressed his fingers down on the keyboard hanging from his shoulder.

"Quill!" she screamed, rain pouring into and out of her mouth as she did. *"Quill of The Nor! Quill, underling of Nimble and Nemu!"*

Quill glared at her from his car. *"Don't call me that! I'm not one of those bastards!"*

"Quill!" The memories and words of Adelaide surfaced in Edith's mind, from when Edith had copied so many of the past Agent's memories after they'd taken down the Axeboy. Edith took those words and mixed them with her own, and with one word from Mars:

"I, Edith Downs, am the Memorian, Protector of the Memories of New Orleans! I am taking you into custody under the jurisdiction of The Agents Of! You have brought nothing but chaos and the threat of destruction to the city, and your song ends now!"

Quill shook his head as he screamed back at her. *"I've already done it! Your words are nothing but delusion! The dreams of the city are already affecting your mind!"*

Edith screamed back at him, *"Quill, underling of Nimble and Nemu!"*

Quill yelled at her as he continued to play, but Edith kept on screaming at him from inside her net of light: *"I am The Memorian, Protector of the Memories of New Orleans! I am taking you into custody* under the jurisdiction of *The Agents Of!* You have brought nothing but chaos and the threat of destruction to the city, and your song ends now!*"*

"*I'm not bringing destruction!*" he screamed, tears flowing from his red eyes. "*I'm giving the city the only thing that can* fix *it! I'm giving the city back its dreams!*"

Edith watched as dozens of mems climbed up the side of his car. She began again: "*Quill, underling of Nimble and Nemu!*"

The mems leaped at his head, at his mind, but the strength of dreams emanating from The Moon and from the pearl on his wrist must have been too strong. The mems stopped in mid-air, fighting the current and trying to *swim* towards his mind. The air around Quill was crawling with the small blue creatures.

Two of the mems swam down into the car and suddenly Edith was free—they'd turned off the net gun. She stood up, gritting her teeth and raising the Extraction Glove. She twisted her hand to power on the glove, the legion of mems struggling to swim towards Quill's mind all vanishing from her senses. She gripped the back of the swinging car with her other hand, her voice horse as she screamed: "*I am taking you into custody under the jurisdiction of The Agents Of!*"

Quill kept playing the keyboard, shaking his head. "I don't know how you turned that off, but it's *too late!*" Green cracks sliced the air between them. "You'll know soon how I'm fixing this city, and you'll *thank me!* The new New Orleans won't even *need Agents!* There won't be *anyone* hurting the city!"

Edith focused on the outstretched Extraction Glove, forcing her breath to slow and listening to the continuous, static noise of the pouring rain underlying all other sounds. Her gaze shifted to Quill. He kept yelling, but none of what he said registered. She leaned forward, her own car tilting perilously beneath her as she pushed the Extraction Glove centimeters closer to him. Her senses strained like aching muscles as they reached out towards Quill, her body tensing up as she willed her mind to connect to his. She'd never accessed memories from a few yards away.

Lightning struck down behind Quill, backlighting him in his rocking car.

Edith pushed, a sharp pain slicing down the center of her forehead, her mind feeling like it was being broken open and pried in half. Still she *pushed*, reaching towards his memories, her body shaking, her teeth grinding, until she screamed out into the surrounding storm.

Then Quill's mind bloomed out of his forehead, his memories flipping like a Rolodex of rotating files.

"*I am the Memorian! Protector of the memories of New Orleans! You've put the city and its memories at risk, and your life...*" Tears streamed down Edith's face as she looked into Quill's eyes—she could feel the *love*, the *conviction* in them. "*Your life is forfeit.*" She pressed a button on the Extraction Glove. "*I have something that belongs to you.*"

The button *clicked* and the memory virus—the one Quill had stolen from Nimble and given to Banshee Dave to take down The Presbytere—streamed across the space between them and dropped down into the files of Quill's mind. She watched the red-streaked cluster of memory lash out at the files around it, infecting them.

Quill reeled back, screaming up into the pouring rain. Edith knew that he was *living* the memory of being a building completely engulfed in flames. He convulsed and lurched against the side rail of the car, yet his fingers still pressed down on the keyboard.

Edith called out, "*You're going to fall off the edge!*"

He continued writhing, unable to see reality through the strength of the virus memories. Edith turned off the glove and climbed out the back of the car, out onto the steel beams of the Ferris Wheel. The beams were soaking wet, and she got onto her knees, crawling across them. She had to stop the Reverie Organ.

She was nearly at Quill's car when he spasmed and toppled over the side. Edith reached out and grabbed one of the Reverie Organ's shoulder straps, Quill's weight quickly pulling her sliding off the beam. She screamed out as she grabbed the next beam down with the Extraction Glove, pain tearing across her shoulders and arms from Quill's weight.

Quill's fingers still pressed down on the keys as he squirmed and screamed underneath her.

"*Stop playing!*" yelled Edith, grunting as she kicked at the pieces of the Reverie Organ strapped to his back, trying to dislodge the Reverie Heart or any of the cords or tubes.

Quill shook violently, pulling Edith back and forth, the Extraction Glove's fingers slipping off the beam. Her screams joined Quill's as they tumbled through the dream-cracked fog, branches and leaves on one side with the beams of the Ferris Wheel on the other.

Pain seared across her shoulders and arms once more as the Extraction Glove was gripped from above, Quill's weight tearing her body in half as she refused to let go of the Reverie Organ's strap.

Edith looked up at the chain of mems—dozens of them braided together, wrapping around the Extraction Glove and holding onto one of the beams. The Reverie Organ's cords spiraled up to the car above them, probably still hooked up to The Moon. Edith and Quill were still rather high up, the fog obscuring the ground below them.

Below her, Quill was still screaming, shaking his head violently as he pressed down on the keyboard keys.

"*Stop playing!*" she screamed. "*Quill!*"

There was no question, no consideration, in Edith's mind. One moment she was holding the shoulder strap of the Reverie Organ; the next moment she let go. The only thing that mattered was the city, and all the lives Quill threatened. She cried out into the rain, having sent someone to their death.

Edith closed her eyes as he vanished into the green fog, the cords attaching him to The Moon unplugged or snapped, smacking against Edith's body in the rain and wind as they followed him down.

Edith looked up, realizing that the shrill notes of the Reverie Organ still pierced the air from above. Squinting up through the onslaught of rain, up past the mems who were holding onto the Extraction Glove and keeping her from falling to her death, she saw the beam of green light still spearing up from the car into the sky. The music of the Reverie Organ was still pouring out of The Moon.

The green beam of light thickened, then ripped open the sky itself. Where the streams of the dream tethers intersected above, the sky broke apart in shards of green the size of city blocks.

File 78 :: [Mars]

Tears mixed with sweat to mix with tears again, all of it pouring from her forehead and chin, searing into her eyes. The waitstaff of the bar held her up as she continued to work, though she could barely see any longer—her eyes were in such pain.

Revel convulsed below her, between Mars' thighs and knees on the bed of pillows.

Mars began working on her with her eyes closed, feeling where the energy needed to be shifted off course, where she needed to hurt Revel.

She fought off wave after wave of nausea, fought off the blackness that beckoned her into the darkness of dreams.

Her body began to shut down. After her ability to hold herself up, after her eyes, next came her fingers. She used the side of her hands to push the energy off course. Then it was her neck as her head lolled down, her chin rolling over her chest. Next came her breath, which came in short bursts as she heard the pounding of her own heart reverberating through her skin.

She whimpered as the shadowy dreams finally took hold, her body forcing her mind into the cool, dark relaxation that those dreams promised.

File 79 :: [Julius Marcos]

Julius roared as he sprinted through the green fog, weaving around an oak tree and dodging the widening green cracks in the waking world. As he broke through the trees, he entered a battlefield. Amidst the thick fog were dozens of Nor and Baku locked in battle, soaked and covered in mud, the sounds of screams, growls, and war cries filling the air. The rain finally let up, still coming down yet not as hard.

A Nor leaped and vanished into a swirl of fog, moving towards the Ferris Wheel, just before a Baku leaped up and pulled The Nor out of the fog with its jaws and tossed the small figure to the mud.

Bursting from the trees came a Baku, charging towards three Nor who spun around, their blades ready. A curved staff hooked around the Baku's neck from behind and pulled it splashing into the mud. Clutching the staff was the animated statue of Little Bo Peep in her bright pink dress. The other guardian, Humpty Dumpty, leaped out of the trees and slammed his large body onto the beast, Humpty's mouth forever etched into a giant smile. The beast was knocked out cold.

A Baku howl erupted from deeper into the trees, and the two guardians ran back into the trees and fog.

Roman was with a cluster of Nor, pushing through the Baku as best they could. The ground was littered with the bodies of the dead or dying, both Nor and Baku. Roman had a glowing blue device in his hand which knocked the giant creatures back from him. Several Baku had been taken out of the fight, wrapped up in nets of light.

Julius called out to Roman: "*Plan B!*"

Roman backed up from The Nor and Baku, slid his device into his coat, and slung the duffel bag off his shoulder, setting it on the ground. "*Nor!*" he yelled out. "*Fall back!*"

A few of The Nor fell back as others relayed his command to their comrades. Many paid him no attention, being deep into the fight with the

Baku, and focused on getting to Quill.

From the duffel bag, Roman pulled Mars' clunky Claw Machine, which Roman had been tweaking in what little spare time he had. The tubes running through the gun, which previously glowed yellow, were now glowing green. Roman flipped a few switches and nodded at Julius.

Roman fired into the battle, the metal claw launching from the gun to splash into the muddy ground amidst the fighting Baku and Nor. He slapped the large button on the side of the device, green energy pulsing through the cables connecting the gun to the claw. The claw itself spurted tons of green fluid out in every direction, mixing with the rain and the mud, making the ground glow green for a thirty-yard radius.

Julius stampeded forward into the battle as Roman slapped the gun's button again. The glowing green ground pulsed bright, and every Nor and Baku suddenly *slammed* into the glowing green mud underneath them. Julius was unaffected as he charged through the chaos.

Outside of the glowing radius, The Nor and Baku continued to fight.

Julius ran and leaped high into the air. He saw a Baku soaring towards him from his left, grabbed it in mid-air with his claws and tossed it away.

He landed on the side of the Ferris Wheel, the whole contraption shaking from his weight. Something fell past him. It was Quill, screaming as he tumbled deeper into the fog, followed by a trail of wires. But the whistles of the Reverie Organ played on. Julius guessed that The Moon was still full of the music, that the music had been storing itself inside of her.

He shifted slightly towards human, pushing up awkwardly with his metal leg and foot, grabbing a higher metal beam with his one fur-covered hand and pulling himself up. He had to get to The Moon.

He nearly lost his grip from the force of a Baku landing on his back. The beast sunk its teeth into him and everything went green. Julius looked around—the Baku had pulled him *into dreams*. "No!" he roared, reaching out for the swimming Baku, but it vanished before he could get his hands on it.

There was only the green glow of dreams in every direction, and Julius was floating.

A slice appeared in the air next to him and the young-looking face of King Nor peered inside, holding her golden dagger with its ability to cut through the waking world. "Come on!" she yelled.

Julius swam over to her, reaching out of the slice and gripping onto the Ferris Wheel, pulling himself back into the waking world. King Nor crawled onto his back. "I'll keep them off you!"

Julius climbed the beams of the Ferris Wheel and King Nor cut slices into the air as the Baku leaped at them, letting the Baku fall into dream and have to travel back out again.

He passed Edith, who was suspended in mid-air, her eyes wide and her body shaking at the sight of Julius. She'd come a long way since that day in the headquarters when he'd transformed while she closed her eyes. She wasn't screaming or crying or cringing. Julius didn't have time to wonder how she was hanging in mid-air, her Extraction Glove stretched out above her head.

Then Julius was climbing to the car, the beam of green light bursting from within and stretching up to where the dream tethers intersected near the clouds. The whole sky looked to be made of dreams now, and it was coming down.

King Nor slid off his back as Julius climbed into the car. The Moon was there, half-delirious with a shard of green dream tether sticking out of her thigh. Julius pulled the shard out and threw it into the fog, then pulled the wires off her. "Wake up!" he yelled, but she was completely lost in dream. Bringing his wrist to his teeth, Julius ripped the bracelet with The Moon's pearl off of himself, spitting it away.

Like a destroyed dam which had been holding back a lake, Julius' hopes and dreams crashed through his conscious mind. Quickly, he wrapped his massive, fur-covered arm around The Moon's shoulders, covering her body with his, taking in and blocking as much energy from the Reverie Organ as he possibly could, taking it into himself so that it stopped going out into the city.

The Reverie Organ pulled out not only his current aspirations, but those from his past as well. Every time he yearned to defend the city, every time he strove to save one of his Agents from destruction, soon it all overwhelmed him to the point that he was blind to the current situation. He was no longer living life; instead, he was simultaneously living every hope and dream he'd ever had.

But the flood did not stop. Soon the hopes and dreams of his past incarnations burst into his mind, flooding him with all their different versions of what they wanted the city to become, along with their versions of what the Agents should aspire to be. He was flooded with so many visions of what so many men yearned for—who they wanted to love, how they wanted their lives to unfold, who they wanted to be in the eyes of Bes, what they wanted to do *as* Bes.

Julius knew, on some level, that he was screaming as his mind was fragmenting, being pulled apart in so many directions, but that knowledge was so far away that it hardly registered.

He was over a dozen men living so many hopes and dreams per man, and there was nothing he could do besides give in to that reality.

File 80 :: [Edith Downs]

Edith dangled, shoved about by the wind, the mems holding onto her Extraction Glove, sweat pouring down her face to mix with the old tears and fresh rain. Her body shook as she watched the beast that was Julius crawl out of the green fog mere yards away, climbing the Ferris Wheel. He was something between a werewolf and a giant black lion, and the throbbing of her heartbeat filled her neck, temples, and chest as her instincts screamed inside her, wanting to be far away from this force. King Nor crouched atop his back, gripping his fur in her fist as she swung out at Baku who flew through the air towards them, cutting the air open with her golden dagger so that the Baku slipped into dream.

Julius' golden cat eyes flickered over Edith as he climbed, his metal leg dented and groaning. He ascended to the passenger car, from which the beam of green light speared the sky. Julius climbed inside, and King Nor latched onto the side of the car.

All at once, the beam was gone, and the music *stopped*. The bracelet with The Moon's pearl stopped vibrating against Edith's wrist. The sky was still broken into shards, the cracks in dreams snaking across the sky in every direction she looked. She wanted to know if it was too late, if there was any chance of saving the city.

A roar broke out above her from the passenger car. The roar scared her more than being right next to Julius in his beastly form. That roar turned into a scream—a long, unending scream which broke into pieces, becoming the scream of *many* men.

Julius, completely naked and human, convulsed at the edge of the car before tumbling off the side. Edith screamed and reached out, but he passed by yards away from her, vanishing into the fog.

Edith looked up at the chain of mems trailing up to the car she'd been netted and thrown into, latching onto each other in order to keep her suspended in the air. *"Can you get me down!? Please!"*

File 81 :: [Roman Wing]

Roman leaped through the fog, catching the falling figure of Quill and bracing himself against the beams of the Ferris Wheel to leap off and land in the mud next to a cluster of Nor. Quill screamed, eyes wide and lost in some sort of dream state.

The Nor and Baku were getting to their feet now that the Claw Machine's effects had worn off.

Roman ripped the Reverie Organ off Quill, the straps breaking. He broke off the brass pipes and wrenched the violet oval of the Reverie Heart from the device. He tossed the Reverie Heart to one of The Nor, then picked up and threw Quill's limp, wounded, and screaming body at the foot of the approaching Baku. "*He's no longer in danger,*" he yelled at the Baku, signaling The Nor to stay their weapons. "*He's safe, now call off your attack!*"

Several of the Baku nudged and sniffed at Quill, running their trunks over his face. One by one, they looked up into the gently pouring rain and howled. Other Baku joined them, their howls rising throughout the fog of Carousel Gardens and Storyland until dozens of howls harmonized together through the shadowy green mist.

Roman heard Edith's scream and spun around, unable to move fast enough to stop Julius' body from smashing into the ground. Julius twisted onto his back, his whole body arching up, his mouth open in a piercing scream. Roman started running to his aid but stopped. Hazy figures burst up all around him like ghosts, each one of them a black man. Roman recognized some of them. The men appearing around Julius, standing around him in a messy circle and looking down upon his writhing body, were his past incarnations. There were well over a dozen of them.

Like cats suddenly seeing a mouse or an insect, the Baku stampeded towards Julius and his incarnations. Roman tried to shove them away but was quickly knocked down. Baku after Baku trampled Roman, their paws crushing down on him as he shielded his head with his arms.

When there was a gap in the flow of Baku, Roman rolled out of their path and got to his feet, bruises welling up all over his body. There was a whole sea of Baku shoved into such a small space. He watched as the Baku ripped apart the apparitions of Julius' past incarnations, all of the figures just standing there and letting themselves be torn to shreds. Roman yelled out, leaping into the fray, but the Baku between Julius and him were so packed together that he couldn't get through them.

Roman yelled into the chaos, tears flowing down his face.

Just as quick as the turmoil began, it was over.

The Baku backed away, bucking like wild horses and howling madly. Some pounded their tusks into the ground as others vanished from the waking world. Two Baku next to Roman butted heads like goats, and Roman could see in their wild eyes that they were disconnected from the world around them. Binging on dreams of the incarnations of an African god must have been much more than their minds and bodies were evolved to handle.

The Nor backed away from the bucking Baku, their swords drawn. More of the Baku vanished, the rest charging into the fog until there were no more around.

Roman stumbled over to Julius and fell to his knees. He knew his friend was alive—Julius had lived through far worse—but he didn't know what state Julius' mind would be in. Roman looked up through the light rain, seeing the beams of dream tethers high above the Ferris Wheel, the broken shards of dream in the sky, and the cracks of dream all around.

The beams and cracks were fading, and Roman put a hand on Julius' shoulder. "We did it, old friend."

Julius' body was torn up but already healing, just as the cracks in the waking world would heal themselves. The metal leg was still in one piece, but would have to be scrapped and replaced. Perhaps some of the smaller pieces could be salvaged and used to make a new one.

Roman heard something splash and turned to see Edith getting to her feet, half-covered in mud and leaning against the Ferris Wheel. "Is he alive?" she asked.

Roman nodded. "We did it."

He barely saw the body below him tense before Julius' arm flew at him, sending Roman flying back into a cluster of Nor. Roman rolled off the struggling Nor and onto to his feet, seeing Julius grow into full lion form, searching about madly. "Julius!" Roman yelled. "*We did it! We stopped the destruction of the waking world! It's over!*"

Julius' muscles flexed under the fur, and he let out a piercing howl which made Edith and The Nor cover their ears. Then he turned lakeward and ran, hobbling on the dented metal leg and leaping well over the fence, further into City Park to vanish in the fog and trees.

"*Should we chase him?!*" asked Edith, clearly using the Ferris Wheel to hold herself up.

Roman shook his head, his heart sinking at the thought of his friend being in trouble—trouble Roman had no way of helping him with. "No. Nothing good would come of finding him right now." He turned to Edith. She was wounded, bruised, and exhausted. He had to be here now, for the other Agents and for the city.

Edith stumbled over to Quill, whose screams had become pitiful moans in the wake of his exhaustion, and crouched down.

"What are you doing?" asked one of The Nor.

"Fixing him," she said, powering on the Extraction Glove.

Roman didn't know what Edith could possibly be "fixing", but he was confident she knew what she was doing.

Green light sliced through the air near the foot of the Ferris Wheel, and King Nor walked out with her golden blade, followed by three bruised and scratched up Nor who carried The Moon. The Nor laid her on the muddy ground, completely unconscious.

Roman heard a commotion among the other Nor and turned to see Keaton hobbling through the metal archway between Carousel Gardens and Storyland. Her arm was around Nemu's waist, helping her walk. Keaton and Nemu were soaked in blood, Keaton without her bowler hat or cane.

A dozen Nor ran at them with their swords and knives drawn, and Keaton shouted at them to stop.

That's when Roman realized that Nemu's eyes were open and that she was looking around in utter terror. Then he realized that the person he saw wasn't Nemu at all; it was someone else entirely.

Keaton told the woman, "Don't worry, please, it's ok. They're not going to hurt you."

Roman crossed the muddy stretch to meet them.

"She's not Nemu," said Keaton to The Nor. "The Baku... I think they ate Nemu."

Roman nodded, looking into the woman's eyes. "I'm Roman. What's your name?"

The woman shook her head, muttering something in Japanese. It had been over sixty years since he'd spoken Japanese, and he only made out a word or two of what she said.

He pointed at himself. "*Watashi wa, Roman desu. Anata no... namae nan desu ka?*" He was fairly certain he was saying, *I am Roman. What is your name?*

Her eyes brightened, and she whispered: "Harumi."

"You're safe now, Harumi," he said. "I wish I remembered more

Japanese, but it's been a long day."

They walked closer to the Ferris Wheel and Keaton broke off from Harumi, running to her brother lying on the ground. His face was red and tear-stained, but he was no longer screaming or moaning. Edith was talking with him in a hushed voice, and Roman overheard the words "fire" and "flames", after which he had a rather good idea of what Edith had done.

Edith stood up and powered off the Extraction Glove.

Keaton fell to her knees. Quill's head rolled in the mud and he looked up at her, then he turned away, looking at the sky. "Hey, sis."

Keaton pulled back her hand and slapped him hard across the face. *"Sis? Don't call me that, you fucking liar! You lied to me, you lied about everything you've ever stood for!"* He tried to raise his arms to shield himself from her next slap, but his arms were too weak.

Slap!

"You'll see!" muttered Quill. "I did this all for you! For The Nor! For the whole city! Everything will be better now!"

Keaton shook her head. "You lost. The Agents Of and The Nor stopped you. You *failed.*"

Quill's eyes rolled up towards the sky above, towards the healing cracks of dreams tearing through the air, and tears streamed down his cheeks. "No, no. I'm so, so sorry. I wanted to give you a New Orleans worth living in."

"I *have* the only *New Orleans* worth living in," she said, getting to her feet and taking a step back. "And I'm done with you. You're no longer my brother."

Quill's eyes shut, more tears pouring down his face.

King Nor nodded to a group of approaching Nor, who walked up to Quill with coils of rope and glowing chain. Roman stepped forward, his fists clenching as his voice erupted from him like thunder: *"You will not put your hands on that man."*

The Nor holding the rope and chain froze, looking back at King Nor, who turned to Roman and pointed at Quill. *"Quill is Nor. He is to be tried as a Nor who betrayed their own kind."*

Roman shook his head. "Quill put the city of New Orleans at risk of destruction and was stopped by The Agents Of. His life, imprisonment, execution, and/or rehabilitation are under the jurisdiction of The Agents Of. We will *not* let you take him. If you attempt to do so you will be acting against the city herself and all aspects of New Orleans which have granted us this power."

Edith limped through the mud, stepping up next to Roman.

Keaton looked back and forth between Quill, King Nor, and Roman, then stepped towards Roman. "I think he's right."

King Nor shook her head of brown dreadlocks. "Quill is one of us, and will be tried by our rules."

"He hasn't been one of you for *ten years*." Roman sensed all The Nor tensing up, their fists clenched around the handles of their swords or knives. He had a couple of devices in his coat that would push the odds in their direction, but the fight would not be favorable to either side.

He heard Edith whispering into her shoulder and realized that she was talking to mems. If the mems helped them, perhaps they could get Quill out of Storyland before The Nor tried and executed him.

Suddenly everything was covered in piercing green light. It was coming from the booths of carnival games. From out of the light walked Revel, her form an endless, dark expanse wrapped in a violet cocktail dress. She was with Mars, the Agent's eyes red and her face looking painfully exhausted. They had their arms around each other, helping each other walk out of dream and into the mud.

Each of The Nor, including King Nor and Keaton, fell to one knee and bowed to Revel as she approached.

Revel's dark eyes looked at Roman, and he bowed his head to her.

"Roman," she said. "It's been a number of decades."

"It has," he answered. Revel had only been in the waking world, as far as Roman knew, three times during the course of Roman's life.

Quill moaned as he sat up, looking at Revel and muttering: "Oh, Revel! I was giving this world to you! I was—"

She raised a hand, and Quill's voice caught. He brought his hands to his throat, confusion crossing his face as he coughed violently.

Then she looked back to Roman. "You are correct, of course, in your assessment of the laws and the situation. But there is something of mine which Quill is in possession of."

Quill lurched forward, coughing and hacking, until he wretched up gobs of green letters and symbols. They poured out of his mouth, floating around him in the air.

When Revel spoke next, she did so to Quill: "You swore an oath to me. You swore an oath to The Nor. Do you remember?"

The green letters and symbols rose up into the air, circling his head.

Then Quill's voice echoed through the air. But it was not the voice of this *man*, it was the voice of Quill as an eleven-year-old boy:

"I take one step out of the waking world, but only to protect it—I will use my connection to dream to defend the sanctity of the city herself. I take one step into the sleeping world, but I will not stray—I will guard the border between the awake and the asleep. I will protect the dream tethers which hold the waking world together. I will watch over the bridges to Carnival, ensuring the forces of Carnival do not mix with the living except during allotted times. I will answer to King Nor, and to Revel, who weaves

*the dreams which hold together the waking world. If I quit The Nor or am
kicked out, I vow to never stand in the way of The Nor or any of their
causes. I understand that by breaking any of these oaths, I would be
forfeiting my life.*"

The glowing green letters and symbols of Quill's oath circled him
faster and faster, closing in and binding his mouth like a gag, binding his
arms and legs like rope. Then the glowing binds pulled him up into the air,
towards Revel, Quill's eyes wide and looking from Revel to the others
present.

Keaton stepped up to Revel, avoiding her brother's pleading eyes.

"You want to know what I'm going to do to him," said Revel.

"No." Keaton shook her head, glancing back at her mother lying in
the mud. "Whatever fate you choose for him, I would choose worse."

Revel nodded. "The Nor would kill him. The Agents Of would send
him to their Riverwalker prison. I will make him *rebuild* the dream tethers,
even if it means dissecting his mind and weaving him into the tethers
themselves."

Quill began struggling in his bindings to no avail.

Keaton nodded. "At least he'll do something good after causing so
much harm."

"It's not too late to become Nor again, Keaton. But you're human
now, and you're aging. You were brought into the Nor at an older age than
most, and you'll be too old within a year. I can feel the waking world
siphoning the reality from your dreams as we speak."

"I... I need some time to think."

"Of course, just don't take *too much* time." Then to Quill, she said:
"Because of you, I've had to endure more *pain* than I've had in over two
centuries, coming quite close to death." With a wave of her hand, Quill
vanished into the bright, green light she and Mars had come out of.

Mars turned to her, looking half-dead—though Roman would never
tell her such a thing, he'd learned nearly a hundred years earlier never to
say that to a woman.

"Well that was dramatic and badass," Mars muttered to Revel.

Revel put a hand on Mars' shoulder. "Thank you, for everything."

"No prob," Mars croaked in a dry whisper. "Any time. You know
where to find me."

Revel turned to Roman and King Nor. "Don't be stupid and go killing
each other." Then she turned and limped back into the dreams of the city,
the bright green light vanishing behind her.

Edith walked up to Mars, grabbing her and hugging her gently. "I'm
glad you're alright."

"Oh, I'm peachy keen," croaked Mars. "Though I could probably use
twenty hours of sleep and five gallons of water."

"Me, too," said Edith.

"Where's Julius?" asked Mars.

"Um... he left," said Edith. "It's a long story. Can I tell you in the ride back to headquarters?"

Mars nodded, leaning on Edith. "Sure." Then she looked over at Roman. "What are we lookin' at, boss?"

Roman motioned towards the scraps of the Reverie Organ scattered around where Quill had been lying. "Gather up the pieces. We'll need them to put the calliope back together."

Mars and Edith nodded, wandering over to pick up the various remnants of the device.

"What?" Mars croaked loudly. "That's my Claw Machine!"

"I told you I was tweaking it," said Roman.

Mars toed the soaked and muddy gun where it lay on the ground, the claw itself over a dozen yards away, lodged into the mud. "You filtered dream through it instead of ghost blood?"

Roman nodded. "Baku were running around. Didn't think we needed it to incapacitate ghosts."

"Huh... and it worked?"

"Splendidly."

She nodded, picking up the gun and activating the reel mechanism inside, which pulled the muddy cable and claw back into the gun's giant barrel.

King Nor walked over to Roman, looking up at him. "If The Nor and The Agents Of weren't working together, the city would have been lost."

Roman nodded.

"I'm sorry," said King Nor. "I didn't see the madness growing in Quill, but I should have expected it."

"No," said Roman. "It's near impossible to see a seed of madness growing in someone you love. The Agents Of know that intimately. The important thing is that we worked together to snuff out the flame of destruction before it took hold."

King Nor held out her hand, and Roman took it.

"May The Nor and The Agents Of always work together in such harmony," she said. "Or perhaps greater harmony..."

"May we always," said Roman. He turned and looked at The Moon, who was still deep in dream, lying peacefully on the ground. "Can you get The Moon back up in the sky when she wakes up?"

King Nor nodded. "We'll get her up there."

They parted and nodded to one another. Roman turned to Mars and Edith, who each had two armfuls of pieces of the Reverie Organ, including the keyboard itself.

Then he noticed Keaton, who approached The Moon and knelt. The other Nor backed away, giving her space. She pulled off her ripped-up suit coat, lifting her mother's head and shoulders to place the coat underneath.

Roman walked up. "If you'd like, you can come with us. Or we'll take you wherever you'd like to go."

Keaton shook her head. "I'm staying with my mom, at least until she gets back up to the sky." She looked up at Roman. "I'm not Nor, but I'm not an Agent, either. I'm not anything anymore."

Roman crouched down and put a hand on her shoulder. "You call us when your mother is safe, and we'll get you a hotel room in the CBD. You can sleep. You can stay there for as long as you'd like, until you figure out what you want to do. There's no pressure. None at all."

"Why would you help me?"

"Keaton, I've known you for a long time. In 1981 you gave the city and I more than just The Moon; you gave us your faith, your belief. You gave us who you really are, and that's only one of many reasons that I would help you."

Keaton relaxed so much that Roman thought for a moment she might collapse against him. She looked over at Harumi. "What about her?"

"We'll keep her safe," he said. "We'll make sure she gets home."

Keaton nodded. "Ok. A hotel sounds nice. And a shower. I probably still smell like swamp and sweat."

Roman nodded. "Whenever you're ready."

Keaton looked down at her mother, pushing wet hair from her mother's forehead.

Roman got up and walked over to Harumi, motioning to the trees they were about to walk into, back into Storyland. "You're safe now, Harumi," he said in the most soothing voice he could muster. "Please, come with us."

Roman walked through Storyland, his arm around Harumi to help her walk, with Edith helping Mars. They traversed the winding pathways, past the nursery rhyme statues and towards the front of the children's park, Henri's streetcar waiting for them somewhere beyond the fog.

File 82 :: [The Function]

Dangling from a rope ladder roughly fifty feet above the streets of the CBD, with skyscrapers and office buildings looming above him on all sides, The Function was finally nearing the ground. The rain had let up to become a drizzle, and he'd somehow managed to dodge all of the cracks in dreams as he descended.

Below him were the bright-shirted tourists, the construction workers, the business people in suits, the oddly dressed locals, all of them lying on the sidewalk or slouched sideways inside their stopped cars, finally stirring. He stopped climbing down, pulled out his binoculars, and used them to look down both ways of the street he dangled above. People in every direction were sitting up, getting to their feet, and talking with one another.

The Function pulled the binoculars from his eyes and looked up into the sky. The dream tethers were no longer visible. The glowing green cracks in the waking world, still all around, began simmering and shrinking like water in a hot pan.

Two emotions moved through The Function's body in waves:

The first was elation; the city, the waking world, was saved. He still had a job tomorrow. Well, he'd *probably* still have a job even if the city had been plunged into its own dreams, but that job would consist of running through dreams and dodging nightmares while doing tasks for Serendipity, and he much preferred how strange New Orleans was *without* being flooded with dream and nightmare.

The second emotion was annoyance; yet again, The Function was shoved to a corner of the city where he was utterly useless during all of the action. Sure, he didn't mind not being hurt or killed (coming back to life really sucked). But when everyone's swapping war stories about whatever happened in Storyland, he's not exactly going to wow anyone with his harrowing tales of swinging from a two-mile-long rope ladder (though he did nearly fall and die twice during the ordeal).

Sliding the binoculars back into his coat, he looked around at the stirring people below. Sure, they were talking to each other about the surreal situation now, but most of them would begin changing the details in their minds over the next hour or two. Pretty soon, the Wonder of the city would kick in, pushed into high gear by all the Wonder devices Roman had spread across the city. People would start talking about how everyone felt strange that one afternoon, assigning it all sorts of reasons— Mercury in retrograde, this or that phase of The Moon, or something in the air that made everyone have a weird day. Perhaps some would come up with religious reasons, blaming it on Catholic Saints or Voodoo holidays.

Basically, everything was back to normal, or at least as normal as New Orleans would ever be.

The Function took a deep breath, feeling all the aches in his body, feeling all the water soaked into his clothes and boots and socks. He looked up at the more-than-a-mile of rope ladder above him.

"Screw it," he said to himself as he began to climb. He didn't have any money on him for buying a drink at a bar, and Albert had two things The Function wanted more than anything else at that moment: Whiskey and a clothes dryer.

One thing was certain: Whether it was Roman, Mars, or somebody else, *someone* was going to create some kind of elevator.

This was *so* lame.

File 83 :: [The Moon]

Some days later, The Moon sat with her daughter on the edge of the roof of a hotel in the CBD. They faced the river, overlooking countless building tops with the dual bridges of the Crescent City Connection and the curve of Algiers Point beyond.

Almost a week had passed since the waking world was nearly tipped upside down into dream. The cracks in the waking world were half-healed and invisible now to normal eyes. The Moon could see them almost every direction she looked, though the cracks were much thinner than they had been.

The stumbling notes of the calliope sauntered playfully through the air, batted about by the wind as they made their way from atop the Steamboat Tchoupitoulas to the far corners of New Orleans.

When the evening songs were done, all was incredibly silent.

"Do you think he's up there, woven into the tethers?" asked Keaton, looking up at a sky half covered in clouds.

"I haven't asked Revel yet," said The Moon. "I'm afraid of the answer. I'm still recovering from what Quill did to me, and I just don't know if I can handle knowing. Not yet."

Keaton sighed. "I can wait a bit longer to find out too."

The Moon put her arm around Keaton's shoulders, squeezing her close. "How are you holding up? Is the hotel alright?"

"It's lonely, but it's nice. The Agents Of have really helped me out. I keep getting panic attacks about being homeless without Quill, but they don't last long, and I think they're going away."

"You've been surrounded by Nor for a long time. And you've never really been alone."

Keaton nodded. "And being human again, it's like my time as Nor is there and not-there at the same time. I was Nor since the '70s, but now it really feels like just last week I was living in the streets with... with

Gabriel."

A tear slid down The Moon's cheek at the sound of her son's original name. When she looked at Keaton, she was crying too.

"All my life," said Keaton, "I've been afraid of this moment. Afraid of the day I lose him. Even when he was infiltrating Nimble, I held onto this *idea* of him, like he was my compass."

The Moon nodded. "But he wasn't your compass."

"No, he wasn't. When he left The Nor, I grew stronger. I just didn't see it, somehow."

The Moon leaned over and kissed her daughter's forehead, whispering: "I saw it."

Keaton leaned her head into her mom's shoulder.

The Moon had no illusions that her daughter was actually eleven years old, yet she cherished this moment with all her heart and being. Moments like this were what she'd squandered all those years ago, swimming in drugs and desperation. Moments like these she simply didn't deserve.

But her children had saved her, perhaps in more ways than she could ever convey, and now these moments were hers to experience. It's like she was living pieces of a past she never had, a past where she'd made different choices.

They sat in the silence above the city for some time, The Moon's arm wrapped around her daughter. There were no animated stories, no harrowing tales—just the wind and the soft scraping of the rope ladder against the roof behind them.

File 84 :: [Edith Downs]

Underneath Spanish Plaza, under the fountain and restaurants and little kiosks, amid the twisting underground hallways of the headquarters, Edith loomed over a wooden Mardi Gras doubloon with her Extraction Glove, pulling out and copying memories[48].

It had been just over two weeks since the incident of Storyland and the Reverie Organ. Scars across her ribs marked where Nemu had stabbed her with the shard of dream tether, and her bruises from the whole endeavor had mostly healed.

The doubloon was one of nearly forty memory items which had appeared inside *The Library*, which is what Edith and Mars now called the memory of the first New Orleans Public Library. The Library was now a safe space for memories, cut off from most parts of the world. Edith had started introducing herself as *The Memorian* when meeting new people as an Agent.

The Memorian—the words seemed to hold such *purpose* in them, and she loved the way that purpose felt.

The city was back to normal, the cracks in the waking world completely healing up within a week and a half. The first week consisted of the Agents tethering themselves to solid structures in the waking world and venturing through the green cracks and into dream, rescuing people who had slipped through the tears. Though the Nor, being adept at traveling through dream, did the bulk of the rescue work.

The Reverie Heart was back in the carousel, with children riding the antique horses and other animals. The calliope was back together and functioning, its songs weaving into the air throughout the day, helping the

---

[48] Most doubloons are aluminum coins roughly the size of silver dollars, thrown along with beads and stuffed animals from the massive floats during the parades of Carnival. Some parades still throw out the older, wooden variations, which are imprinted with a rare ink excreted by certain river and lake creatures.

flow of Wonder through the whole city.

In some ways, everything was back to normal for the Agents, though Julius hadn't returned. There were sightings of a monster roaming the swamps outside of smaller towns south of New Orleans, and Roman had his contacts in the Riverwalker tribes keeping an eye out for him.

Whenever asked about Julius, Roman would merely say, "He'll be back when he's ready."

Roman and The Agents Of had spread rumors throughout the city that Julius was on a series of missions in the swamps, going back and forth from the swamps to the city. Their hope was that the more malicious powers of the city didn't see the Agents as being weakened.

A loud *boom* came from the table next to her, and Edith turned to see Mars hunched over a device with her VR Goggles strapped over her eyes, a surgical-like tool clenched in each of her hands. "I'm alright!" she yelled without looking up.

Dust-o-Bot 5000 crawled into the lab on its clicking crab legs, climbing up the wall next to a trash can to empty its contents. Then it scurried down the wall and back out into the headquarters.

Edith sat back on her stool and switched off the Extraction Glove, stretching her arms. She'd copied fifteen memories from the doubloon so far, and there were at least a few more. She turned and looked across the sea of lab tables at Keaton, who stood facing a stone wall with her hands in the air. Golden glowing symbols and letters floated above her hands, transforming into crudely drawn pictures suspended in the air, then transforming into audible words describing a streetcar traveling under giant oak trees, then becoming floating symbols once more.

Sheets of paper were taped all over the wall that Keaton faced. With a wave of her hands, the symbols darkened and pressed themselves into the sheets of paper like ink, their lines thick, reminding Edith of tribal tattoos. Keaton moved her hands back, and the symbols peeled off the paper and into the air, leaving the pieces of paper blank and white again.

It had taken just over a week of living in a hotel room for Keaton to call up the Agents and ask if Roman was serious about her joining up. Keaton said she needed to work, to move, to find a sense of purpose again. Above all else, she needed to feel like she was doing something beneficial with her time. She wanted to help the city.

Roman already had her in his plans, theorizing that her abilities to manipulate the form of story may work on memories, specifically the memory files that Edith had been copying for months now. Whether or not she wanted to be an Agent, he was going to ask if she'd attempt to convert memory files into text. She'd only been at it for a week, struggling with turning visual story into words, but she was really close.

Soon the first of the memory files would be in text form. They'd be gathered into volumes, recording the exploits of The Agents Of as well as the history of all the past incarnations of the Agents.

Roman was finally getting his wish—his goal of having a documented history of the Agents was actually attainable.

Edith's thoughts were interrupted by the shrill ring of a payphone.

"Got it!" said Mars, shoving her goggles onto her forehead, getting to her feet and wandering over. She picked up the phone. "The Agents Of, how can we save your city today?"

Keaton closed her hands together, the symbols in the air turning to light and condensing into a single square of light between her hands, becoming a memory file once more. She turned and placed the memory file into a glass and metal box, not unlike an aquarium, meant to keep the file stable.

"Uh huh, of course, I remember you," said Mars into the phone. "Wow, yeah, that sounds bad. How many? You said Magazine Street? Ok, thanks for the call. We'll see you in five-ish."

She hung up the phone. "Grab your gear!"

Edith hurried to the door, beside which hung three long duffel bags. Edith slung hers over her shoulder, threw Keaton's to her, and grabbed Mars' bag.

Mars picked the phone back up and hit the intercom numbers. Her voice came through the speaker system wired through the entire headquarters: "Roman, we got a situation. Meet you at the ramp in twenty seconds. I'll explain on the way."

Keaton swung on her sleeveless suit coat and slung her bag over her shoulder.

"Don't forget this," said Edith, picking up Keaton's bowler hat and tossing it to her.

Keaton did a backflip, kicking the bowler hat twirling into the air, and when she landed, it *almost* came down on her head. She reached out and caught the hat instead, pressing it down over her braids. "*Almost* got it that time!"

Mars slung her own bag over her shoulder. "Oh yeah, take this!" Mars grabbed the device she'd been working on and tossed it to Keaton. It was a black wooden cane with a brass dragonfly perched on the end for a handle.

"What?!" yelled Keaton. "You made me a cane?" Edith thought the decades-old eleven-year-old was going to cry. Keaton turned it in her hands, revealing a series of tiny buttons below the dragonfly handle.

All three of them walked into the hallway, towards the ramp.

"Uh... it's not exactly finished," said Mars. "Just don't hit the blue button. It might blow up... or something. Actually, maybe you should just hit the yellow one for now. That one should be safe enough."

"Got it," said Keaton, twirling the cane to figure out its balance point.

Mars walked up to the sleek, black motorcycle parked in the hallway, grabbed the handles, and kicked up the kickstand, pushing it towards the ramp door. She'd been teaching herself to ride Nemu's old motorcycle, since Nemu no longer existed.

Edith walked up to the underside of the fountain, the giant aquarium set into the wall with dozens of hoses and dials pumping Wonder into the fountain's water.

She pulled the lever, and the ramp lowered, daylight spilling into the hallway and onto the three Agents. Roman was approaching from behind.

Mars elbowed Edith. "*It's your turn,*" she whispered.

Edith smirked, using the best serious voice she could muster:

"*Time to save New Orleans.*"

Acknowledgments

First I would like to thank Caitlyn Watson, Aime' SansSavant, James Smith, JJ Kellogg, and Zachary W. Mohr for listening endlessly to my ideas over the years as I put this story together, as well as for their help beta reading and editing this book.

I would also like to thank Chuck Cook, Aaron Damon Porter, Corrinne Almeida, and Kayla Drummond for their help with beta reading and editing.

I want to thank Julia Y for helping me revise the book and for encouraging me while the world stopped and inspiration was hard to find, as well as for helping me become a better artist while I worked on the cover for this book. The cover wouldn't look nearly as good without her artistic expertise and unending kindness.

I would like to thank Mark Brown, who has been supporting me on Patreon for years now, for believing in me and for sharing his poetry, short stories, and artwork with me throughout the years.

A special thanks to Mr. Raphael Gratch for being so kind as to lend me the use of his name for Julius' nephew.

And thank you to Ariel Gratch, who invited me to write weird stories for an online magazine once upon a time. Those stories followed the strange character of The Function, along with Scape and Serendipity, and they were the birth of this New Orleans world I love so much.

Thank you to New Orleans, with all of its dreamers. This city and the people here are everything to me.

And thank you, reader/dreamer/friend, for going on this escapade with me.

Until the next adventure…

--Andy

Andy Reynolds was a gambler born in New Orleans in 1898. He lived a very messy yet deliberate life, and despite surviving numerous brushes with yellow fever, died quite young in 1936—an event involving at least one street magician, five insidious cats and a stained glass window. Three incarnations later and he again resides in New Orleans, this time as a writer of fiction and an imbiber of whiskey and local knowledge.

Find out more about his writings at: AndyReynolds.net
& also: Facebook.com/AndyWritings

Watch & listen to him read poems and other such things on his YouTube channel called AndyWritings.

Check him out on Patreon at: Patreon.com/AndyReynolds